BEKA WESTRUP

Demons and Roses

THE ETERNAL BRIDES

1

First published in the United States of America April 2024 by Beka Westrup

Cataloging-in-Publication Data is on file with the Library of Congress.

ISBN: 979-8-9863087-5-3 (paperback), 979-8-9863087-4-6 (e-book)

Editor: Alexa Thomas (The Fiction Fix)

Cover: Selkkie Designs (insta: @selkkiedesigns)

Internal Art (first page): Stephanie Sabarez (insta: @stephydrawsart_)

PLAYLIST

1. cowboy like me - Taylor Swift
2. Bitchcraft - Jax
3. Hungover - Mothica
4. Panic Attacks in Paradise - Ashnikko
5. cardigan - Taylor Swift
6. bloody valentine - Machine Gun Kelly
7. Hateful Ever After - Ellise
8. Sucker - ari hicks
9. Anti-Hero (ILLENIUM Remix) - Taylor Swift
10. Unlock It (feat. Kim Petras) - Charli XCX
11. Nonsense - Sabrina Carpenter
12. Until I Found You - Stephen Sanchez & Em Beihold
13. Wonderland - Taylor Swift
14. R.I.P. 2 My Youth - The Neighbourhood
15. Under My Bed - Ellise
16. Stfd - TeZATalks
17. Love the Way It Hurts - Cloudy June
18. Can't Help Falling in Love (feat Brooke) [Dark] - Tommee Profitt
19. "Slut!" - Taylor Swift
20. I Put a Spell on You - ari hicks
21. Wide Awake - Katy Perry
22. Labyrinth - Taylor Swift
23. Work Song - Hozier

Author's Note

This is a dark demon romance.
The monsters fuck. Please proceed with care.

Content Warnings:

Explicit Sexual Content
Smoking/Drinking
Emotional & Verbal Abuse
Blood and Gore
Torture/Murder
Mention of Human Trafficking
Brief Mention of Rape
Mention of Cancer & Parent Death
Brief Reference to Child Abuse &
Pedophilia (Not Graphic)
Fictional Human Sacrifice (not based on any real
life religion or cult)
Fictional Demonic Rituals
Dubious Consent
Anti-Religious Rhetoric
Gun Violence
Active Shooter Situation
Removal of Birth Control Without Consent

Kinks:

Primal
Breeding
Exhibition

For the nasty little demons within each of us

CHAPTER 1
BE WARY OF RUNAWAY GOLF CARTS

My husband is almost always an evil fucking bastard, but most especially when he's golfing.

I lounge in the driver's seat of the black golf cart, my feet propped up on the dashboard, the edges of my white tennis skirt fluttering in the breeze. The material is so sheer, you can see the lace of my underwear through the shorts. I hate it, but there's a dress code for the club. Plus, my husband likes it when all the wrinkly, rich men at the club admire my legs. He likes being reminded that he has something others want, even if that something is me.

I'm wearing the designer sunglasses he shoved into my hands this morning, and I haven't complained once, even though they tint the world an irritating shade of yellow.

The sun beats down on the plastic top of the cart, its heat trickling around me like rain. I wish it was real rain.

It's an unexpectedly bright and warm fall Saturday in Boston, and my chest is damp with sweat. My dark hair slides forward in frizzy clumps thanks to the humidity.

On days like this, I long for winter. I long for thick

sweaters and tights, for holiday travel and a blessed reprieve from these dull visits to the club. If it was up to me, I'd spend all autumn visiting the nearby farms, picking pumpkins and apples, exploring corn mazes and the best haunts in our state, of which there are *plenty*.

But it's *not* up to me.

"Rose."

I sigh, lowering my book to glower over top the wrinkled pages.

The romance in my current read is finally heating up, so I don't appreciate the interruption. I don't appreciate my husband's presence *at all*, really, but he's disgustingly rich, and I'm his pretty little trophy wife, so what's a girl to do?

He stares at me from the foot of the grassy hill I parked our cart on, his golf club braced across his shoulders, his blond hair slicked back with a thick layer of gel. I hate when he styles his hair like that—it makes him look twenty years older and twice as stiff. He's not a bad-looking guy. In fact, I'm pretty sure anyone who passed him on the street would think he was absurdly handsome, in a serious-prep-school-boy-turned-business-mogul kind of way.

I certainly thought he was handsome once, but I see a lot more of him now.

Walter stands in the sand pit he's been trying (and failing) to hit his ball out of for the last several minutes. For someone who drags me to this hellscape week after week, he's a pitiful golfer. The books I bring serve to entertain me, but they also keep me from laughing in his temperamental face. Two birdies, one stone.

My husband never misses an opportunity to ridicule me for my reading habits in return.

Unrealistic whore is his favorite descriptor as of late.

I fully expect those words to fall from his lips now,

considering the way his eyes narrow in on the bright pink novel in my hands as his thin lips purse in irritation. Walter's mood has been terrible enough today to warrant that insult and more.

He surprises me by simply shaking his head and demanding I bring him a different club.

This is my burden every Sunday: to drive him around this grassy wasteland and practically choke myself while fetching things for him like a dog on a leash.

He'll need more than a change of clubs to get himself out of this one. I can't even see the golf ball anymore.

Logically, I know it will be easier for us both if I just get up and do it, if I just count my blessings and continue playing my part in this façade. That's all it is really: a façade. A loving husband and his doting wife, a blissful marriage—I gave up on that fantasy a long time ago. The truth is, he's a powerful man, and I am a possession.

As a child, I was taught to cherish my possessions, but it's not the same for him. He takes everything he has for granted, and damn anyone who tries to take his toys away. I'm the little beanie baby gathering dust under his bed.

Luckily for me, no one is around right now to see the truth, our unhappiness. I don't need to pretend. "Get it yourself," I reply as I promptly return to my reading.

Sometimes, I resent my mother for being poor.

Not in the way I thought I would, though. I didn't mind actually *being* poor. There's a lot to be said about growing up with nothing. I valued my education. My friendships were meaningful. I learned the value of community, donating my time to shelters and food pantries because at least that meant I could get out of our tiny, shitty apartment for a few hours. I learned to be grateful for the things I *did* have, and my mom made up for all the time she spent working by giving me every joy she could spare—she loved me intentionally and fiercely. I met many kids in our low-income apartment complex who weren't so lucky.

The *problem* with my mom is that she convinced me marrying rich was the only way to be happy, that a man was the only way *out*.

It was the only thing my mother believed in—the only truth, Holy Bible be damned. Becoming the valedictorian at my high school graduation? Not good enough. Getting into an Ivy League college on a full goddamn ride? Nope. It was all preparation for the *real* mission: *find a good man (aka, a really rich one) and know the prenup like the back of your hand.* I used to laugh at her when she said things like that. At least, until I realized it wasn't a joke. Until she got sick. After she died, it didn't seem funny at all.

She went to sleep that last night in hospice, and it was like I woke up.

I was left with nothing. Everything we had was lost over the course of her treatment—a treatment that didn't even work. I walked into foster care with little more than the clothes on my back, and I learned what the world was like without my mother to stand between it and me. I learned what true poverty felt like, with no love to soften it.

All I had left were the things she taught me, the things she wanted for me. I couldn't let them go. I was only sixteen then. Her body was donated to science, the way she wanted—giving, even in death. There was no funeral, no family to share the grief with. Only her words remained, and they had carried me to this point.

She was right, of course. Life is easier when you want for nothing.

So, here I am, reading about love on an immaculately landscaped golf course with thousands of dollars' worth of gold jewelry weighing me down. Only seven more years of this torture, and I can walk away with the money my mother so desperately wanted for me, what she secretly wanted for *herself*. My future alimony will buy peace for us both.

I do wonder, sometimes, how much of me will be left to enjoy it.

Walter stomps a quarter of the way up the hill and snarls, "Get off your lazy ass and do what I asked, Rose."

I slide my sunglasses down my nose and raise a caustic brow at him.

A sharp retort springs to my tongue, but he's already talking again, his neck and face reddening from the rage he instills into every word. "Do you want someone to see you acting like this? This is how rumors spread, and I do not have time to put out a fire before the next board meeting. I swear to God, you have to be the stupidest bitch I've ever met."

My feelings might have been hurt if he didn't say shit like that every other day. I'm used to it now, and none of it is true.

I'm not lazy, and we're so far from the club right now that no one would hear us if we *screamed*. Walter always insists on renting out the entire course because he doesn't want the untouchable 1% in this city to see his terrible swing.

I curl my lip at him and push my glasses back into place.

In my silence, Walter practically starts smoking with anger. The air around him looks like it's *vibrating*, but that has to be the heat. "Don't make that disrespectful fucking face at me," he points my way, and I feel a shiver spear down my spine, "or I'll find a way to reverse the plastic surgery you've had on my dime before sending you away."

He likes to threaten that too. Divorce. It's an empty threat, though. I know as well as he does that if he divorced me, I'd find a way to ruin his life. I've been carefully documenting his bullshit for years, and he's a fool if he doesn't realize it.

Even so, I snap my book shut and sit up, my sneakers squeaking loudly as they slide across the dash of the cart.

I don't know how he always figures out which buttons to push to make me react, to make me feel like going absolutely *psycho*, but the plastic surgery comment did it. I got lip filler *once*. "You know what? Go fuck yourself, Tiger Woods."

Leaping out of the cart, I let Walter's continued verbal assaults hit my back, tuning out his voice as I set my sights on a shady patch of grass up ahead. I'll hide out there while he plays his remaining holes. He can drive *himself* around.

I don't intend on glancing back, but a sound cuts through the blood pounding in my ears: a high-pitched squeal.

I spin around just in time to watch the golf cart hurtle down the hill and slam into Walter.

It happens in slow motion, an honest-to-god cinematic cut scene. My eyes prickle, but I can't look away. The cart hits Walter so fast, surprise doesn't even have a chance to register on his face. Then, his limbs are wrapped around the front of the cart. His skull knocks off the metal with an audible thwack, and one of the front wheels catches on his tan trouser to pull him under. I swear, I hear every bone in his body breaking as the cart chews him up and spits him out the other side.

From a distance, I can't see much—only his body landing in a heap as the cart rockets into the sand pit, only a gleam of red soaking through his blond hair.

"Walter?" I whisper.

His body is too still, too warped. It's obvious that he's dead. There's no fantasy clouding my mind, no great love or desire for him that keeps me from accepting the truth. He's gone... and I am free. My body feels lighter than air, like I can finally breathe after a decade of slow suffocation, but that relief is brief. Reality hits, and I mull over my fate.

They'll say I killed him.

What if I'm arrested? What if I'm charged with murder?

I frantically attempt to replay the last few seconds in my head, but my brain isn't working right. Everything is fuzzy, jumbled from the adrenaline. *Had* I done it? Did I jostle the cart out of park without realizing it? I was so upset, I can't recall anything but needing to get away before I completely lost my shit.

Now he's dead, and I feel... nothing.

That's not right. I shouldn't feel nothing, even if I hated him. He's a person—a mean, angry, miserable person, but a person, nonetheless.

Should I leave?

I could purchase a plane ticket and disappear before the body is even found. It's so early in the morning; I have hours yet. Those panicked thoughts are fleeting, though, and soon, they fade as well. I shouldn't leave. I *can't* leave.

The paralysis in my legs and arms lift, foaming out of me until, at last, I can move.

My book tumbles to the grass, and I trudge forward a step. Yeah... There's no way I'm going to be able to walk back to the club like this, much less board a plane. The golf cart is bloodied, the wheels turning crookedly as it lies on its side in the sand pit. I need to call someone. Yes, that's it. If I wait any longer, it'll only seem like a confirmation of guilt.

My hand flies to my side, and I realize I don't have my phone on me; there's no place to put it in this skirt. My throat swells as my eyes drift to the pit.

I left my phone in the cart.

Swallowing hard, I start to stagger down the steep hill. I move carefully, trying not to fall and skid into the body.

In fact, I try my best not to look at the body at all, or at the blood pooling in the grass beneath him. It's a lot of fucking blood.

When I step into the sand pit, the golf cart is spitting black smoke and gasoline, so I try to be quick about finding my phone. I had set it in the center console, but it isn't there anymore. *Of course it isn't.* Heart in my throat, I walk to the other side, peering through the metal frame.

"Fuck," I rasp when I spot a glimpse of black glass pinned under the cart's side.

I kneel to dig out the sand around it, sweat beading on my temple, the sun raking angry claws down my back. I curse again when I finally free the phone, discovering the screen shattered. Half of it looks completely inoperable, but I try anyway, the broken glass cutting into my fingertips as I push off my knees. I don't even notice which direction I'm headed until my shins collide with a dirt wall and I tumble forward, falling palms-first into the slick grass.

A whimper curls in my throat as I raise my hands in front of my face.

Crimson liquid coats them, dripping from my fingers like strawberry syrup. My eyes slide forward, and I see him. Walter's lifeless body. His blood on my hands. I recoil from the mangled corpse, leaving my phone behind. "No, no, no," I mewl.

His body looks like a balled-up piece of paper, his neck bent out of shape and his features brutalized beyond recognition. There's no explanation for how a golf cart was able to do *that*. He looks like he was run over by a tractor, one of those spiky, gargantuan ones.

A warm breeze whistles in my ears, and I could have sworn it whispered, *yes, yes, yes.*

A wave of blistering heat blasts me in the face, and I

squeeze my eyes shut against it, the warmth washing over my body as my skin erupts in gooseflesh. A low, drawn-out moan surrounds me, deep and distorted, as the swirling heat intensifies. I gasp, and it feels like swallowing hot coals.

I'm being *burned alive*.

But then a heartbeat later, the heat evaporates, its absence a cool relief to my skin.

My eyes flutter open, and I instantly wish I'd kept them closed. Walter's bones break again. I watch as they snap and contort, as his back arcs off the grass and his limbs lengthen as if rods are being speared through them, resetting his joints. That groan I heard before... it came from his mouth. He makes another one, and it gets louder, turning into a growl as his head oscillates wildly against the ground.

With a final crack, his head snaps toward me. His eyes flash open, and I scream.

The whites of his eyes are bright red, the vessels in them erupting. His irises, once a deep blueish-gray, are now black, and his whole body shakes from the force of his growl. I'm not sure how he's making such a sound, only that I wish it would stop.

I cover my eyes and cower in the sand, unable to look any longer.

Gases. That must be what this is. His body is releasing all those weird death gases, and that's why he's moving. Either that, or he's not as dead as I thought he was. Oh god, what if he's suffering? I begin to sob; I don't know what else to do. That terrible voice in the back of my mind pipes up again, hoping he dies soon, if he hasn't already, just to put us both out of our misery.

After what feels like a small eternity, the world beyond my hands goes quiet. No snapping joints. No growling. No wind. Even the soft trickle of gasoline from the golf cart has stopped.

Slowly, I peek between my fingers.

Walter sits on that patch of bloody grass, his body shockingly whole, his white shirt stained a dark red. It looks like he fell into a vat of cherry juice.

He's staring at me, and he's smiling.

I can barely breathe as my hands fall into my lap. What the fuck just happened? Am I hallucinating? Did the gasoline fumes get to me? Maybe I'm dreaming. Maybe I've been dreaming this whole time, and if I wake myself up, I'll be home, safe in my bed. I pinch myself and hiss at the pain.

Still, he remains—my husband, watching me with red and black eyes.

"Ar-are you all right?" I ask tremulously, because what else can I say? I thought he was dead, and he's not. For a moment, I thought I was free of him, but unfortunately, I was *wrong*. I wonder if he can tell that I'm disappointed.

Walter's lips quirk into a lopsided smirk as he tilts his head, considering me. The black of his eyes seem to ripple, and I shiver under the weight of them. I've never experienced such an unnerving stare before—then again, I've never watched someone get run over by a golf cart either. Maybe it's the head trauma.

"Oh, baby," he finally rumbles, his voice deeper and darker than I'm used to. "I've never been better."

CHAPTER 2

ALWAYS LOCK THE DOOR

The shower spray hits my face as I scrub away the day's grime. My thoughts whittle down to the scalding water and the tiles beneath my feet, the humidity of the bathroom, and for a moment, I forget about this day and the horrors that came with it.

Nope, shit. There it is again—the memory of Walter's broken body glowing red behind my eyes.

Stepping back from the spray, I gasp for air and hug myself. Several times today, I've found it hard to breathe, like the events of the day are sitting heavily on my chest. I shiver despite the warm air and stare at the tiles on the wall, trying to sort through the confusion of the last several hours.

Walter and I spent the rest of the day at the emergency room, getting him checked out despite his protests. It was a goddamn miracle—he had no broken bones or internal bleeding. The doctors treated a few surface cuts and hydrated him through an IV, but they'd looked at both of us a little funny when they saw the state of his clothes. They did a few extra tests to be thorough, but it resulted in nothing. Or, at least, nothing I wanted to accept.

When the hospital psychologist turned her attention on me, I knew it was time to shut up about what I saw. I knew that look. I've *given* people that look before. So, I backpedaled and lied my ass off until they finally let us go home.

The most unsettling part of the day had nothing to do with my husband's miraculous recovery, though. It was his behavior.

He was silent in the hospital. Usually, he deals with strangers with the enthusiasm of a salesman. He needs to be liked, admired. But today, he didn't speak a word more than required. He didn't look at anyone or anything but *me.*

As soon as we got home, I used the blood beneath my fingernails as a means of escape from his watchful gaze.

Now, I scowl at the frosted glass door of the shower, knowing I can't stay inside much longer—the water is getting cold. Reluctantly, I turn off the water and dry off with a towel from the heated rack. When I'm finished, I exit the shower naked, half-expecting to find my husband waiting for me, since he's refused to leave my side most of the day. To my relief, he isn't. I walk into the closet to dress for bed and stop short.

He wasn't waiting in the bathroom because he already found the bench to lounge on in the closet.

When I enter, he looks up from the book in his lap with sleepy eyes and a small smile. The nurse insisted on him showering at the hospital, so he's easier to look at now. His eyes are still darker than I remember, more of a charcoal rather than a blue-gray. Every time I look into them, a chill crawls up my spine. Something isn't right about that, but when I brought it up at the hospital, they gave me no explanation. They didn't care. They wouldn't even refer him to an optometrist, for fuck's sake.

The cotton robe he changed into at the hospital is tied loosely around his waist, and I can see the hard edges of his upper torso from here, can see the thick muscle of his thighs.

My husband closes the book, exposing the cover to me, and my jaw drops. It's one from the stack on my nightstand. My *special* stack. Crossing my arms over my bare chest, I snap, "What are you doing with that?"

Any other day, I might have said it nicer, might have tried harder to keep the peace, but I'm completely worn out. If I have to listen to one more insult about my primary source of happiness and pleasure these days, I'm going to lose it. *He'll wind up with a heel shoved through his eye this time.* I stiffen at the violent thought and frantically shove that piece of me back down.

He only shrugs and sets the book down, unbothered by my attitude. "Biding my time. Reading about a woman being railed ten ways by three different men isn't a bad way to do it." His eyes crinkle in amusement, and my head empties out. He's being sort of... pleasant, and I don't know how to react to it, so I don't react at all. His gaze doesn't stray from me; it leisurely peruses the length of my body, down and then back up. "Though I'd much rather be participating."

Blinking, I shift on my feet, the hairs on the back of my neck standing on end.

If I was a more self-conscious woman, I might have covered myself with the closest item from my side of the closet, but I've never been shy about my body, and I won't start hiding it now. I study my husband carefully, trying to determine how he's messing with me. He must be. He likes playing mind games in the most underhanded ways possible, so that I don't even realize he's insulting me until the punchline drops and I walk away feeling more of a fool for it. I can only imagine he's dangling sex in front of me just to rip it away when I reach for it. Though, I have no clue why he thinks that would tempt me. We stopped having sex years ago.

Rather than walk into his trap, I turn and rifle through my nightgowns, pulling out a scarlet silk teddy and leisurely shimmying into it. As I slide the straps into place on my shoulders, I spin to face my husband again. He's still staring—staring *harder*, if that's even possible. He cradles his jaw in one hand, his thumb absently tracing his lower lip.

I fold my arms, glaring daggers at him. "Do you have to watch me like that?"

"Is there any reason why I shouldn't?" he counters with a cock of his head.

"It's creepy as fuck."

He smiles, which only serves to unsettle me further.

I shake my head, stalking toward the bedroom. "You clearly sustained a concussion or something. I don't think the doctors did enough for you."

Walking through the bathroom, I make a point to *not* meet his eyes in the mirror, though I feel his gaze on me all the same. My feet sink into the lush carpet as I enter our bedroom. I approach my vanity and scoop up my lemon-scented lotion, squirting a generous amount into my palm. As I massage the cream into my arms, I smile, the citrus scent wrapping me in a happy little cocoon.

My smile falls as Walter leans against the wall beside my vanity, directly in my line of sight.

"You're so concerned about my well-being today," he says in a low, rough timber. "Are you feeling bad about what happened to me, Rosie Posie? Are you feeling *guilty*?"

My blood freezes.

Rosie Posie...

My mother is the only person who ever called me that.

I don't speak to Walter about her or my childhood, never have, so I don't know how he learned *that* particular gem. It feels like he's just ripped my spine out through my stomach and nicked my heart in the process. I start hemorrhaging memories of her, her jewel blue eyes and wrinkly smile. Her favorite beaded necklace that I lost my first year of grad school and still cry over to this day. The musky perfume she always wore that she really shouldn't have been able to afford —the only nice thing I remember her ever buying for herself —and its bottle that I added oil to again and again as I used it up, until it eventually smelled like nothing at all. Her weak hand squeezing mine as we laid in her hospital bed, surrounded by empty jello containers and a half-finished crocheted blanket that would never be completed.

It always happens like this. One trigger, and all of that grief comes flooding back.

Sometimes, it quiets to a low rumble, hibernating in my heart like a bear in the dead of winter. But it always returns, and when it does, it's an unpredictable, vicious creature. It has claws and fangs, and never fails to defend its territory.

I glare at him through welling tears, and then the rest of what he said hits me like a train.

Guilty. He wants to know if I feel guilty.

I wasn't sure how much he remembered about the accident; he hadn't said a word about it until now. I'd hoped he'd hit his head hard enough that he didn't remember the way I stood there and watched it happen, the way I smiled when I thought he was dead. He was knocked unconscious when the cart hit him, so he couldn't know, right? Maybe this is just his way of prying for more information.

Walter would do terrible things to me if he knew how

little sadness I felt over his death, how little I did to help him. He's already terrible enough.

"I don't know what you're talking about," I reply tightly, severing our eye contact.

I turn to watch myself in the vanity as I prop a foot on the chair and slather my thigh with lotion. My hair hangs in dark, wet strings around my shoulders, my skin red from the exfoliating I did in the shower, highlighting the brown beauty marks speckling my flesh.

Angel kisses, my mom used to call them.

"Sure you don't," he mutters, moving to crowd me from behind.

His hands close over my hips, and I jolt, but he holds me in place as he presses even closer. His body radiates intense, *feverish* heat. He must not be feeling well, and that's why he's acting so strange. His breath warms my scalp, and that heat spreads to my ear as he whispers, "*Sweet menace.*"

That threatening tone...

Does he remember what happened at the golf course? The moments before it hit him? Does he think I'm to blame?

I lift my foot to leave, but his hand flies out and seizes my thigh, keeping me in place. I'm suddenly very aware of my center, spread and bare beneath the nightgown. I forget to breathe as my body coils tight, and I can't tell if it's from fear or just general surprise. He hasn't touched me in years. He lost interest once he moved on to younger, more eager women, and I was glad for it.

"Stop, Walter." I place my hand over his where it grips my thigh, digging my nails into his flesh.

His hand tightens, and I hiss, lurching away from him.

He grabs my neck with his free hand and wrenches my face toward his. His teeth flash in the dark room, his eyes nothing more than portals of midnight, threatening to swallow me whole.

That stare stills me, my fight, and my thoughts.

"I told you to call me Levi. I won't remind you of that again." I bite down on a shudder as his fingertips squeeze my neck—not enough to cut off airflow, but enough to make his point. He smiles, and I feel like crawling right out of my skin. "Not *nicely*, anyway," he adds.

When we were driving to the hospital, he asked me to address him by that name, but he didn't bring it up again, and he didn't correct me when I gave the professionals his information. I wrote it off as a product of his injuries, a brief confusion. Apparently, it wasn't.

I lean back against his shoulder, trying to find the slightest bit of relief from his grip. "Let me go."

"I don't have to," he taunts. "And would you like to know why?"

"Because you're a *prick*," I snarl.

He chuckles, his hand loosening, turning into a feather-light caress down the length of my carotid. "Because you're *my* wife now. *Forever*."

Before his words can fully register, he releases me, and I fall forward. I catch myself on the vanity, breathing embarrassingly hard as I watch his silhouette retreat across the bedroom through the mirror, disappearing into the dark hallway beyond it. I wait until I hear his footsteps on the grand staircase, and then I run across the room and shut the door, locking it.

That does little to soothe me, though, and my hands tremble against my stomach.

What the hell was that all about?

My heart pounds against my ribs. I wait for his shadow to

reappear beneath it, but it doesn't—that's only my fear talking, and the longer I watch, the sillier I feel.

The dark is feeding my imagination.

I flip the overhead light on and return to my vanity. As I moisturize my other leg, I try to reason with myself. My husband had a difficult day. Tensions are high, and we're both deliriously tired. I'm sure he didn't *mean* to scare me. I'm sure he remembers very little about what happened on that golf course.

I didn't mean to take the cart out of park. Really, I didn't. For all he knows, the cart could have been defective. There's no reason for him to suspect *me*.

By the time I separate my wet hair into two sections to braid it, I feel a little calmer, but only barely. A worm of unease continues to wiggle around under my skin, traveling lazily from limb to limb. At least this day is over. Opening the top drawer of my vanity, I pull out a little green prescription bottle—my sleeping pills. I shake out one of the white tablets and return the bottle to its drawer before ambling to my nightstand and swallowing it with a sip from the glass water bottle I keep there.

With a heavy sigh, I walk back to the door and unlock it.

It's better if I don't make my husband any angrier with me. Nothing good will come from locking him out. If we slept in separate rooms, like most unattached and unhappy couples, this wouldn't be a point of contention, but Walter has always been insistent that we share this space. We have company over too often for him to allow me that level of independence, that level of *comfort*. Plus, if I lock him out tonight, it'll only fuel his animosity once he's well-rested and back to normal.

Once he's back to hating me as much as I hate him.

I climb into bed, turn on my white noise machine, and wait for sleep to claim me.

————

*W*AKE UP.

Those words reverberate through the darkness, glimmering in my mind like fireflies flickering. Awareness. Faint at first, but building brighter as I stir out of sleep. Waves crashing into a shore. Seagulls crying.

The voice speaks again. *Come on, Rosie Posie.*

At once, I've fallen back in time to my childhood home. I'm nestled in my canopy bed, surrounded by pink curtains and stuffed animals. Instead of the ocean, I hear trucks rumbling past our 900 square foot apartment. *Home.*

The voice is almost my mother's. *It's time to wake up, baby.*

I peel one eye open.

I'm lying belly-down... but not in my childhood home. Instead of a lumpy mattress, I'm on memory foam and down pillows. My vision is blurry, but I know right away that it's too early to be awake, no hint of sunlight peering through the windows.

I blink a couple times, and my vision clears enough to make out the blue numbers glowing on my nightstand. 3:33 *A.M.* The white noise machine is still on, but it's quieter now, as if someone turned down the volume. I may have done it in my sleep; it wouldn't have been the first time.

This *is* the first time my sleeping pill has failed me, though.

I groan into my pillow, debating whether I want to try falling back to sleep or not. The pills are the only things that keep me from dreaming, but I can't take two of them in one night. They're too strong. I was prescribed the tablets just over a year ago, when my nightmares really started bothering me. In my dreams, dark shadows chase me down corridors and laugh at me, monsters envelope me in flashes of violence, bloodshed, and raw, carnal pleasure. They were sometimes wonderful, sometimes terrifying, but *always* vivid. I would wake up feeling as if I hadn't slept at all. I became an insomniac for a few months just to avoid them, but when I started hallucinating due to sleep deprivation, I finally went to my doctor.

Nope, I'm not going to risk it. Best just to get up early.

As I flip over, I see a shadowy figure towering over my side of the bed.

I gasp in surprise, my body jolting against the mattress. My heartbeat spikes, thundering in my ears as all of my limbs lock up. I can't roll away. I can't do anything. All I *can* do is stare wide-eyed at the figure as a wicked chuckle fills my ears.

When a wide grin pierces the dark, I finally see who it is.

My husband.

I force myself to blink, and the finer details come into focus. The moonlight silhouettes his naked body, creating a silvery sheen on his skin. When I look down, I realize water is dripping from him, and there's steam curling through the open door of the bathroom. He must have taken a shower, but why now, in the middle of the night?

"What are you doing?" I demand breathlessly.

His head tilts ever so slightly. "I just wanted to say goodnight, baby." His voice is an unholy thing, deep and menacing.

I swallow my dread and choke out, "Oh. Ok then. Goodnight?"

He leans forward, his hands sinking into the mattress on either side of me. I'm trapped. He brings his smirking face millimeters from mine, until all I can see is the utter blackness of his eyes and the red scratch on his cheek. Is that new? Or has it been there all day and only reopened in the shower?

His voice slithers around me, cutting off my line of thought. "Say. My. Name." Each word is a commandment, and I so badly want to obey.

"Goodnight, Levi," I breathe.

He drags a finger down my cheek. "Good girl. Now, go back to sleep before I forget my patience entirely."

I feel my brow bunch in confusion, but he's already pulling away. As he rounds the bed to his side of the mattress, I'm paralyzed. I stare at a divot in the ceiling as he settles in beside me. There's no fucking way I can go back to sleep now, not after that *delightful* wake-up call. I'll have to wait until he passes out, and then I'll get up. I'll call the hospital; there's something seriously wrong with him.

Levi shuffles across the mattress to me, and his hand caresses the braid lying across my shoulder. "By the way," he purrs, tugging on the hair hard enough that a star of pleasure shoots through my center, "I really, *really* like these. You made a pair of pretty little leashes just for me."

I don't know what to say. I don't know what to do, other than clamp my thighs together and flip off my cunt for double-crossing me.

I should have kept the bedroom door locked.

As my husband's breathing evens out and the sky lightens around us, he holds on to that braid, anchoring me to him and this bed as my eyes continue staring at that mark in the ceiling. A nick in the paint that looks a little too much like his new smirk.

CHAPTER 3

TEST THE PIGGIES FOR POISON

Miraculously, I fall back asleep.

When I wake again, the sun is shining, and I'm alone but that doesn't totally surprise me. My husband is usually up before dawn. I glance at the time and scramble out of bed. It's mid-morning; I forgot that my phone is still broken, and I didn't set up a secondary alarm, so now, I'm late.

Scowling at the braids as I destroy them, I quickly tug my hair into a bun before I dress for the day in a ruby-red blouse, black pencil skirt, and my favorite pumps.

In the burgeoning light of day, my concerns from last night seem a lot less serious. My husband clearly sustained a concussion of some sort. He was up doing god knows what for hours but he's gotten some sleep now, and if he went to work this morning, then things must be returning to normal. Thank fuck.

As I make my way downstairs, the scent of breakfast and espresso wafts over me. I walk a little faster, almost tripping over my own feet as I rush through the dining area.

If I don't get some form of caffeine into my system, I might drop dead on the freeway. As I enter the main kitchen, though, I skid to a stop. Our personal chef is *not* the one cooking.

"What are you doing in here?" The question bursts from my lips before I can think better of it, and even I can admit my tone was far too accusatory for ten in the morning.

My husband turns from his position at the stove, cracking a crooked smile that makes my heart thump harder. "What does it look like, Rosie?" He gestures at the pan in front of him. "I'm making breakfast."

He's in gray pajama pants, his chest bare and rippling with toned muscle.

I pause to catch my breath.

Breakfast? I've never seen Walter even use a *toaster* before, but I guess Levi feels differently about a man laboring over a stove. He certainly *looks* different.

He doesn't usually walk around the house like this; he wears suits so often that at social events, I like to joke he was born in one. And he seems larger this morning. It's not his body that grew, but rather the man inside of it, like there's some kind of energy ballooning under his skin, pressurizing every inch of his presence. He fills the room.

"What about work?" I ask.

He shrugs. "I think yesterday permits me some time away from the office, don't you?"

The events of yesterday flash through my mind like some overplayed horror film, almost comical now with a night between us. He's right. After what happened, I should have expected he might want to stay home. If a golf cart could bloody him up like that, his anxiety about driving a car must be astronomical. Even a workaholic prick can be traumatized.

I give him my signature *I-hear-you* nod. "Of course. Why,

exactly, are you monopolizing our kitchen, though? Where's our chef?"

"You're that skeptical of my ability to feed you?" he teases.

I give him an impatient look, and Levi sighs, waving his spatula at the French doors behind me. "The chef's checking on the garden." He returns to the pan, poking at whatever is sizzling in it. Despite my better sense, I stroll around the island to stand beside him.

"What *are* you making?"

He leers at me with a smirk. "Piggies in a blanket, baby."

I survey his work. There's a plate filled with sausages steaming beside the stove, and he's in the process of cooking a few pancakes. He's made a mess with the batter, but there's a light-heartedness about his self-imposed task that stuns me.

When I don't respond, he leans in to add, "I was inspired after seeing you in your pigtails, all bundled up in the comforter this morning. You looked good enough to eat."

My head snaps up to meet his stare, my lips pressed together as I wait for the punchline, but after a heartbeat, I realize he's serious. There's a wickedness in his eyes, and the words... there's sincerity in them. *Good enough to eat.*

That pressure under his skin seems to pulse, and my attention is drawn to his eyes, as black and endless as space. They haven't returned to normal yet.

None of this is normal. A shiver threatens my composure, so I quickly step backward, putting space between us.

Levi turns back to the stove, flipping the pancakes onto a plate as I slowly back away. I don't know how my hand finds its way to the landline telephone, but it does. I turn slightly, shielding my actions as I fill in the number for our county's psychiatric hospital. It isn't ethical—using my license to admit him—but that feeling in the pit of my stomach has returned, the total wrongness of him.

I'm not sure how I'm going to explain it. What do I say to get them to understand? How do I say that he's being unusually *nice*, flirtatious, and borderline creepy? We're married. How do I explain that we aren't a regular couple? That he may have suffered brain damage in an accident that might have been my fault, and his body has retained no actual proof that it ever even happened?

A drastic personality change like this after head trauma is... not good, to say the least. If left untreated, there's no telling the long term effects.

Faintly, I hear the worst bit of myself whisper, *why not wait and see what happens? If he loses his life or enough of his mental faculties, the money is yours. All of it. That's better than alimony. Haven't you earned that? Don't you deserve more than the bare fucking minimum?*

As my thumb hovers over the call button, my eyes flick up and catch on the small television mounted in the corner of the kitchen, the screen lulling that voice back to sleep.

Our chef likes to watch the news every morning. It's muted right now, but the picture and headline is enough to make me drop the phone on the counter.

"Oh my god," I gasp.

"What about him?" Levi steps up behind me, close enough that his breath puffs against the nape of my neck.

I swiftly grab the landline and clear the number on the screen before he can see it, and then I snatch the remote with my other hand to unmute the television.

The news anchor's sharp voice blasts from the speakers. "—businessman, Callum Smith, was confirmed missing early this morning when his wife found an unmarked package on their doorstep. The authorities are not sharing details at this time, but a reliable source reported to SVTV that the contents of said package includes severed fingers, possibly belonging to Mr. Smith, and a note that suggests his involvement in a trafficking ring—"

"Oh my *god*," I repeat, my stomach churning.

Glancing over my shoulder, I expect Levi's face to reflect the surprise I feel, but his expression is cold, unreadable. Levi tears his gaze from the screen and returns my stare. His hands slide over my hips, squeezing slightly, and then he shrugs, as if adjusting the company to Callum Smith's disappearance won't bother him in the slightest.

"If what they said is true, then good riddance," he says.

My brow furrows.

Callum and my husband have been the best of friends, both in business and beyond. Callum is one of his top advisors, and they sometimes disappear on work trips together for weeks at a time. Hearing the disregard in Levi's voice now, I have to wonder if something serious happened between them, if there has been a falling out of some sort.

What kind of person doesn't blink when a business associate goes *missing*? Did he not hear the part about Callum's fingers being *severed* and delivered to his wife like a goddamn present?

Levi plucks the remote from my hand and turns off the television. "Come on, that's enough." He herds me around the island, intense heat seeping through my pencil skirt from his palms.

It becomes clear to me then that he's guiding me to the breakfast bar, and I try to shake him off. "Would you stop manhandling me? I'm not hungry."

A low rumble vibrates from his chest into my back. He's *laughing* at me. Hooking his arms around my waist, he smoothly sweeps me off my feet before depositing me on one of the stools and leaning in to purr into my ear. "I'll manhandle you if I need to. There's no use lying to me when I could hear your stomach growling in our bed."

Scowling, I pry his arms from my waist so I can scoot off the chair, but his hands fly up to seize my shoulders. His grip is firm, almost rough, as his thumbs dig into the muscles of my back. I gasp, gripping the counter in front of me, and I groan involuntarily as he applies more pressure, massaging his way down the length of my spine.

He chuckles again. "You see? I know what you need, menace."

The hell he does.

But I moan again anyway as his focus narrows in on a knot behind my shoulder, his knuckles finessing their way into places I didn't realize they could.

"And you, my beautiful wife," he says in a heated whisper, "are *hungry.*"

He drops a blistering kiss to the nape of my neck before stepping away. My back tingles from his touch as he stalks around the island and gathers food onto a clean plate for me. I can't move; it's like Levi has wrapped chains around my spine and anchored me to this seat.

His touch is a spell, and I am bound by it.

Levi sets the plate on the island between us before taking a toothpick and impaling one of the sausages after sandwiching it in a pancake. He grabs the strawberry syrup and pours a generous helping on top. Sloppy, but effective. He slides the plate and fork across the counter to me, and I frown at it.

The piggie in question looks like it was wrenched from bed and slaughtered, fileted of its skin, its corpse now lying in a pool of blood.

"Eat up," Levi commands, licking a dribble of syrup off his thumb.

Treacherous warmth fills my cheeks, despite the fact that nothing about him should have the power to make me *blush*. I pick up my fork, deciding I would rather eat the breakfast than let him think he succeeded in making me feel uncomfortable—or worse, flattered.

Scooping a bite into my mouth, my eyes bulge as flavor bursts across my tongue, both savory and sweet. I think he put cinnamon into the pancake batter. As I continue to chew, I raise my gaze to his, my eyes narrowing in suspicion. Considering I've never seen him so much as butter his own toast, I'm surprised. Another glance around the room draws my attention to the cookbooks open on the counter behind him. Well, that makes sense.

After swallowing, I mumble, "It's delicious. Thank you."

"You're very welcome." He leans forward, resting his forearms on the counter.

My skin prickles under the weight of his stare. "Are you going to eat too, or are you just going to keep staring at me like that?"

His head tilts. "Like what?"

"Like *I'm* your meal."

Levi pauses, pursing his lips to mask a smile. "Well, you're right about one thing," he admits quietly. "You are the only thing I wish to feast on right now."

My stomach rolls, the compliment lost on me as I quickly shovel one last bite of breakfast into my mouth before I leap up and aim for the coffee maker across the kitchen.

"Sorry to disappoint, but I don't have time to spread my legs for you." Besides, we both know he can get it elsewhere, and usually, he does, with whatever female employee is tolerating him best at work.

I grab a thermos from the cabinet and fill it with coffee and almond milk as Levi leans against the edge of the counter with a pinched brow.

"Where are you going?"

"I have a few errands to run today. You know, lady stuff. I'll be back later." I place the lid on my thermos and quickly turn away, my heels clicking across tile and then wood as I enter the narrow hall leading to the garage.

He pursues me. "Well, no, I *don't* know, but now I must."

I pull my jacket on without looking at him—which is difficult, considering the mud room is the smallest area in our entire house. "I'll be busy for most of the day, so I'll just see you at dinner time, okay?"

"Do you have to leave? I thought we could spend the day together."

Ugh. I'd rather be run over by a golf cart. I bite back a wince. I really shouldn't think things like that. Smiling tightly, I lift my purse off its hook. "You know what they say: idle hands are the devil's playground."

He scoffs. "Trust me, a devil's hands are never idle."

I step up to the door, and suddenly, he's there. Levi's forearm appears in front of me, bracing the door to prevent me from opening it.

"Hold on, *menace*," he drawls, his voice liquid fire. "Aren't you forgetting something?"

I twist toward him with a huff. This is getting annoying. I don't know why he insists on being in my way at every turn this morning. Maybe he *knows* it annoys me. I'll admit, it's better than his usual methods of humiliation, but that doesn't make me any less combative.

"What?" I cross my arms under my breasts.

His eyes drop to survey my cleavage, a mischievous grin

dancing over his lips as they slowly slide back up to my face. "A kiss goodbye for your dear husband?"

I blink. This may be the first time he's ever *asked* me to kiss him. We kiss in front of other people, sure—for appearances—but he never has to actually ask. And never in our house, alone, with no one to perform for but each other. I can't recall a single real kiss since we got married and all the pretense officially fell away. What kind of twisted game is he playing?

I don't have time to examine his intentions; I'm late and running later by the minute. So, with a roll of my eyes, I lean in to give him a quick peck on the lips. Or, at least, I try.

The moment my lips touch his, he strikes.

Both of his warm hands plunge into my hair, pulling dark strands free from my bun as he twists and shoves me up against the door to the garage. One hand shifts to firmly cup my jaw, and a growl radiates from his chest—so loud, it makes me shudder. A small moan escapes me, and I resent the sound as soon as I make it. The fingers around my throat tighten, and I drop my thermos to grab at his wrist, momentarily overcome by the irrational fear that he might try to strangle me.

His tongue teases the seam of my lips, on the cusp of invading me but not quite crossing that line. Instead, he pins my lower lip between his teeth, scraping and tugging, *commanding* a response. I don't know how, but I wind up responding. Suddenly, I'm closing my eyes and kissing him back in earnest.

Because this is more than a kiss—it's war, and I have never been one to back down from a fight. I'll take anything he gives me and make him wish he had more.

But the instant I start kissing him back, he pulls away.

He's smirking at me when I open my eyes, pride and

amusement swirling in the blackness. "Mmm," he hums. "Just as sweet as I remember." Then, his tongue darts out, flicking over his lower lip, savoring the taste of me.

My eyes latch onto the movement, because I feel it too, the lingering phantom—a tingle that assures me my lips are swollen and pink now that they've been thoroughly worshiped. I can't remember the last time I was kissed like that. It's been a long time.

Levi's hand loosens on my jaw and trails down the length of my neck. When he reaches my collar, he steps back and bends to retrieve my thermos from the floor. I'm still in a daze, my chest heaving as he returns it to my hands. "I'll see you soon, baby."

Then, he turns on his heel and exits the room, leaving me overheated and disoriented in the drowsy bowels of my own personal un-caffeinated hell.

CHAPTER 4

ALWAYS CARRY A CRYSTAL IN YOUR BRA

"I'm glad you haven't been kidnapped, murdered, or crashed into a ditch on the way here, which are really the only acceptable excuses for being *this* late to the clinic *we* decided to open together." Astra is on a roll already, and I've barely entered the office.

I turn to hang my jacket on the coat rack, rolling my eyes. My best friend is being a little dramatic this morning.

Every corner of the staff room is billowing with aromatherapy diffusers. Today, it smells like frankincense and citrus—not the worst scent she's experimented with this month; it's actually pretty nice. Overgrown plants curtain the only window in the room, tinting what little light seeps through an almost magical green. Crystals of varying shapes and hues decorate the kitchenette and the short tables scattered throughout the room.

I walk around the large cushions meant for resting, beelining for the coffee machine in the corner.

"Don't think I can't hear your eyes rolling like boulders

into the back of your marvelous head," she grumbles as she follows close behind me.

I heave a sigh of relief when I see she's already brewed some for me. She can't be feeling too murderous, then. Maybe she poisoned it, but if that's my fate, so be it. My head is still fuzzy from sleeping in, or maybe from the interruption to my sleep. Or that kiss. Either way, I feel the sleeping pill lingering like curdled milk in my bloodstream.

I refill my thermos, barely leaving a cup-worth behind. No one else here drinks it. This coffee machine is the only item my partner let me contribute to the "refined aesthetic" of our clinic, and only barely. Caffeine wreaks havoc on cortisol levels.

Astra is always *very* concerned about my cortisol levels.

As if I haven't been chronically anxious my entire life. Then again, my mom let me drink coffee from the age of ten, so maybe she's onto something.

The lights in here are dim, which means Astra started her meditations earlier than usual—my absence must have driven her to it. Shit. That sort of makes me feel bad. She cares too much about me, but that's always been our thing. It's not that I don't care; I just worry that telling her how much she means to me too often will inevitably drive her away, like she'll see right through me to my insecurities and decide I'm right. I'm not capable of loving anyone well enough to keep them around for a long time.

I know that's not fair to believe that, but most fears aren't fair or rational. We feel them even when we hate them—*especially* when we hate them.

Astra calls the break room our "astral sanctuary," and she heartily encourages the staff to explore other *dimensions* in their free time. While I'm the realist in our friendship and our clinic, Astra is the dreamer, the spiritualist.

The miserable housewives in the area cling to her while offloading their troubled kids onto my couch. It's an efficient —and *profitable*—system.

I discreetly sniff the bean juice to make sure Astra didn't try to trick me with decaf before dolling it up with a little oat milk from the fridge. She didn't give me decaf, that angel. *Yeah, I definitely feel bad for stressing her out now.*

She glares at me as I take a long sip, and I use that time to gather my thoughts. I know better than to lie to her. She has a built-in lie detector that would put the polygraph to shame. Once I place my thermos back on the counter, I pull her stiff body into mine for a hug. She smells good, as always, like coconut and caramelized sugar. I rest my chin on her shoulder, my face buried in her pretty dark curls as I wait for her body to soften. After a few moments, she sighs and snakes her dark brown arms around my waist.

"I'm really sorry," I say. "I've had a chaotic weekend, and I'm pretty sure I had a weird reaction to my sleeping pill last night. I'm all over the place right now."

She grunts noncommittally. "I've been calling you all morning."

I disentangle from her and return to my coffee. "My phone was crushed by a golf cart yesterday," I mutter.

Her perfect brows stitch together, and I take a deep breath as I decide to share the rest. "Walter was as well. We spent the whole day at the hospital."

Her mouth pops open. "Oh my gods."

"He's fine," I add quickly.

She brackets her hands on her hips with a frown. "Damn, talk about a missed opportunity for karmic justice." She shakes her fist at the ceiling. "Get it together, Universe."

I have to make a conscious effort to swallow the coffee in my mouth rather than spit it out.

"Oh, don't give me that look," she grumbles. "We were both thinking it; I'm just the only one allowed to say it as your best friend in this stepford wife horror show. I'm the Bobby to your Joanna." A thoughtfulness crosses her face, and she abruptly spins to look around the room. She leans over to snatch up a crystal from the tabletop beside her and stuffs it into her bra as she turns back to me, releasing a heavy breath. Maybe she thinks that little lump of mineral will negate any negative karma accrued from wishing someone dead.

But didn't I wish the very same thing yesterday? Maybe I need one of those pretty rocks to bruise my tit too.

Taking another sip of coffee, I ask, "Are we talking about the actual book, or the 2004 Hollywood adaptation here? Because trust me, there's a difference."

She folds her arms and smiles prettily. "The one where we reap sweet revenge on the patriarchy and run away to live in a little cottage in the forest together."

"Uh-huh," I say through a laugh. "Well, you let me know when you find a way to revert the entire city's programming, and then we can start plotting our vengeance."

"No plotting, only anarchy!" she exclaims with a raised finger. A warm smile graces her face as her hand drops back to her side. "Well, seeing as you have a perfectly reasonable explanation for pissing me off, I guess you're forgiven."

Splaying a hand over my chest, I say, "I live for your forgiveness. *Thank you.*"

"Don't sass me, Rose." Her eyes narrow to slits, but she's still smiling.

I nod sagely. "Yes, ma'am."

Astra turns to her window of plants, flicking a marbled leaf. "As much as I wish that stupid prick had gotten what he deserves, I'm glad you're not being forced to take bereavement leave right now." Her breath catches, and her eyes flick to mine as the energy between us shifts. She's just remembered something. Through her teeth, she says, "Because you have a new client. She's waiting in your office."

I jolt, nearly dropping my thermos again. "Wait, *right now?*"

She grimaces. "Been waiting a while."

I leap away from the counter and walk briskly across the room. "Christ, Astra, why didn't you say that ten minutes ago? Why wasn't she on my schedule?"

She replies, "I was waiting to see if I needed to fire you first."

"Ha. Ha."

Sighing, Astra follows me out of the staff room as we rush through the shiny white hallway to the back of the building where our clinical offices are. "I didn't know about the client myself until about an hour ago. Then I started worrying about you, and I forgot. I really was afraid you got into a car accident or something. I've been scrolling through the real-time traffic reports for the last thirty minutes."

My heart breaks a little hearing her say that. "I'm so sorry, Astra."

She forces a small smile. "It's fine. You're okay, I'm okay. Do you remember that nosy monster of an investor who attended our last fundraiser? Blue suit, killer eyes."

My brow furrows as I try to recall that night. There had been a champagne fountain, and I'd been drinking enough to forget we were spending a small fortune to raise a slightly larger fortune for the clinic—but we'd met all the investors we needed that night. I pluck a flickering memory out of that drunken fog.

"What—the one who wouldn't stop following us around?"

"Yup." Her mouth pops on the p. "Turns out, he and his

wife adopted three little girls. That's why he took an interest in our clinic. They foster as well, and the newest foster kid they took in is having a rough go of it. His wife strolled in here this morning demanding we treat the kid and threatened to pull funding if we didn't."

I spin on my heel as Astra returns my wide-eyed stare, finally letting me see her exhaustion. The early meditation wasn't because of me after all. I should have noticed it sooner—the slight redness of her eyes that suggests she's been dealing with angry tears.

"You let her push you around like that?" I demand.

She shrugs. "I got a few words in edgewise, but it's like you said, babe—we're fighting the city's programming. We can't afford to lose his funding and, honestly, the kid looks pretty damn miserable."

I pinch the bridge of my nose. "I could never say no to a hurting kid," I mutter into the stars behind my eyes. "But this doesn't bode well for dealing with them or their friends in the future. It sets a precedent."

When I drop my hand, I find Astra back to her regular self.

She smiles confidently. "I know. Don't worry; I just need a little time to figure out what we should do, possibly to find a replacement investor." She places her hands on my shoulders and steps forward to lean her forehead against mine. Her honey brown eyes drill into me, as if she were attempting to transfer that same feigned confidence through our eyes or skin cells. Actually... that's probably exactly what she's trying to do, and that's really sweet. I place my hands over hers, pretending to receive it.

"Go work your magic," she whispers forcefully. "And I'll work mine."

Astra spins around without another word, sweeping back

up the hall, and I turn to my office. I was given no time to prepare for the session, but there's nothing to be done. I'll have to assess on my toes.

I roll my shoulders back, swipe on a smile, and enter the room.

The child on the couch jumps at the sound of the door. They look to be about thirteen or fourteen, with long blonde hair and aqua eyes. They sit on the edge of the cushion, hands pinned beneath their thighs and one foot bouncing against the carpet.

I smile a little brighter and walk across the room to set my thermos down on my desk. Then, I slowly approach the chair sitting across from the couch.

The child doesn't keep extended eye contact with me. Instead, their eyes flick down over my outfit and then around the room, catching on the small comforts I've placed throughout it: fluffy decorative pillows, soft knit blankets, a narrow bookshelf in the corner filled to the brim with *Chicken Soup for the Soul* books.

I thread my hands in front of my stomach, foregoing any attempt to shake their hand as I say, "I apologize in advance for not knowing your name and for being so late. I'm Rose. What are your preferred pronouns, and what name would you like me to use to address you?"

They lift their eyes to mine, their leg still bouncing, shaking their entire slender body. "My name is Sam, and she is fine."

"Alright." I sit down in the chair across from her. "It's lovely to meet you. Do you know why you're here today, Sam?"

"Do *you*?" The question is laced with hostility.

I pretend not to hear it. "I'm sorry, I don't. This session is as last minute for me as I'm sure it was for you. What motivated your foster mother to bring you in during school hours?"

"I'm homeschooled," she replies. "And Mrs. Busch is not any kind of mother to me."

"I see." I cross my legs and clasp my hands in front of my knee.

I wait patiently for her to answer my initial question, ignoring the awkward silence that unfolds between us. I've already prompted her a couple times, and she doesn't seem to respond well to that. She doesn't like being guided. She probably just needs some time to get comfortable with me, or uncomfortable enough to fill the quiet. Either way, she needs space.

Sam scoots until her back is pressed into the cushion of the couch, and then she crosses her arms tightly over her chest. Before she can speak, I hear her stomach gurgle, and I watch her hands drop to cover her stomach. She's hungry—whatever brought her here also caused her to miss breakfast. Very interesting.

I lean in and whisper conspiratorially, "I keep a private stash of junk food in here. You can have some if you promise not to tell anyone about it."

Astra would blow her lid if she found out how much corn syrup I eat in here behind her back. It's all herbal tea and fancy crackers out in the lobby.

Sam's eyebrows furrow, but she doesn't object right away, so I rise from my seat and retrieve the wicker basket of snacks from underneath my desk. I carry the basket back to Sam and present it to her. Her eyes scan the colorful plastic bags, the wide array of chips and sugary treats. I don't have to encourage her any further; Sam quickly plucks a bag of spicy red chips from the basket and opens it.

"Good choice," I mutter, grabbing a bag for myself and

setting the basket down on the coffee table between us. I pull out two sets of disposable chopsticks from my desk and hand her one before she can dig in. She looks at the proffered utensils in confusion, so I explain, "To keep the chips from leaving stains on your skin. Red fingers would be a dead giveaway."

"I don't know how to use chopsticks," she murmurs.

"That's alright. I can show you how."

A few minutes later, she's caught on enough to get the chips all the way to her mouth without dropping them in her lap. Another minute or so, and she's wielding the chopsticks like a pro. "You're a quick learner," I comment through a grin.

She ducks her head, her cheeks reddening.

There's a long silence while we eat, and I try to put her more at ease by carefully keeping my gaze averted, allowing her a sense of privacy while she determines how she wants to open up. When she runs out of chips, she says, "I don't think Mrs. Busch likes me very much."

"Oh?" Setting aside my own bag, I return her stare. She doesn't seem quite as angry now. Resigned maybe, but not angry. "What makes you say that?"

Sam shrugs. "She doesn't like dealing with me."

"Do you think her bringing you here was meant to be a punishment?" I venture.

She shrugs again, looking away.

"Well, regardless of her intentions, I'm going to do my very best not to feel like a punishment to you. I promise."

"Yeah?" Sam grumbles, looking down at the chopsticks in her lap. "And how much of what I say will get back to them— my foster parents?"

"Not a word. What you say here remains between you and me, in full confidentiality. You're a ward of the state, so I'm not required to report to your foster parents. Besides, I may as well give up my license if I broke your trust like that.

You deserve privacy." I rarely break that promise to any client, child or not. Unless they're in danger, of course. Giving her those chips was my attempt to show her that there were secrets I can keep, secrets I *want* to keep for her.

She smirks, tossing the stained chopsticks on the table so she can cross her arms again. "I'm surprised you even have a license. A real one, I mean."

Her meaning is clear. She's questioning the legitimacy of our clinic, and I don't blame her. I know how this place can seem. It took a long time for me to take Astra seriously, but I learned my lesson. Belief is as powerful a transformer as psychology. In fact, I'd even go so far as to say that the two are often tightly wound together, inseparable.

"I know our clinic is a little... unconventional, but rest assured, we are all qualified to heal, some in equally unconventional ways and some not." I gesture to the wall decorated with my diplomas and licenses.

Sam squints at them for a long minute, and I start to wonder if she needs glasses and refuses to tell anyone about it.

"You went to Stanford, huh? I guess that explains how you can afford those Choo Choos on your feet with a therapist's salary." When she turns her sneer on me, I only smile. I allow her to get it all out. "Exactly how long do you plan on riding out your trust fund so you can comfort poor little orphans like me? Does listening to us cry make you feel better about yourself? Are your mommy and daddy just *so* proud of you for following your dreams?"

It doesn't hurt to hear her say that. She's in pain herself. She's bitter. I understand.

"What do *you* dream of, Sam?" I ask quietly. "After you leave the system behind, what do you want your life to look like?"

She recoils an inch, blinking rapidly.

Before she can respond, the sound of footsteps echoes from the hall, and the door to my office swings open. And there he is.

Levi.

CHAPTER 5

SOMETIMES FORGIVE, BUT NEVER FORGET

Levi pauses at the threshold of my office, his wide black eyes raking across the room until they land on me, his face pinching in confusion.

"I did not realize you had a job."

I force myself not to react, but internally, I'm screaming. I've kept this clinic a secret from my husband, and for good reason. I'm afraid of what he might do to ruin it for me. Walter's family believes a woman's place is at home; any profession outside of housewife and mother is a disgrace, and he told me as much before we got married.

For years, I've been keeping up on my licenses and attending conferences when I could manage to line them up with Walter's work trips.

Astra and I had dreamt of this clinic since our senior year of undergrad. It was happening for us, whether he wanted it to or not. It was just easier for me if he didn't know so he couldn't harass me about it.

So much for that.

Calmly, I stand and walk to him, closing the door to my office as I lead us into the hall.

After a few long strides, I swing around and hiss, "What the fuck are you doing here?"

He shrugs with one shoulder. "I was bored."

"Bored?" I huff a short, bewildered laugh. "You're *bored?* You have an entire company to occupy your time, so why on Earth are you following *me* around?"

"I don't give a shit about that company," he says with a curl of his lip, effectively shocking me. The company has always been the *only* thing he cares about, and our wealth proves it. Before I can process that admission, Levi leans toward me. "My wife's distractions are far more interesting to me. Look at this place—it's charming." He nods at the colorful drawings on the wall around my door.

Charming. Not a word I ever thought he'd utter in a place like this.

"It's a clinic," I bite out.

His eyes return to me, consuming the very breath in my lungs. "And you are its healer?" It's not a mean question. It's not even skeptical. There's genuine curiosity in his voice.

I push him backwards, farther away from the office in case Sam tries to listen in. We settle next to the massive window looking out over the walking trails that intersect with our building and the parking lot. "I listen to people," I say blandly, "and they heal themselves."

"Is it ever truly that simple?" He gives me a disbelieving look.

"You're not going to keep me from working, Levi."

His brow furrows. "Well, of course not. It's obvious that this place is important to you." Those words knock the wind out of me all over again, but Levi only shakes his head, his expression turning thoughtful. "I do wonder, though, why you bother trying to help people who are broken. Don't you ever tire of it?"

I take a step closer to him, anger fizzling through my veins.

"They aren't broken." I speak viciously, but softly enough that it doesn't carry down the hallway. "I work with children, so yes, they're sometimes a little confused and scared, but they are *never* broken. Now, I need you to go."

"What if I want to stay?"

"You can't."

"Why not? You have to take a break at some point, and I can spend time with you then." He looks down at me with such eagerness that, for a moment, I don't know what to say.

Why does he want to spend time with me *now*? Why does he want to spend time with me at all? We have an unspoken agreement: our private lives are separate. I don't have the energy to deal with him crossing these lines.

I take a deep breath. "This is my place of occupation, Wal—," his darkening expression makes me choke.

"*Levi.*" I correct myself. "And you just barged into one of my private sessions with a minor. I could have you escorted off the property by the authorities if I wanted to. In fact, that option is still very much on the table, so if you don't want to spend the day in a boring cell instead of our boring home, you need to leave. *Now.*"

I expect him to react with equal irritation, but he only smiles. He looks delighted by my threat. *Tickled fucking pink.*

Before I can ask him what his problem is, honking draws my attention to the parking lot. In the distance, I see my husband's Tesla parked sideways in the center of the thoroughfare with several cars backed up behind it.

I point at the scene. "Levi, why are you parked that way?"

"Why not?" His voice is entirely nonplussed.

"It's congesting the entire parking lot. You stopped two literal feet from an open parking spot. For Christ's sake, your front wheels are touching one of the lines."

He rolls his eyes. "Lines are so arbitrary, aren't they? Imaginary. It doesn't make much of a difference for me if I park within the lines or in the middle of the road. I'm parked."

"Other people are affected by your choices."

"I don't care for other people or what they think. The only person I care about is standing right in front of me." Levi takes a step forward, and suddenly, we are much too close. His hands wrap around my upper arms, his fingertips overlapping as his presence bears down on me.

I'm overwhelmed by his largeness, by his *more than*. That energy under his skin crackles, those black eyes pierce through to my soul, and it doesn't matter that he's frowning, that he seems conflicted about something. For some reason, my body responds to him. My compassion responds.

I cup his cheek with my palm. "Are you sure you're okay? You're feeling well after yesterday?"

"No, I'm not well. I'm hard as fuck for you, and you're sending me away."

I immediately drop my hand and step away from him. He doesn't get to say things like that. He doesn't get to make me feel desire for him anymore, not after everything that's happened between the night we met and now. "Well, *husband*, that's a problem you've proven you are more than capable of taking care of without me. How about you get the fuck out of my clinic and look for someone who cares?"

His eyes flash with surprise before a laugh erupts from him, deep and hearty. "Oh, you've got thorns in the shape of claws, Rose. I *like* them."

I swallow hard and shut my eyes to get him out of my head. I'm suddenly exhausted; arguing with Levi wears me down faster than fighting with Walter ever did. The back of my neck prickles, and I grimace at the way I'm thinking of him—*them*—like two separate people. "Just go," I sigh.

As my eyes flutter open, I see Levi has finally contained his amusement. He's backing away slowly, his lips twitching. "I'll be waiting for you at home then. Don't make me wait too long, or I'll be forced to come looking for you again, and I might not be so understanding next time." He winks and returns down the hall, glancing at me over his shoulder before turning the corner.

With a low grumble, I walk back into my office.

I groan when I open the door and find the couch empty, the window behind my desk wide open. Sam made her escape while I was distracted, and she took a few snacks from the basket with her. I stalk over to my desk, glaring at the phone like it might come alive and strangle me.

Should I call someone? Or should I allow her to get away?

She didn't seem like the kind of girl who would run off to get herself into trouble. She seems like the kind of girl who *is* in trouble and doesn't want to talk about it. I don't know what happened this morning between her and Mrs. Busch, and I'm worried that if I make that call, I'll only worsen the situation.

Do I risk it? It's a risk either way, I suppose.

"*Fuck me.*" I collapse into my ergonomic desk chair, plopping my face into my palms. I shy away from making a decision, distracting myself with my other *big problem*.

My body pulses with fury and desire.

How did he make me feel this way *again*? First when he tugged on my braid last night, and now at *work*. There has to be a deeply disturbing psychological explanation, or… maybe it's the season for reminiscing.

I met Walter at a college frat party approximately nine years ago on Halloween.

The memories return to me in flashes, softened around the edges by resentment and time. I was wearing expensive lingerie and devil horns, and I smelled of French perfume I'd received from an ex-boyfriend. Walter walked in with his friends, the friends who are now his business partners, and I knew it was time to make my move.

I was also fresh off the worst breakup of my life.

I've only fallen in love *once*. I blame my naivety for most of it, and sheer dumb luck for the rest. I was 21, nearing the end of my undergraduate degree, and I'd been forced to consider entering a more "serious" relationship. I needed cash for grad school soon—my scholarship ran out after my sophomore year, and my student loans were already maxed out.

There was someone I'd been seeing casually at the time. We used to take long drives and fuck in the back of his car, and then he'd drop me back off at my dorm in the early hours of the morning. He didn't live on campus, and I don't even think he attended his classes most of the time—just the parties and football games, since he played for the school— and his family was a massive donor, so he got away with it. He was nice—a little dull sometimes, but able to carry a pleasant conversation.

In my desperation, he seemed decent enough to marry.

That was, until he finally brought me back to his "place", and I discovered he was living in his father's pool house.

He had no passions, no aspirations, and he'd already blown through his trust fund at the ripe old age of 23. The moment he passed out on his sweat-stained sheets, I rushed to throw my wrap dress back on, not caring to tie the dress closed or brush the knots out of my hair before tossing it into a bun, and *ran* out of there, suddenly feeling extremely grateful he was the type of guy who liked to smoke weed and talk after sex.

I emerged from the pool house, and there he was. His father, taking a midnight swim.

The underwater lights illuminated his body and silver-streaked hair in a cool, blue hue as he swam to the ladder, and I'd like to say I had no idea who he was as he lifted himself out of the water—as I admired him shamelessly from the threshold of the pool house—but I did. The resemblance was there.

He tossed me a smile as he retrieved his towel from a lounge chair. "I can't believe my son allowed a girl as beautiful as you to sneak out of his bed at this hour," he said.

"He's asleep," I said in a clipped voice. I was irritated, but who could blame me?

His smile shifted, souring. "I'm sorry to hear that. If you were in *my* bed, I'd be doing everything in my power to keep you until morning."

The words had been so brazen and sure; it was shocking, really. It stirred something in me, something that made my core flutter and my toes curl, something that forced all the thoughts in my head to fly away like a flock of frightened birds. I'd never experienced desire like that before. Maybe it was because of my daddy issues (in that I didn't have a daddy at all), but I suddenly wanted to get closer to him. I wanted to press up against his chest and feel his arms wrap around me. I wanted to feel his weight on top of me, crushing me until I could no longer breathe.

It was an alarming compulsion, but exciting too.

I did my best to push that desire away. I knew it was a

dangerous idea, even then. Pulling the door to the pool house shut behind me, I muttered, "Not much point in sleeping over when I have no intention of coming back."

His brow furrowed, and then he dropped his towel back to the lounge chair before ambling toward me. "So he didn't please you?" His tone was conversational, polite, even if the question was sorely inappropriate.

I secretly *loved* that it was inappropriate. I'd been focused and serious for *years*—preoccupied with my studies and my seasonal jobs and the endless line of strategic flings that were all the same, same, same.

He was new. He was rich. He was... sinfully tempting.

I only scoffed before I confessed, "No one ever pleases me."

"You can't be serious."

"And why not?" I crossed my arms under my breasts, not-so-subtly pushing them together.

With a wicked glint in his eyes and a promising smile, he replied, "Because I can tell from the look of you that you'd be delicious."

Then, he ate me out on the edge of the pool, and I had to muffle my cries as he made me come outside his son's bedroom. It was hot and dirty, and I knew in that moment that I never wanted to fuck some inexperienced stoner in the back of a Mercedes ever again. Not when I could have *that*.

I had *him* for an entire summer—Charlie.

In hindsight, I probably should have known he was married. I should have suspected it at the very least, but I think I so badly wanted it to be real that I allowed myself to live in delusion for a while. A delusion where I loved him and he genuinely loved me back. A fantasy where we could have been together forever and nothing would try to tear us apart. I didn't think about the pale outline on his finger, the evidence that became so painfully obvious to me in the pictures of us I eventually burned. I didn't wonder why we never stayed at his house beyond the night we met. I turned a blind eye to all of it, living in blissful ignorance until the record screeched to a halt on our whirlwind affair. It happened that August, when his wife showed up at our hotel room in Aspen and slapped me across the face, and I was promptly tossed on the first redeye flight back home.

When he walked me to the town car, he told me I would never see him again, and when I asked him why, he only shook his head and said, "It's my wife." As if that was the only explanation necessary, he gave me a hundred-dollar bill before slamming the car door shut in my face, and I used it to buy a handful of cocktails at the airport bar.

A week later, I found out that Charlie had paid my tuition for grad school. He paid off my student loans too, so at least I was paid back for all the tears I shed over him, right?

That was when I *knew* love was a poison to women, and that marriage was a safety net.

That was the day I decided I was going to marry someone I could never fall in love with, because if all I needed to do to protect myself was be a rich man's wife, I wasn't going to get my maimed heart involved. Why complicate things?

When I set my sights on Walter, I knew he was exactly what I needed.

I stalked him (really, there's no better word for it) for weeks before we met. I learned his schedule and habits, attended the same parties he did and studied him from a distance, struck up a temporary friendship with one of his ex-girlfriends and talked to friends of his friends until I finally fit all the pieces of him together. Business savvy and charming, self-absorbed enough to easily flatter, he came from a family that enforced "wholesome" values while living lives that quietly contradicted their beliefs. Everything done in public was calculated, and as long as you looked good from the outside, it didn't matter what happened behind closed doors. Family was a label, and divorce was the ultimate scarlet letter.

He was the perfect man for me.

After my mother died, I figured out how to use sex to my advantage, against horny rich boys in exchange for rides across town or new clothes, free meals and easy access to comfortable beds. Seducing Walter was just another necessary seduction.

I certainly didn't expect to *like* it as much as I did.

That first night with him was incredible. He'd been sweet once we were alone, removing my clothes with unhurried gentleness, wringing pleasure from me with sharp kisses and possessive fingers. I didn't think I would be capable of feeling pleasure like that after Charlie, and I was so frightened afterward, as Walter held me in his arms and we watched each other fall asleep. I wasn't ready to fall in love again. My heart couldn't fucking take it.

I worried that all the time I spent preparing to meet this man had been in vain.

But then the sun rose the next morning, and I found myself alone in his bed. He texted me several hours later asking me if I wanted to have dinner with him, and I said yes. Even though we slept together that night and the next, and those nights turned into weeks, he kept me at a distance. There was no more romance, and no more fear. He brought me to Sunday dinners with his family. He arranged for me to move in with him without asking me if I actually wanted to. He proposed to me on my 25th birthday, and I said yes. Once we were married, he treated me like a trophy he'd won, a task he'd completed. He set me on a shelf to stare at sometimes with a pompous look on his face.

I didn't mind, though, any of it. This was what I wanted, what I *needed*. He'd offered me stability and a ring, so did the rest of it really matter in the end? My mother never told me to hope for love from my husband. Love was what I found with my friends, with my family. I only found love in men who broke my heart.

My marriage was exactly what I hoped for. That is, until today.

Maybe that collision with the golf cart jostled something loose in my husband's brain—sent him back to that night when we stood in his dark apartment and stripped each other bare as the twinkling city lights watched us through the window. When he pushed me into the bed and feasted on my body like a god unleashed. If I'm honest with myself, I don't think I would mind a repeat of that night. It's been a long time since I felt that satisfied, that *wanted,* and I don't even have to worry about falling in love with him now.

I know him, and I *hate* him.

It's settled, then. I should enjoy this while it lasts, before the sun comes up and my husband reverts back to an evil prick. When I get home, I'm going to milk this good mood of his for all it's worth.

I throw open the door to my husband's home office, not bothering to knock. He hates when I do that, but I don't plan on making myself agreeable to him tonight if he wants to spend time with me. For once, I'm the one with leverage here, because I finally have something he wants. I just never thought that something would be *quality time*.

Before I even lay eyes on Levi, I announce to the room, "If you want to spend the evening together, I need a greasy hamburger and ice cream."

It's a test I came up with on the drive home, after I figured out what to do about Sam (which is nothing at all, at least for now—I saw her being picked up in the parking lot by who I presume to be her foster mother).

My husband hates fast food, so if he agrees with my dinner choice, that means he's still playing nice and I can probably tolerate him for a few more hours, but my test is quickly forgotten when I see what he's doing. He's lounging on the leather couch tucked between two bookshelves, some machine vibrating loudly in his hand. His pants are off, which honestly isn't that shocking to me. I always imagined he masturbated in here. What else does he really have to do in the middle of the night? But the thing in his hand right now...

It's a tattoo gun, and that *does* surprise me.

Levi lifts the needle away from the skin of his knee and looks up at me with a broad smile. "It's a deal, baby. Let me go get changed, and then we'll go."

He stands up to turn off the machine, and my mind fills with static.

Levi is stark naked from the hips down. I hadn't realized at first, but his boxers are missing too. His dick bobs as he moves, partially erect and long. My God, has it gotten *bigger* somehow? I guess that serves to remind me of exactly how long it's been since I last saw it. I shake my head and look away. It's not like I *want* to be intimately familiar with its exact length and girth until the day I die, because I don't.

"Why are you tattooing yourself?" I ask the wall.

Levi shrugs, tearing off his shirt and tossing it onto the couch beside his discarded jeans. I'm watching him from the corner of my eye. I can't stop. "Does it matter?" His chest ripples as he stretches his arms above his head, and I pretend not to notice how hot he looks with only the tattooed skin bleeding on his knees.

The tattoos are a conglomeration of lines and symbols, swirls and angles, and I have no idea what it's supposed to resemble.

"Well, yes. For two reasons, actually." I cross my arms, forcing myself to look at his face as I lift a hand to count the reasons on my fingers. "One: usually people get tattoos that have meaning to them, and two: they usually have a professional do it."

He smirks. "I'm perfectly capable of carving into my own

skin for fun, menace. Besides, what if I'm the only one who can draw exactly what I want? Maybe the vision is locked up inside my head."

Levi ambles toward me, and I try to inch away, but the way he's closing in on me pushes me farther into the room.

"I'd say I think you're having a mental breakdown," I snipe.

Who decides to start tattooing themselves with no prior experience or desire to do so? This is the man who had an issue with the very cute cartoon heart I had tattooed on my ankle when I was eighteen. He paid for me to have it removed during our engagement.

Levi eats up the space between us, his absurd body heat instantly seeping into my side. "Then I'd say I think you're pretending to be far too shy right now, sweet menace. Since when have you been afraid of this cock?"

I'm all too aware of that appendage, fully erect now and practically glaring at me from below, like some demon spawn crawling up from the pits of hell. I refuse to return its stare, so I keep my eyes on Levi's smirk. "I'm not afraid of it. I'm *disgusted.*"

Levi tilts my chin up with his pointer finger and whispers, "Your weeping cunt says otherwise."

My every sense narrows in on the truth in those words, the challenge in his smile. I allow him to lure me closer with that finger under my chin, drawing me in like a fish on a hook, and I realize what I'm feeling—the carnal heat spreading through me.

There's no doubt he can see it flushing my cheeks.

"I—you don't..." I huff in frustration. "You can't say that to me."

His smile turns downright wicked. "Why not? I'm right, aren't I? If I wasn't sure before, I am now. Look at how flustered you are. Do you like it when I talk about your pussy, Rose?"

"Stop it."

"I will never stop when it comes to you," he says, his expression hardening. "And you'll be glad for that someday." I just glare at him, crossing my arms as he studies my face for a few long moments. "You know what? I'm suddenly feeling a bit famished myself. Meet you in the car?"

Before I can respond, he turns on his heel and walks out of the room.

I watch him go, wondering *what* exactly he's famished *for*. Because the way he said that didn't make me think of food. I told myself he didn't deserve my desire, but I haven't orgasmed under someone else's touch in a long time, and my vibrator just doesn't feel the same after the thousandth time in a row. It wouldn't take much to convince me to ride his dick. I can pretend he's someone else while I do it if I need to; they all feel the same. I shift on my feet, squeezing my thighs together as I cast a lingering look at the couch.

Tattoos. Skipping work. Walking around the house naked.

He's almost a regular fucking person.

My eyes catch on the sleek device laying next to the tattoo pen: he left his phone on the couch. I roll my eyes. It figures that *his* phone would survive that crazy accident while mine didn't. Lucky bastard. As I approach the couch, I realize the screen is lit up, and my heart skips a beat. He left it unlocked.

Maybe I'm the lucky one.

I stride across the room and scoop it up. He was looking at pictures of car washes. Weird. I immediately navigate to his bank app. Then, I send an email to change his password, which I promptly delete after using. Immediate access to his accounts. *Easy.*

It started a while ago—the stealing. I've been squirreling money away for years into my own offshore accounts. A little here, a little there. Walter grew up filthy rich. His mother is the type of woman who has a hundred pearl necklaces gathering dust in her jewelry case, only bringing them out when she feels like clutching them. It was easy to convince my husband that I needed to order new designer clothes every week. Losing a few thousand every other day is nothing to him.

In fact, when I hacked into his laptop last summer and moved an entire five-figure account, he didn't even notice—or if he did, he didn't suspect me. I took precautions, of course, just in case he tried to track the hacker down, but nope... I never heard a word about it.

Granted, he was busy fucking one of our neighbors around that time too.

The distraction was appreciated.

My husband's alimony will keep me comfortable, but I want more. I want *power.* I want to take everything I can from him. It gives me a spiteful, delicious kind of satisfaction and makes these next seven years of hell feel a little more bearable. With his head injury, this might be the perfect opportunity to *really* do some damage.

He won't even know what hit him.

CHAPTER 7
EAT AND BE EATEN

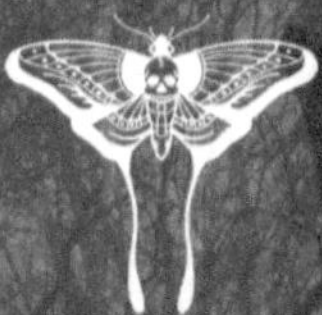

I've just finished devouring a double cheeseburger and hand-cut fries from a local mom and pop joint down-town, *and* I have an ice cream sundae in hand (with that hard shell chocolate stuff smothering it), so really, I'm as placated as can be. I don't even care where Levi is driving us, or how sharply he takes every turn.

I'm surprised by how easily he chomps down on his own burger. He's positively ravenous, moaning quietly after every bite, and after it's gone, he licks his fingers clean.

Who the hell is this man, and what has he done with my husband?

My mind short-circuits as I chuckle to myself, reminded of the way I've started to compartmentalize this new person-ality of his. Soap operas profit on the evil twin trope all the time, but I think I'm experiencing the opposite right now—Walter's good twin is sitting in the driver's seat, and the evil one is nowhere to be seen.

Levi glances at me, swerving in his lane on the highway as he does. My hand flies to the oh-shit handle.

"Are you laughing at me, menace?"

"Yes. I've never seen you eat so fast," I reply. "Your mouth turned into a vacuum."

Usually, my husband eats with the speed of an outdated, rusty machine—oiling his parts every couple of bites with a top-shelf red wine. I learned to match my pace with his to avoid being called some variation of slur related to starving children. It was an agonizing process, and particularly insulting, because I actually *did* happen to be a hungry child once upon a time—not that he knew that.

"It's been too long since my last real meal," he murmurs.

I feel my brow crease. I suppose I didn't see him eat this morning or last night, which meant his last meal, to my knowledge, was sometime before the golf cart incident. Breakfast at the club that morning? That *was* a while ago.

Scooping another spoonful of ice cream into my mouth, I stare out the window as we make a turn without signaling into the parking lot of a car wash.

I frown as the chocolate slowly melts against the roof of my mouth. He drove an extra ten minutes out of the way for *this?* Why? There's at least three other car washes on our route home.

When I look at him, Levi flashes a boyish grin. "This is the longest tunnel in the entire state. The Google said so."

Ah, that would explain the search on his phone when I picked it up.

"Okay..." I say slowly.

He's practically vibrating in his seat, his eyes alight as we pull up to the kiosk. Levi rolls down the window and deals with the kiosk worker, paying for all the add-ons. Then, we pull up to the opening of the wash, and he follows the instructions flashing overhead with alarming focus, as if he's afraid of making a mistake. It's as if he's never done this before, but I guess that wouldn't be surprising—he has people to do it for him.

The attendant at the opening of the tunnel waves us forward, and Levi drives up onto the tracks a little too fast. When the employee yells at him to stop, he puts the car into park and the tracks begin screeching beneath us. Levi looks around in confusion, as if searching for the source, and my face burns as the attendant shouts at us again.

"What are you doing?" I demand, anxiety straining my voice. "Put the car in neutral."

His brow furrows but he pulls the car out of park... into one of the lower gears. Then into another gear. Then back into park. His foot is on the brake too.

With a growl of frustration, I reach over, place my hand over his, and put the gear into neutral myself. Then I slap his thigh and say, "Foot off the pedals. I can't believe you've never been in a car wash before; this level of ignorance should be illegal." My last comment was a little mean and I regret insulting him the instant it leaves my mouth.

He only moves his foot like I commanded and smiles sheepishly in return. "Thank you, baby." Then, he lifts my hand to his mouth and kisses my knuckles.

My neck prickles at his sweet tone, and I rip my hand out of his, scooting as far away from him as the passenger seat will allow. This vehicle feels too small in the dark, with his black eyes staring at me the way they are.

As the tracks tug our SUV into the tunnel, Levi folds up the center console between us and removes his seatbelt. Before I can anticipate his intentions, he reaches over, releases my seatbelt, and wraps a hand around my calf to drag me toward him. I yelp as my skirt rides up, my upper body colliding with the passenger door.

"What are you doing?" I snap as I try to sit back up.

But he's already gathered both of my feet in his lap and is pulling my heels off, discarding them on the floor. "Settling in for the show. *Relax.*" Then, he does the very last thing I expect and starts rubbing my feet.

I'm frozen for a moment, my jaw dropping as I stare at my foot between his fingers. *What is happening right now?*

His thumbs press deeply into my arch, and I moan, my eyes fluttering shut. I set the ice cream down in my lap and slump against the passenger door, my head leaning back on the cold window as we enter the tunnel. The hum of the machinery enveloping us vibrates into my skull. I hear the misters and the soap sprayers, but all I can really focus on is Levi's dextrous touch.

When Levi grunts beside me, I peel my eyes open to find him frowning at the cotton-candy-colored windshield.

"Is something wrong?" I ask.

He squints at the foam and the lights seeping through the soap that illuminate the car in a reddish-pink glow. "I thought this would be more... terrifying."

I huff a small laugh. "What do you mean?"

"Well," he gestures in front of him with a hint of irritation, "this looks like quite an elaborate torture room from the pictures on the Google, does it not? The darkness and chemical soap and all of the wet whips."

I don't have a response to that. Why would he want a torture chamber? Every ounce of ease in my body evaporates as I try to pull my feet out of his lap, but Levi catches my ankles, and I still at the silent warning in his eyes.

Clearing my throat, I stab at the ice cream with my spoon to occupy myself. "I'm feeling very concerned about you right now." I attempt to say it lightly.

He flashes a wide grin. "It's sweet of you to worry about me, but I'm alright. I'll just have to search for something else that will suit my needs. Now here, hand over that treat in your hand before it melts entirely." He leans over my body to take the cup, and I let him have it.

Something that will suit his needs? He *needs* a torture chamber? For what? He has to be messing with me. He must know more about the incident on the golf course than he's letting on. This is another game. Another joke.

If he's trying to unsettle me, it's working.

I fiddle with the hem of my skirt, trying to pull it down without moving my feet and incurring his silent wrath. When I'm unsuccessful, I clear my throat again and whisper, "Are you mad at me, Levi?"

He only tosses me a puzzled look. "Certainly not. Why would you think that?"

Somehow, I think he means it, so I don't dare push the issue. Maybe I don't want to know why he brought me here. Chances are, he would just say something else I won't quite understand. His head is jumbled, and nothing he's saying is making sense. I start to wonder if he'll ever fully recover.

Although, that might not be too bad for me.

He's been kind of sweet today—last night, too. I mean, he's rubbing my feet for Christ's sake, and if this head injury means he's liable to do it again, maybe I'm happy the golf cart hit him. My throat swells as I realize what I've just admitted. God, what a selfish thing to think.

But I know I'm a selfish person, at least when it comes to men like him. I've had to be.

Levi brings a spoonful of ice cream to his lips, spreading the cream across his broad, flat tongue as he holds my gaze. It's borderline pornographic. I wiggle in the passenger seat and look down at my fingers. They're pale after holding the ice cream cup for so long, reflecting the red lights of the car wash like aluminum foil. They look like they're covered in blood.

I can feel Levi's eyes lingering on me, and my skin crawls.

"*So,*" I venture, trying to break the tension. "You really don't care that I work in a clinic?"

"I care because you care," he says.

I peer at him from beneath my lashes. He's still looking at me, but not with quite as much intensity (or insanity). There's a thoughtfulness to the set of his mouth as his fingers drag the spoon through the melted pool of ice cream, around and around. "I'm interested in anything that makes you happy," he mutters.

"No, I mean," I rake in a deep breath, "you aren't going to do anything to destroy it or try to get me to quit?"

"I wouldn't dream of it," he says immediately.

My body relaxes a fraction. It wasn't a promise, but the way he said it feels like one. Time will tell whether he means it. "Okay."

"But I do have a question," he adds.

I grimace. Questions can't lead anywhere good. "Shoot."

His brow furrows as he glances down at the ice cream, taking a moment to gather his thoughts. Then, he lifts his head and squints at me. "Do you feel like you truly help people? Those who are lost, like you said."

That's not what I was expecting. "Well... I *hope* I do."

Levi's black eyes burn. "Have you ever met someone who was really, *truly* lost? Someone who was so far gone that the chances of their soul being found were near impossible?"

I shrug. "I don't touch people's souls. I'm not even sure we have them, really. There's no evidence to support it."

"Say there was," he counters.

I huff a laugh. "Hypotheticals would require me to

believe it's possible. Souls are more Astra's line of work, not mine."

"Then what do you fix?"

"Their minds," I pause. "A lot of times, people just need someone to talk to, someone to trust, someone to listen and lead them back to themselves. But... for the sake of your question, I don't believe anyone is hopeless, if that's what you were trying to get at."

"Hmm." His head tilts. "So your goal is to make the people you treat happier?"

I think about that. "Happiness isn't the goal. Happy is just a feeling. I hope that anyone who leaves my office feels like their life has worth and purpose and hope, though it's difficult to ensure that for every client, or every session. People doubt their worth and purpose when they are hurting. Healing from that hurt takes time, and it's rarely linear."

After a long moment, he asks, "Does it make *you* happier? To help them?"

I blink at him. I understand what he's asking—it's the same question Sam asked me today. Does the work make me happy? And honestly... no, it doesn't. If anything, it makes me hurt alongside them. Carrying that burden is a responsibility, and it doesn't always bring me joy to do it. I shake my head. "It gives my life meaning, and that's all I want."

Levi nods slowly. Then, with a small smile, he asks, "What about me?"

"You?"

"Would you work your healing on *me* if I asked you to?"

I swear, my heart is beating so hard, he can probably see it shaking my entire chest. Is he asking me to be his therapist? "Why? Do you feel like there is something inside you that *needs* healing?" I ask in a daze. I can't believe he would admit such a thing.

He tilts his head, pondering my question before he nods. "I feel confused sometimes, about my existence. About my future. About what I feel. Not around you, though. When I'm next to you, everything seems so perfectly clear. If there *is* something hurt inside me, I think you might be the only one who could mend it. If not, then it is I who must change you."

It takes a full minute to wrap my mind around his request, and he waits patiently for me to recover.

I don't understand everything he just said, but I know one thing with absolute certainty: Levi is dangerous. Our entire marriage, I've been careful to keep myself from empathizing with my husband. It would ruin everything if I cared for him. I know the dangers of loving a bad man—a man who pretends to care for you long enough to get you hooked on his affection. Then, the abuse or abandonment happens, and you have no defense, no exit plan, because you fucking *loved him.* And who in their right mind would make an exit plan for love?

Me. I would.

I watched love happen to my mom several times. She always fell head-over-heels and then walked away with a little less. Less stability. Less heart. Less of herself. When it happened to me, I felt myself break in the same ways she had. It was the most terrifying experience of my life.

If I had to be with a man like that, *he* should be the one to suffer, the one to be used.

Walter fell right into my lap like some kind of karma-ordained present. I'm not going to waste it. I'm not about to hope that he becomes a good man, because, honestly, I don't think it's possible, and I wouldn't want him even if it was.

Eventually, I reply, "That would be a serious conflict of interest for us, so no."

"So you say no one is hopeless, but you are conflicted about healing me?"

I shake my head. "If you want to see a therapist, go right on ahead." Not that it'll do much for him. The statistics don't favor remorseless narcissists. "Your counselor just can't be me. It's against the rules."

"You and your rules." Levi leans toward me, bracing his hand on the back of my headrest. "What if I bribed you, baby?" His breath is hot and smells like vanilla, and fuck, I want to taste it.

Instead, I give him a chastising look. "Even then."

"We'll see about that," he murmurs.

Levi turns his attention to the ice cream in his lap. He lifts the spoon, melted cream dripping from the plastic as he wraps a hand around my ankle and hooks it over his shoulder. I gasp as he drags the cold spoon along the inside of my calf.

Before the cream can drip off my skin, Levi leans forward and drags his tongue across my flesh, sending a bolt of lightning straight to my core.

"What are you doing?" I gasp, desperately trying to get control of my twitching hips.

But all hope is lost when he looks at me.

His smile is blistering, his eyes darker than black, death and lust twined together in a perfect symphony. "The ice cream tastes better on your skin," he purrs before he licks up another trail of cream, his piercing gaze trained on my face.

Heat radiates from my cheeks—I must be visibly flushed right now, and that only eggs him on. He drags the spoon higher, past my knee, and his tongue follows. It's a war of temperature; the cream is cold, but his mouth is hot, and his fingertips are a brand on the outside of my leg, matching his steady journey north. My legs try to clamp together, but he keeps them open with his shoulders as he nestles between my legs, his mouth on my inner thigh.

He pushes my skirt over my hips, and I try to scoot away. I'm slick and dangerously close to writhing, to begging.

"Wait," I whisper urgently, grabbing his shoulder.

He doesn't pull back, but he does lift his face an inch to look at me. His eyes are drugged. "Do you want me to stop?" It sounds like a threat.

The ice cream bowl has tumbled to the floor, white cream creeping across the rubber mat as his fingers dig into my flesh. I glance up at the scrubbers pummeling the windshield, whipping the foam in circles, the motions teasing me.

I try to swallow the rock in my throat.

My head is confused, but my body is not. It doesn't want Levi to stop. I can't even remember the last time someone ate me out. I try to concentrate, because now I'm determined to know. Walter did it for my birthday a handful of years ago— unenthusiastically. I definitely didn't come.

I want to come now.

Why shouldn't I let him do it? Sure, he's an absolute prick and impossible to deal with ninety-nine percent of the time, but so what? That doesn't make coming on his tongue any less appealing. Don't I deserve a little bit of pleasure for what he's put me through? A mere hour ago, I was transferring thousands of dollars out of his accounts, taking the only thing he cares about away from him—he's a little bit poorer than he was yesterday, and I'm richer. The thought only makes me wetter.

I'm the one in control here. I'm the one using him.

I give him a sly smile and remove my hand from his shoulder, opening my legs a little wider. "No. I don't want you to stop."

"That's good to hear, baby," Levi growls with a feral grin. "Because I already told you I won't be stopping when it comes to you."

I should be furious at him for saying something like that after I've already given my consent, but he buries his face between my legs before the words can sink in.

Then, all I'm thinking about is his tongue.

He hooks my underwear to the side and drags his tongue up my center, my flesh parting easily for him. It feels so *good*. My nails dig into the leather seat. He licks me again, slowly, this time swirling the tip of his tongue around my clit and flicking at just the right angle to make me cry out.

His tongue thrusts into me, and I moan.

He groans in tandem as his tongue reaches impossibly deeper. Then he pulls back long enough to say, "I want you to be my first and last meal on Earth, Rose."

Levi starts pulling my underwear down my legs.

My head is spinning too fast to think of a suitable

response. I watch as he brings my black panties to his nose and breathes me in. I gape at the soft smile blooming on his lips, the wickedness in his eyes. After stuffing my underwear into his jeans pocket, he settles between my legs. His mouth closes over my center and sucks. The pleasure is insurmountable; I don't think I've ever been so ready to come. His tongue is playing with the trigger. I'm right on the edge, but before I can fall over it, Levi draws back and pulls my legs even wider, pinning them to the seat as he proceeds to trail kisses along the creases of my thighs. The skin there is overly sensitive to his afternoon shadow.

He didn't shave this morning.

My body convulses beneath him in a desperate attempt to bring his mouth back to where I want it, and I'm barely aware of what I'm doing, let alone what I'm saying.

"Oh, *please*," I moan.

Levi chuckles, his fingers digging into the meat of my thighs—he's going to leave bruises behind, I just know it. God, I love that. He draws back even farther, turning his gentle kisses and nips to my inner thighs. I hate that he's teasing me. The car wash could end at any second, and then it'll be over.

Maybe this is a torture chamber after all.

My stomach jumps as a terrible thought occurs to me. What if that was his plan this whole time? That would be just like him—well, the old him. The *real* him? I don't know.

I whimper; I just can't help it. *"Please, Walter."*

His teeth sink into my thigh, and I yelp as I try to pull away from him, the haze of lust parting for a heartbeat. My core flutters as I peer down at him between my legs, my body pulsing as the pain bleeds into pleasure, and I'm paralyzed by Levi's angry black eyes.

I don't know why, but his glare turns me on all the more.

He has a mouthful of me, and he doesn't look eager to let go. The muscles of his jaw feather, and I'm struck with a sudden fear that he may swallow me whole.

That's when my error hits me: I called him Walter. "I'm sorry, that was an accident," I blurt out. "I wasn't thinking."

Levi doesn't blink. After a moment, he unlocks his jaw and tilts his head in an alarmingly animalistic way. My eyes flick to the marks he left in my skin, and my pussy clenches hard around nothing, the emptiness almost painful.

He says in a quiet voice, "My name is Levi. If you ever make that mistake again, you'll suffer for it."

I shake my head fervently. "I won't. I swear."

Without another word, he returns his mouth to my clit and sucks it between his teeth, rolling the electrified nerves with his tongue, and a filthy noise leaves my mouth that I didn't realize I was capable of making.

"That's it, sweet menace," he rumbles against my clit. "I want to see those beautiful eyes roll."

My pleasure is a slower climb this time, but I think that's Levi's intention. He ravishes me for a few brief moments before resorting to tender, feather-light kisses. Again and again, he lifts me higher and then denies me, smiling as I squirm.

I don't complain. I'm too scared that he'll punish me if I do, and then I won't get to come at all.

He caresses my inner thigh with his fingertips, and then slowly slides one long finger inside me. I'm teetering on the edge as he sighs against my swollen clit. "Mmm, and you still clench so tightly for me, like a naughty little snake looking to suffocate your prey. I would let you suffocate me, menace, as long as I can remain right here, between these sexy fucking legs of yours. I'd die here if I could."

He moves his finger, giving me a few shallow thrusts, and I whimper.

"Do you accept the truth now?" he says lowly, menacingly. "You *love* when I talk about your body, especially this pretty little cunt." He pulls his finger out and then shoves two in deep.

The moan that erupts from me is guttural as my body tingles all over. I'm *right there*. Maybe this time, he'll let me have it. I dare to hope.

Levi sits back abruptly and pulls me into his lap.

He reaches forward and manually releases the back of the driver's seat to lay it down flat before he starts pushing me up the length of his body. "Crawl until you're sitting on my face. Grab onto the backseat to steady yourself."

I do as he says, my mind swimming, my body swaying precariously as our car continues to be pulled forward by the tracks. How long do we have left in this car wash? It feels like we've already been in here for a small eternity.

The thought of being caught like this makes my heart hammer even harder.

As I grab onto the backseat, Levi arranges my knees to hang off either side of his shoulders, framing the headrest. When I glance at the window beside me, I see that it's cotton candy pink. We've been in here for several minutes, and we're still being pummeled with colorful soap? I could have sworn we've been through the soap and the brushes a couple times now.

But I can't give that any real thought as Levi grips my thighs and lifts them just enough to get his mouth back on me. In the same breath, he slips three fingers into my cunt from behind.

"*Oh fuck*," I moan. And then I do nothing *but* moan as I ride his face.

The harder I ride him, the harder he fucks me with his fingers. It's rough and wet and warm, and for the briefest of seconds, I fear that I might actually suffocate him, but then I remember I shouldn't care. He can lose consciousness buried in my pussy for all I care.

I use him. He uses me. It's our thing.

I lose myself in the sensation of his stubble chafing my sensitive skin, the sharp edges of his teeth as I grind myself against him, the flick of his tongue moving in tandem with his fingers.

This time, he doesn't stop. I come all over his face, panting and mumbling incoherently as my arms tremble, on the brink of giving out. I'm ready to stop now, but when I cease my grinding, he grabs my hips and moves them for me. Sparks of fresh arousal roll down my spine as he provokes my sensitive clit, and suddenly, I'm gushing into his mouth. My legs shake and clamp around the head rest to no avail. Oh my God. He isn't stopping.

I remember his promise. *I will never stop.*

"Again," he commands, his teeth grazing my flesh.

I whimper. "I-I can't."

He growls, sending vibrations through my clit. "Yes. *Again.*"

His palm strikes my ass, the connection a sharp sting that bleeds into pleasure, and my body bursts with velvety surprise. My body comes for him, the heat sweeping through me, swift and hard, scraping my arteries and hollowing me out. I can't say anything once it hits, can't even scream as my mouth goes slack, as I writhe and gasp desperately for air.

When I come back to, I'm laying in Levi's lap. His seat is upright again, and he's cradling me, gazing at me as he twirls a lock of my dark hair between wet fingers.

My mouth is bone dry, but I manage to croak, "Oh my God."

Levi's hand slides to the back of my skull, fisting my hair as I gasp at the delicious tug. "God has nothing to do with this," he says just before his lips capture mine.

The kiss is brutally conquering, but edged with the sweetest warmth. Vanilla cream and me.

I want my husband to stay this way. I know it's a foolish thing to wish for, but I want it. At least long enough for us to go through the car wash one more time.

A loud knock on the window startles us.

Levi and I break apart, and I lurch off Levi's lap when I see it's an employee of the car wash, smiling awkwardly through the window. We're at the end of the tunnel. I don't know exactly how long we've been here, but judging from the look on this lanky guy's face, it's been long enough. He makes a motion, urging Levi to roll down the window.

As I fix my skirt and blouse, Levi jerks the gear into drive and pulls out of the tunnel, ignoring the employee completely. "Nosy waif," he snarls to no one in particular.

I quickly buckle my seatbelt before he can crash into something. His erratic driving is worsened by his obvious irritation, and now I'm wishing we never came here. The orgasms mean nothing if I die on the way home.

"He was just doing his job, Levi," I snap.

Levi glances at me from the corner of his eye, his knuckles whitening around the steering wheel. "Yeah, well, he's lucky that kiss was the only thing he saw."

I clamp my mouth shut; his sudden shift from warm affection to violent anger is disorienting. When I glance at the clock, my jaw slackens. Three minutes? There's no fucking way we were in there for only three minutes, and yet...

I pull out my phone, shaking my head in disbelief when I see that it says the same thing.

"What is it?" Levi asks. "Is something wrong?"

"No. Nothing," I reply quickly, tucking my phone away. *Nothing, except that my husband might not be the only one losing his mind.*

CHAPTER 9

NEVER LET MEN SEE YOU CRY

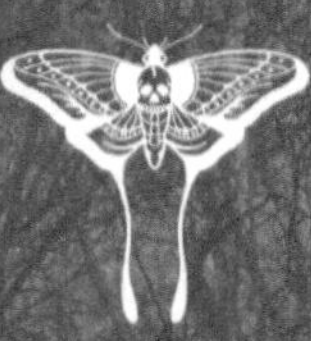

I wake to the sensation of warm fingers combing through my hair in slow strokes. The touch sends delicious sparks swirling down to my toes, curling in my belly as I shift my body, still heavy with sleep. Something rustles in my ear—paper, I think, or… is it plastic?

"I'm going to keep you forever," someone whispers in my ear.

I shiver, rising even quicker out of unconsciousness. In my grogginess, I come to the realization that the voice belongs to my husband, though it's deeper than I'm used to, velvety soft. *Levi.*

His balmy lips press into mine, and I respond, moaning as his fingers tighten in my hair.

"I want to fuck you again, my sweet little snake. You're too tempting." He kisses the corner of my mouth and then my cheek, my temple and my closed eyes, returning to my mouth with renewed purpose as he rolls me onto my back. He rumbles against my lips, "And you're soaked for me already, aren't you? I can smell it."

The bed rustles as I wiggle beneath him, the same sound from when I was first waking. My arms twine around Levi's neck and I find his hair damp as I run my fingers through it. His body lowers to mine, and I realize that his chest is wet too. He groans into my mouth, and my legs part for him, hooking around his waist as he grinds against me in a slow, sultry thrust.

I gasp as his body moves with mine. "That feels so good."

"So do you," he whispers. "You're the best thing I've ever felt."

He rolls his hips again, and paper crinkles under my back. *Oh fuck, my papers.*

My eyes flash open and I shove Levi off me as I sit up. "Shit. I fell asleep."

Levi is so shocked that he backs off a foot or so, watching as I vault off the bed, flick on the bedside lamp, and gather up the files scattered across the comforter.

I passed out while reading Sam's history (and damn, there was a lot of it). Usually, I wouldn't crack open a file at home, but Levi left me alone for some kind of emergency meeting, and I was already behind. I barely received Sam's full transcript before the end of the work day, and our next session is scheduled for tomorrow afternoon. I didn't mean to fall asleep before putting it away, but our *activities* in the car wash completely exhausted me.

Straightening the stack of papers, I turn to toss them into my computer bag along with my laptop and slide it under my nightstand before turning to face my husband.

He's kneeling naked on the bed. The first thing my eyes land on are the tattoos on his knees, the ink vivid against his red skin. He must have finished them at some point tonight. There's a beauty about them in their completion; it doesn't look like nonsense to me now. No, they look like an intricate hieroglyph, the kind you would expect to see in Egyptian tomes.

My eyes slide up the length of his body, over his hard abdomen and muscled arms. His wet blond hair drips water onto his broad shoulders, and the droplets roll down his exquisite physique in a way that makes my mouth water.

He smells like sex and soap, and a sense of dread touches my gut. "You were in the shower," I murmur.

"I just got home." He leans over with a smirk and fists my silk nightgown at my hips, using it to tug me toward him. "I needed to rinse off before coming to bed."

My heart stutters.

I glance at the clock on my nightstand, and my heart sinks into my stomach, my guts hardening around the organ. He's been gone for hours. His hot hands greedily bracket my waist as he trails a line of kisses up the skin between my breasts. I can tell he wants to continue where we left off—he wants to fuck me, and maybe a minute ago, I would have let him. A minute ago, I wanted him to.

But now, my body feels cold and empty, because I can guess where he's been.

Pushing his hands off my waist, I take a step back, my breath coming faster until I'm on the brink of hyperventilating. "It's three in the morning and you took a shower?" My voice grows louder, angrier. He was out this late yesterday evening too, and I was stupid for not realizing it then.

Levi chuckles, clearly not understanding just how dangerous it is for him to do so—it stokes the flame in my gut. He gives me a patient smile and says, "Yes, baby, I think that fact has been thoroughly established."

He reaches for me again, and I slap his hand away. His face falls.

"I seriously can't believe you," I hiss before I turn and

stalk toward the bathroom, intending to lock myself inside until he leaves, but he leaps from the bed and cuts me off.

He frantically scans my face. "Hold on—what am I missing here?"

I cross my arms over my chest and smile, though I feel closer to crying than I have in a long while. "I realize that I haven't cared about your affairs up to this point, but it's a low blow for you to rub my nose in one now, especially after what we did yesterday."

Levi's eyes flash like polished onyx. "What are you talking about?"

It's true—up until now, I haven't cared who my husband screws behind my back, when or where he did it, because at least he had the decency to try and hide it from me. But tonight, he kissed me right after washing away the filth of whatever corporate whore called him away, and the betrayal burrows its way under my thick armor.

I hate to admit it, but this one hurts. There isn't a lot of good to be said about the old Walter, but he never would have done something like *this*.

"Who have you been fucking?" I sneer. "No, wait, let me guess. Your new assistant? The marketing manager I saw you making eyes at during the last company banquet?"

Levi's nose flares. "You're the only one I've fucked, Rose. You're the only one I want."

"Then where have you been?"

His eyes pinch, and a long silence stretches between us. "I can't tell you yet."

"Yeah." I turn away with a scoff. "Sure."

Levi grabs my upper arm and spins me around to face him. His grip is tight, painfully so, and every trace of levity and lust is gone from his eyes as he growls, "You best believe me, Rose."

"Or *what?*" I challenge.

His whole face darkens. "Or I'll be forced to prove just how devoted I am to you, whether you like my methods or not."

A thrill runs up my spine. "Is that a *threat?*"

I know he has something downright sinister in mind when his hard expression cracks and he slowly smiles at me. "It's a fucking promise, baby."

I take a small step backward, and he follows me, his smile only growing as I back up into the wall. He advances carefully, tilting his head in that way that scares the living daylights out of me. "You know, I received an interesting phone call a couple hours ago. Apparently, a lot of our money has gone missing from our bank account. You wouldn't happen to know anything about that, would you, little snake?"

My heart thunders.

I clean up after myself. There's a reason I took so many computer courses in college, classes I didn't need to graduate. I know he doesn't have any proof, but now he suspects me, and that's no better. What's he going to do about it? How is he going to punish me?

He laughs softly, looking me up and down as he closes in. "Are you afraid of me, sweet menace? Whatever for?" He doesn't sound angry. No, his tone is warm, teasing, but the look in his eyes makes me think he's moments away from grabbing me by the throat, makes me think he's about to pin me to the bed and brand his devotion upon my skin with his teeth. I can imagine him doing things I never believed my husband capable of.

Before he nearly died, I remind myself.

He's not the same person at all. He's worse. He's *better.*

I would let him do those things he promised with his

smile. Despite what he did tonight, I would enjoy every thrust, every kiss, every dirty word. Those black eyes are turning into my kryptonite; I can't let them touch me any longer, or I might do something horrible, like let him in.

I point at the door. "Get the hell out."

His head jerks to the side, almost as if he'd been stung by a bee. The temperature of the room spikes, and the air between us seems to burn as his eyes meet mine again. His irises are larger; I see them growing still, slowly overtaking the whites of his eyes.

"Rose," he growls.

I shudder at the violence in his voice. No. I can't show weakness, or he'll pounce on it. "*Get out*," I shout.

He falls back a step, then another. He takes stilted steps backward until he's finally standing on the threshold of the room, gripping the sides of the doorframe with white knuckles.

"Fine," he says through gritted teeth. "I have some work to do anyway. I'm leaving on a business trip in the morning; might be gone for a couple days."

"Great," I shoot back. "Be a doll and close the door behind you?"

He scowls but leans forward to grab the doorknob. The door is halfway shut when he pauses, and his gaze softens as he says, "Tell me you want me to come back."

The hair on my arms stands up straight. Is that *fear* in his voice?

When I don't respond right away, he continues in a whisper, "Please, Rosie, I need you to say it, or at least show it to me somehow. You don't really want me to disappear, right? You want me to come back to you?"

As furious as I am with him, I can't bring myself to say no.

I'm thinking of the way his mouth sucked on my skin earlier. The way he spoke to me. The way he made me feel. I have no way of knowing where he was tonight. I have no way of knowing if I was wrong. What if he told me the truth?

What if I'm really the only one he wants?

The words sit heavy in my chest, even though I'm sure it's just a lie. I'm not a fool—I know the kind of man he is, but if he doesn't come back to me, the money might disappear too. Now that he's aware I might be stealing from him, the power has shifted again, right into his waiting hands.

Reluctantly, I nod, and relief rushes over Levi's features. His lips twitch up in the semblance of a smile, but he seems so indescribably sad as he mutters, "Then I'll see you again as soon as I can." With that, he leaves me alone, closing the door gently behind him.

"Welcome back, Sam. Go ahead and take a seat; grab a snack if you want." I smile at her from behind my desk and quickly finish typing up a note.

Sam perches on the edge of the couch as I grab my notebook and make my way to the chair across from her. She ignores the basket of snacks on the table, even though I replaced all of her favorites this morning.

I settle in, smoothing the skirt of my dress down my thighs before I cross one leg over the other. "Did you have a nice afternoon yesterday after our session?" I ask politely.

Sam shifts in her seat. "I'm sorry."

Jumping right into it, then. "Why are you sorry, Sam?"

"I'm sorry for sneaking out. I just—I didn't want to be here."

"I know."

After a moment, she asks quietly, "Why didn't you call Mrs. Busch?"

"I already told you I have no intention of punishing you, or of breaking your trust. I meant that." I shrug. "Besides, I wanted to extend some trust to you too. I believed you wouldn't do something that would justify my tattling on you, and this is a fairly safe area of the city."

Her eyes drop to her lap. "I just walked around the trail for a while, and then I called Mrs. Busch to pick me up in the parking lot."

I gesture at the basket. "You really can have a snack if you're hungry."

"That's okay," she said, stuffing her hands beneath her legs. "Mr. Busch took me to lunch today, and I'm still stuffed."

That must be why she was half an hour late. "Does he do that often?"

"More often lately. He likes me better than Mrs. Busch does."

"Well, that must be encouraging."

She shrugs. "I guess so." I can feel her hesitation.

"Do you like him?"

Sam brow furrows. "What do you mean?"

"It's nice that he takes you to lunch, but I imagine the meals would be difficult to endure if you felt uncomfortable around him."

I had foster parents who did that. Some of them treated me to special meals and gifts as a form of charity, and I could tell they expected me to shower them with gratitude in return. They served their own ego, and I found no happiness in accepting anything from them. They offered fleeting, inconsistent joys... and all it did was drain me.

Foster families who seemed to care always expected something in return for their kindness. That's how I learned how easily men could be bribed, manipulated.

There was one day I came home from school and refused to scrub baseboards instead of sitting down with my homework, and the foster parents I was living with sent me to my room without dinner. My foster brother surprised me by sneaking a plate of food into my room. Then he pulled out his dick and told me to suck it, and I did. Because I was starving. That boy taught me that nothing is given to girls like me for free.

That was the only time I let myself be on the defensive side of getting what I needed. From that point on, I took what I desired, and I willingly offered the world what it needed as payment for my happiness—if you could even call my survival of the system that.

Sam wiggles in her seat, reaching up to tuck a lock of blonde hair behind her ear as she murmurs, "No, he's fine. He's very nice to me."

Interesting...

A tinkling melody carries toward us from my desk. My phone.

I finally picked up my replacement this morning, and the store managed to restore most of the data from my old one. I must have forgotten to mute it, but then again, I rarely have a reason to; I don't know anyone who would call or text me during work hours.

I try to ignore it, but the melody repeats again, then again.

"I'm sorry; one moment." I stand and walk to the desk, picking up the phone to flip the switch on the side to mute it. As I do, I see the messages appear on the screen—I haven't had a chance to change the privacy settings.

Four new messages from my husband.

> I can't stop thinking about your pretty cunt.

The way it tastes.

The way it feels.

The way it convulsed around my fingers when you came. I want you to suffocate my cock next time, little snake.

Jesus Christ.

I slam my phone down so hard, I wince at the sound it makes against the glass desk. There's warmth creeping into my cheeks as I turn to face Sam, and I have to swallow a couple times to clear my swelling throat.

Sam has snatched up a bag of chips and is chewing on one loudly, smiling as I return to my chair. "Juicy gossip?" she nods at the phone.

I force a chuckle. "Something like that. Let's talk about what happened yesterday morning—what made Mrs. Busch drop you off here so suddenly?"

Sam's hand tightens around the chip bag, audibly crushing the contents as she clears her throat. "I don't know. Nothing I do is ever good enough for her. She tries to talk down to me a lot and doesn't like it when I speak my mind, which I refuse to stop doing, so... I guess I pushed her a little too far yesterday."

I can tell that she's only telling half of the story, keeping details to herself. She's not ready to talk about it, so I smile and nod, carefully redirecting the conversation to her studies, which she offers up enthusiastically. Twenty minutes later, her hour is up, and I send her away with a handful of snacks so I can prepare for my next session.

After the door shuts behind her, I twist to survey my empty office—the glass surfaces and plush cream carpet. My gaze catches on the shiny, rose gold device on my desk. With a sigh, I cross the room and scoop up the phone, collapsing heavily in my desk chair as I unlock the screen. My stomach flutters as I reread the messages, and I don't think too hard about my response.

> Bold of you to assume there will be a next time.

The typing bubbles pop up instantly.

> Tell me that wasn't the best orgasm you've ever had, baby, and then you can lie again and say you don't want to ride my cock as badly as I want to fuck you on it.

My body clenches all over, and I bite my lower lip. Before I can even touch my screen, another stream of messages come through.

> I'm going crazy without you.

> If I could, I would never be away from you again.

> I would breathe only the air from your lungs, feel only your touch.

> I would be so close to you that we would live in the same skin.

I scoff, but my chest is suddenly too tight, and my eyes are burning. How can he say such sweet things to me after I threw him out? He should be *angry*. I woke up this morning to find he was already gone, and I figured there would be radio silence for the entire trip, which is normal for him when he leaves the state after any sort of disagreement.

I'm not so sure he was with someone else last night, not anymore.

All you had to say was "I miss you"

A long minute passes before his text bubbles pop up again, and I find myself wondering what he's doing. He's never been totally transparent about what he does on these trips. Is he in and out of meetings? Chatting up new investors at a nice restaurant? Is he wearing one of his tailored suits that clings perfectly to his broad shoulders and muscled torso?

Maybe he's wearing khakis. Maybe he's playing golf. The twisted thought makes me chuckle.

Finally, a new message.

What I feel in our separation is so much more than that.

I stare at the words, trying to think of a response. It's hard to dislike Levi when he says things like this. Half of me wants to flirt back, while half of me wants to ignore him.

Before I can decide on one or the other, a high-pitched cry drifts into my office.

With a frown, I slip into the hallway and follow the sound to the front of the clinic, to one of Astra's treatment rooms. This area in particular is left open to the rest of the clinic, with nothing but crystal bead curtains hanging in the doorways—Astra insists on having an exit route for any "low vibrational energies" she may encounter during reiki sessions. It helps that most of our alternative medicine clients like being looked in on anyway. Appearances are everything.

There's something different about this crying, though. I can hear the anxiety in it, the panic and pain.

A blonde woman sits cross-legged on a large blue cushion next to Astra. I don't recognize her right away. She's wearing sweats, and her hair is piled up on her head, unbrushed. Her eyes are red and puffy, startlingly blue. She looks like a hot mess Barbie.

Astra is doing her best to soothe her, her hands hovering over the client's chest and shoulders, pulling invisible threads away and waving positive energy toward her.

When the young woman throws her head back to project another sob to the ceiling, I finally see who she is—the wife of one of my husband's angel investors. I've seen her at banquets and charity galas over the last year—she's his third wife, young enough to be his daughter, maybe even granddaughter. Her name is Ashlee or Amber. A... something.

Regardless, I shouldn't be watching them.

I quickly turn away, but before I can leave, the woman sees me. "*Rose!*"

Sighing through my nose, I plaster on a smile and face the room as the woman staggers over to me, silent tears still streaming down her cheeks. She bursts through the curtain and throws her arms around my neck. "Oh, it's so good to see you. You wouldn't believe the day I've had. It's terrible—just utterly, unbearably terrible."

I fight the urge to push her away. She's about a foot shorter than me, and her damp face is now nestled in my chest. "I'm sorry to hear that, Aaaah—"

I meet Astra's gaze and try to convey my desperation to her. Crossing her arms, she mouths the name *Allie.*

"—llie," I finish, gently withdrawing from her. "I see you're in very good hands, though. I'll let you two finish up."

Allie completely ignores the attempt to excuse myself. "I just can't believe this is happening to me. It's so awful. The police department refused to take my report this morning, so now I have no idea what to do. I've been crying all day. I just feel so *helpless*."

"I can see that," I say through a grimace. "I'm sorry, but I don't fully understand what you're talking about."

"My husband didn't come home from work yesterday. He said he would be working late, but I woke up this morning, and he still wasn't back. I have the worst feeling," she starts sobbing again, "that something truly terrible has happened to him."

My grimace bleeds into a frown. This is the first time, I guess. Her husband finally decided their honeymoon phase is over, and now he's falling back on old habits—the lying and cheating, the disappearing for days at a time. I've heard all about his predilections from the last wife. She was quite the talker at parties.

Astra reflects my pitiful expression behind Allie's back as she steps forward and places a comforting hand on the woman's shoulder. "Deep breaths, honey. We just have to take this day one heartbeat at a time and have faith that the universe will work it all out."

I force a small smile. "Astra's right. The police know best." *AKA, they know his history.*

None of that seems to comfort Allie, but she wipes her face and nods. "Yeah."

"I have another session starting here soon, so I have to go," I say gently. "But I hope you have a better evening, and that you get a phone call soon to let you know where he went. Who knows, maybe he ran off with my husband to that last-minute business trip early this morning. It seemed pretty urgent." Though angel investors rarely tag along on those kinds of things.

Allie's eyes light up instantly. "You think so?"

"Maybe," I repeat.

Then I turn around and walk back down the hall before she can snare me in another hug. My phone buzzes before I reach my office.

Don't forget to change my name in your telephone device.

Astra and I sprint from her car to the hidden alcove of the best dive bar in Boston. The narrow black hallway winds back into a dim room, pool tables on one side and a karaoke machine set up on the other. It's a fairly crowded night, for a Tuesday.

The bouncer nods at us in greeting as we pass, smiling warmly. He's a gruff-looking guy, with a shaved head and American traditional tattoos covering his arms, but he's nice to the regulars.

Astra leads the way, weaving through the bar-height tables to one of the booths near the back. It's been recently vacated and still has glasses scattered across the table, but Astra doesn't miss a beat. She stacks up the glasses, and I help by cleaning up a small spill with napkins as I slide into the round booth. Then, she slides in across from me.

We're creatures of habit in this place. Same time, same booth, same drinks.

One of the female bartenders swings past us and scoops

up the glasses, swishing away again in her tight black shorts and knee-high boots.

Astra stares after her, mindlessly tugging her vape pen out of her purse.

"You're no better than a man sometimes," I tease her, crossing my arms as I sink back against the worn plastic cushion.

"Oh, I am *definitely* better than a man." She smirks as she pins the pen between her pink lips and takes a long pull, her shoulders visibly relaxing as she exhales.

For all her passion for wellness, she hasn't given up this particular vice.

She offers me the pen, and I automatically accept it. The only time I smoke is when I'm drinking with Astra. My mom used to smoke, and sometimes, I wonder if that's why it's so comforting for me, to breathe in poison and feel like the smoke is hugging my lungs. It's terrible for me, and yet I can't say no, because it's secretly a little good for me too.

The tingly blend of citrus and menthol coats my mouth as I exhale.

As I hand her the pen back, I ask, "Were you able to calm your client down? I hope she didn't drive home like that."

"I got her an Uber. Poor thing." Astra shakes her head. "I'll be ducking out of the office tomorrow to drive her car back to her house. I'm going to do a little home visit to get her set up with an astral kit while I'm there."

I fiddle with my burgundy ruched dress, hiding my grimace.

We don't see eye-to-eye on everything. That's to be expected, considering the differences in our clientele. It usually doesn't bother me, but I simply can't see a purpose for astral travel in this situation. To be fair, I'm not exactly sure what astral travel even entails. It's Astra's newest hyper-fixation.

A small chuckle draws my attention back to Astra, who hides a smile behind her vape, her brown eyes flicking between me and something outside of the booth. "Look at who's working tonight."

I follow her gaze to the bartender walking our direction. *Jake.*

Jake has been working here almost as long as we've been coming. He's young and handsome, a bone-fide James Dean lookalike, right down to the coiffed dark hair and sterling blue eyes. We've grown familiar with each other in recent months. It's hard not to be friendly when I'm so often drunk, and he's so flirtatious with me.

This time, though, I see him, and my stomach drops.

Actually, now that I think about it, I'm pretty sure something happened between us the last time I was here. I scramble for more clarity, but my brain offers me little. He had escorted me to my Uber after Astra left the bar with a pretty girl, and I was falling all over him. I think I might have kissed him, but I can't really remember—and really, who could blame me if I did? I hadn't been kissed for several months at that point. Walter had just fired his last assistant, and I knew why. It didn't mean anything to me—in fact, I forgot all about it until now.

I feel the sudden urge to crawl under the table, but Jake has nearly reached us now.

His eyes latch onto mine. "Hi, Rose."

I force myself to look away. Astra gives me a smug smile, and I'm tempted to flip her off. "Hello, Jake," I mumble without glancing up.

"Astra, it's good to see you too." Astra hums in reply. "What can I get for you ladies? The usual?"

I refuse to look up, even though I can feel his stare. I just nod. Astra nods too, and Jake walks away to get our drinks going.

"He's so obsessed with you. It's kind of cute."

I roll my eyes. "He is not. Are you sure that's the best idea?"

"What? You and pretty boy? You know I'm not one to judge."

I shake my head. "No, I'm talking about Allie. Astral travel."

Astra squints at me. "Yes, Rose, I'm sure."

"Sorry, I just meant to say that it feels a little counterintuitive to teach her to avoid her reality instead of discussing it."

Astra huffs a laugh. "I'm not teaching her to avoid anything. It's not like she's jumping dimensions or visiting someone's dreams, or anything complex like that. I'm just teaching her how to explore herself. Her reality is perceived from within, so doesn't it make sense to draw her attention to the lens she's looking through in order to alter her perspective?"

Jake reappears with our drinks, and I make the mistake of glancing up. Our eyes meet, and he winks at me. *Fuck.* I quickly return my gaze to Astra, who is too distracted licking a drop from the outside of her glass to notice what just happened.

I sigh as he leaves and give Astra a small smile, the most apologetic one I can muster. "I suppose that does make sense. Forgive me for overstepping."

She lifts her glass in the semblance of a toast. "Drink, bitch."

And we do.

Approximately four gin juices and a laughable game of darts later, I putter my way to the bathroom while Astra orders us another round of drinks. She drank her first slowly, and I'm finally slowing down, so I think this is our last call. My head is light and fluffy, but my body isn't. Liquor just doesn't keep me partying like it used to. I feel the urge to devour an alarming amount of canned whipped cream and pass out on the first comfortable surface I can find.

Plopping down on the toilet, I pull out my phone to entertain me, only to see the messages right away.

> Still angry with me, menace?

> Are you thinking of me too?

The last text is attached to a video message.
A video? *Hmm.*

I tuck my phone away for a moment to clean up and stumble to the single sink. As the water runs over my numb hands, I look into the mirror. My dark brown hair is fluffed, with several flyaways floating around my head, as if I stuck a fork in a power socket and weathered the shock. My cheeks are bright red, and my eyes are droopy. I try to open them wider, but that makes me look insane.

As I turn off the water and dry off my hands, I lean back against the wall across from the door into the bathroom. Raising my fingers to my cheeks, I close my eyes and relish in the sensation of cold fingers cooling my skin. After a long minute, I remember that I'd been in the middle of looking at my messages, that Levi had sent new ones.

I look around the small bathroom (two stalls separated from the sink by frilly curtains), and then lean my shoulder against the wall as I pull my phone out of my bra. I stare at the still shot on video. It's black, so either he filmed something outside in the dark, or he covered the camera for whatever reason. I tap play before I can think better of it, and a low, breathy moan fills the silence of the bathroom.

My jaw drops.

Levi moans my name, then a string of nasty words about my pussy, and my already damp panties become *soaked*. The camera is definitely covered. He's in a bed, touching himself with my name on his tongue.

I'm both mortified and incredibly turned on.

I can't be listening to this here, in the middle of a dive bar bathroom—can I? I don't want to stop. My body is aching, and without meaning to, my hand slips under the hem of my dress. I close my eyes, and then I jump as the bathroom door swings open. I nearly drop my phone into the trash can, but I juggle it precariously until I finally get a good grip and spin to see who came in.

Jake smiles at me, the door slowly closing behind him. "What are you listening to in here, Rose? Sounds like you're having fun."

I hide the phone behind my back. Luckily, in my dropping it, the video stopped playing. "Oh, no, it's nothing." Common sense finally returns to me as I ask, "I'm sorry, is there something wrong?"

"Why would there be anything wrong, beautiful?"

"This is the women's bathroom," I say with a frown.

"I know." He runs a hand through his hair. "I followed you in here. I noticed you've been staring at me all night, and I thought you might want a repeat of that night a few months ago. If you do, the bathroom gives us a little more privacy than the street."

Jake takes a step forward, and I retreat until my shoulder blades hit the wall. He braces a hand over my shoulder and gives me his best panty-dropping grin. I'm still aroused, my mind spinning from Levi's video, and for the briefest of seconds, he almost tempts me. I'm still thinking of Levi, though, about how all I want to do is go home and watch his video again.

I huff a nervous laugh. "I'm not so sure that's a good idea. I-I'm married."

"That didn't stop you from kissing me before."

"I was very drunk then."

He shrugs, stepping even closer. "You're very drunk *now*."

And just like that, all of my attraction to him evaporates. If drunkenness is enough consent for him, then he's a selfish prick in bed. Fear creeps through my chest and sticks in my throat. I'm alone with this creep; he's blocking the exit.

"Wow," I say tersely. "How heroic of you to notice and take full advantage."

"Oh, come on, Rose." His blue eyes sharpen. "It's not like you're some innocent, faithful wife. You think I didn't pin your type the moment I met you? You're a bitchy little gold digger who snagged a big fish. Good for you. But it would be a shame if your husband found out about the things you do in this bar when his back is turned. What's his name again? *Walter?*"

My stomach rolls. "You're blackmailing me just to get your dick wet?"

He shrugs. "You have a tight golden snatch, don't you? I just want a turn with it."

Vicious anger flares in my veins, sobering me instantly. This is exactly why I don't fuck around with regular guys. They're as horrible as the rich ones, minus the money, with twice the trauma.

I lean in and hiss, "If you think I'm going to let you threaten me into a quickie in some dirty bathroom stall, you are fucking *delusional*." He blinks, recoiling an inch. Yeah, I bet he wasn't expecting a fight. He should have researched his target better. "If you threaten me one more time, if you even *look* my way again, I'll report you for assault. I know who you are. I know where you work. You will be charged and thrown in jail, I assure you."

His jaw slackens. "I'm *not* assaulting you."

"You're trying to coerce me into sex. That's rape." My voice is rising, and I can tell he's getting uncomfortable. The bar is loud, but it won't be loud enough to drown out screaming. "I doubt any cop is going to believe a piece-of-shit bartender over a pretty, rich woman with a PhD. So, here's *my* idea: you leave this bathroom and return to your shitty ass job, and we'll pretend we've never met. Or hey, you could go ahead and test your luck, but I won't offer you another way out if you don't take this one." I bare my teeth. "I'll ruin your entire fucking life if I have to, and I'll smile while I do it."

His face flushes as red as my dress. He probably thought I was a girl he could scare, but he had no idea who or what I really was. Now, he knows.

The bartender formally known as Jake spins on his heel and storms out of the bathroom.

I bend over once he's gone, collapsing until I'm sitting back on my calves. Why are men always so goddamn disappointing?

My breath slows, and I quickly stand and return to the mirror before my panic attack fully settles in. I start to fix my hair, only to realize I'm still holding onto my phone. I see that it's... displaying a phone call. *Oh my god.*

I'm on a phone call with Levi.

The time lapse in the corner is ticking past four minutes. I must have accidentally called him when I fumbled the phone—that's why the video stopped playing. Slowly, I lift the phone to my ear, turning away from my red-eyed reflection.

"Levi?" I whisper.

There's a long silence, and I almost begin to hope he didn't hear anything, but then his voice comes through the speaker, ice cold. "You're lucky I'm not within driving distance of you right now, menace."

There's a whole boulder in my throat. "I turned him down," I croak.

"You hesitated," he retorts, and my stomach churns violently as another pause stretches between us. "The next time I see you, I'm going to ensure you never hesitate like that again."

The call ends, and I lurch for the toilet to puke my guts out. It makes me feel better, but not by much.

After my belly is empty, I do my best to make myself look presentable before leaving the bathroom. I linger at the front of the bar until Astra spots me. When she sees me, she knows something is wrong and abandons our drinks.

We leave the bar in total silence.

I don't think I'll ever be able to come back here again.

Astra can tell I don't want to talk about what happened and drives me home without saying a word, giving me a kiss on the cheek before watching me walk up to my front door. I wave at her before closing the door behind me.

The house is dark and large, and I feel like an unwelcome mouse in the center of it as I walk up the stairs to the bedroom.

I don't bother with changing my clothes or washing my face. I manage a quick swish of mouthwash before I collapse on the bed and curl up on my side, staring quietly at my phone. He hasn't texted since the accidental phone call, and after his many messages today, I feel like that speaks volumes.

I hurt him. I hadn't meant to—I didn't even know it was *possible* to hurt him, or that I would care this much about doing it.

Right now, I really wish I wasn't alone.

I wish he was here so I could explain, so I could make it better, but he's not, so I do the only thing I can think of. I type out a message and send it before tossing my phone to the other side of the bed, leaving it just out of reach before I close my eyes.

> I miss you too.

CHAPTER 12

RUNNING IS FOR SUCKERS

Something is chasing me.

Some*thing*, because it's not a some*one*. If it was a someone, it would call after me; it wouldn't snarl like a wild hound. If it was a someone, I would hear footsteps pounding behind me instead of this... horrifying absence of form. I know it's there only because I can sense the presence, the unrelenting pressure bearing down on my spine.

Mine, it whispers into my mind. *You are mine.*

I'm running. The faster I run, the more ground I gain, but I always look back to find that shadow catching up to me. I look to either side to find more of the same—more darkness and bramble, more of the same, same, same. Where am I running? Why?

I don't know.

I just keep running, hoping I find some safety up ahead.

There must be a way out, but an awful certainty is seeping into my bones, and I know this thing is going to catch me. When it does, it will do whatever it desires to me.

Mine, mine, mine.

Anticipation takes the place of my fear. Those two emotions feel so similar, with my thundering pulse and the rod in my throat—the thinking too much and too quickly without really knowing anything at all. There is no peace until it happens.

The dark sky collapses.

As the presence crashes into me, we hurtle to the ground, and I quickly twist to face it before we hit the earth. It hovers over me, panting, a nothing dressed in darkness and heat. It pins my wrists, and as it leans in, caressing the skin of my neck with its breath, wisps of sensation travel down the length of my body, like fingernails dragging across my skin.

You're all mine, and you will never forget it.

"Yes," I moan.

You will let me in.

Of course I will. Don't I always?

The darkness settles between my legs and shoves inside. I cry out, tingles spreading outward from my core as it invades my body, stretching and pushing, deeper and deeper, until it feels as though I might split apart. My moans turn into screams, but it doesn't stop, and I find that I don't really want it to. The pain is edged in the most intense pleasure, and I give myself over to it, allowing my body to soften and accept every inch of the intrusion. As I surrender, it burrows itself through my stomach and into my chest until it's fully inside me, inhabiting my skin, whispering against my heart.

Yes. What a very good girl you are. My girl. Mine.

My stomach flutters and clenches, creating a sphere of tension on the verge of exploding—

I jerk awake.

My eyes peel open to reveal the dark ceiling of my

bedroom. The pleasure coursing through my body ebbs, and I could cry in disappointment. My cunt is throbbing; I need to come. As my eyes drift shut again, I replay the dream in my head, memorizing every second of it before it fades from my memory.

I slide my hand down between my legs until my pointer and middle finger rub small circles over my swollen clit.

Mine, it said. For a moment, I let myself believe I belonged to somebody, even if it's just to a *something*, a dark figment of my dreams. It's not difficult to pretend the presence is still with me, inside this room. Every thrust of my fingers drives me closer to release, but not quite close enough.

Nothing compares to the dreams—that's why I sought sleeping pills to stop them. This is far from the first time I've dreamed of such terribly wonderful things.

I flip over and grapple with the drawer of my nightstand, and I don't even bother opening my eyes all the way. Pulling out my vibrator, I settle back against the bed, my thumb finding the buttons. My hips jerk at the familiar vibration, and I set a fierce rhythm, turning everything to the highest settings.

I can almost hear that familiar whisper in my head. *Mine-minemineminemineminemine.*

I'm coming within seconds, but it does little good, because I'm not satisfied. There's a hollowness in my abdomen, a deep, endless need.

Turning off the vibrator, I lay there for a minute and catch my breath. I sit up and toss my legs over the side of the bed, preparing myself to get up and clean the device, but as I lift my head, my eyes lock onto the mirror of my vanity.

I see another face beside my own staring back at me, a black figure with burning green flames for eyes.

A scream tears out of my lungs as I scramble backwards across the bed, and I promptly fall over the edge of the mattress. My shoulder collides with the ground; it probably would have hurt like hell if my body wasn't surging with adrenaline. I consider staying there on the floor, either for forever or until I'm murdered by the intruder sitting at my vanity, but the dark abyss under the bed actually scares me just as badly as whoever is on the other side of the room. I can't stop imagining something crawling out of the darkness toward me.

I quickly roll onto my back and sit up, my eyes trained on the mattress just barely obstructing my view. *Come on*, I tell myself. *Get up, grab your phone, and make a run for it.*

Better to die fighting than to just let it happen.

I lurch forward, pulling myself up by the comforter I didn't turn down before passing out. My phone flies toward me, and I snatch it up, but I pause when I see... nothing.

There's no one at my vanity.

My heart is still hammering as I glance around the room. The sliding bathroom door is closed—I would have heard it move if the intruder retreated through it. My lip trembles, and I bite down on the soft tissue for some semblance of control. I unlock my phone and navigate to the security app to see if anyone's used any of the doors, only to find that the last register was me coming through the front door hours ago. Everything is still locked.

Maybe it was all my imagination?

It takes me another minute or so to break free from my paralysis, and I return to the bed, still feeling uneasy about what might be lurking beneath it.

There's no way in hell I'm walking to the bathroom right now.

I consider calling the police, but what would I say when they got here? I would have to tell them that I think I'm losing my grip on reality, and they would pack me up and send me away. A danger to my own health, they'd probably say.

Insane.

And maybe, just maybe, they'd be right.

CHAPTER 13

YOU CAN LOOK, BUT DON'T TOUCH

I park my SUV in the garage, turn off the ignition, and let my head fall back against the curved headrest as the garage door rolls back down.

It's been the longest day of work, possibly ever. I blame it on the fact that I didn't go back to sleep last night. There was nothing and no one in the house except for me, I knew that, but that didn't stop me from cowering on top of my comforter all night. My sessions today dragged, wearing on my thin patience and empathy. It's difficult to feel compassion for others when I barely have enough energy for myself.

I pluck my phone from the middle console and check my notifications.

Still no new texts from Levi.

My stomach sinks. I sent him another message this morning asking when he would be coming home, but I think that phone call in the bar was the final nail in our coffin. He's ignoring me. I should be used to that by now, but this time, it feels different. Everything feels different.

I make my way into the house, toeing my heels off the

second I'm through the door, resolving to clean up after myself later, maybe in the morning. As I hang up my purse, my stomach rumbles—I skipped lunch because I got too busy. Maybe I'll have the chef freeze whatever meal she made for tonight, and I can get some fried chicken delivered; I'm craving something greasy and hot. My mom always used to bring home fried chicken after a stressful day at her back-to-back jobs. When I do it, it almost feels like she's still here, comforting me.

Walking into the kitchen, I see that the chef isn't here at all, but still, there's music playing through the smart speakers, instrumental and a bit listless. The shades are drawn, the only light in the room coming from the pendant bulbs above the kitchen island and a glow emanating from the table lamp in the hallway beyond. It's not much to see by, but it is enough to see the flecks of red scattered on the floor.

Rose petals.

I remove my blazer, suddenly feeling *very* warm. Folding the pinstripe material over my arm, I walk to the white marble island and lay down the jacket there, then follow the trail of petals down the hallway and up the stairs. I'm nearly to the top landing when I notice it's leading me to the bedroom, soft light flickering over the threshold of the partially-closed door.

Entering the bedroom, I finally see the source of that warm light.

Dozens and dozens of black candles are lit throughout the room, some on the hardwood floor and others spaced out across every flat surface. Several small black columns line either side of the rose petal path as it winds toward the bathroom.

I amble farther into the room, completely aghast.

I'm forced to walk on top of the roses, and it feels like

walking on silk. The petals stick to my sweaty feet—I don't know why I'm so damn nervous. My eyes scour the bedroom for Levi but he's not in here, so I continue into the bathroom. As I peer through the archway, I hear a bath running and spy a handful more candles placed on the bathroom counter and around the tub.

Steam curls through the room. The tub is only halfway filled, and I think some kind of bath bomb has been tossed into the bottom, because the water swirls with a dark red pigment, becoming a deeper crimson than the rose petals floating on its surface.

As I stare disbelieving at the tub, I feel the atmosphere shift behind me.

A hand appears at my waist as a nose buries in my hair, breathing me in. A soft chuckle that I recognize. Levi—I missed him, his touch, his overwhelming presence. The room feels smaller now that he's in it. His energy crowds around me, making me feel safe, and that burning hand slides around to press against my belly to wrench me back into his hard abdomen.

I stifle a gasp.

"Hello, little snake," he whispers into my ear. "Are you happy to see me?"

For a moment, I'm not sure. This offering—the bath and the romantic trail of petals—is so at odds with how he acted on the phone at the bar. I'm a little scared—I'm not sure how he plans to punish me with it. He was clear: he's going to do something to me.

Levi nuzzles my hair again, heating my scalp and making my skin erupt in gooseflesh. The hand on my stomach travels in feather-light circles up between my breasts.

Maybe he did all of this to get laid. I'd be okay with that, actually—more than okay.

I twist in his arms, intending to launch myself at him, but before I can, his other hand lifts a brown bag between us, and I fall back a step. "What is that?"

He grins. "You didn't expect me to forget to feed you?"

The smell of the fried food smacks into me, and I smile as I snatch the bag from his hand. When I see the chicken nuggets inside, I start bouncing in delight. I'm totally happy to see him. "Oh my god, it's like you read my mind." I reach in and grab the cardboard box, backing up to lean against a section of the bathroom counter without candles.

Levi sweeps me off my feet, earning a squeal as he deposits me on top of the counter. "I wish I could read your mind," he murmurs.

He takes a step back but rests his hands on my knees as I dig in. My pencil skirt has ridden up my thighs, so his palms are on my bare skin, and that's when I notice the rings on both his hands. They aren't silver or gold. No, they're heavy iron rings. I never thought I'd be so attracted to a man wearing jewelry, but they're... masculine, somehow. Rough and raw, just like Levi, and they highlight the thick veins running through his hands. It reminds me of how his fingers felt inside me, and how they might feel now.

As I eat, Levi's thumbs stroke the sensitive spots just below my kneecaps. It tickles enough to make me want to clench my legs together, but I resist. I want him to keep touching me like this.

It scratches a little itch inside my brain—the casual intimacy.

After the long night and day I've had, it's nice.

I devour my nuggets and fries in record time. The tub reaches an optimal level by the time I'm done, and Levi leaves my side to turn off the faucet.

I'm sucking the salt from my fingertips when he turns

back to me. His black eyes narrow in on my mouth, and I can't stop the coy smile from spreading over my lips as I cock my head. "What do you have planned for me now, husband?" The words leave my mouth like a challenge.

I'm curious what his plan is—no, I *need* to know. Why would he feed me and run me a bath when he was so upset with me before?

Levi doesn't approach the counter like I expect. He walks backward instead, and it's only as he slowly lowers himself that I realize he brought my vanity bench into the bathroom. "I'm going to sit here and watch you undress," he murmurs, reclining until his shoulders hit the wall behind him, parting his legs in a relaxed but dominant position, "and then I'm going to watch you bathe."

My stomach flutters.

"Is that so?" I slide off the counter and cross my arms, piquing a brow to give the illusion that I don't want to give him exactly what he just demanded. "And what's in it for me?"

His voice comes out in a low rumble this time. "Don't you want to please me, menace? Don't you realize that the more you please me, the more generous I will be in return? I'd like to be so very generous, if you'd let me."

I hear what he doesn't say: this is my penance, and if I don't give it to him, he'll find another way to take it. He's giving me a choice, but the balance of power is leaning heavily in his direction. The problem is, I missed him. His touch is a drug, and now I'm itching for another hit. I want him, and he knows it.

I reach up and start unbuttoning my silk cream blouse. By the time I undo the first two buttons, he starts clicking his tongue and shakes his head. "Slow down, baby. Let me enjoy you."

My abdomen tightens; I know I'm moving too quickly—I'm nervous. For all the things I've done with my body to get me here, I've never needed to strip for anyone. Sex is just sex. This is... *intimate*. I swallow the saliva in my mouth and lift my chin, staring at him down the length of my nose as I lean back against the counter and slowly make my way through the rest of the buttons. When the blouse is open, I tug the hem from my pencil skirt and shrug it off.

Levi's ebony eyes brighten as they roam the skin I've just exposed, and I pause to let him admire my neck and petite shoulders, the breasts swelling out of my balconette bra. I'm glad I wore my matching lavender lace set today.

When I move on to my pencil skirt, I lean forward as I pull the zipper down, flexing my chest as the material slowly loosens around my wide hips.

Levi's expression darkens, and I bite my lip and flutter my lashes as the skirt pools around my ankles. "How was that?"

"Perfect," he whispers.

I reach behind me to unhook my bra, but Levi stands up and shakes his head. He raises a hand and twirls his pointer finger in a circular motion. "Turn around."

I turn and watch him approach through the mirror, his dark eyes burning straight through me. All my senses sharpen under his attention; I can smell the honeyed wax of the candles all around us, the musk emanating from his skin. I can feel the warmth of his body as he draws up behind me, but still, he maintains a sliver of space between us. The space is unbearable.

I sway toward him without trying to.

Levi slides a hand into the hair at the nape of my neck and tugs my head to the side, knocking me off balance. I grab hold of the counter to keep my footing as a growl rumbles in

Levi's throat. He leans in and drags the tip of his nose from my collar to my ear, the intense warmth of his breath making me shiver.

I wait for him to say something, but he doesn't. In the mirror, I watch as his eyes sweep up to trace the profile of my face as his own glows in the candlelight, his body highlighted by long shadows on the wall behind us. That mysterious energy under his skin whirls and pulses.

"Please," I murmur.

He blinks, meeting my gaze briefly in the mirror. His fingers loosen in my hair, and then his hand drops to my bra. In one swift motion, he unhooks it, and then his fingertips skate along my ribs in front of me. The rings are cold, but his skin is hot, and I watch his eyes darken in the mirror as he looks down at me over my shoulder. I arch to lean into his touch, craving more, but he backs away, stuffing his hands into the pockets of his sweatpants.

"Not yet. Keep going." His voice is dark and commanding, sending a spark of excitement skittering under my skin. Levi doesn't sit back down, but I can tell he has no intention of touching me any further.

I let my bra drop to the counter. Then, sick of moving so slow, I hook my thumbs under the sides of my mesh thong and shimmy it down my legs, turning to face him as I raise my eyebrows, daring him to complain.

He traces a thumb over his lower lip as his gaze travels up and down my body. Once he's had his fill, he nods at the tub. "In you go."

I step into the scarlet water, the oils of whatever bath bomb he used clinging to my skin. The water is right on the verge of scalding, but I welcome the heat. It smells amazing—cinnamon and apples, with a very subtle floral undertone.

"Mmm," I moan, closing my eyes as I lower myself the rest of the way into the tub. "It smells like autumn."

"Do you like it?" Levi presses.

I smile at him. "Yes. Fall is my favorite season, ever since I was a kid."

He returns the smile, sitting down on the bench. "Really?" He seems so damn pleased with himself that I keep talking.

"The scent of apples always reminds me of when my mom took me to an orchard." I look down at the red water. Cupping the oily surface, I pull the water toward me and let it splash up over my chest. "When we got there, it was really dark, so we were basically picking them off the trees and the ground blind. We spent the next three days sifting through bags upon bags of them, and the house smelled like apple pie for months." I smile at the memory, but it falters a bit as I add, "She never told me we were stealing them. I figured it out later, when I was cleaning out the pantry after she died and I found a leftover jar of the apples she canned."

I dare a glance up to find Levi's eyes trained on me, listening. There's no sign of judgment or disinterest, but I hesitate anyway.

The only person I've ever talked at length to about my mother was Charlie, and he had nothing kind to say when I finally opened up. He *hated* her. That should have been a bloody red flag to me, but at the time, I had thought it was sweet how much he seemed to care, that he thought I'd needed protecting and coddling. It was only after we broke up that I realized it had been another way for him to break me down, to make me feel like I *needed* him. It was all too easy to forget the good—and that's not to say there wasn't bad too—but I found that missing my mom was easier if I held on to the worst.

Charlie made my mother the villain so that I would feel grateful to him for liking me, for thinking I was... better than her.

I never quite forgave myself for allowing someone to put her memory down like that. It gives me a sick, slimy feeling, even now, like I'm no better than the asshole who knocked her up and left her to raise me alone, or the people who tolerated her at church while rolling their eyes the moment her back was turned. No one ever hid their disdain for her from *me*. They glanced at me with pity, as if we were all in on some kind of twisted joke at her expense, and I never said a word.

I was no better than the cancer, betraying her in silence like that. And I was her fucking daughter.

"Anyway," I say through a forced laugh, through the guilt. "I like the smell of apples."

I dunk my head to break the tension, holding my breath as the red water envelops me. When I come back up, I smooth my hair back and rub the excess from my eyes before I reach for the soap, only to find Levi still staring at me. I don't think he's even blinked.

"Do you miss her?" he asks.

I squirt the liquid into my hand and begin lathering it up. "I do. More than anything."

When I glance up at him, he's frowning at his hands, but as I rub myself down, he returns his gaze to me, watching as I lift my legs from the water one at a time.

A wickedness gleams in his eyes as I massage my breasts.

As I rinse off, he seems to shake his arousal and asks in a strangely soft voice, "Will you tell me more about her—your mom?"

I feel my eyebrows stitch together. We don't talk about our families, or our pasts, or anything meaningful, really.

That was Walter's preference too—he didn't like talking about his parents. After meeting them a few times, I understood why. But with Levi, just like everything else, talking about her felt *different*, like a chance to talk about the good, to talk about what she was like beneath the world's opinion. So I say, "What do you want to know?"

He shrugs. "Whatever you wish to share."

I lay back against the porcelain slope of the tub. "She was strong," I whisper. "Resilient and goofy and hopelessly optimistic. I never had to wonder if she loved me, because it was obvious in everything she did, everything she sacrificed for our life together. Children can be selfish sometimes, though it's not like they can help it; it's simply their nature. My mother let me be selfish with what little we had, and it wasn't until I was older and she was gone that I realized how wonderful she was for that. For all of it."

Levi smiles tightly. "She raised you. I think that is very telling of how wonderful a person she was."

I blink at him. *What a very sweet thing to say.*

People had a lot of vitriol for my mom when I was growing up, both spoken and implied. They blamed her for all the bad things that happened to her, the divorces and the string of jobs she couldn't keep and... the cancer. Especially the cancer. They looked at her and all they saw was a single mother. A sinner. A thief. A disappointment. A whore. An *inconvenience.*

They never saw the good, because they never bothered to look. It was easier for them to turn a blind eye.

I look away from Levi, because I can't keep staring into those black eyes. I'll start crying if I do, so I quickly grab the conditioner and begin massaging it into my hair, closing my eyes and humming at the sharp sensation of my nails.

"Do you look forward to seeing her again?" he asks before I can dunk my head.

I pause, my brow furrowing. "What do you mean?"

His lips purse. "Well, when your time is up here on Earth, do you look forward to joining her, wherever she went?"

"Like, when I die?" He nods, and I huff a little laugh. "I-I don't know. I'm not really counting on it. I think if there's an afterlife, I would be shocked."

Now it's his turn to look confused. "Would you? Why?"

"There's not a whole lot of evidence for it. I don't mean to say that it *doesn't* exist, but I think something like that is better left to be discovered at death. Why waste time worrying or guessing about it? If I see my mother again, that would be a marvelous surprise, but I have a whole life to live before then. I can't abandon the present."

Something shifts in Levi's eyes, like fog clinging to the coast on a winter morning.

I submerge myself in the water and scrub the conditioner out of my hair. Levi is deep in thought when I emerge, gazing toward the large mirror above the counter. Of course I just had to go and ruin the mood with talk about my dead mother. I fold my arms over the edge of the tub and force a bright smile. "I think it's *your* turn now."

He looks at me, his face pinched.

I let my gaze drop to his fully-clothed body. "I think you're overdressed."

That earns me a small smile. "Oh. You think so, menace?"

I nod, pouting.

Levi stands then, holding my gaze as he pulls his long-sleeved shirt over his head. My mouth salivates at the sight of his chest and stomach, not only because they look even more toned than the last time I saw them, but because they're now covered in tattoos. It's more of the same "nonsense" lines that he tattooed on his knees.

My eyes bulge a little as I sit up. "*What did you do?*"

Levi only tosses me a devious grin before shoving his sweatpants off. He's left in a pair of black boxer briefs, the material clinging to every glorious inch of him as he folds his arms over his chest. "That's all you get, baby. Drink your fill."

I frown. "But... you got *me* completely naked."

He chuckles. "Yes, well, I don't trust you to keep your hands to yourself."

"And why should I keep my hands to myself?" I demand, standing up as well. Red water sluices from my body, and Levi is noticeably distracted by its descent as I reach for a towel.

He still hasn't recovered by the time I step out of the tub and start squeezing my hair dry. I refrain from wrapping the towel around me as I walk, and as I halt in front of him, I smirk and drop the towel entirely.

"I've given you everything you asked for so far," I whisper. "What more could you possibly want?"

Levi leans in, almost close enough to kiss me. "Sweet girl, I want *everything.*"

"Then take it," I return with equal softness.

I lift my hands to his chest, and he allows me to push him down on the bench. His hands find my waist, and I stare into his eyes for a long moment, our mouths inches apart, before I brace my hands on his shoulders and lift my knees to the bench, settling them on either side of his thighs.

My new plan is simple.

If I can't steal what I want from him, I'll take advantage of his recent obsession with me instead. I'll seduce him all over again, buy myself enough time to get what I need. The next time he loses interest in our marriage, I'll be ready. I'll have him declared unfit, get him admitted to a psych ward. With the way he's been acting, it would be hard, but not impossible. I can plant the evidence if I must. If it works, I'll get the money and my freedom, and he'll never be the wiser, not until it's too late.

Levi's hands roam over my body. They caress my ribs and my spine, one reaching up to tangle in my wet hair. Once he has a grip on the nape of my neck, he leans up to graze his nose against mine, and I lean in too, wanting to kiss him, but his fingers tighten in my hair to keep our lips from touching. He continues teasing me, his breath warming my cheeks as he chuckles. His other hand tightens on my hip as he pulls me down against him, rolling his hips. His cock is erect and nearly bursting out of his boxer briefs—when I glance down between us, I see the reddened tip peeking out from under his waistband.

I whimper, and he laughs louder.

He grinds against me, and I moan. His hand holds me firmly so I can't move on him the way I want to, the way I *need* to.

Levi moves purposefully, his touch soft and sensual as he trails kisses down my throat and across my chest. My arms wrap around his neck, and I surrender to his torture for a few minutes. There's only so much torture I can endure, though, which is why, when he makes a second pass across my breasts, I peel back and slide a hand between us. With a swiftness that surprises even myself, I swipe a thumb over the tip of his cock, swirling it in the precum beading there.

My body clenches, knowing there's so much because of *me*.

I barely get a chance to enjoy it before Levi snatches my wrist and pulls my hand away. His fist tugs painfully on my hair, forcing me to arch my neck as he growls against my skin, "You naughty girl. I knew you couldn't be trusted."

I like it when he pulls on my hair. "I needed *more*," I say breathlessly.

His teeth graze my skin. "I will decide when you can handle more, little snake. You don't want to choke on more than you can swallow."

My legs tremble, his body the only thing keeping me upright.

"I've decided you can wait a couple more days," he says with a vicious laugh. "Fucking you again on Halloween is too perfect an opportunity to pass up, and I have a full night of fun planned for us." Before I can respond, he lifts my hand and slots the thumb I used to touch him into my mouth. "Suck, baby, because that's all you get tonight. Show me you appreciate it."

I suck on my thumb while holding his gaze, savoring his salty arousal.

Levi stands and carries me into the bedroom. He lays me down and braces his hands on the mattress to either side of my head, his eyes trained on the thumb in my mouth.

"Next time, you won't hesitate," he murmurs.

I nod, and he leans in to press a lingering kiss to my cheek.

CHAPTER 14

MONSTERS ALWAYS COME OUT ON HALLOWEEN

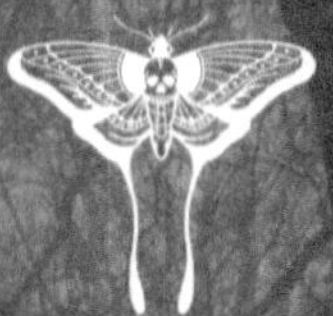

A pop song rumbles up my spine through the passenger seat of my husband's sleek Tesla. It's the last thing I expected to listen to as we drive past city limits, but Levi bobs his head to the beat, smiling and rapping his fingers against the steering wheel.

I wring my fingers in my lap and watch the sun set outside my window.

Levi was waiting with a slutty witch costume in hand when I got home this evening, which surprised me—not the costume, but the fact that he's actually taking me out tonight, on Halloween. My husband *hates* Halloween. One October, I bought a throw pillow with a Ouji board printed on it, and he lost his fucking mind, tore it up and burned the pieces in our fireplace. He always seemed a little bit frightened of everything around this time of year. Usually, I spend the holiday handing out candy alone while he stays out all night drinking with his friends.

I've been waiting for him to get spooked and cancel our plans all week.

Levi left the house after our fun in the bathroom on Wednesday, and then he was gone again last night. He blamed it on work emergencies, naturally, but at least it's Friday now. We have the whole weekend together, and I won't let him disappear again under the guise of business.

As I tug a loose black thread out of the hem of my minidress, the song ends, and the radio hosts begin talking to each other over the air. Levi's eyes flick between me and the traffic ahead, his eyes warm pools of ink. "Are you going to tell me where we're going now?" I venture.

"We're nearly there," he replies after a moment. "I found out about a haunted farm from someone at work this week. I thought you might like it."

"The Haunted Realms?" Excitement swells in my chest as Levi nods.

I start bouncing in my seat—I've tried to get Astra to check out this haunted house for years, but she's not into the creepy stuff. Her practice leans more toward crystals and incense rather than doom and gloom, and she refuses to entertain even the *illusion* of welcoming dark energy to follow her around for a night. That's fine, but it meant I never had a chance to explore the haunted attractions throughout Massachusetts, and I love creepy shit.

As I turn to Levi, planning to tell him exactly how excited I am, I see a frown forming on his face. His eyes lock onto the radio, the car veering into another lane. Luckily, these roads are mostly empty.

Shifting my focus to the talk show, I realize that they're talking about my husband's company. Specifically, about the executives going missing. As in, *more than one*. As the newscaster lists off three familiar names in addition to the first who went missing on Monday, my eyes bulge, and a cold weight settles in my stomach. That's all I hear before

Levi's hand flies forward and turns the volume all the way down.

I guess that explains why he's working so many late nights. His partners...

"Why didn't you tell me more of the executives went missing?" I demand.

He smiles tightly, his eyes retraining on the road. "I didn't want to worry you, baby. It's not your problem. I'm sorry you had to hear about it in the first place."

"You should have told me." I shake my head in disbelief. "Is someone targeting your company?"

I'm not shocked that there's someone angry enough to come after the executives. There's been a few lawsuits filed over the last couple years. I've heard whispers—*only* whispers, because their company lawyers were quick to get gag orders into place and most of the prosecuting parties had already signed NDAs anyway, but the bits and pieces I've heard aren't pretty. They burn through assistants like they grow on trees. The lawsuits may not get far before the company settles them, but this is beyond legal process now. People are getting hurt.

Levi could get hurt.

"Is that why you've been so busy this week?" I press. "Please tell me you've increased security around the office. I don't feel good about you spending so much time there at night if you haven't."

Levi scoffs. "You don't need to panic, baby." When he glances at me, his smile has spread, and his eyes are crinkled and warm. He seems so sure.

But how is he going to defend himself against someone who has already gotten to a handful of his friends? Why isn't he more concerned? It has to be his head injury.

He still isn't thinking clearly.

I open my mouth to argue further, but his hand grips my thigh, squeezing hard enough to make me yelp. I try to scoot away, but he slides his hand higher, and my chest clenches as my back arches off the seat.

He chuckles softly. "You're adorable when you worry about me, menace, but it's not necessary. I promise you, we're safe. I will *always* keep you safe."

His fingers loosen and slip into a few of the holes on my netted tights, and I freeze, staring at the greenish-blue veins bulging in his hand. His fingertips draw tiny circles on the inside of my thigh, soothing me with so much sweetness, I can feel my teeth forming cavities. I sigh, letting my worries go for now. It's impossible to argue with him anyway.

Levi keeps his hand on my leg for the rest of the drive, his palm hot against my skin.

As we pull into a very busy parking lot, I perk up and watch the flickering lights in the distance. A blend of red, purple, and white spears through the dark sky from the attractions beyond the fence—I can't see more than that from here. The parking lot is barely functional, without lines or concrete. It's just a long stretch of dirt and hay. We drive behind other cars all searching for a spot, and when the other cars turn farther out into a secondary field, Levi turns down a different lane.

This aisle gives me a view of the entrance, of the endless line of people waiting to pay for tickets. I groan; Halloween has to be their busiest night.

"We're going to be waiting hours to get in," I gripe, falling back against my seat. We'll probably be looking for a parking spot for hours too at this point. We're stuck behind at least a dozen cars in this aisle alone, and it's stop and go.

Levi doesn't say anything, but when I look over, he's smiling to himself.

"You're alarmingly cheery today," I mutter, crossing my arms over my mesh-covered cleavage.

"Would you like me to be a grump, instead?" He shoots me an exaggerated glare, and I laugh.

His fingers dig into my skin, dragging higher up on my thigh. Instead of trying to wiggle away from him, I part my legs, daring him to continue. If we have to be in line for most of the night, we might as well have some fun.

"Hungry little snake," Levi muses, squeezing my thigh once more before pulling his hand away to wrap around the steering wheel.

I bite back a discontented sigh.

Then, he mutters in a deeper voice, so quiet that it might have been to himself, "Perhaps I'll have to catch some field mice to feed you."

My face pinches as I try to interpret the meaning of that, but honking draws my attention forward. There's a truck attempting to pull out of a space right in front of the entrance. Unfortunately, the car in line before us sees it and nearly backs into us to give the truck room to reverse, effectively claiming the spot that should have been for us.

"Asshole," I mumble.

The Tesla hums beneath me, simulated engine sounds rumbling out of the speakers. We surge forward, connecting with the bumper of the car in front of us as it starts turning into the empty space.

I jerk forward at the collision, inhaling sharply. "*Levi,* what the hell?"

"Exactly." He's already reversing.

The car's tail lights in front of us light up, and the driver's side door swings open. A guy in a cowboy costume jumps out, looks at his dented bumper, and raises his arms as he turns to our Tesla. "What the fuck, dude?"

Levi rolls down his window and leans his arm along his door, smiling like a maniac.

"*What are you doing?*" I seethe.

The guy approaches our window, his face red as a beet—he looks about ready to grab Levi by the collar and drag him out of the car. My heart creeps so far up my throat, I'm practically choking on it, but before the guy can even reach us, Levi drawls, "Hey pal, how about you let us have this spot? You can take the next one."

The guy halts a few feet from our car, his forehead creasing. "What?"

"You don't mind if I take this one, right?"

I stare wide-eyed at Levi. I'm sure my face looks as bewildered as the cowboy's. I can't believe he just asked for this parking spot after tapping the guy's bumper.

The stranger takes a moment to collect his thoughts, and then he shrugs and says, "Sure."

Sure. That's it. He smiles as he says it too.

My jaw slackens.

"Much appreciated, partner," Levi says in a mocking southern accent. "Now, get in that steed of yours and giddy up."

The guy staggers backward and turns to his car. Within seconds, he's pulling away from the parking space and driving forward, leaving the open spot for us. I'm still gaping at Levi as he parks and turns off the ignition.

"What was that?" I breathe.

Levi tosses me a sharp smile. "Was my parking performance up to your standards this time?"

"No," I growl, nodding at the truck now disappearing up the aisle. "What the hell was *that*?"

He shrugs. "I can be *very* persuasive, baby."

Without giving me a chance to respond, he jumps out of

the car and walks around to open my door. When I step out, he leans around me to grab something from beneath my seat. As he straightens, he pulls the item over his head. "What do you think? Like my costume?"

My skin chills at the sight of it.

He's wearing a metal devil mask. The horns curling at the top look long and sharp enough to disembowel someone, and the smile on the front is unsettlingly wide as his dark eyes pierce into me through the holes on the mask. *Creeeeeeepy*. It makes me want to squeal in delight. The rest of his outfit makes sense now: he's wearing a silken black ensemble, with slacks and a button-up left open at the collar, topped off with a waistcoat, a deep purple handkerchief peeking out from his breast pocket, and his hands laden with those iron rings.

He looks hot as fuck.

"I like it," I tell him. The only thing I don't like about the mask is that I can't kiss him, and I suddenly *really* want to kiss him.

Levi takes my hand and drags me toward the line, but surprisingly, not the back. No, he ambles toward the entrance, where tickets are being sold.

I slow down. "Levi."

I try to get his attention by tugging on his hand as people turn to glare at us, but he ignores me, continuing to pull me along. Someone shouts at us from down the line, and Levi ignores them too as heat crawls up my neck.

The lady inside the podium spots us and calls out, "Sir, stop. You have to pay first."

It's only when we're walking under the archway into the farm that someone physically stops us. It looks like security, though it's hard to tell—they're in costume, too. "Whoa. You two need to go to the back of the line and wait your turn."

I start to say, "Yes, of course," only to be interrupted when Levi counters with, "You misunderstand."

His voice is almost... *musical.* The words twinkle on his tongue like the stars hidden above us.

Security immediately takes a step back, and Levi turns to the ticket worker. "I have an agreement with the owner. He told me to come straight in when we got here, no tickets needed. I'm sure he told you to keep an eye out for me?"

As if anyone could recognize him with that mask on.

The employee stares at him for a long moment, her eyes glazing a bit before she nods, the movement stiff. "Yes, sir. My apologies. You can go on in."

My stomach flips. *The fuck?*

Several people waiting in line start to complain when they realize we're about to cut, but security steps aside without another word, and we continue on our way. The angry voices fade as we navigate the crowd of fake blood and myths, and I try to work out what just happened. Maybe the employee *had* been told to let him in, but I somehow doubt it.

It felt like some kind of interactive stage play, like those people were just actors on a stage, and he'd directed them into the positions he wanted.

I shake my head, scoffing at the thought. That's not possible.

Stop analyzing every second of your life, I tell myself, the voice sounding more like Astra's than my own. *Live in the moment before it turns on you. Let yourself enjoy tonight.*

I forcibly put away my confusion, my thoughts. I don't need them right now.

Astra would be so proud if she could see me. Well, except for the fact that I'm walking through a haunted farm without so much as an evil eye talisman to protect me.

There's three sections mapped out on the farm's direction

board: the House, the Yard, and the corn maze. The House and the Yard are fully staffed tours, while the corn maze is a self-guided walking trail that stretches for miles out behind the main attractions. I can see the maze from where we stand in front of the map—it's deserted, no one going in or not.

I'm guessing the only time people go in there is when they want to fuck. We have plenty of time for that later.

Levi's black eyes scan the map, and then he turns and leads us to the Yard. We squeeze our way through the crowd gathered around the entrance, and when we reach a woman with a clipboard, Levi tells her we're already at the top of her list. She doesn't argue, and I start to wonder if Levi paid off the entire farm. Maybe this was all carefully orchestrated, right down to the ticket worker at the front. That would make a lot of sense.

The actors on the tour are decked out in realistic and horrifying costumes, animatronics and real people jump out at us at every corner, and I cling tightly to Levi's arm, giggling at every scare. Levi, on the other hand, seems confused. Every time something pops out at him, he doesn't even flinch. He just stares at them with his shrewd black gaze.

By the time we're halfway through, the other members of our group are sprinting, but Levi only wraps his arm around me and starts laughing as we continue at a leisurely pace. Haunting music and jarring sound effects play from the speakers above us, but Levi's laughter drowns it out. I can tell the actors are getting annoyed with him.

So instead of trying to scare *him*, they come after me.

An actor with a chainsaw singles me out. Logically, I know it's not real—I know there's no chain on that machine, but when he swings it like he's about to saw us apart, I *freak*. I leap away, and the rest of the actors descend on me with their twisted smiles and menacing props, cutting me off from

Levi completely. The guy with the chainsaw comes at me again, and I run as he chases me up onto a bridge. At the peak, I glance back, trying to see over the actor to where Levi went. I don't have to look far; he appears behind the chainsaw guy and shoves him off the bridge into the shallow creek below, and I stagger to a stop. Levi stalks up the bridge to meet me, his eyes darkened, his mouth set in an angry line.

The chainsaw guy groans from where he fell in the creek.

"Levi, why did you do that?"

He halts in front of me, some of his anger fading. "He was targeting you. They all were."

"That's the whole point," I scoff. "Their job is to separate the weak ones from the group and scare the shit out of them. That's what we're all paying for."

After a moment, Levi's eyes lighten. "I see." He takes a step closer to me, raising a hand to tuck a loose lock of hair behind my ear. "Let me just make one thing perfectly clear to you, Rose. You are not weak. You never have been and you never will be."

I try to think of a response to that, but I'm without words. His eyes are so much darker in this moment, his voice deeper, and it feels like I'm standing face-to-face with a stranger—a dangerous, beautiful stranger. That twisted part of me hovering in the recesses of my mind revels in this feeling—in the fear and exhilaration that comes along with Levi. She loves the way he surprises me, the way he scares me.

I'm no longer certain I can handle him turning back into the Walter I knew. I might crack.

My gaze drifts to the actors we left behind. They stand together in what looks like the same place we left them, each one staring at us with their heads cocked at identical right angles.

That's certainly one way to creep a girl out. Good job, guys. *A+ performance.*

"Sorry," I sing over the edge of the bridge. Then, I grab Levi's hand and drag him out of the Yard before they can run at us again or worse—throw us out of the farm entirely.

The House is better for Levi.

He's finally caught on to the novelty of haunted houses. He lets the actors have their fun with me and watches calmly the entire time, his eyes glittering behind the devil mask. It's a blur of fog machines and neon lights, tilting rooms and moving walls, and by the time we squeeze through the exit together—through an inflatable jumpy house hallway that kind of feels like being birthed by a condom—I'm gasping for air from all my giggling and screaming.

I haven't had this much fun in ages.

Once we're both out, I spin and launch myself at Levi, wrapping my arms around his neck. "Thank you," I whisper.

His hands land on my back and draw me closer. "For what, baby?"

Tears well behind my closed eyes. "For... making me feel like you understand me." I pull back an inch and grip the bottom of his mask, sliding it up so I can touch my lips to his.

As I kiss him, everything shifts.

His fingers dig into my back, and he lifts me off the ground. Without breaking the kiss, he carries me around the side of the House, a direction we're not supposed to go, but I can't bring myself to care as he pins me to the wall. He breaks the kiss and shoves his mask up on top of his head to look into my eyes.

The smile he gives me is sinful. "You like being scared, don't you? It turns you on." He presses one of his thighs between mine, applying just enough pressure to drive me wild.

"Shut up," I mutter, but I hear my own breathlessness.

His head moves in a slow, predatory tilt as he grips the bottom of my dress, exposing my lacy underwear to the night. He doesn't hesitate to slip his fingers under the waistband, and I gasp, exhaling shakily as his fingertips dip into the peak of my wet slit.

Leaning in, he whispers, "I think you like being targeted, being chased, knowing something dark and violent could happen to you if you're caught. The proof is right here, soaking my fingertips." Two of his fingers rub slow circles around my clit, and I grip his shoulders to steady myself, swallowing back a whimper.

He trails kisses up my jaw, his tongue dancing across my skin as his free hand hooks behind my right knee and lifts it to circle around his waist, giving his hand easier access. I can barely breathe as his fingers change pattern. They move up and down over my clit, his nails flicking before he returns to circling faster, with more pressure.

Levi's hot mouth finds my ear. "We can put my theory to the test, you know. *I* could chase you. I could be rough with you, if you want me to be."

I swallow dryly. "Stop it."

He chuckles, his chest vibrating against mine and sending tingles all the way down to my toes. "Why? Because you think it's wrong? There's no such thing as wrong with me. No one's here to judge us, baby. On All Hallow's Eve, even God closes his eyes. I can mark you as mine. I can slap and choke and bite you, fuck you hard enough to make you see stars, and no one needs to see it. All you have to do is ask."

Levi starts kissing my neck again, my collar, my hair. He lightens his touch against my clit, and I know he's doing so to stave off my orgasm. He's waiting for an answer. It doesn't feel like a question to me because I feel no hesitation—I want him to do what he said. I want him to do all those depraved things because I know he'll make me like it. I trust Levi with my pleasure.

What's more surprising is, in this moment, I think I might be able to trust him with more than that.

I arch into him. "Please."

He brings his mouth a millimeter away from mine. "Please what?" he taunts.

"Chase me," I beg him. "Fuck me."

"What else?"

I whimper as his touch grows more forceful, more resolute. "Whatever you want."

He stills his fingers. His other hand disappears from my thigh and grasps the underside of my jaw, holding my face in place as he looks down into my eyes and speaks onto my mouth, his lips brushing mine with each word. "You have no idea what you've just agreed to, baby."

I'm falling into his eyes, into the endless darkness with him. "Teach me then."

Levi smiles slowly, and then his mouth crashes into mine, our teeth clinking as his body crushes me into the cold wall of the house. He hitches my thighs around his waist, and I wrap my arms around his neck, pulling him against me as his hips roll and his hand finds its way back to my cunt.

He rips my underwear off, and there's nothing gentle about how his fingers fuck me this time.

He shoves two fingers in, pausing briefly to scissor them and stretch my muscles, and then he thrusts into me with sharp, fierce movements, curling his fingertips toward my belly button with every plunge. The heel of his palm rubs against my clit, and I squeeze my eyes shut as I grind myself against it. Cool metal kisses my cunt with every thrust. His rings are wicked.

Everything sparkles white behind my eyes as I break the kiss and lift my head, gasping for air. "Levi, I-I'm—"

"I know, baby," he rasps against my cheek.

Stars explode all over my body, and my cunt clamps around Levi's fingers as I come. I'm vaguely aware of the moan erupting from my mouth, but then his lips cover mine, consuming the sound as his tongue thrusts into my mouth, claiming, absorbing every vibration of my voice. He pins my lower lip between his teeth and tugs, sending a spear of painful pleasure straight through my core.

Levi shifts his fingers, rubbing my swollen clit, and I can feel myself rising again, reaching for the peak I've just fallen from. It shouldn't be possible. *There's no way—not so soon.* Then, Levi bites the side of my neck, and I do.

My cunt squeezes around nothing, but Levi doesn't stop his assault on my nerves. I'm coming and still climbing, and it's as if I haven't quite hit the peak somehow. I bear down, desperate for any relief. Release spreads through me as I feel the gush of arousal. I can't control it. I can't stop it, and I don't want to. This is the most pleasure I've ever experienced, and he's not even inside me yet.

It takes longer to come down this time.

Heat is the first thing I register: the burning arms wrapped around me, the scorching fingers in my hair. My damp legs are the only part of me that's cold. When I open my eyes, I find Levi staring at me like I'm the most beautiful thing in the world.

For the first time in a long while, I start to believe that it's true, that maybe I *could* be that beautiful to someone.

Our bliss is cut short by a rustle in the brush beside us.

My head whips toward the sound, and my stomach drops when I see the gangly middle-aged guy staring at us from the corner of the house. Judging from the cock in his hand, he's been watching for a while. I suddenly want to vomit.

Before I can do or say anything, Levi drops me and lurches for the man. The peeper takes off around the back of the house, and Levi chases him. It takes me a few moments to recover my balance and senses enough to follow them, and by the time I turn the corner, I hear the distinct sound of flesh and bone colliding.

Levi has one hand gripping the guy's collar as the other fist swings forward to smash into his face again and again. A terrible ringing floods my ears. My eyes water, and yet I can't blink. The energy under Levi's skin explodes outward, radiating off of him into the air. I hear the familiar sound of bones crushing, of my future dawning.

That vicious voice in the back of my head tells me to stop, to wait, to *think*.

This is an opportunity, one I can't ignore. I might never get a chance quite as perfect as this again. The violence... I should be recording it. With shaking hands, I withdraw my phone and start recording a video, and then quickly darken the screen and tuck it into my bra, with the camera peeking over my cup.

Then, I sprint to them, grabbing Levi's shoulder.

"Walter!" I say his name as loudly and as clearly as I can. "Walter, quit it. The next round of people are going to come out of the House any second. You're going to get us kicked out, and he's not worth it."

Levi isn't listening to me. Suddenly, I worry that he's never going to stop. I didn't want to record a *homicide* tonight. After the next punch lands, I squeeze myself under Levi's arm, putting my body between them. Levi's eyes land on me, and the anger in his face falters. His bloody fist falls away, and he allows me to push him backwards, but he glares over my shoulder as the peeping tom scrambles up and away.

"Hey," I lift my hands to his face, "look at me."

His black eyes flutter, the depths swirling.

"What happened?" I implore. "Why did you attack him like that?"

"No one gets to take pleasure in you except for me," Levi growls, his hands wrapping around my waist and tugging me toward him until our chests meet. "He forfeited his ability to breathe when he looked at you that way."

My breath catches. Eventually, though, I manage to say, "That guy was a creep. Let's take a minute to cool off before we make any more rash decisions."

Levi's eyes narrow, and he redirects his gaze over my head, as if he's watching the crowd in the distance for something. Every muscle in his body is coiled, tense; it was a miracle no one else saw what he did, but I'm not surprised. This is a place that manufactures terror. It's easy to ignore screams.

When his eyes return to me, they're hard as granite. "You called me Walter."

My chest squeezes. *Whoops.* I didn't think about the fact that he would hear me call him Walter—I'd simply needed to catch it on the recording. I force a smile, laughing off the threat in his voice. "It was a slip of the tongue," I lie. "Come on, there's gotta be something better to do than stand here and stare at each other."

He looks me up and down. "I can think of a thing or two, yes."

Stepping forward with renewed purpose, Levi wraps a hand around my upper arm and drags me into the crowd, toward the corn maze, and I don't stop him. I *did* suggest a cool off. Once we're shielded on either side by corn stalks, the chaos and clamor of the crowd falls away. There's a few stragglers and couples in here with us, but we soon out-walk them.

When the last trace of footsteps and voices dissipate behind us, Levi stops, turning to me with a dark expression. "We need a word."

"What?" My brow furrows in confusion.

Levi's eyes are hard as obsidian. "If things become too much for you, if I scare you too badly, just say 'leviathan', and everything will stop. That's your word, menace."

It finally dawns on me what's happening, and my heart skips a beat. I nod eagerly. "Okay. Leviathan it is."

He smiles, his chest expanding in a deep inhale as he steps forward and wraps his hands around my arms. His lashes sweep low as he drops his gaze to my mouth. "Say that again, baby."

"Leviathan," I repeat in a whisper.

He wrenches me forward and crushes his mouth to mine in a brief, hard kiss. When he pulls away, he nuzzles my nose. "Good girl."

My stomach flutters. I love that he's pleased with me.

Levi steps back. "You're going to have ten seconds." He takes another step backwards, and then another. The air around me feels so cold without him in it.

"To do what?" I ask.

A chilling smile spreads across his face, too wide to be real. Levi slides the devil mask down over his face, his eyes the only thing anchoring me to the knowledge that there's a man behind it. Whatever man it is, I never want to let him go.

His head slowly tilts to one side. "Run, Rosie. Run."

CHAPTER 15

NEVER LOOK AT THE DARKNESS
BEHIND YOU

By the time Levi says nine, I'm running.

"*Eight.*" At the next split in the maze, I take a right, but I meet a dead end and have to turn around, scrambling in the opposite direction. "*Seven.*" I sprint down a long, straight path and follow it to the left. "*Six.*" I glance over my shoulder and catch a glimpse of his figure rounding the corner behind me. "*Five.*" I take another right. His voice is as deep and dark as ever, and I hear the whisper of his steps beneath the counting. "*Four. Three. Two.*"

My lungs burn in the cold night air. What's the point in running when I know he's going to catch me? Isn't that exactly what I want him to do? I slow, willing to tempt fate. "*One.*"

"Ready or not," he roars, "here I *coooome.*"

God, I hope so.

I glance back, watching Levi sprint around the corner. His eyes are black pits—I don't think I've ever seen him so hungry, so furious. This isn't a game to him. He's chasing me down for a reason, because he *wants* to. He could do anything to me once he catches me. That's what he said.

The realization sends a spike of fear down my spine. Adrenaline rushes in, and I force myself to face forward, running faster, ignoring the cramp building in my side.

His voice thunders through the air, close enough that I can feel the heat of him. "You better get off the path, baby, or I'll punish you for spoiling our fun too soon." The corn. He wants me to run into the corn.

I veer into the stalks before I can second-guess it. My ears fill with the rustle of dry fibers scraping against my body, the wind whistling loudly above me. I sense a body crashing into the stalks somewhere behind me, pursuing me.

A giggle bubbles up and out of me.

I can't help it.

It's like riding a rollercoaster. Danger and excitement wrap around my lungs and squeeze the sound from me like a goddamn squeaky toy. What is he going to do when he catches me? He gave me a *safe* word. What does he have in mind that would possibly make me want him to stop? I can't imagine anything.

I'll take anything he gives me.

I hear something running alongside me in the corn, just far enough away that the movement could be a phantom. The world is so dark, I can't see what it is. My heart is pounding, my tongue bone dry. It's as if Levi is in multiple places at once, but that's not possible.

Is there someone else in here with us?

My smile fades as I veer away from both of them, but those footsteps follow me seamlessly. I can't breathe. I can see it in my head—the shadow from my dreams, here in the maze with us, chasing me.

Mine, mine, MINE.

I know it's not real, that it *can't* be real, but that doesn't stop the fear from restricting my lungs, from flooding my head. Something massive rustles to the right of me, and there's a loud growl. A thud. Mind-numbing, body-chilling silence.

I run a few more steps before I realize nothing is following me anymore.

Twisting around, I attempt to peer through the stalks. My breath billows in a white cloud as I stand there, scanning the pillars of blue-tinted corn, and it almost feels... serene.

Until a scream pierces the air.

It digs into my ears, raising the hair all over my body. I'm running again as a second scream follows me—a deep, guttural screech. There must be someone else out here with Levi and me. Maybe it's another actor, stationed out here in the maze to terrorize unsuspecting patrons. That would make sense, but I'm certainly not going to seek out the source to find out for sure. As I continue to run, the screams fade, and then they abruptly cut off.

Fear bleeds down my back, even as I try to reason with myself.

It was probably just a group of teens trying to mess with me, but they aren't chasing me anymore. Nothing is chasing me. I'm alone.

But that also means Levi doesn't know where I am. *Shit.*

I slow, my breath sawing in and out of me. I'm thinking about turning around to try and find my way back to the path, but I'm pretty sure I would just make myself more disoriented and confused if I tried.

Up ahead, I finally glimpse a break in the stalks. The blue glow of the moon bounces off a dirt path as I leave the maize and return to clear ground, taking a few deep breaths.

Squeezing my eyes shut, I try to calm my racing heart.

It was nothing. I'm fine. I should just walk back to the farm and wait for Levi there. I should see if he's tried to text me or something, actually. That's when I remember that my camera is still on. Digging the device out of my bra, I turn the video off and save it, uploading it to a safe place. I don't have any messages.

The game is over now. I lost him. I win, but this isn't a victory I wanted.

Thoroughly disappointed, I turn in the direction of those faint lights dancing above the corn. The wind dips to stir the hair at the top of my head. Without the rustling of the corn right up against my body, or the pounding of feet behind me, the night air almost feels... stale, like something has sucked all the oxygen out of the atmosphere.

My skin tingles as I look up from putting my phone away.

There's a figure standing at the end of the path, his legs spread and his arms hanging stiffly at his sides. *He found me.* His black silk vest is torn open and hanging off one shoulder; he must have caught it on something. The devil mask gleams silvery-blue in the moonlight. I take a step toward him, smiling in relief, but he raises a hand.

"Why aren't you running from your demon, baby?" His voice is red velvet.

I cross my arms.

Because my side aches and I'm sick of running, honey.

Levi tilts his head toward his other shoulder, and strained laughter fills the space between us. "Ah, I see. Eager to wrap yourself around me, little snake? Think you could suffocate me before I swallow you whole?"

I smile wider.

"So desperate for the kill," he croons. "Well, I'm sorry, baby, but if you don't run, I won't play with you, and I'm in a *very* playful mood."

His fingers twitch at his sides, but he doesn't come any closer. That's when I notice something strange about his mask: there are dark flecks on it.

Dirt? Did he trip?

I quirk a brow at him. "If you want me to run, then scare me."

Levi shakes his head, chuckling again. "All right, menace. Just remember, you asked for it." He raises his hands in front of him and takes a step forward, and it's as if the earth beneath my feet pulls me toward him.

A strange humming fills my ears.

I stagger back a step, confused. My stomach churns as he takes another step, and it happens again. I stumble back a few more steps, my arms flailing, and that's when I realize that the humming is actually words, words I don't understand.

Levi is chanting beneath his mask.

Fear rips its way into my chest, wrapping around my heart like barbed wire. My nipples harden painfully against the thin mesh of my costume as Levi's voice rises above the whistling of the wind, the consonants of his words throaty and round. My chest squeezes so hard, it hurts. If I don't get out of here soon, I think I might have a heart attack.

When Levi lifts his foot to take another step, I turn on my heel and run.

I only make it a few feet before he catches me; it's almost as though he glided to me in the span of a heartbeat—I didn't even hear the footsteps before I felt his arms. He chants into my ear as I leave the ground.

Horror coils tighter around my organs, squeezing and twisting, leaving me breathless, and I have to force the unbidden scream rising in my throat back down.

This is Levi—he won't hurt me. He won't hurt me, right?

I grapple with the arm he wraps around my neck, but

then he hooks a foot around my leg to bring me to the ground. He flips me over, and I lash out, smacking his torso, knowing he wants a fight, *a struggle*... and knowing I want that too.

There's something wet on his shirt that clings to my knuckles as I struggle. The chant echoes through me, multiplying in my head until it's almost too much. I try to shove him away, but he pushes my thighs open with his knees and settles between them.

"What are you saying?" I gasp out. "Stop. Yo-you're scaring me."

Dark laughter rumbles out of his chest, distorting his voice, but the chanting doesn't stop. If anything, it gets *louder*, and I know why. I didn't say the word that would save me. I'm slick and hot, and I'm only getting wetter. I'm frightened, and he's right—I love being scared. It turns me on.

Our eyes meet, and I stop fighting.

He's still chanting, but I don't care as I fall into his eyes, hanging on to every syllable. I want more. I want all of him.

I reach up and grip the top of his shirt, tearing it open. Buttons go flying, hitting my face and chest as I slide my hands lower, pulling the two sides apart until his abdomen is fully exposed. My fingers splay over the muscle, coasting greedily up over his chest. As I drag my hands back down, I realize I'm smearing something dark and red over his skin.

My brow furrows. Where did he get fake blood? Did he have it in his pocket this whole time?

Faint purple veins pulse and spread through the skin of his chest, undulating as he hitches the hem of my skirt. The veins aren't just on his chest—they're all over his body, his neck and hands, the arrows of muscle leading under the waistband of his pants. I squeeze my eyes shut and shake my head, trying to clear my vision, but when I look again, the moving veins remain.

Is this real?

Levi's fingers find my soaked slit, and I forget all coherent thought. He flicks my clit with his thumb, and my hips arch, my eyes fluttering closed. Sliding his fingertips down to my entrance, Levi circles the ache there too.

My hands clutch at his sleeves. "Please. Fuck, Levi, *please*. I need to feel you."

The chant matches the pace of his fingers as they circle once more and then sink into me as I moan. There's a rustle of material, and then Levi removes his fingers to press something larger and hotter to my entrance.

He pauses the chant to growl, "That's right. Say my name as I make you mine."

Levi lifts my hips off the ground and pushes the head of his cock inside me. I gasp desperately around the thickness of him. He definitely feels bigger than I remember. Panting, I feel myself accept him, my pussy relaxing and drawing him deeper. He pulls back an inch, then pushes his hips forward to claim the rest of me.

My head kicks back as I groan his name.

"Look into my eyes," he rumbles.

I tilt my chin forward, anchoring my gaze to his. He can have anything he wants—anything he asks for, I will give to him.

My eyes. My heart. My entire fucking *soul*.

He resumes his chanting, his tongue forming syllables so quickly, it sounds like he's grown a dozen or more tongues. They click and curl and vibrate as he starts to fuck me in earnest, his hands manipulating my hips as he wrenches me up and down. Every push knocks his cock against the perfect spot inside me. It's pain and pleasure—more pain, more pleasure, black eyes and a silver smile. That energy rumbles out of his skin and envelops me, and I can *taste* it. Summer nights by the sea—salty and warm, watery, sharp and sweet. It sinks under my tongue and into my jaw as my entire face starts tingling.

His eyes darken. I can barely see the whites anymore.

All I can do is whine incoherent nonsense as his thrusts get rougher, my voice rivaling his chant with my own mindless pleas as I reach for that insidious peak. It's so close, I can taste it. Salt and heat. Sulfur and the musk of sex.

I start begging, needing this release more than I've ever needed anything.

Levi leans down and gathers me up in his arms, lifting me so I'm straddling his lap. I let out a choked cry as he sinks even deeper, not allowing me time to adjust as he continues fucking me. I run my fingers through his hair, and I swear it's longer, as blue as the moonlight around us. The new angle sends me soaring into a violent orgasm—it rips through my stomach like a blade, bleeding into my legs as I go limp.

My arms slide around his neck as he continues to use me, offering no signs of stopping anytime soon. I don't want to stop. I would remain here, doing this, forever if I could.

I press my hands more firmly against his back as I recover, already building to another peak as he tilts my hips to his liking. My core tightens and sharpens to a needle point as his skin radiates heat into my chest and my palms. His... *shifting* skin. My eyes flash open; it feels like something is literally *moving* under his skin, like little bugs scuttling and swarming just beneath the surface. I sit up, intending to figure out what's causing it, but before I can, one of Levi's hands slithers down to my clit.

He pushes me over the edge one last time, following after me with a harsh groan. His cum paints my inner walls, *hot, hot, hot*. Sweat covers my body as we ride out the aftershocks together, our hips rocking in tandem as my heart slowly evens out. He hums against my ear, soft moans and murmurs that tell me exactly how pleased he is. His skin is still burning, but it's not moving anymore. Maybe I'd imagined it.

I turn my face toward his.

He seems to have the same idea, because he pushes his mask up to capture my searching lips. He teases my mouth open, our lips sliding together gently, sweetly, as his tongue plays with mine, and I become a helpless mess draped across his chest.

Trailing kisses to my temple, Levi whispers in my ear, "This was worth the wait." He slowly pets my hair.

My chest is tight, and my eyes are hot. There's something strange happening inside of me, something scarier than haunted houses and runaway golf carts and nonsense words being chanted in my ear. I'm scared of my husband for all the wrong reasons—or maybe they're the right ones.

I don't know anymore.

Wiggling closer, I bury my face in Levi's neck and match my inhales to his. I know I'm holding him too tightly, that I'm showing him too much of what I feel, but I can't help it. I want to be closer to him.

Levi presses a kiss to my hairline. "What is it, baby?"

After a long moment, I peel myself away from his chest. "Nothing. We should get back to the farm. I don't feel like being seen like this for a second time tonight."

He pinches my chin in one hand and brushes dark tendrils of hair out of my face with the other. "Let's go home so I can worship you in our bed." I shiver as he cups my ass, squeezing, rubbing my sensitive clit against him.

"Okay," I murmur. More mind-blowing sex is a welcome distraction from whatever I'm feeling right now.

He rises with me in his arms, and with surprising gentleness, he ensures my feet are steady beneath me before tugging the hem of my dress back down. His hands attempt to smooth every wrinkle out of the cheap material before they rise to frame my face and pull me in for a kiss.

A kiss that leaves me breathless, feeling cherished and tingly all over.

My head is still spinning as Levi takes my hand and leads us back to the farm. It's less busy now; I can see the exit all the way from the entrance to the corn maze. We must have been in there longer than I thought. Levi pulls his mask back over his face as we navigate the thinning crowd, his eyes intent on the archway leading to the parking lot.

As we near the exit, someone screams behind us, and I glance back as a young blonde runs out of the maze. "*Someone call 911!*" she screams as she sprints up to a nearby employee, repeating that frantic demand.

I trip to a stop, but Levi's hand tightens on mine as he walks faster, tugging me along.

"Levi, wait."

But he's dragging me again. He weaves deftly around the people turning toward the woman, some jogging past us to her aid. "It's nothing that concerns us, baby," he says firmly. "You're tired, and I'm eager to feast on you."

I don't argue with him—I *am* tired.

We walk under the wooden archway and veer toward our car, my feet dragging, but halfway there, Levi halts unexpectedly. I watch fear flicker across his face, and I follow his gaze to some person standing a few cars down from ours, dressed in a shoddy resemblance of a grim reaper costume. The robe looks more like a dress, tattered up to the thigh. Black combat boots shine with moonlight against the dusty road, strapped around brown, golden-sheened legs. The hood is large and structured, completely shrouding the person's face and shoulders. Long brown arms lead to an old, wicked-looking scythe.

Levi only hesitates for a heartbeat, and then his hand tightens on mine as he drags me across the rest of the parking lot at a run.

"What's wrong?" I ask breathlessly. "Do you know them?"

He shoves me into the passenger seat and slams the door in my face. After he gets into the car and starts the car, he mutters, "No, it's nothing." But as he peels out of the parking lot, it doesn't feel that way.

Not at all.

"Maybe his tiny prefrontal cortex was damaged when the golf cart hit him, and instead of the trauma turning him into a psychopath, it did the opposite." Astra tosses a stress ball into the air, watching it twirl as it falls back into her hand. "Maybe it swelled to a normal size."

I stare at her from where I'm reclining in one of the few structured chairs in the break room. Chewing on my salad, I stab a few more leaves onto my fork before I swallow hard and reply, "Wishful thinking."

I told Astra a little bit more about my situation—nothing about his new name or the chanting or his weird eyes, but I did finally explain his extreme personality changes and the at-home tattoos. I figured I should do it before she saw the ink up close. It was all over him now.

This last weekend had been a dream. A delicious, smoldering, rose-tinted dream.

He worshiped me in our bed just like he promised. And on the kitchen counter. And in the walk-in closet, the bathtub, the sunroom, the office couch. He lived between my legs as if the flavor of me was his oxygen.

I shift against the fluffy chair cushion, crossing one leg over the other.

It wasn't just the sex. It was the other things too, like the way he washed my hair for me when we took a shower and then rubbed lotion into every inch of my skin before putting me in bed, the way he played with my hair until I fell asleep draped across his chest. All the time he spent in the kitchen, cooking our meals throughout the weekend. The way he laid his head on my lap, kissed my belly, and napped as I read the Sunday afternoon away. Then, when he woke up, he feasted on me again as I read my favorite scene out loud.

It was too good. A voice in the back of my head whispers that this can't possibly last, and I do my best to ignore it.

"I don't know," Astra continues. "I mean, if trauma can make someone worse, is it so crazy to think that it could also make them better? Kinder? More compassionate?"

I frown at her. "He was hurt, Astra. Very badly. For a minute, I thought he was dead."

She catches the foam ball out of the air and sits up, twisting to face me. "And now he's acting like an actual human being. He's treating you the way you deserve. Maybe the universe gave him what he needed to change for the better." She shrugs.

I sigh, running a hand through my hair. "I don't know, something feels... off about him. I can't put my finger on it."

"I *saw* him when he dropped you off this morning, the way he looked at you. His vibes were," she pauses, searching for the words with a furrowed brow, "lighter than before. Weightless, like floating in water."

"If you say so." I stuff a too-large bite into my mouth.

Astra tilts her head, considering me. "Are you sure you're not just scared?"

I almost choke on a crouton. Smacking my chest, I demolish the saliva-coated bread between my teeth before grinding out, "Of *what*, exactly?"

Astra has always been very good at reading people, sometimes to the point of coming across as paranoid, but she's rarely wrong. Her keen intuition is one of the many things I admire about her. If she wants to take on the heavy lifting of the emotional turmoil I've been burying all weekend, I'll welcome her piercing stare.

She squeezes the ball a few times as her eyes flick away to scan the empty room.

The diffusers are running, and it smells like roses and sandalwood. The overhead lights are off, but the lamps around the room have been turned to their lowest settings, and they glow a soft blue. For whatever reason, Astra seems... nervous.

I set aside my bowl. "What? Just spit it out, bitch."

Her brown eyes slide to me. "Could you maybe be afraid of investing in a real, meaningful relationship? Of actually *loving* someone?"

My throat tightens. "I love people," I murmur. "I love *you*."

She rolls her eyes. "You know what I fucking mean."

I lean back in my chair and let my gaze lift to the ceiling, only to find a tapestry of shadows and bruises. Could I grow to love my husband the way he is now? I've already accepted that I don't hate him anymore, but could I... fall in love with him? I really don't know.

I can't say I've ever truly been in love with anyone. Even things with Charlie felt inauthentic once it was over, like I wanted it so badly, I gaslit myself into thinking it was real.

Lost love doesn't feel the same once you realize it was one-sided.

What would my heart require to fall in love with another person? I fear I might require too much. I fear I won't be able to really give anyone that kind of power over me.

A knock across the room startles us.

Astra stands gracefully from her floor cushion, and I perk up in my chair as we turn to the couple standing on the threshold of the room. Both are dressed impeccably, with clean white button-ups and pantsuits.

"Hello, can I help you with something? This area of the clinic is for employees only." Astra approaches slowly.

The woman at the forefront of the duo steps forward with a smile, slipping her hand into the inside pocket of her navy-blue blazer. "Yes, actually, I think you can." She presents a black leather folder, flipping it open to reveal a gold badge and an identification card. "Federal Bureau of Investigation. I'm Agent Diaz. This is my partner, Agent Peregrine."

I lean forward in my seat, curiosity setting fire to my nerves.

The male behind her marks my sudden movement, his blue eyes snapping to me over his partner's shoulder. I feel vulnerable under his gaze, though I really don't understand why. He's wearing a yellow-brown suit, a terrible choice for his pale, freckled skin. I quickly look away and watch Astra halt a foot or so in front of them.

The female agent decides to speak again. "We need to speak with one of the psychologists on staff here. Perhaps you can point us in the right direction?"

Astra's smile turns brittle as she extends a hand. "My name is Astra. I'm the owner of this clinic and I'm more than happy to help, but I have to warn you that you may need to be patient if my employee is with a client. Who are you searching for?"

"I believe we've already found her," the male agent interjects, gesturing past Agent Diaz to where I sit. "Mrs. Rose Burroughs?"

I blink, my body stiffening. "Y-yes, that's me." I stand and walk over to them even though my legs feel numb. Astra's stare is a brand on my skin, Agent Peregrine's too. I choose to meet Agent Diaz's gaze instead, her hazel eyes wary but kind.

"What can I do for you?" I ask, settling in at Astra's side.

"We'd really like to speak with you alone," Agent Diaz replies.

Agent Peregrine moves in beside her, forcing me to meet his gaze, however briefly. His expression is stoic—I get the feeling he doesn't smile often. There are no lines in his cheeks to suggest he's ever smiled before and, judging by his silver hair, that's a long time to be so serious. "Do you have an office we could move to?"

"No need," Astra interjects brightly. "You can go ahead and use this room. I'll close the door on my way out. Everyone's out to lunch or in session right now, so you won't be disturbed."

Astra waves the agents into the room, skirting past them to leave before her eyes meet mine behind their backs. She winks, and I know that's her attempt at comforting me. Her brother is an attorney, so she knows a fair deal about dealing with the authorities—I'm guessing she wants me to avoid bringing them into my office for whatever reason.

"Can I get you some coffee?" I ask as Astra shuts the door. "I just brewed a fresh pot."

Agent Peregrine shakes his head as Agent Diaz says, "Please."

I direct them to a group of large cushions across the room

and join them a minute later with two mugs in hand. After I give Diaz hers, I cradle mine in both hands, happy to have something to hold as I settle into a cushion across from them. I'm sure the three of us look ridiculous, sitting on the floor in our business clothes, surrounded by spiritual garb and ethereal blue lights. I sip at my cup, my eyes flicking between them as I wait.

Whatever they're here for, I get the feeling I'm not going to like it.

Peregrine is still staring at me with an intense lack of emotion while Diaz takes a slow, delicate sip of her coffee before setting it aside and returning her gaze to mine.

"We're sorry to interrupt your workday, but this is an urgent matter." Diaz folds her manicured hands in her lap, her red hair swinging from the ponytail at the back of her head. "I'm sure you've heard about the disappearance of several associates from The Exeis Corporation."

Ah, so that's what this is about. I release the breath I'd been holding and nod. "Sure. It's all over the news."

There's a moment of silence as the agents exchange a look.

My relief slips away as quickly as it came. "What would I have to do with that?"

Diaz turns back to me, but she's no longer smiling. "When was the last time you saw any of the men who are currently missing?"

I think for a moment. "A couple months for most of them, at the last quarterly company dinner, but Callum Smith came over to our house a few weeks ago. Why?"

"Mrs. Burroughs," Peregrine says my name like it hurts to have it on his tongue, "it was brought to our attention that you believe your husband took Callum along on a business trip last week. That would make your husband the last person to see him."

My stomach drops. "Did you hear that from Allie?" I ask, even though I already know the answer.

They don't reply.

I sigh. "I only said that because I didn't want to hurt her feelings. I thought her husband had disappeared on another drug bender."

"So you lied?" Peregrine snipes.

I turn to him. "Lying is not the worst thing one person can do to another. On the contrary—sometimes, it is the kindest thing you can do."

Diaz clears her throat. "Unfortunately, we don't have the luxury of kindness, so I'm going to be blunt with you. We're here to determine how involved your husband might have been in these disappearances."

I stare at her, waiting for her to start laughing, because this has to be a joke. To my great chagrin, she doesn't. "Are you serious?" I exhale.

"We want to know if you've heard or seen anything out of the ordinary recently," Peregrine interjects. "Has your husband been acting strange? Has he been absent from the home for long periods of time, particularly at times that coincide with these disappearances?"

I gape at both of them. For a moment, all I can think is *no, there's no way*, but... he has been acting strange. He's been absent. He's been so different since the accident, and I hoped it was for the best, but Astra's comment returns to me. She was right. Trauma to the frontal lobe has been proven to affect memories, emotions, personality, impulse control.

What could he be doing in the middle of the night when I'm not around? He already swore to me he isn't cheating.

I'm careful not to let any of those thoughts creep across my face. "No. I haven't noticed anything," I say evenly.

Diaz's mouth tightens. "I see." I don't think she believes me.

"Why would you come to me about any of this in the first place?" I wonder aloud. "We're talking about my husband here. I'm not exactly your ideal witness." Turning on him could ruin my life. It would cause all sorts of unwelcome repercussions, both socially and financially, even if he proves himself innocent later. Plus, spousal immunity is definitely a thing.

"Well." Diaz glances at her partner. "We are aware that you and your husband are not the happiest couple."

My neck prickles. "And where did you hear that?"

"Here and there," Peregrine replies with a smirk. He seems kind of amused, in the way some seltzer water is kind of flavored.

And here we were, Walter and I, thinking we'd fooled everyone. We clearly hadn't.

"We thought," Diaz continues quickly, "considering your strained relationship and your choice of occupation, that you'd be willing to speak with us if you thought we were on the right track in our investigation. To prevent anyone else from getting hurt."

They think my morality would demand it from me—morality and marital spite. Too bad for them, though, I'm not an unquestionably moral person. No, I'm a smart one. If they'd asked me to do this to Walter, it might have been a different conversation, because they're right about one thing: our relationship *was* strained. He was a terrible husband. I was eager to get out, counting down the days until the prenup would let me take alimony.

Now that Walter is Levi, though, I'm feeling an unexpected devotion to him. I don't want to believe he's capable of this, not until I have hard proof.

I shake my head. "You're wrong. My husband wouldn't do something like this. He wouldn't hurt his friends." Even if they were total pricks.

I've disappointed Diaz; I can tell by the darkening of her eyes.

With a loud sigh, Peregrine stands. He isn't looking at me anymore, and it feels like he's totally finished with me as he brushes his hands across his blazer and trousers. It's clearly a signal, because Diaz stands up too.

"Wait." I stagger to my feet. "Is there something else going on? Something you're not telling me that makes you believe he's behind this?"

Peregrine clears his throat. "Thank you for your time, Mrs. Burroughs."

"Here, take my card, just in case you remember anything." Diaz steps forward, pulling a piece of cardstock out of her blazer. "I answer my cell anytime, day or night."

"If you have any concerns, you'll call us." Agent Peregrine's tone is cold.

It wasn't a request.

My throat is swollen, so instead of trying to talk, I nod. I walk them out of the room and to the front door of the clinic, and as the agents climb into their unmarked sedan, Astra appears beside me, her arms folded tightly over her chest.

"If they come around to harass you again," she says, "I'll call my brother."

"They won't," I murmur. Or at least, I hope they won't.

My mind refuses to accept that Levi is behind these disappearances. The thought is too terrifying to consider.

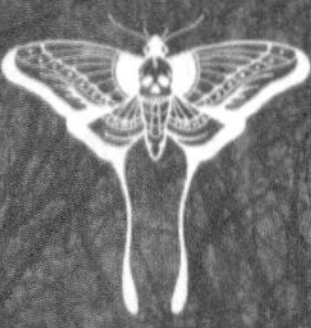

CHAPTER 17

I stand naked in front of the bed, staring in disbelief at the clothes Levi laid out for me.

Tonight, we're expected to attend a company event for Exeis. Since most of the executives travel around the holidays, they've gotten into the habit of having a huge company party at the beginning of November. It's Christmas before Thanksgiving. I ordered a dress for it months ago—a modest blue cocktail dress that covers everything I love about my body.

As much as Walter liked to flaunt me in what he deemed the appropriate setting, he was adamant about my modesty at company functions. I think he knew how many of his partners genuinely wanted to bend me over and fuck me on the banquet table.

The dress glaring up at me is *not* modest.

For one thing, it's sheer. Skin-tight. Made of black mesh with barely enough satin backing around the intimate areas. On top of that, every inch of the dress is covered in tiny crystals. It's beautiful, actually. He's been a bit obsessed with dressing me up lately, like a doll, and the attention to detail in his choices is a total surprise.

I wake up every morning to a new outfit waiting for me, some entirely brand new with tags on, and some from the back of my closet—things I haven't glanced at in years, form-fitting and slightly girlish. Not that I'm complaining... I like not having to make as many decisions before I've had my morning coffee.

Besides, his taste *has* been rather impeccable.

On the bed, in addition to the dress, Levi laid out new heels, a sequined garter belt, black tights with lines running down the backs, and lace panties with interesting black straps criss-crossing on the inside of the crotch. There's a pair of black, elbow-length gloves too.

I'm not sure whether he's trying to dress me like a movie star or an expensive prostitute tonight. Either way, I like it.

I pull on the underwear and the dress, careful not to ruin my makeup or the fresh curls in my hair. I tug the tights up my legs, attaching them to the garter clasps hanging down to the top of my thighs, the hem of the dress barely covering them.

When I turn to look at myself in the full-length mirror next to my vanity, my lungs catch. I blink, tilting my head as I twist my body back and forth, sunlight bouncing off the crystals and refracting rainbows onto the walls of my bedroom. It fits me like a glove, the narrow straps on my shoulders drawing attention to the hollows of my collarbone and a cluster of birthmarks trailing up the column of my neck. As I turn to look at how the dress hugs my ass, I catch a glimpse of movement in the mirror.

Levi ambles into the bedroom, dressed in a blue tux, a small black box in hand.

I wish I could say I feel excited as that familiar, wicked

smile spreads across his mouth, but I feel apprehension more than anything else. He's been disappearing in the middle of the night again, all week. He probably thinks I haven't noticed, but my sleeping pills ran out on Monday, and I haven't refilled them. I haven't *wanted* to refill them. He's been waiting until I fall asleep before slipping out of the house. After the first night, when I woke up to an empty bed, I only pretended to sleep to see if he would do it again.

I've considered following him, but I'm not brave enough.

The FBI's visit lingers in my mind, terrorizing my nerves. I know I can't remain in this state of paralysis forever—I'm going to have to confront him, just... not yet.

Levi tosses the box on the bed and stalks to me, wrapping his arms around my waist. His face nestles into my neck as he breathes deep, and for a heartbeat, I let myself melt. His body is so warm, and I'm so cold and anxious apart from it, especially today.

Sam didn't show up for her session this morning, and when I called Mrs. Busch to ask why, the woman snapped, telling me she and Sam had something else to do today and that I had no right to bother them. Never mind that I'd been sitting there, waiting for Sam to arrive, for over an hour. Never mind that we have a zero-tolerance no-show policy. What does it matter if Mrs. Busch can afford the fee? The entire situation settled strangely in my gut.

Levi pulls back, takes my hand, and spins me under his arm, smiling at the explosion of light and color on the walls. "Look at you. You're a galaxy, baby." He presses a kiss to my temple. Under his breath, he adds, "You're my entire world."

I smile and take a small step back. "Thank you for the dress," I murmur, "but are you sure you want me to wear this to the party? Everyone will see me in it."

"Yes. You look beautiful," he replies. "And you deserve to be appreciated tonight."

His eyes are twinkling nearly as bright as the crystals on my dress. Sometimes, I really wish I could climb into those black eyes of his and hear what he's thinking. Before I can ask outright, he starts tugging me toward the bed. "Come on. Let me help you into your shoes, and then I have one more surprise for you."

I smile, despite my worries. *Another one?* Christmas before Thanksgiving indeed.

When I sit down on the mattress, I lean back on my palms and ask, "Is it jewelry?" I eye the box beside me, trying to imagine what kind of metal and stones are hidden inside.

"It's better than jewelry."

I blink at him in surprise as he cups the back of my calf and guides my foot into the heel on his thigh, the heat of his palm seeping through the sheer tights. As he fastens the clasp on my ankle, I mutter, "That's a tall order, husband. After all, diamonds are a girl's best friend."

He skims his fingertips up either side of my calf as he leans in to kiss my knee, looking up at me from beneath his lashes. Lowering my foot to the floor, he picks up my other leg to repeat the same process, staring into my eyes as his fingers work the ankle strap. He's thinking again. Brooding.

When he finally speaks, his voice is soft. "I want to be many things to you, menace, but a friend is not one of them."

My brow furrows. What's wrong with being my friend? It makes me wonder if he's ever had a friend—a real one, that is. Not someone who liked his money or connections, but someone who liked *him.* I doubt any of his business partners could be considered true friends, and maybe that's why he doesn't care that they went missing.

He wasn't losing anything real.

I'm far more willing to believe that he's gained sudden self-awareness rather than that he's to blame for all those men going missing.

Levi kisses my other knee before removing my foot from his thigh. He plucks the box off the comforter and starts turning it over in his hands. "I'd like to play another game with you," he admits with a smirk.

"What kind of game?" I whisper.

"A game with rewards and consequences. A wager."

"What exactly are you wanting to wager on?"

His smirk deepens into one cheek. "Your pleasure."

He lifts the lid on the box to reveal a sleek black vibrator. The shape of it is interesting, the front side flatter than I'm used to, and the piece intended for internal stimulation narrow and curved to touch the G-spot. I lean over it and notice a small hole on the inside of the flat section, which I'm assuming is supposed to be placed over my clit—that has to be for suction. I can't see any buttons, so it must be controlled remotely. It suddenly dawns on me what all the straps on my underwear are for.

"You want me to wear this all night?" I breathe.

Levi nods.

"Why?" My voice sounds a little panicked, I have to admit.

He smiles. "I want you to feel me inside of you while everyone is admiring you. I want you to walk around that party wondering when you're going to feel me next, not knowing when I'm going to touch you with my hands or my cock. I plan on fucking you in the middle of the party some-where, and I want you to *beg* for it."

I rub my thighs together, attempting to scoot back away from him and his intoxicating gaze, but his arm snakes around my hips to keep me close.

I shake my head. "We can't do that *there*, surrounded by all those people."

"Why not?" Just like on Halloween, he's challenging my sense of right and wrong, desire versus morality. Who decided what morality looks like anyway? Men? Morality has always sprung from desire, just not the desires of women.

And well... I desire this. I think that should be enough.

"What do you want out of it?" I ask, because he has to want *something*. That's why he wants to make it a game, why he wants to lay out consequences and rewards, so what does he want this badly? And why is he so sure I wouldn't give it to him if he simply asked?

"If you beg for relief by the time we finish dinner," he drawls, tugging my ass closer to the edge of the bed, "I get to tattoo whatever I'd like on you."

My breath catches. He wants to tattoo me? That's a lot more reasonable than I expected. He could have asked me for a baby or something else that would affect the way I live my life. Letting him prick my skin a thousand times or so? That's easy enough.

He did alright tattooing himself; the fine-line tattoos crawling up either side of his neck are proof of his capability.

I cross my arms, feigning disinterest. "And if I don't give in? What do *I* get?"

Levi's whole face lights up, his hand tightening on my hip. "How about a weekend trip to our vacation home in Maine? If you win, we can leave the moment you get off work tomorrow, and you'll have my full attention the entire weekend."

My chest flutters. I love that house. I love Maine, the forest and worn roads, the oceanside towns with ice cream parlors on every corner, the preserved old-world charm.

I swallow the saliva gathering under my tongue. "Where?" I demand.

His forehead creases. "Hmm?"

"Where will you tattoo me?"

He stands up slowly, holding my gaze as his nose brushes mine. Then, he brings his hand to the center of my chest and presses me back into the bed, his fingers splayed across my sternum. "Right here."

Levi stares into my eyes, barely breathing, waiting.

"Okay," I whisper, surprising even myself.

His intense gaze melts into a smile, and he slides down my body until he's kneeling between my legs. "Lift your hips, baby."

I do as he says, and he slides his hands under my dress. After pulling my lace panties down to the tops of my garters, he arranges my heels on the edge of the bed, spreading my cunt for him.

Looking at me between my legs, he opens his mouth, glistening spit dripping in a thick string over my clit. His saliva hits my sensitive skin, and I gasp for air as his thumb follows, swirling the slickness.

"You have the prettiest pussy, menace, and it's even prettier with my spit. I like making you slick and soft." He lifts his hand and brings it back down, slapping my cunt, and a yelp rips out of me as I flinch. I hadn't expected it, but now, I want him to do it again. It made the loudest, nastiest sound as his rings bit my flesh. It hurt, and yet a wave of arousal slowly seeps out of me. The pain scratched a dormant itch in me, his touch spreading like venom beneath my skin, raking across my nerves like possessive claws, and the urge to feel him becomes that much stronger, that much more dangerous. If I even like it when he *hurts* me, then I'm well and truly fucked. That's like begging for punishment, for heartbreak. And yet, I know I'm past the point of no return. I will accept anything he gives me, because now, that twisted thing inside me wants to know the limit—the point at which I finally break. She wants to know what will happen once I snap, who I might become on the outside.

I shove that piece of me away, slamming the door in her smug face.

That's not what I want to think about right now.

Levi leans down, and his breath hits my skin before his mouth, the spark before the scorch. When his tongue slides against my center, I throw my head back against the bed as he moans in appreciation. "So wet already. So ready to *play*."

His free hand slides across the comforter, and I hear a faint buzzing start up. Levi slides the head of the vibrator over my clit, and I bite down on a groan as my hips jerk. The vibrator slides easily over my flesh, up and down, teasing relentlessly until he finally slips it into my cunt. I moan as he settles the dormant suction over my clit.

Levi orders me to lift my hips again, and when I do, he wiggles my underwear back up, securing the vibrator in place. The change in position presses the dildo more firmly against my G-spot. It's not the type of vibration that would make me come on its own, but it's enough to stimulate me, enough to make me clamp and gush with arousal, everything warm and fuzzy.

I can already tell that the next few hours are going to be a special form of torture.

Without warning, the suction spurs to life, and I cry out, writhing as I force my eyes open. Levi stands at the edge of the bed, looking down at me, his face lit up from the blue LED of his phone. He looks downright ethereal—blue looks good on him.

He taps on his screen, and I feel everything intensify as I hold back a scream.

Levi laughs, returning the phone to his pocket as the vibration and suction fade. "We're going to have one hell of a night, aren't we, little snake?"

CHAPTER 18

ALWAYS HAVE LEVERAGE

The company event hall is as extravagant as ever. The ceiling drips with ivory curtains and crystal chandeliers. Every round dining table is set with porcelain and silver, and the centerpieces overflow with fall flowers—sunflowers and marigolds and fiery mums, pomegranates and vintage gold accents hidden amongst the foliage.

Soft instrumental music drifts down from the speakers, some rock single on piano.

The tables are arranged around a small stage, set up on the far end of the room, black curtains drawn around it, cutting it off from the rest of the room. Lights glow along the front edge of the stage—that's where they make the pretentious annual speeches about how the company is doing, how many percentage points they've grown by, *blah blah blah.*

At least there's an open bar.

That's the first place I report to when we arrive, ordering a gin and tonic strong enough to burn my eyelashes off. Levi follows, leaning against the bar top as I take my first sip.

The cold of the glass seeps through my sheer glove. I turn

to Levi and, at the same time, a voice calls to him from across the room. The HR manager, Cindy, races toward us, her floral print dress bouncing as she jogs, her worried eyes narrowed in on my husband.

She's a nice lady... sort of. Well, she's nice to my husband at least, which is all that really matters. Cindy is a decade or so past middle-aged, and sometimes, I think she was brainwashed into believing my husband is the reincarnation of Jesus simply because he's a man.

I sigh around the straw of my drink as she stops in front of us. "Hi, Cindy," I mumble.

She ignores me. I'm pretty sure she thinks I kick dogs in my free time.

"It's about time I caught you, Walter," she says in a sweet voice. "I've been needing to talk with you for a week now."

"Then you can go ahead and wait a couple days longer," Levi says smoothly, wrapping an arm around my waist. "No shop talk in front of my beautiful wife."

She looks at me with the usual disdain in her eyes. "Alright, sir."

The vibrator spurs to life, and I jump, nearly dropping my glass. Levi's hand tightens on my waist, and I bite my lip and lean into him, willing myself to remain quiet and still.

Cindy looks around in confusion. "That's strange. Do you two hear buzzing?"

I glare up at Levi and catch the smirk that flits across his face before he composes himself. "I can't say I do."

"How odd. I hope the speakers aren't acting up."

Cindy keeps talking, but I can't focus on what she's saying. Levi chuckles quietly, and I realize why as the vibrator slowly intensifies. I have to grind my teeth to keep from whimpering, my hand tightly gripping the front of his tux as I gaze up at him, my eyes heavy. At least he's not wielding the suction against me. Yet.

"Levi," I seethe as his eyes slide to meet mine, narrowed in amusement.

Cindy sighs loudly. She's annoyed that I interrupted her, drew his divine attention away, but it's not like he was really listening to her anyway. The device turns off abruptly, and my muscles loosen.

I don't get a chance to relax, though, because I see who's approaching his other side. My husband's newest assistant catches my stare, and her red lips spread in a tight smile. She wears an equally tight crimson cocktail dress, and as her hand slides up over Levi's shoulder, I fight the urge to reach over and snap her wrist.

"Walter," she purrs.

I push aside the tiny black straw and gulp down the rest of my drink. To my chagrin, Cindy notices, proceeding to shoot me a dirty look.

Levi shrugs out from under his assistant's touch, looping an arm around my waist again to pull me closer. My stomach flutters; it feels good to watch him react like that. Maybe he told me the truth. Maybe he really *is* done fucking around on me. Either that, or he's putting on a *very* convincing show.

His assistant's smile weakens as she looks between the two of us. Lifting her chin, she delicately clears her throat. "Head of the Board is looking for you, Walter. He wants to talk to you about making a speech since Callum is—uh, since he's still missing."

"Not interested," Levi replies.

Her mouth flaps open in confusion, so I smack my hand into Levi's stomach, and he looks down at me with a furrowed brow. "Are you turning down an opportunity to make the entire room fawn over you, husband?" I tease.

His eyes soften. "Are you trying to flatter me, little snake?"

I roll my eyes at the hint of arrogance in his voice, but still, I'm smiling. "I know how much you like an audience."

Levi's eyes darken.

I don't feel like smiling anymore when I realize the assistant is still watching us. She shifts from foot to foot, obviously uncomfortable. My stomach churns; if he hasn't fucked her yet, it certainly seems like she thought he would eventually.

"Fine. If my wife insists," Levi mutters, removing his hand from my waist to wave her forward. "Lead the way."

The assistant turns on her heel to face the front of the room. A group of board members talk around a table next to the stage, a few of them looking our direction; it looks like that's their destination.

Levi attempts to take my hand to drag me along, but I pull away. "You go ahead," I say, shaking my empty glass. "I need to grab another drink, and then I'll come find you."

"I'll join you," Cindy interjects. "I'm feeling a bit parched myself."

I can barely keep the annoyance from my expression.

Levi's eyebrows stitch together, but before he can insist I go with him, I turn away, striding towards the bar as I sense Cindy following right on my heels. My smiles fade as I reach the bar top and order a gin martini—I'm going to need something a little stronger for what I plan to do next. I also need to ditch this old lady somehow.

Cindy orders a club soda and gives me the judgmental side-eye as I eagerly accept my drink from the bartender. I don't care. I don't want to be sober right at this second.

Did my husband fuck this new assistant of his or not? I can't tell. I don't like the way she looked at him, the way she touched his arm. My chest hurts just thinking about it. But I also can't imagine a world where Walter *wouldn't* want to screw a woman that young and pretty. Her red dress is almost as indecent as mine.

As I lift the martini glass to my lips again, the vibrator surges to life.

I squeeze my legs together, leaning my arms against the bar, focusing on my composure as the intensity slowly builds. I focus on sipping at my gin, trying not to spill it, but then the suction spurs on, and I have to cover my face with my hands to endure it. The seconds feel like hours as my body trembles, a simmering tension building in my belly. When the suction goes still, I continue to feel the phantom of it on my clit.

The vibrator turns off, and I gasp for air.

"Are you sick?" Cindy asks from the stool next to me. I look up and find her watching me, her eyes lingering on my belly. Maybe she thinks I'm pregnant. *Ha! Not even in my worst nightmares.*

"I'm fine." I stand up straighter.

She continues in a chastising tone, "If you're feeling sick, you shouldn't be here, drinking and spreading your germs to the entire company. Is that why Walter's been out of the office for two weeks—he's been at home, taking care of you?"

A chill trickles down my spine. "What?"

"Really, Mrs. Burroughs," Cindy sighs, shaking her head as she taps an acrylic nail against her glass. "When you're sick, you see a doctor. It's not right to monopolize your husband's time. He has a company to run, a company that helps ensure you stay comfortable and healthy, I might add. The least you could do is not be a burden."

How can someone sound so kind while saying such terrible things?

Cindy raises her eyebrows as she waits for a response, but

I can't think of one. My husband hasn't been working over the last two weeks like he said he was, which means he *has* been lying to me. He's been doing something else late at night.

"I'm not sick," I repeat, my voice icy. "And I'm not a burden." If anything, I'm an *opportunist*. The men I take advantage of deserve everything I do to them, Levi included. I can't forget that.

Turning away, I stride purposefully out of the banquet hall, sending a text to Levi as I go.

Getting some fresh air.

As I walk down the hall, the noises of the party fade. The walls shift from plaster to glass as I enter the lobby, just as my phone buzzes.

Giving in already, baby?

My breathing stutters, and I type out my response.

Hell no. Don't bother following me. I'll BRB

BRB?

I trip a step, frowning at my phone.

Be right back?

You better be, quickly.

The vibrator turns on to accompany his text, but I can barely feel it through the nervous energy swirling in my belly.

There's no one in the lobby. I figured there wouldn't be—everyone is getting drunk in the banquet hall, so security is watching that room. It's an unspoken rule that the rest of the building is off-limits. I call for an elevator and step inside, pressing the button for the top level, my neck burning as I ascend to the twenty-first floor.

All board members have offices up here, but my husband's is the largest.

The city lights twinkle beyond the glass windows as I enter the room, scanning the sparse modern furniture. His desk is on the far end of the room, arranged diagonally in the corner, the glass walls stretching to either side of it. I would get to that in a moment. Turning to the wall behind me, I start looking beneath the hanging photos and paintings, and then, finding nothing, I move on to the bookcases. I quickly scan the shelves at eye level, grimacing at the finance books and other non-fiction. *Borrringg.* I grab the sliding ladder and start exploring the higher shelves. There's a few leather volumes here with strange swirling letters and brittle yellow pages. I'm not sure what languages these are written in, only that they're none I've ever heard of or seen before. I vaguely recall my husband mentioning his fascination for dead languages, but that was so long ago I'd forgotten. He certainly doesn't talk about it as often as I would expect someone like him to. Which is a pity, because this might be the most interesting side of the old Walter.

Bingo.

Found the safe.

Removing the books from in front of it, I climb another rung and brace my upper body on the shelf to reach the keypad. I knew it had to be here. We don't have a safe at home, which honestly, was pretty smart on Walter's part—I would have found a way into it. But that also tells me there's something interesting inside; valuables, to be sure, but what I'm really looking for is information. Leverage.

I type in his birthday, and the keypad blinks red, denying me access. Right at that moment, the vibrator roars to life, nearly shocking me off the ladder. I bite my lip, ignoring it the best I can. There's only so many times I can try to get in before I risk an alarm of some sort. Walter would have put precautions in place.

After a moment, I punch in the last four of his SSN. Red again.

Fuck. I lower my forehead to the shelf, waiting a few more long seconds for the vibrator to turn off. I grow wetter as my body responds to the stimulation, my legs beginning to shake.

When it's over, I sigh and pull back from the shelf. I can't fail the code again. Bad things usually happen at the threshold of three. It's okay. Simply knowing the location of the safe is sufficient, as long as he never finds out I've been here. I put the books back into place and quickly climb down, turning my attention to the desk in the corner. I don't know how much longer I have until dinner is served, until Levi starts looking for me and realizes I'm not outside.

Reaching up, I remove the small USB drive I had pinned in my hair and walk around to the front of the desk, turning on the computer and inserting the drive.

The little miracle of technology is going to hack through the password protections for me. This lovely bit of software was a little beyond my coding background, but it was easy to find someone willing to make it for me. Thank fuck for those Ivy League connections. It's the same drive I used to get into his home computer when he was screwing the neighbor. Once I make it into the desktop, I search his files, using keywords to find all the financial reports for the company. Then, I scan his most recent downloads and documents, paying attention to the legal ones especially, and copy them over to the drive too. I don't have time to stop and read; I can do that later.

There's a reason why the FBI thinks Levi is involved with all these disappearances, and I need to know what it is. I need to know what I might be helping to cover up. I need to prove both his innocence and my own.

I hear footsteps approaching the office, and my blood pressure skyrockets.

Heart pounding, I turn off the PC and pull the drive out of the USB port in the same swift motion. Then, I walk out from behind the desk and lean against it, crossing my arms. At the same time, I slide the drive under the hem of one of my gloves.

Cindy suddenly appears in the doorway, her brows furrowing. "What are you doing up here?" she demands.

I raise an eyebrow. "I could ask the same of you."

I keep my voice steady, acting like I have every right to be here, sitting on my husband's desk. Shouldn't I?

"I *work* here," she grumbles, her eyes narrowing.

"And now you've ruined our fun," I retort in a bored voice, pulling my phone out of the clutch tied to my wrist so I can pretend to send a text to my husband. The insinuation in my tone is clear: *Walter sent me up here to wait for him.* It's not such a wild idea, knowing what he's like.

I notice the way her eyes flick around the room when she thinks I'm distracted. She glances back at the bookcase; I'm surprised she knows where it is.

What the hell is in that safe?

Seeing nothing amiss, Cindy's wary eyes meet mine again as she approaches the desk. I refuse to move even an inch for her, and she has to reach around me to pick up the folders stacked there. "I came to grab a few files from Walter's desk. He told me he won't be coming back to the office this week, so I need to pass them on to someone else to get taken care of."

I'm pretty sure she's lying to me.

I return the phone to my clutch and push myself off the edge of the desk. "I don't care," I sigh. Hopefully, I already have all the information I need.

The USB drive burns against the inside of my arm as I leave the office behind.

The elevator dings, opening up to the main floor, and I stride into the lobby. I hear a second elevator arrive behind me, and then the sound of heels clicking as Cindy races to catch up with me.

"Mrs. Burroughs?"

I keep walking. The drive is pinned up in my hair again, so I'm not as anxious to get away from her, but I was hoping I would be able to beat her back to the party. I don't want to talk to her. I don't want to talk to *anyone*. I just want to eat dinner and leave, to win this stupid bet so I can spend a relaxing weekend in Maine. I'll look at what's on the drive and decide what to do with it while I'm there, after a little bit of R&R.

"I'm hungry," I throw over my shoulder, walking faster, hoping that'll be enough for her to get the point and leave me alone.

As I walk over the threshold into the banquet hall, she finally catches up to me. "Can I give you some motherly advice, Mrs. Burroughs?"

I open my mouth to tell her no, but she's already talking again as she points to my dress. "You shouldn't be wearing that here. It's disrespectful to not only yourself but also your husband. I hate to imagine what your mother would think if she saw you now, God rest her soul."

My jaw slackens, and unwelcome tears sting my eyes.

Before I even realize what I'm doing, I grab Cindy's arm, harder than I think I mean to as I lean in and snarl, "Don't talk about my mother. *Ever.*"

She doesn't know my mom, who she was, what she was like. No, all she knows is that she's dead, and I hate that Cindy even knows that much.

I won't let her use my mother against me. Too many people used her while she was alive—used us both.

"Oh, *sweetie*," Cindy gives me a pitying look, "don't take that the wrong way. I'm only speaking out of respect for Mr. Burroughs and my love for you."

I scoff. "That's a load of crap. You speak from your *ego.*"

Releasing her arm, I turn and cross my arms. I wait for her to leave, to go talk to my husband about me some more, seeing that they've clearly talked about me before.

Levi's voice suddenly booms directly behind me. "What's going on?"

I spin and find him towering over us, glaring at Cindy like he wants to set her frizzy blonde hair on fire as his hand reaches for my waist.

"Nothing," I say, smoothly stepping away. I've already said my piece.

But, of course, Cindy isn't finished.

People like her are never satisfied by how much they say in judgment towards someone else, how much they insert themselves into places they don't belong. They aren't satisfied until the entire world is beneath them.

"I was just giving your wife here some advice," she informs him with a warm smile.

"What could *you* possibly instruct *her* on?" His voice is glacial.

"Oh, you know." She laughs nervously. "Life things."

He takes a step toward her, his head tilting in the terrifying way that's quickly becoming familiar to me—like a predator surveying his prey. It's not seductive when he does it to someone else. "My wife is the kindest, most resilient, and most brilliant woman on this Earth. If anything, *you* could learn a thing or two from *her*."

My heart skips a beat, and the skin all over my body tightens.

His voice is edged with venom as he leans in closer to Cindy, making her shrink away from him. "She may not stand up for herself surrounded by people who choose to misunderstand her, but *I will*. This woman has dedicated her life to finding lost souls and leading them back to themselves, so you would do well to realize who the fuck you dared to talk down to tonight. She is my fucking *queen*."

I can't look away from him as he seethes the last word. He's beautiful right now, believing in me, *seeing* me. How could he be capable of what the FBI thinks? He shifts his dark eyes to me, and I smile as my heart pounds in my ears.

When Cindy finally replies, I barely hear her. "I'm sorry I offended you, Mr. Burroughs."

Levi's gaze whips back to her. "Don't apologize to *me*."

I have to forcefully tear my eyes away from Levi to look at Cindy. She's trembling, twisting her fingers in front of her stomach. I sigh. "It's o—"

"No," Levi hisses. "It's *not* okay."

Cindy swallows hard, nodding. "I-I'm sorry, Rose."

I can't bring myself to do anything but nod in return.

"Good," Levi says brusquely. "Now leave."

Cindy blinks a few times, the blood draining from her face. "Excuse me?"

"You heard me. *Go.*" He nods in the direction of the exit. "Walk out of this building before I throw you out myself."

Cindy lowers her head and does just that.

Before I can turn back to Levi and demand answers, the vibrator and suction turn on, *hard,* and I have to grip the front of his tux to keep myself upright. Levi's laughter fills my ear as he wraps an arm around me and guides me to one of the tables near the back.

I allow him to be my anchor as we find our seats.

He doesn't end my torture until I sit down fully, and the movement presses the suction firmly enough against my clit to make me yelp. As the vibrator falls silent, the other people around the table turn to look at us. They wear smiles and mildly curious expressions despite their bewilderment, because my husband is still the CEO, whether I embarrass us or not.

I lower my face and pull the red cloth napkin down into my lap.

Pomegranate is the theme for our meal. Juicy scarlet arils are scattered over the leafy salad, its sour-sweet tang permeating the vinaigrette. The wine provided is deep crimson and infused with a tart concentrate. The sugary glaze on the duck breast is more of the same.

I have to pause multiple times throughout dinner as Levi assaults me with more vibrations, more suction, each session stretching longer and growing more intense. Several people swing by our table to say hello to Levi, but he quickly waves them away. He's too distracted watching me. My clitoris is swollen and my core aches, but I know I'm not even close to orgasming. I won't be able to until he touches me.

I so badly want him to touch me now, and he has been very careful to keep his hands to himself since we sat down. It doesn't matter how I respond, or if I don't respond at all... it's becoming too much.

Thank god the dress I'm wearing is black and encrusted with rhinestones, or I would be worrying what the back will look like when I stand up.

As servers come by and place panna cotta topped with syrupy pomegranate jam in front of us, Levi makes it happen again. It's at full strength now as tingles spread through my body, sparking like fireworks down into my fingertips and toes. My hand flies out to grasp his leg underneath the table.

Levi raises an arrogant brow at me, asking the silent question. *Giving in now?*

My grip tightens on his thigh, and I sway into him, nodding. I've had enough.

Levi reaches over and trails his knuckles along my jaw, a soft smile crawling across his lips. He buries his nose in my hair and inhales before whispering into my ear. "I'll meet you in the hallway in two minutes."

I shiver as his teeth graze the outer edge of my ear.

Then, he stands and heads for the exit behind us, the employees at our table pretending not to notice. As I watch the antique clock on the wall, I count down the seconds. A minute and a half later, I stand and walk to the hallway, but I pause just outside the door when I see Levi isn't alone.

His assistant just emerged from the bathroom across the hall.

Levi hasn't noticed her yet. He's standing farther down the hall, tapping away on his phone as she walks toward him, her back to me, her hips swaying as she says, "What are you doing out here, Walt? Getting ready to make your speech? Or are you just hiding from your wife?"

Levi lifts his gaze to her, his eyes burning with annoyance. He catches sight of me immediately, and he doesn't even bother to look at his assistant as he replies, "I'm not hiding at all."

The assistant scoffs, inching closer to him. "Where have you been? I've been calling and texting you for days. You missed our scheduled work dinner, and trust me, there was a *lot* of work for you to do this time. You left me hanging all weekend."

My heart plummets, and my eyes slide shut as I come to terms with what she just said, the *way* she said it. He did fuck her—maybe not in the last two weeks, but definitely before that. It's been two weeks, only two weeks since he was sleeping with her behind my back, and it's not like he bothered to fire her either, the way he usually does when he gets bored with one of his affairs. He's been lying to me this whole time. Maybe he's been cheating on us both with someone new. Where else would he be going at night?

A familiar feeling of detachment settles in my chest, spidering green roots into my heart.

For so long, I've diligently tended the roots that were already there, that have been there since my mom died. They were thick and hardy, unbreakable. Charlie snipped a few vines, but he didn't get through, not all the way. Then Levi showed up and started hacking at them with his obsidian eyes, and against my better judgment, I let myself hope for the impossible: someone I could love, who I could allow to love me back.

What a fucking joke.

In a handful of days, Levi managed to make a dent in my hatred, but I shouldn't have been so foolish. My heart grew those thorns and brambles to protect me. I am the only one I can depend on, and it will be that way until the day I die.

Before any tears of betrayal can seep out of me, I clear my throat, making myself known, my heels clicking against the tile floor as I walk to them.

I tsk at the assistant. "Don't tell me you actually expected my husband to be loyal to you?" I force a cold chuckle as she spins to face me, her blue eyes wide. I pause a few feet from her and cross my arms. "Trust me, he's not the fidelity type. He belongs to no one but himself."

I refuse to look at Levi, but I can feel his stare fixed on my face.

Offense burns in the assistant's eyes. *Poor thing.* She's losing her temper. "No," she spits. "I just didn't expect him to fuck *you* again. He fucking hates you."

I do my best to push away those words and the terrible things they make me feel. I was so stupid to let him in. I can only imagine the lies he's told her about me, and it's not even her fault. How can I be angry with her for believing them?

New, thorny brambles crawl through my chest, threading between my ribs to curl toward the bruised and battered organ at its center.

Then, Levi is there, seizing his assistant's arm in what looks to be a painful grip. "What I feel for my wife is *not* hatred. Hatred is cruel, blinding and destructive and murderous, and if I feel true hatred for anyone right now, it is *you.*"

He pushes her, and she staggers back. Her eyes well with tears, but before they can fall, she turns on her heel and retreats into the bathroom.

Levi closes the distance between us, and it takes all my willpower to remain where I am, to meet his gaze without flinching. He lifts his hand as if he might touch my face, but I step back; I don't want his touch distracting me.

"What do you want from me?" I demand.

His eyes narrow to slits before, without a word, he grabs my hand and starts dragging me down the hall.

"What are you *doing?*" I try to pull away from him, but my heels don't have the best traction, and he's too strong.

Levi leads us to a black door at the end of the hall. He opens it and tugs me through, and as the door shuts behind us, I have to blink a few times, waiting for my eyes to adjust in the dim lighting. We're behind the stage—short black curtains are spread throughout the room, and there's a full wall of them up front. Directly behind the main curtain, there's an almost gossamer white screen spread taut from floor to ceiling, like something a movie would be projected on.

I barely have a chance to glance around at our dark surroundings before Levi grips my biceps and covers my mouth with his. I surrender for a moment—his intoxicating heat and conquering tongue are damn near irresistible, but I *have* to resist.

I need answers. I need *space.*

Shoving at his chest, I break free and stagger back a couple steps, rubbing his kiss from my mouth with the back of my hand. The material of my glove chafes my swollen lips, and my chest heaves as I glare at him. I hesitate a second, but then I'm stalking toward him, jabbing a finger at his chest. "You can't just *kiss* me like that and expect everything to be okay. You screwed that woman, I know you did. You've screwed a dozen or more behind my back."

His eyes glitter with amusement. "I'm not that man anymore, menace." He steps forward, every shift of his body a sensual promise. "You know that."

"Do I?" My voice is bordering on hysterical now. "How do I know you aren't going to turn around and go right back to what you usually do? You've been lying to me already. I know you haven't been working late, that you haven't been working *at all* the last two weeks. When you sneak out in the middle of the night, I'm awake—I wait hours for you to come back home. So what's really going on? If you aren't the man you used to be, then who are you?"

He strikes, burying a hand in my hair and wrenching my head back as his other arm wraps around me, his mouth an inch from mine. "I am Levi, and I am *yours*."

"That doesn't mean anything," I exhale shakily.

"It will."

I shove at his chest again, and it takes a little more fight this time, a little scratching for him to finally let go of me. When he does, I shout, "What the fuck does that mean? Why won't you tell me?"

"Because everything I've done over the last two weeks, I did for you," he growls. Running a hand through his hair, he continues speaking through gritted teeth. "If you find out too soon, it would ruin *everything*, all of my work. There's no way I could start over in time."

I'm a little too aware of my next inhale, my lungs burning as I hold it and consider his words. That didn't sound like a man covering up his sins. No, it sounded like a man with a secret, a good one. My body softens, my fists loosening.

"So," I slowly respond, "you're planning some kind of surprise for me?"

Levi stares unblinking at me for a long moment before his eyes drift down the length of my body. "I mentioned the vacation house earlier because I've been preparing the property for weeks now. We were going to leave tomorrow night, whether you won this bet or not."

The exposed skin of my chest begins prickling. "Oh."

Levi's phone buzzes in his pocket, and he quickly diverts his attention to it.

"Excuse me," I protest. "We're in the middle of a conversation."

"It sounded like we were done." He doesn't even bother to look up from his phone.

"*I* wasn't." I take a couple steps closer to him, but he quickly finishes whatever he's typing on his phone and puts the device away, looking up at me expectantly.

I brace my hands on my hips. "Let me get this straight, just so that it's perfectly clear—you've been driving out to Maine and back every night, and that's why you've been sneaking out? That's it?"

He shrugs. "Pretty much."

I'm about to tell him that's not the definitive response I wanted, but he's already skirting around me, headed for the corner of the side-stage. He picks up a black chair pushed up against the wall and walks past me, headed for center stage behind the massive white screen.

"What are you doing?" I demand. Damn, I sound like a broken fucking record tonight.

Levi sets the chair down facing us before he turns around to smile at me, his arms crossing over his chest. "I'm just preparing, little snake."

"For what?"

He leans forward and whispers in my ear, "For you to turn around, lift your dress, and bend that beautiful ass over the chair for me."

My lungs catch.

Levi remains stone still, his hot breath warming my ear and stirring my hair. Without even thinking about it, my hands find his shoulders, and he chuckles against my temple.

"I thought you wanted me to beg," I murmur. Suddenly, I feel weak, lightheaded.

"Do bodies not beg as well as mouths?" he drawls, his

voice like velvet and crackling fire. "If you offer up your glistening pussy to me, that's just as good as words."

My mouth has gone dry. "I can't," I rasp. "You'll win."

"Baby, don't you see?" Levi's hand cradles my jaw as his eyes drill into mine. Without blinking, he leans in and grazes my lips with his. "I already have."

He's right. I gave in earlier, before we were interrupted. I want to give in again now, despite the unanswered questions and the confusion I feel over who exactly my husband is, over what he's capable of.

Levi backs away with an arrogant grin, and I do what any horny wife would in my position.

I turn around, lift my dress, and bend my beautiful ass over the chair.

As I wrap my fingers around either side of the plastic chair, I feel Levi's immense heat caress the back of my thighs and seep into the soaked material between my legs. My arousal is sliding down my thighs at this point, and for a moment, I want to laugh at the ridiculousness of it. I thought that only happened in romance novels and highly-edited porn.

But the proof is there. My body is screaming for him.

The promise of his warmth is almost a relief—almost, because he doesn't fucking touch me. Tightening my grip on the chair, I close my eyes and listen to his shoes thump against the floor, back and forth, like a pacing feline. All my senses sharpen as my legs start to tremble, the muscles in my thighs burning from how they're being stretched. The air blowing from the vents above us is suddenly too cold, and I can hear the company on the other side of the curtain beside us, the low rumble of conversation underlined by music.

"Do you have any idea how exquisite your sex is, little snake? Just the scent of it..." His voice is a melody as he continues pacing behind me. "You call to me everywhere. It's hell and heaven intertwined... and I think that's why I can't bring myself to let you go. I can't resist you. You are everything divine in mortal form, two worlds in one beautiful body. You will be my eternal devotion."

I shudder, the effects of his confession sinking in as it plummets like cement in my stomach. His heat crawls up and over my back in the same heartbeat, making me shiver, but he's very careful not to touch me. Instead, there's only the wish of it, the need.

What is he waiting for?

As I drop my head to look between my legs, I witness him dropping to his knees. My blood pumps hard, foaming in my ears, and I squeeze the chair so tightly, my fingers start to go numb. His first contact makes me jump: a feather-light graze of his fingertips up the backs of my thighs, but they fall away before they reach the swell of my ass.

The vibrator whirs to life, and I startle again, instantly shaking. My body clamps around the intrusion, but it's not anywhere close to enough. I figured I wouldn't be able to come from the vibrator alone, but all this anticipation—his teasing and distance and the desperate need building in my core—might make it possible after all.

His breath whispers across my damp center. "You are the only creature I will ever get on my knees for, Rose. *My* Rose, how sharp your talons and sweet your sap."

Is my husband reciting fucking *poetry?*

Levi's palms cradle my thighs, and before I can process the words, his thumbs travel up the insides of my legs. He nudges my stance wider, and I bite back a moan. It's worse that I can't actually see him—I can't read his face or anticipate his next move.

I'm at his mercy.

I hope he gives me none. No mercy. I'm not sure how much more I can take of this before I explode, but maybe this is just how I'll die, detonated like a bomb and splattered all over the floor of this dark fucking stage.

As his hands reach the slope of my ass, he leans forward, pressing his nose into the soaked material of my panties. He inhales before dragging the tip of his nose from the vibrator up over my asshole, then across to the center of my right ass cheek. He sinks his teeth into my flesh, and I yelp.

Levi catches my hips with a chuckle, licking the hurt of his bite away. "It's too late to run away now. I've got you in my hands, and I am never letting go."

The suction flips on, and I groan. He doesn't give me a moment to acclimate to the sensation before he hooks a finger in my underwear and pulls it to the side, his thumb massaging my wet entrance, circling the vibrator base.

My vision warps.

I hear him murmur, "So tight and warm, so very welcoming of the darkness between us. I never forgot this, *you*. Your existence defies the order of the universe, little snake, and you deserve to be rewarded for that, don't you?"

I want more. I push back against his touch, rising on my toes, but of course, I never get exactly what I want with Levi. Granted, I've been getting something better.

Without warning, he removes his fingers from my center. "I need to ask you something."

The vibrator is still pulsing, and I have to really focus in order to consider what he said. "What?"

His heat is all over me, coating my skin like a sheet and shoving its way down my throat as I gasp for air. As he stands up and leans over me, all I want is for him to be closer, so close that he's a permanent attachment. An extra chamber in my heart, bloody and strong and fierce.

"Do you like the idea of being watched as I fuck you?"

My body is buzzing as hard as the vibrator. Did he really just ask if I have an exhibition kink? "*What?*" I repeat, trying desperately to understand.

His hand slaps my ass and kneads the supple, stinging skin. Whimpering, I try my hardest to concentrate as he explains, "You seemed to like it at dinner. Your face turned the most beautiful shade of pink when everyone at the table looked at you. You loved it when I fucked you at the farm. Is that something that turns you on? Do you like being watched?"

I might have tried to deny it if I had even one coherent brain cell left in my head, but I don't. He's right: this little game tonight was fun because it was *here*. Tonight, he'd admired me and stood up for me and made me feel like I was the most important person in the world. He made me feel like anyone would be lucky to be with me, and that's a confidence I'd been slowly losing over the last few years. There's something powerful about an unhappy man like Walter—they drag everything down with them.

Even if no one knows what we're doing here behind the curtains, just the fact that they *could* find out is exciting.

Because it's *him*. The good twin. The possessive and violent and terrifying twin who can summon orgasms from the hell inside me. The fact that he wants me to experience the fullest pleasure I can, however I need it, makes me feel cared for, makes me feel heard and *understood*.

"As long as the only person touching me is you," I rasp.

Levi inhales sharply before a dark chuckle wraps around me. "That was the exact right answer, baby." His hands leave my skin, and I hear his belt buckle clink as I push myself up onto my toes, my heels leaving the ground. Levi grabs my hip and I force myself to relax, waiting for him to turn off the vibrator and remove it.

He doesn't do that.

Instead, I hear the distinct sound of Levi spitting, and then the head of his cock presses against my cunt, right on top of the vibrator. I gasp as he starts pushing in. "What are you —oh, *fuck!*" Every inch of him spreads me wider. My muscles clamp around him, but he keeps moving. I didn't know I could stretch this much, but then, I'd never tried. It's glorious —the stretch isn't quite painful, but it's close. Levi's hand slips around to my front, pressing the suction firmly against my clit, and the pain bleeds into *ecstasy.*

Through fuzzy vision, I see droplets hitting the chair underneath me. I'm crying.

"That's it, sweet menace," he hisses, bottoming out. "You stretch so perfectly for me. You're going to do so well when our time comes."

Our time?

He pulls out and thrusts back in with one, sharp movement, scattering my thoughts. An orgasm crashes over me like a goddamn tsunami, setting fire to my veins, electrifying my nerves, every element combined. He's wrong—I'm not his world. He's *mine.* My forehead presses against the plastic seat of the chair, and my thighs tremble as Levi holds me upright.

His movements lengthen and slow, and he fucks me as if he has all the time in the world.

The suction cuts off, and I wiggle as my clit tingles from the overstimulation. I have no idea how he's juggling me and his phone right now, but he's managing it. My body isn't done yet, even if my mind is mush. After a few moments of recovery, Levi revives the suction and turns it to the highest frequency before he starts driving into me harder, the chair scraping across the floor in time with his thrusts, and I have no control over my next orgasm.

I cry out as I spiral through what feels like a thousand layers of blissful, velvet relief.

As it fades, the vibrator turns off, and I hear a voice nearby. I think someone is talking through the speakers in the banquet hall, but Levi isn't finished. I guess he told them to make the speeches without him.

I smile as Levi's fingers dig into the flesh of my hip, hard enough to bruise.

I'm starting to think this side of my husband is worth all the worry that comes with him. Maybe I *could* love him, eventually. Maybe I *could* trust him. I already trust him with this, my *pleasure*, more than I've ever trusted anyone before.

And if he can change, maybe I can too.

That realization is interrupted by a loud hum. The large curtain to our right parts, and light floods us from the back of the stage, casting our silhouettes up onto the white sheet between us and the banquet hall on the other side.

"Wait, what's going on?" I demand breathlessly.

My arms are too weak to push myself up, so I crane my neck to look back at Levi, and he meets my gaze with a serpentine smirk.

"I'm giving you everything you've ever wanted. I'm showing them I'm yours." He rolls his tongue over his lower lip. "One more time, Rose. Give them a good show."

My gaze flashes back to the space between the curtains. I can barely see through the screen, but I know the room is there. I know they can see us. They can see our silhouettes at the very least. It turns me on, and I know it shouldn't —all those men, all those strangers seeing us like this. I'm about to turn around and shove Levi off me, but the suction returns, blinding me to anything but the pleasure he's giving me. I'm going to come again—there's no stopping it.

"*Oh my fucking god.*"

"Yes, I am," Levi grits out, thrusting into me hard.

I come at the same moment he erupts inside me, his hot cum spilling out around the vibrator as I fall through space and time, cocooned by a million burning stars. Levi pulls out as the vibrator turns off again, and then he wraps his arms around my body and guides me to my feet.

His cum slowly seeps out of me as I stand, and I swear, my entire core is *tingling* because of it, warming me from the inside out. All I want is more. More of him. More of this. All the eyes on us mean nothing to me in this moment, because he's inside me. The sensation is rocketing straight to my head, making me feel light-headed and almost euphoric.

But I shouldn't be feeling that way—should I?

Levi straightens out my dress and combs my hair out of my face as I sway, clinging weakly to the front of his jacket. His eyes are soft, affectionate, but the room on the other side of the white sheet is silent.

I catch Levi's hand as he traces my lips with his thumb. "You did this?" My voice is high-pitched, frantic, but honestly, who can fucking blame me?

That's why he was on his phone earlier.

He was letting someone know he was ready to give his speech, and he dragged me back here, knowing they would see. That's why he asked those questions—it was his twisted way of getting me to agree, I think.

"We both did, baby." Levi smirks at me, and I suddenly can't feel anything but the warmth spreading through me. He said it like he was so damn *proud* of me.

Before I can recover, he tugs me around the white screen, to the front of the stage.

I'm too confused and pumped full of hormones to fight him. I just don't get it. *Why would he do this?* The last time someone watched me come, he beat them bloody for it. There's a pit in my stomach, the depths churning with warmth and pleasure and snapping teeth, and I try to sort through how I feel. Mostly, I just feel... *good.* I feel vindicated. He gave me exactly what he promised, and now everyone knows exactly who he belongs to: *me.*

As much as I like it, it's hard not to succumb to shame as we cross the main stage and every single pair of eyes in the room locks onto us.

We approach the microphone, and Levi's free hand swings out in a grandiose gesture as he takes a bow, grinning like a rockstar finishing his setlist. All I can do is stare out at the frozen crowd, my scalp prickling like there's larva hatching in my hair follicles.

Levi's assistant stares daggers at us, her eyes red and puffy, one of the other girls from the office comforting her on the edge of the room.

"I know I'm supposed to make some kind of inspiring speech," Levi begins with a scoff, "something to comfort you all about the state of this company and those going missing, but I won't be doing that. You will find no comfort in me." His gaze slashes to the table of board members, and a few of them shift uncomfortably, exchanging glances. "Evil requires punishment, and this is only the beginning."

In their shocked silence, Levi smiles as his words pull me out of the lust-addled fog. That was definitely a threat, but who was it really aimed at? He's looking at the rest of the room, chucking softly. The laughter is not joyful, though. It is not kind. "Now, if you sorry bastards will excuse us," he growls.

Levi turns and throws me over his shoulder, and I forget

how to breathe as he stalks across the stage and leaps over the steps into the banquet hall.

A giggle bubbles out of me before I can stop it. It's all so absurd. I feel like I'm in a dream.

Everyone in the room remains seated, their heads swiveling as they follow us out of the room. The synchronized motion sends a shock up my spine, but I can't stop my laughter. I've never liked anyone at this stupid company, but I endured them because he demanded it. After tonight, I'm not sure we'll ever be expected at one ever again. Relief floods my body, and I feel light enough that I might simply float away.

As we cross the parking lot, the giggles die in my throat.

How is he supposed to continue running this company after what we did, after what he said? Was this his way of quitting? *Can* CEOs quit?

Why would he throw away everything he's worked so hard for? This could ruin us, both financially and beyond. If the FBI hears about what he said, they could view it as a confession. What's going to happen to us? To him?

He didn't hurt anyone. He couldn't have.

Levi unlocks the SUV and opens the door with me still over his shoulder. As he deposits me in the passenger seat, I catch him before he can pull away, cradling his face in my hands.

"Levi," I say hoarsely, "are we going to be okay?"

His eyes liquefy, turning to pools of swirling ink as they scrutinize the panic in my face. He reaches up and covers my hands with his own. "Yes, little snake," he whispers. "As long as we stay together, everything will be okay."

CHAPTER 21

BREATHE THROUGH IT

"Is there any possibility of talking my way out of this?"

I know better than to think I might get a positive response, but now that I'm standing in Levi's office, watching him prepare the tattoo gun, I'm nervous. He's not a professional—he could make a mistake, or his tools could give me an infection, or I could get stuck with something ugly on my chest for all eternity.

Though, I suppose none of the tattoos he gave himself are ugly.

Levi took his shirt off, and now, I can admire the full impact of them. He added more last night and over the last week. Black ink stretches across his torso, up over his shoulders and down onto either arm. It's a pattern of sharp lines and strings of circles, arranged together like a strange game of Tetris. It looks like what I imagine a computer might print if asked its thoughts, or one of those crop circles people like to make. They're definitely alien-like and *really* hot.

Levi straightens and turns to look at me. "No."

No smile. No mercy.

"Careful. I'll use my feminine wiles on you." I slip my leg out of my satin robe and wiggle it like some boneless burlesque dancer.

He's fighting a smile. "Robe off, sweet menace."

Levi beckons me toward him with two fingers, the iron of his rings glinting in the dim light, and it's both the hottest thing I've ever seen and the scariest. He won't let me off the hook for this one; this tattoo is happening, whether I lay down happily for it or not.

I sigh and push the robe off my shoulders, letting it cascade to the ground.

Before he can order me around anymore, I lower myself to the floor, reclining where he's prepared a pillow for my head. The wooden floor is cold, and my nipples harden into rosy red pebbles, the rest of my abdomen breaking out into gooseflesh. At least I can still wear my underwear. In fact, Levi insisted on it.

I can understand why when his gaze catches on my bare chest and lingers. I smile at him, not that he's paying any attention to my face.

He quickly shakes away his fascination as he kneels over me, messing with some items above my head. It is clear that he doesn't want to be distracted, and neither do I. Mistakes happen when people are distracted, mistakes like burning dinner or brushing off a weird freckle on your skin or... falling in love. Those kind of mistakes can't be made right.

Tattoo gun in hand, Levi flicks on the power supply and swings a leg over my hips so that he's straddling me. His free hand spreads over my sternum, his thumb and pinkie finger resting on the swells of my breasts, his skin hot and the rings ice cold. His eyes glaze over as he studies that valley of cream flesh—he's thinking, planning.

I don't interrupt.

After a long minute of him tracing his fingertips all over my chest like he's memorizing every inch, he bends, resting his elbows on the floor to either side of my chest. My hands instinctively wrap around his biceps, and my thumb skims over one of the raised lines of healing ink on his skin. It hits me then, just how straight and precise the lines are—and he's not working off marker and transfer paper either, like most artists do. He's doing all this free hand.

He dips the needle into black ink then stretches my skin with gentle fingers as he begins.

The sting of the needle isn't a problem. No, it's the vibration of the pen—it feels like the buzz is radiating down into my bone marrow. My hands tighten on his arms, and he keeps working, undisturbed by my reaction. I glance down, watching as his hand moves swiftly and delicately across my skin.

It's the position of the tattoo; there's no fat or muscle to absorb the sensation.

Levi moves over a particularly sensitive spot, and a strangled whimper escapes my lips. He pauses. "Are you okay?"

His words from the haunted farm return, swirling in my head like the sweetest high. *You are not weak.*

Gritting my teeth, I nod. I can do this. It's just a little pain, a temporary discomfort. It will pass. "Yeah, it's just... a lot in the silence. Can you, like, talk to me or something? Tell me about the tattoo. What is it?"

The skin around his black eyes crinkle in amusement. "Are you sure you want to know?"

"It's *my* skin. Of course I want to know."

"Alright." He returns the needle to my skin, and I squeeze my eyes shut, focusing on my breathing.

Then, he starts talking, invading my pain-addled thoughts with his dark voice. "Say, for a moment, that you believe in the afterlife. You told me you don't, I know, but just stay with me. Say there's a heaven for people who are generally good, who have reached their highest self or tilted the scales enough in the right direction, or however entrance to paradise is rewarded." His voice is bitter as he says that, and he pauses. I don't know where this is headed, but I nod encouragingly, and he continues in a gentler voice. "But then say there is a hell, an underworld, a place for those who have done terrible things with no remorse, a place of retribution. What would you imagine a place like that looks like?"

He pauses again, and I can tell he wants an answer.

"I don't know," I manage.

Spots of white bloom behind my eyes as he touches another vulnerable stretch of skin, but I push aside the pain to focus on his voice. "You see, many people accept the existence of Heaven's Gates. Without even realizing it, they acknowledge that death is a transitional state, that there must be movement into something other, but what most people don't realize is that it's the same for hell. There's another gate. Those on Earth who *do* acknowledge such a thing call it the Hellmouth."

I've heard that before. Back in college, I took a cultural arts class, and there was something that depicted what people believed to be the entrance to hell. "Are you talking about that thing with monstrous jaws?"

Levi huffs a laugh. "The real thing is not as terrifying as you might think. That would negate its purpose. It's meant to draw in and capture those who belong there, so it appears lovely and pleasant on the outside. It's the honey catching flies."

I grunt, because I'm pretty sure if I open my mouth again, I'll groan. He's on a rib.

"Unfortunately," he says softly, "this also carries the risk of the Hellmouth capturing souls who belong elsewhere—lost or wandering souls. So, to prevent those innocent souls from walking into the depths of the Underworld, it is said there exists a magical labyrinth, watched over by a prince of Hell. The labyrinth swallows souls and transports them to the other layers of Hell, but for innocent wanderers, it can also confuse and misdirect, cutting them off from the prince in order to keep them safe. Whatever the prince finds, he absorbs."

He shifts the pen down into slightly less tender territory, and I manage to rake in a deep breath. "That's probably the most unique take on hell I've ever heard," I rasp. "But what does that have to do with my tattoo?"

After a moment, he says, "The labyrinth. That's what I'm tattooing on you."

His tattoos do look a bit path-like now that I think about it, a complex network.

Levi's forehead creases as he focuses on drawing a string of circles in a loop under one of my breasts. When he crosses over my ribs, I can barely contain my agony—I'm pretty sure my nails are breaking the skin on his arms. I need to think about something, *anything*, else. "So," I seethe, "your theory about hell—I have one issue with it."

"And what is that?"

I groan through a long line. "What happens to the souls wandering in the labyrinth, the ones who don't belong there?"

He hesitates and then mutters, "In a perfect world, they find their own way out."

I see through his careful words. "And in a less than perfect world?"

Levi lifts the needle from my skin, shifting his gaze to mine. "They wander until they find a way. Forever." His voice is cold, unfeeling, the voice of acceptance, and he holds my gaze for a long moment, studying my reaction.

"What about the prince watching over the labyrinth?" I ask. "Can't he intervene to help them?"

"Leviathan is not a shepherd."

My chest tightens. That word... it's our safe word from the farm. Now that I hear it spoken in context, I realize I've heard it before, in Sunday school when my grandma used to guilt me and Mom into attending church. This little theory of his is getting more and more interesting.

"*Leviathan* is a demon prince in charge of the labyrinth? I thought he was a beast."

He grimaces, his eyes flicking to mine for a fraction of a second before he returns to his work. "Leviathan is only one of his many names," Levi eventually murmurs. "Leviathan, Cetus, Jörmungandr, Akurra, Ouroboros." He recites them like a professor, each word taking on a unique accent and lilt as they fall from his tongue.

I'm frozen with curiosity and simmering surprise. He's done a lot of research on this, and I suddenly want to know more, want to know *why*. I can't shake the feeling that I've just stumbled across the key to his broken psyche. This is the most he's revealed about himself since... well, ever.

With a shrug, he explains, "Leviathan just happens to be the name people most recognize. He is none of those creatures, and yet, all of them at once. When someone hears the name Leviathan, they might think of a powerful weapon from Norse mythology or some primordial beast from the Bible, and those, perhaps, are closest to the truth. Leviathan is a beast. He is a weapon."

A skeptical laugh huffs out of me. "Because *you* would know what the truth is?"

"Yes." He looks up at me through his lashes, smiling arrogantly before tearing into more of my skin, and I screw my eyes shut to endure it.

Luckily, his dark voice sweeps in to comfort me again. "The full truth is that Leviathan—the *real* one—has been around since the dawn of this universe. When this world first exploded into being, there he was, along with several hundred other Eternals who were given charge over life and death and everything in between. He quickly learned he had a natural ability to manipulate the veil between life and the afterlife, that he existed outside of time. When humans implored for intervention from shadows, he was the one they summoned. In addition, he could break down souls more efficiently than most other Eternals—could redistribute their energy into other parts of the world that needed it. To avoid the inner cities of the Underworld, he took on the responsibility of the Hellmouth. He rules there, unhappily."

I absorb his words, my mind spinning with this delusion he's created. "If he chose the Hellmouth for himself," I wonder aloud, "why would he be unhappy?"

"Haven't you always known you wanted to be a healer, or at least known you were inherently good at it?" he asks in return. When I nod, he continues, "It's the same for Eternals. Watching over the Hellmouth was a choice, yes, but it was also his purpose. Still, that doesn't mean it makes him happy. Sometimes, we must accept that we can still long for things beyond our purpose—we can discover cracks, wounds in ourselves, that prevent us from real contentment. We can have a purpose and want more. We can have a purpose and desire *meaning*."

His words sink into my skin along with the ink. I think of my mother, how her purpose in life had always seemed to be caring for me. Above all else, that was her primary focus. It was a good purpose, a noble one, the best focus a mother could have if she's able to, in my opinion. But despite her purpose and success in loving me well, she was unhappy. She would spend days in bed if she didn't have work, smoked three packs a day. Any moment that wasn't dedicated to me was wasted on nothing. She didn't do anything meaningful for herself, and I watched her mental health dwindle year after year.

Maybe what she was lacking in her life wasn't purpose but meaning.

Wasn't I doing the same? Until Levi came along, I was biding my time. I married rich because that was the only purpose I had after my mother died, because that made *sense*. Then, love came along, and it wasn't enough. What was the meaning behind this marriage, behind all these years I'd willingly signed away? Was there any meaning to it at all? The only thing I have is the clinic, and the hours I spend there don't even make me happy. They weigh on me.

That realization spurs a sick, empty feeling in the pit of my stomach.

I turn from the truth because I can't face it. Instead, I redirect my attention to the story Levi's spinning, to the grand fantasy of it all, and I let the hurt I'm feeling latch on to it.

"Well," I grumble, "I think this prince of hell must be awfully content if he can so easily turn a blind eye to innocent, suffering souls."

Levi lifts his pen away from my chest and sits back, his black eyes searing into mine.

In a gruff voice, he whispers, "In the labyrinth, there are no disguises. There is only *truth*. Innocent souls are specks inside that darkness, just as they are specks in the universe, and Leviathan is a black hole designed to consume them if he gets too close. It's not that he *doesn't* want to help, but rather, he is afraid to. He destroys every-thing he touches."

I blink up at him, suddenly feeling very small and sad under his gaze, the indignation inside my heart slowly seeping out of me.

His chest expands in a deep breath, and as he exhales, his eyes soften. He shakes his head, leaning forward to dip the needle and continue his work. "It's miserable being a demon," he says toward my bare breasts, "especially one like Leviathan. Imagine being the gatekeeper of hell, living in a place that lures the darkest souls in the universe, spending century after century subjected to the agony of consuming evil and avoiding good. It is an empty existence, and he is a prince of hell who must work alone."

The tattoo gun crawls up my sternum, and it's a struggle to breathe again. "Why alone?" I gasp. This part of the tattoo is brutal; it feels like my entire rib cage is vibrating.

"Because he does not have an Eternal mate," he explains. "Some Eternals are lucky and were given mates at the dawn of time—when the world started turning, they found their perfect counterpart standing in the ether beside them. Others have to search for that match. For millennia, sometimes, they wait. They wait for the ether to break open again and bring their mate into the right universe, or rarely, they discover their mate has been born mortal and must do extraordinary things in order to claim them."

The pain sharpens my thoughts to razor-sharp clarity.

I take a deep breath and peel my eyes open, waiting for him to look up at me. When he finally does, his eyes are wary. "You seem to have thought about this a lot. Do *you* feel like a Leviathan, Levi?"

Levi. Leviathan. That's why he chose that name.

Whatever mental break he experienced after the accident

is tied to *this*, to death and the life after it, the dream of a demon who may yet discover the meaning of his life.

He averts his eyes, though I catch the flicker of pain in them. I've struck something true. Another few minutes pass in silence, save for the buzzing of the pen, and then he clears his throat. "So much so that sometimes I wonder if there's any way to separate myself from him."

I lift my hand, intending to cradle his cheek, but he pulls away. Levi sits up and reaches forward to switch off the tattoo gun, and as he slides off me, I have no choice but to drop my hand, using it to push myself up from the floor.

He's not looking at me, and fuck, I so badly want him to look at me. He sets the gun down and reaches for the ink to clean up his workspace, but I catch his arm.

Slowly, his gaze slides up to mine.

I reach up and sift my fingers through the hair falling over his forehead. He's letting it grow out, and I like that; it softens his appearance. "Well, there is one way in which you two are very different."

Levi's eyes shift back and forth between mine. "What is it?"

"You are not alone." I smile gently. "You have me."

It isn't a lie. If Levi is the future of my marriage, then I don't see any reason to leave it. He made a future together *possible*. This version of him would always have me.

With a sad smile, he abandons his task of cleaning up and gathers me into his arms, pulling me into him, his back pressed up against the front of the couch. As my legs settle on either side of his hips, he buries his face in my hair and whispers, "I hope you always feel that way."

I swear, I feel his heart beating inside my chest. For a minute, I just hold him, and I allow him to hold me, to cut me open just a little bit more. "Why did you do it?" I whisper.

Levi smiles against my neck; he knows what I'm asking about. The banquet. The stage. "I wanted you to know how proud I am to be yours, and that I will do anything to make you happy, to make you feel desired and worthy and satisfied. I will ensure that anyone who looks down on you regrets it."

My brow furrows, even as heat bleeds through my heart, burning the brambles around it to ash. "You can't force respect or adoration, Levi."

"If they do not, then they will burn," he promises.

My heart skips and squeezes painfully. I'm assuming that means he'll fire them all if he must—if he ever goes back to the company, that is.

I sigh and wrap my arms around his neck. "Thank you for standing up for me today, for wanting to protect me," I whisper in his ear—there's nothing else to say. My chest is flush with his, my blood smeared all over him, but he doesn't care. He isn't afraid of my pain, and I wonder, for a brief moment, if this side of him is ever afraid of anything.

His fingers thread into my hair, holding me closer. "Always, little snake."

CHAPTER 22
TRUST YOUR GUT

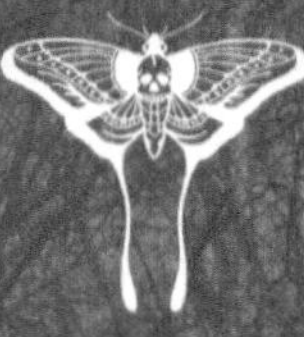

Sam is late to our next session. *Again.*

For the first twenty minutes, I watch the door, bouncing my foot and tapping a pen against the blueish glass of my desk.

I've tolerated more than I usually would from this family, more than I should, and my reasoning goes beyond their contribution to the clinic. I truly feel like I can help Sam. The more she opens up, the more I see it—how similar we are. I was where she is now fifteen years ago: a teen in the system, a kid who just needs a safe place, needs a safe *someone.*

Still, I can't help if she doesn't show up to our appointments, and I can't keep sitting here, alone, doing nothing. I don't do well with nothing.

As I watch the clock tick past thirty minutes, I shift in my desk chair, grimacing as my bra rubs against the tattoo. It's been bothering me all day. Thirty-three minutes late; I doubt she's coming. Even if Sam does show up, we'll barely have enough time for her to relax and talk about her day. Thoroughly irritated, I stand and close the door to my office, locking it.

I jerk off my blazer and remove my bra through the loose silk of my blouse. After tugging it through my sleeve, I drop it onto my desk and walk to the other side of the room, where a vintage brass mirror hangs on the wall. Lifting my blouse, I examine the skin between my breasts.

The sight of the tattoo enchants me, just as it had this morning when I looked at it up close for the first time. The lines are beautifully precise and stark against my reddened skin. I tilt my head and inch closer to the mirror. Now that I know what it's meant to be, I can start to decipher the walls of the labyrinth, the dead-ends and the meandering paths. Each one leads to the same place: the epicenter. My fingertips brush over the interlocked loops Levi tattooed between my breasts, and I wince. No more constricting clothes on my chest for at least a week.

A shuffle hits my ears at the same time the door to my office starts shaking. Someone pounds their fist against the other side, and I think I hear crying. I drop my shirt and rush across the room, my mind racing with worry. Is it Sam? What happened?

The door swings open and reveals the broad-shouldered man waiting on the other side. He doesn't hesitate to push past me into the room. Sam is right on his heels, definitely crying, choking on sobs. The man's icy blue eyes narrow in on the bra on my desk before he turns to me with a furious frown.

Fuck...

I rush over and swipe the bra into my chair before turning back to the man seething in my office. "Mr. Busch," I say in greeting, stepping forward to offer him a handshake. "I wasn't expecting you to come in with your foster daughter today."

He glares at my hand until I drop it. I glance at Sam, only to see that she's staring at the floor, her nails absently picking at a cuticle. She's not just sad. *She's scared.*

Mr. Busch's scowl deepens as he side-steps into my line of vision. "No, I imagine you were not. Do you often undress yourself during my daughter's sessions?"

"No, of course not," I gasp. "I wasn't sure Sam was even going to—" Before I can dig too far into a defense, I shut my mouth. There's no point in defending myself to this man. It's obvious he arrived in a rage anyway. Anything I say will only fuel further misunderstanding on his part. "It seems like you came here to discuss something with me, Mr. Busch," I say evenly. "Let's focus on that."

Judging by the hardening of his eyes, he doesn't appreciate my non-answer, but he folds his arms over his chest and moves on. "It came to my attention today that you've been counseling my daughter without consent."

My brow furrows. "But Mrs. Busch has been bringing her in."

"Sam belongs to *me*, not my wife." He bares his straight white teeth at me, and a shiver spiders up my back.

Sam recoils from his aggression, and I try to catch her gaze.

I fear I know exactly what's going on here now.

Mr. Busch points to himself with his manicured thumb. "*I* am the one who needs to be aware of her activities. If she has a desire to talk to some shrink, that is something we discuss as a family, not something she does behind my back."

What kind of fucked up relationship has Mr. Busch been forcing onto Sam? I can't quite hide the anger in my voice as I say, "Sam doesn't belong to anyone but herself. She's not yours, Mr. Busch."

Mr. Busch takes a measured step toward me, and it may have been intimidating once, but I can't feel intimidated by *anyone* after Levi. He's given me nerves of steel. "You will not be seeing my daughter anymore," he hisses. "And if you know what's good for you, you will keep whatever she's said to you about our family to your fucking self."

He's worried Sam has told me what they are.

Sam finally lifts her head, and her eyes meet mine, swimming with hurt before flicking to Mr. Busch. "Please, Matt. I didn't say anything."

He shoots her a threatening glare. "Shut up, Samantha."

I can tell by the look in her eyes that she hates that name. She probably hates *him* too, but it's the horrible kind of hate that feels a little like love. She has no idea what she's doing. Or, more importantly, what *he's* doing: lying and manipulating her, taking advantage of her because she's an insecure, angry teenage girl without a home. I have to intervene.

"Sam, look at me—"

That's all I get out before Mr. Busch is stalking back into the hall, his hand wrapped around Sam's arm to tug her along after him. I lurch into action, following them, keeping up with Sam's staggered steps as we approach the front entrance. "You don't have to go with him, Sam. You can stay here. Please, stay here."

"We're leaving," Mr. Busch growls as he shoves his way through the glass door.

Quickly squeezing past Sam, I position myself between the two of them, pushing his hand away from her arm as we step into the cool, fall air.

Sam's eyes flick between Mr. Busch and me, and I can feel him closing in on my back, preparing to push me aside to get to *her* again. I fight the urge to draw her into a hug, to guide her inside and keep her safe until her mind slows down enough to process all this. She looks so lost, so frightened, but I can't force her. I can't force anyone to do anything.

"I mean it," I say quickly, training my eyes on hers. "I think you should stay here with me. There's no shame in it. There's no shame in *any of it*, not on your part."

Mr. Busch crowds in on us with a mocking smile. "Oh, really? Is that your *professional* opinion, Dr. Burroughs? I have to say, I thought I was supporting a clinic that put their client's wellbeing first. How are you accomplishing that by meddling in our lives? How are you doing what's best for Sam by keeping her from the only person in this world who gives a shit about her? Without me, she'd be rotting in a foster home, just like you did."

When he finally tears his gaze from me, I'm trembling, gasping for air. I knew I shouldn't have let Astra talk me into giving a speech at the charity ball. Any vulnerability I show to the world is bound to be used against me. I'm only an exception to their rules until they don't want me anymore, and then, I'm trash.

"Don't listen to her," he says to Sam. "The moment I leave here without you, she'll call someone to pick you up and take you away. You'll be put back into the system. Everything you've built with me, with our family, will be destroyed. She doesn't care about you."

I cross my arms and snap, "I'll be reporting you regardless, Mr. Busch."

"And when you do, our lawyers will take care of it." His eyes tell me he has no fear of the system. I have no doubt that he has connections that protect him; men like him always do. It's not like there's anything convincing I can report to CPS anyway—all I have is suspicion and cloaked words, and the horrible feeling in the pit of my stomach. He turns to Sam, offering her his hand. "But if you stay here, Sam, I can't guarantee anything. Now, come home."

Her gray eyes are misty.

"Sam," I whisper, trying to capture her attention.

She doesn't look at me, though. What Mr. Busch said scares her too much. I can't blame her, because she's just a kid. She just wants stability and a family and a place to call home, and that's what he offers her. That's what rich men offered me too, but not at sixteen.

Sam takes his hand, and he smiles at her—a proud, revolting smile.

Then, his eyes flick to me, burning with anger and satisfaction. "You'll be hearing from my lawyer," he growls.

Mr. Busch proceeds to drag Sam away, and I watch as they approach their vehicle, my chest so tight that I can barely breathe. My gaze blurs and I shake my head in disbelief, catching sight of Levi approaching the building. He glides towards me, a brown paper bag in hand. Lunch. But I can't feel happy to see him right now. I can't feel anything but violent anger.

Sam is getting into that manipulative creep's car.

Hot, fat tears streak toward my chin as they tear out of the parking lot and disappear down the highway.

"What was that?" Levi demands as he reaches me.

It's only then that I see the fury in his face. He saw some of that exchange, but exactly how much of it, I can't be sure. My throat is too swollen to respond with words, so I turn on my heel and retreat into the building, new tears brimming over.

Levi follows me inside, his footsteps pounding into the tile behind me.

Astra appears on the threshold of the break room, stepping out into the hall when she notices my tears. "Rose? Are you okay?"

Her footsteps follow us into my office, and I'm barely inside the door when I double over and allow myself to sob.

There's a gaping wound in my chest that seeps pain from every infected tissue. I can feel Sam's hurt inside me, a vicious, angry, desperate thing, and I should've seen it sooner. I should have been able to help her. Maybe, if I had asked better questions, or if I hadn't been so distracted by my own issues the last couple weeks, I would have noticed.

Bad things happen when people are distracted.

Levi's hands appear on me, guiding my arms around his neck so I can sob into his chest, and I'm too miserable to resist.

"What happened?" Astra asks.

Levi shakes his head, his chest rising and falling in sharp bursts. "That's what I'd like to know." His voice is magma, liquid and deadly.

"I failed her," I cry.

"Who, baby?" He starts petting my hair, and it's like his fingers are drawing out the ache, making it easier to let go.

"He could ruin us. He *will*," I rasp, knowing I'm not making any sense but unable to get my thoughts in order to speak coherently. Not only have I failed a very lost young girl, I've also failed Astra. I've failed this clinic. "I'm so sorry."

"Christ," Astra breathes, stepping closer and touching my arm as she turns to Levi. "I'm guessing this is about Mr. Busch and his foster kid. He's one of the clinic's donors. I saw him on his way in and knew something was wrong." Then, she looks at me again, grimacing. "*I'm* sorry, Rose. I should have been there."

Levi's chest vibrates with a soft growl. "I've got her," he says over my head. "Can you, uh..."

"I'll get some lavender tea steeping," Astra offers and then returns to the hall.

As soon as she's gone, Levi picks me up and carries me to the couch. He sits down with me on his lap and tucks my face in the crook of his shoulder as my chest hiccups from lack of air. "Shh." His fingers brush through my hair. "Once you're ready to talk about it, I'm here."

By the time Astra returns with the tea, I've run out of tears. I latch onto the hot mug and sit up, Levi's hands clasping my hips as I sip the floral, fruity tea—this is the only tea Astra has ever convinced me to drink. The liquid soothes my raw throat and warms my chest, giving me enough strength to fill Astra and Levi in on what happened. I don't tell them the details about what I suspect Sam's been through, but I tell them enough—that the circumstances are bad enough to report the family and that we will likely lose the money Mr. Busch pledged to us for the coming year, in addition to any legal fees that may crop up from his anticipatory lawsuits.

Levi's eyes darken as I talk, the vibration in his chest growing louder, while Astra becomes pensive and distant. She's as worried as I am, but she does her best not to show it. After I'm finished, she takes my empty cup and excuses herself, letting me know that she needs to do some damage control. I'm guessing she's probably going to call her brother to prepare for any arrows Mr. Busch plans to send our way.

As the door shuts behind her, Levi presses a soft kiss to my mouth. He doesn't give me an opportunity to melt into it, though; it's a brief, distracting kiss. Then, he moves me off his lap and grabs the paper bag from where he placed it on the side table. The burger and fries are cold, but they're salty—they taste incredible after all that crying.

By the time my lunch hour is up, I've finally composed myself enough to do what I must.

Levi gathers me into another embrace on his way out the door. "He'll get what he deserves, little snake. I promise."

His words send a shock through my body, and as he sets me back on my feet, I force a small smile. I heard the darkness in that threat, and yet, the unease in my chest lingers as I shut the door and return to my desk. I brood over his words as I call in my report. When I hang up the phone, I stare at my computer, wrestling with the fear rising inside me. I turn it on, open a browser, and pull up the search bar. I type only a few words, and then I push enter.

My heart stops when the results load. I stare at the screen for a few long minutes, reeling at the first page that pops up.

It's a news article.

Dead body found at local haunted farm on Halloween—Monster or Murderer?

CHAPTER 23

BELIEVE YOUR EYES

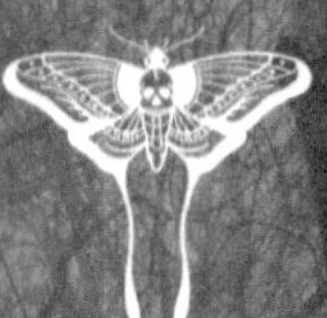

Maine is gorgeous, even in the dreary weather of November. On the way up the coast, the occasional cities and piney woodlands part to grant me a clear view of the granite cliffs bordering the Atlantic Ocean. The trees are mostly bare, but the evergreens stand strong against the sunset. There's a rugged beauty to this coast. Here, there is rarely a stretch of beach to wiggle your toes in. There's only lighthouses and rock and foam, the coastline a steep drop in some places and pebbled slopes in others.

It's usually soothing, being this close to the ocean. Or, at least, it *would* have been if I wasn't terrified about being trapped in this car with my husband.

He could have done it. He really could have killed that man at the farm.

I read the whole article a dozen times. The picture accompanying it revealed what I feared most: the person who died there had been the creep who watched Levi fuck me behind the haunted house. He'd been torn apart in the corn maze. In fact, his corpse was left in such a state that the authorities haven't ruled out a wild animal yet, but that doesn't comfort me. There's a twirling in my gut that warns me against writing this off so easily. How many coincidences can I ignore before I become a willing accomplice?

I looked at the USB drive. I had to.

What I found was evidence that Exies is a cover for some kind of private operation. Money flows in and out of the company at an alarming rate—none of the reports I read specify where it comes from or where it goes, only that it happens every week. The legal documents were more alarming: case after case of sexual assault, allegations levied against almost every single board member. What frightens me most, though, is that I only got through about half the documents before Levi picked me up.

My heart aches as I think over everything I've learned, and I choose to suffer quietly for most of the drive.

I don't dare accuse him of anything. If I do, and Levi *is* the one responsible, then I've just confessed I suspect him, putting myself in a perilous position on these deserted roads. And if he *isn't* guilty, then I've just told him I believe he's capable of murder. It could ruin all the progress we'd made over the last couple weeks.

If he didn't drive me to work today, I don't think I would be in this car right now. After starting the drive, I wanted to disappear, and only a single strand of logic amidst my fears kept me from doing just that.

How could he treat *me* so tenderly?

If he felt the sudden urge to kill someone, why wasn't it me? He hated me before that golf cart hit him. Men kill their wives all the time. We're the victims of easy access and situational prison. If he was a murderer, why would he decide to rekindle our relationship and kill a stranger instead? Why would he go after his business associates? I don't have answers, and I fucking *hate* not having the answers.

Levi is fully aware of the shift in my mood.

I was cold to him when he picked me up. When he kissed me, I didn't kiss him back. When he reached over to wrap his fingers around my thigh as we drove out of the city, my body stiffened, and I shifted my legs away from him. I'm certain he attributes the dark cloud over my head to what happened earlier today with Mr. Busch, because he doesn't react. He doesn't push me to talk about it.

He takes my silence so well, I almost feel guilty for it.

As the sunset bleeds into dusk and paints the world a cool lavender-blue, we turn down the road leading to our vacation home. I can see the Atlantic through my window, its black water lining the horizon behind the pines and naked trees that tower over us. This stretch of road is secluded, miles from the nearest town in any direction. Out the driver's side window, the iron fence of one of Maine's oldest and largest cemeteries blurs behind Levi's profile.

He changed clothes before picking me up. Earlier today, he was wearing a long-sleeved tee and jeans, and now, he's wearing a shirt and pants I've never seen before. The shirt is large on him, linen and billowing, while the pants are dark and tight, leather.

Levi meets my gaze from the corner of his eye, and I quickly look away.

We finally crest a hill, and the entrance to our private lane appears on our right. Levi pulls onto the road, braking in front of the massive iron gate. He rolls down the window, and the cold pours in around him as he types in the security code. The light on the keypad turns green as the gate swings open.

As we drive up to the house, I see that, even though Levi has been visiting, the staff that usually cares for the property while we're here hasn't been called in yet. The trees that line either side of the lane are bare, their leaves a muddy brown carpet on the road and surrounding yard.

It's a grim setting for this beautiful house.

I love it. I love the seclusion. I love its massive sloping yard. I love the view of the Atlantic and the private beach access on the back side of the property, and I especially love the ruddy red brick and stark white columns, the sturdy two-story colonial architecture that fills my chest with a warm, fuzzy feeling every time I lay eyes on it.

It's the house I dreamed of as a little kid. I rarely desired anything before the age of ten, but even then, I wanted this.

It reminds me of the house my mom would drive by on Christmas Eve every year on our way home from the food bank. The roof would be lit with twinkling lights, the yard guarded by snowmen. Every time, my mother would slow down and point, saying it was ours. *Someday, it will be ours.* I thought the house was so beautiful, I chose to believe her. Years later, when she was bald and retching into a plastic bag on our way home from her chemo, when I had driven past it just to humor her, she had said the same thing. I was too old to believe it again, but I'd indulged her fantasy. *Yes, Mama, it's going to be ours.*

If she could see me now, pulling up to this mansion, I imagine she would be happy. I did it. I made it mine, and in the divorce (whenever that happens), I would fucking keep it.

Levi turns off the car and looks at me. I'm so lost in thought, I forget I'm trying to avoid him, and our eyes meet. "Are you okay?" he asks softly. I want to look away, but it's too late—I'm caught up in him. So, I just stare at him for a few long moments, resting in his attention.

His gaze is too sweet for what I feel in my heart.

"Yeah," I murmur, forcing myself to turn away. "I'm just tired."

I grab my door handle and shoulder the door open before he can say another word, stepping into the frigid air. The last threads of dusk are fading from the sky, and the first stars blink to life above us. "Wow, the stars are so bright to—"

Heat crashes into my side, announcing Levi's presence milliseconds before a large hand plunges into my hair and tilts my face higher. I squeeze my eyes shut at the delicious pull on my scalp, and a trickle of warmth worms its way between my legs.

"Look at me, little snake," he hisses.

When I do, his gaze is dark, two pits of black with no flicker of emotion. His hand loosens in my hair as I obey him, and then his other hand joins the first, holding me firmly in place. With the lightest pressure, he scrapes calming circles across my scalp with his nails, and my eyes threaten to roll at the sensation. I grasp the front of his shirt despite myself, using his strong body to hold mine up. I'm no better than a kitten when he touches me.

He chuckles. "I know you've had a difficult day. I don't expect you to pretend to be happy when you're not, but I *am* asking you to set aside the bad for me, if only for just a little while." His gaze swallows me, cradling me in that place where I haven't a clue who he is or what he's capable of. All I know is that I need to be with him. I need to be a part of him. In this moment, I dare to wish for one more night of happiness.

I smile weakly. "I can do that." *I hope.*

"Good." His fingers twist in my hair and pull me closer before he kisses the tip of my nose. "Because there's a surprise waiting inside the house that I want you to fully appreciate."

I rake in a steadying breath and then nod. "Okay. I'm ready."

Levi grabs my hand and leads us up the stairs to the front door. He left it unlocked, apparently. The house is dim when we enter, but a small light glimmers around a corner up ahead, past the narrow staircase to our right.

Christfuck, it *reeks* in here. It makes me wonder when the last time the groundskeeper was here—because it smells like something's crawled into a vent and *died*. I imagine a carcass rotting in the vents and have to swallow down a gag. The first thing I'm doing in the morning is calling our staff.

Levi leads me farther into the house, not seeming to notice the smell at all, walking towards the small light in the other room. His mouth parts in a brilliant grin as we turn the corner, his eyes flicking to mine as I stare at what he's done. The archway in front of us is decorated with a curtain of roses hanging down to the hardwood floor, the light seeping around the petals radiating a soft red glow. I didn't realize it until now because of the dark hallway, but there's a trail of burgundy petals leading into the next room as well.

He gestures me forward, urging me to enter.

The room beyond the curtain is our formal sitting room, but the space is large enough to hold pretty much anything. Unable to temper my curiosity any longer, I walk over the threshold, parting the rose curtain with my fingertips and ducking through. As I take a step inside, the tentative smile slips from my face.

My feet stagger a few more steps, but I'm not quite in control of myself anymore. My mind is unable to process what I see: plastic tarp has been plastered to every inch of the room. Heat floods my body from head to toe, and my chest tightens until I can no longer breathe.

I look around at the lumps of flesh and bone lying in a

large crescent around the room, but it takes far too long for me to realize that they're human beings.

Living and breathing, but only barely.

One of them twists to stare up at me with bloodshot blue eyes. He can't speak through the duct tape on his mouth, but he's trying to scream.

My head shakes back and forth, and I start retreating from the horror in front of me, one of my trembling hands raising to cover my mouth. My back collides with a hard body, and I startle, jumping as I turn to face it—as I turn to face *him*.

The man who abducted his friends and tied them up and kept them here, in our vacation home that I love so much.

Correction: the house I *loved* so much.

"Look at the bouquet of flesh I've gathered for you, my bride." His smile is swollen with bloody sin, his voice velvet. "We will feed on their rotten souls together."

My vision blurs, and I lift my hands to my cheeks to discover tears spilling down them as acid bubbles in my throat. My heart is thudding hard enough to bruise the inside of my ribs, I'm sure of it. This can't be real. I must be dreaming, because this is a brand-new nightmare, and the monster is standing right in front of me this time. All the shadows are gone.

Spots overtake my vision. My head balloons as the world tilts, and the ground rises swiftly to meet me.

CHAPTER 24

IF YOU HAVE A WEAPON, KEEP IT

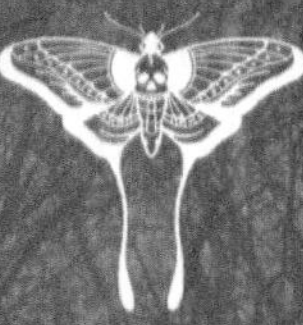

The first thing I notice when I flutter back to consciousness is my aching head, then the hard floor beneath it. I *fainted*. I've never fainted before, and honestly, I'm not inclined to ever do it again, because this fucking sucks. It's like a hangover on steroids. My mind is fuzzy, my body heavy; I can barely turn my skull to one side as I surface the rest of the way.

I peel my eyes open and try to understand my surroundings.

Plastic walls. Flickering black candles and rose petals. A pair of loafers tremble on the floor beside me, and it all comes rushing back. Levi did it. He really did it. He kidnapped his business partners, and now I'm certain he killed that man at the farm. I'm lying in the middle of our vacation house's sitting room, which has been transformed into a bonafide "Dexter" room.

I used to like that show, used to admire the efforts the fucked-up protagonist put into his kills, but it doesn't seem so novel once you're inside one. It's horrifying.

Motion in my periphery draws my attention to someone stepping around my head and then crouching to loom over me. It's Levi. He smiles down at me, naked as the day he was born—well, aside from the tattoos that now glaze a fair percentage of his skin.

"Welcome back, baby." His voice is a low rumble as he reaches out to touch my face, but I jerk back. Or, at least, I *try* to.

As I lift my arms, I see that they're tied at the wrists with a silk ribbon. I can feel the silk wrapped around my ankles too. Craning my neck to look down the length of my body, I see he changed my clothes. My legs and arms are bare, plagued with gooseflesh, and the short gown covering my torso is made of black satin, with lace bordering the hem and tickling the tops of my breasts. A rope is wrapped around my waist, anchoring me by a pair of large iron nails embedded in the wood floor to either side of me. I feel like a damsel in an old black-and-white film, strapped to a railroad with the freight train drawing ever closer.

But there's no hero to save me.

I squeeze my eyes shut against the welling tears. "This can't be real," I cry. "This can't be happening."

Levi chuckles. "Trust me, sweet menace, it's real. It's time to open your eyes." His thumb and forefinger catch my chin, forcing my face toward him. "It's time to *wake up.*"

The pad of his thumb shifts to brush across my lips, and I can't stop my anger from bubbling to the surface. He shouldn't get to touch me like this, not with hands that have done such horrible things. I bite at him, but he pulls back quick enough to avoid my teeth and laughs again, his dark eyes twinkling like the night sky. "By the time this is over," he drawls, "you'll realize that nothing is as real as this, as real as *us.*"

Levi stands, his body blocking the overhead light as he smiles like a lunatic.

"Who should I gut first, sweet menace? Do you have a preference—is there one of your husband's friends you particularly dislike? Or shall I play a game of Eena, Mena, Mona, Mite?" With each word, he gestures idly at four of the bodies around us.

Before I can respond, he turns away and walks to the front of the room, out of my line of sight. There's a rustling sound, like he's rifling through a bag, and then he ambles back to my side holding a large, serrated knife.

"Please," I gasp around a panicked sob. "Please, don't do this. Think of their families, their children."

Levi kneels again, his free hand bracketing my jaw as his smile slips into a scowl. "Their families have nothing to do with this. Each man is responsible for the fate of their own soul. Their choices and consequences are dealt out individually. A pure child does not spare the father, just as the sins of the father does not taint the child. The universe is fair in this way."

All I can do is cry and shake my head.

He grimaces in return, his eyes darkening with something like disappointment. "I'm surprised, little snake, that you would encourage such an imbalance of favor, especially considering you are a healer of the human race. You will need to do better as my mate. I will teach you."

Fuck no. "I'm not your mate," I snipe, attempting to wrench my chin out of his grasp.

His grip only tightens, becoming almost *painful* as he brings his face closer to mine. "You will be," he whispers. "You don't realize it yet, but this unholy union has *always* been about us. You love me, menace, and you'll admit it soon enough."

Love. I want to laugh. I want to cry.

How could I love a murderer? Loving him would be my fall from grace. If I loved him, how would I ever recover from my broken heart when this nightmare is over? When he kills me, or when he leaves me? I will have broken every rule I've ever created for myself, along with all the rules of human decency too. Loving him, knowing what I know, is an unforgivable sin.

"Don't kill them," I beg, the words strangled. "Please. I'm begging you. Let them go—if not for their families, then for me."

He releases my jaw and stands with a frown, slowly backing away. "No. I'm *killing them* for you. These are bad men, baby. You shouldn't waste your heaven on them." He turns to one of the bodies, fidgeting with the knife in his hand, flipping it over and over in his grasp, as if he were getting used to the feel. He glares down at the body for a moment then twists to look at me. "I'll tell you what has earned them this fate if that is what you desire. Would that appease your lovely, bleeding heart?"

"No—" I croak.

"Too late," Levi continues in a sharper voice, pointing the knife in my direction. "I've decided I like that idea. There's something poetic about having their misdeeds be the very last thing they hear." Then, he slips a hand between two panels of plastic against the wall and pulls a thick rope forward.

The man lying on the ground in front of him is attached to that rope, and he's swiftly hauled into the air by his ankles. He startles awake, his hazel eyes flashing open.

Even from this angle, I recognize him—Callum Smith.

I have to admit, that's where I would have started too, if I *had* told Levi where to begin. A memory slams into me: Callum, cornering me in the house one night when Walter was passed out drunk on the couch. He wouldn't leave me alone. His eyes had been bloodshot and wild, looking a lot like they do right now. If our chef hadn't decided to stay late to keep an eye on him—if she hadn't appeared in the living room and given me a way out—there's no telling what might have happened to me.

I'd locked that night away, forgot about it, because there's no point in remembering terrible things when you don't have a way of making it right.

Walter never would have believed me if I told him, so I didn't. I would have been blamed, so I kept my mouth shut. My brain must have decided that now is the perfect time to dig that memory up—and an electrifying thrill accompanies it: this bastard is getting what he fucking deserves, and I'm here to witness it.

Callum's blood will look good on this floor.

I bite the inside of my cheek, trying to cleanse my mind of that terrible thought. The vicious part of me is rejoicing—she loves Levi's violence, his anger. She's ready to spread her legs and get herself off as he spins that knife in his hand.

There's something seriously wrong with me.

I don't feel pity for the men around me, not really. I feel anger—deep, burning, unending rage. I'm fucking drowning in it. It's not just Callum; it's all of them. Every man who hurt my mom. Every boy who used me as I used them. Every church pastor who told my mom she was welcome before loudly condemning her behind her back as the elders laughed.

I'm terrified of Levi, but I'm even more terrified of myself right now. Of this anger.

Levi ties the rope around another railroad nail driven into the floorboards. As he straightens, he cocks his head at me.

"Do you know what all these men have in common, Rosie Posie?"

I glare at him, silently fuming.

"*You*." He points at me with the knife again, and I feel a phantom of it against my throat. "These rotten souls surround you because you radiate life. You draw them in with the promise of a balm to soothe their evil urges. It's not a conscious decision on your part, of course." He waves the knife in a dismissive gesture. "It's only fate. Your soul is endless and all-consuming, like mine. They are the walls trying to close you in, trying to cage you. They are your labyrinth."

"You're not making any fucking sense," I seethe, trying desperately to hold onto my anger instead of giving in to the fear crowding in on the edges of my mind.

Levi steps toward me. "The prick with this fucking face," he points at his own snarl, "created a company with my help, a company he used to cover up a system that has abused thousands. He got you too, because of me. Because *I* was drawn to you. Because you are *mine*. You were never his."

The muscles in my body that have coiled with fury and fear suddenly weaken, and a chill webs through me as I realize what he's admitting to. I know he's telling the truth about the company, because I've read several documents today that prove it. The money. The sexual assaults. The note sent to Callum's wife along with his severed fingers, accusing him of being involved in a trafficking ring.

It all connects.

I knew my husband was an evil bastard, but I had no idea he was capable of *this*, of hurting women and children. There it is again, bubbling its way to the surface: my anger. It's so overwhelming, I can't find the words to respond to him.

There is nothing in my head but the violence I wish to give him.

"These humans." Levi gestures around the room. "They are men who indulge in the corrupt pleasures their company hides. You told me once you believed your purpose was to help others. You said you wanted to make a difference, but you were never going to accomplish that with these men surrounding you, negating every small good you give to the world with their overwhelming evil."

Evil. That's right. That's exactly what he is.

Levi draws closer, his head tilting back and forth like a charmed snake. "If I wasn't here, wearing this skin, they would have taken you too. The moment Walter was gone, they would have pounced on you. *That* is what they are. Do you understand?"

Chilling horror rushes through me. Is he insinuating that they wanted to feed me into the trafficking system? I'm more unsettled by the way he's talking about it: detached, like he's observing it all from the outside. His mental break must be deeper than I thought. He's snapped entirely, like a worn rubber band under too much strain. My thoughts spiral as a vicious smile graces Levi's face.

He shrugs, almost boyishly. "I think it's only right I stole them out of their homes after they supported the abduction and rape of thousands upon thousands of people. Now, I get to punish them. We both do."

He turns to Callum, red-faced and fighting the ropes as much as he can, though his arms are bound against his body, his mouth gagged with a dirty cloth. He's thinner than I remember. Considering he's been here for two weeks and there's no telling the last time Levi fed him, I imagine he'll run out of fight soon enough—not that it matters.

Levi plunges the knife into Callum's stomach and rips him open.

My lips part in a soundless cry as I watch Callum's guts spill onto the floor. The veins in his head bulge through emaciated skin, and he promptly passes out. I wish I was so lucky; I don't want to see this. I don't want to be *alive* anymore if I have to witness this.

Twisting away, I whisper, "Just kill me already. Kill me first, please."

"I'm not going to kill you, little snake," Levi says quietly, his tenor highlighted by the sound of blood hitting plastic. "I would have to be a heartless monster to hurt my mate and, contrary to popular belief, I carry that bothersome organ around the same as you."

What the fuck does he mean by that?

"I found this one passed out drunk in his bed," Levi continues, his voice hardening. "It was easy to carry him out. His wife was asleep in their guest room with all three of their children beside her. Can you imagine how cruel he must be for her to hide away behind a locked door every night? No one came to check on him when he screamed. I did them a favor."

There's a loud, wet squelching, and I know without looking that Levi has a hand inside Callum's abdomen. A small whimper travels through the room as Callum is brought back to consciousness with more muffled pleas and screams.

"I want you to share in the ecstasy of absorbing them, Rose. It's the last piece to the transformation, both yours and mine," Levi says calmly.

There's a lot to decipher in that, but my mind catches one thing in particular. "What do you mean, *absorb* them?" I rasp.

Does he *eat* them? Has my husband's mental break gotten him to eat not only red meat, but *human flesh* too?

"Look at me," he demands.

Fearing what he might do if I deny him, I open my eyes and lift my gaze to his. His hands and arms are dripping with scarlet syrup as his body vibrates. Those varicose veins are back, spidering across his body like a neon light show under his skin. The body behind him is twisted in agony, innards hanging down to the floor. Callum isn't dead, not yet, but he might as well be.

Despite the horror, Levi's eyes are soft and warm as they look down at me.

"I absorb their souls, baby," he explains. "What they suffer at my hands is the *ultimate* death. Once they enter hell, their souls will be broken down and used to keep the Underworld's river of power flowing anyway. Their fate is the same, whether faced here or in a few decades there. At least this way, they can't hurt anyone else."

His voice has simmered into a sticky, resinous thing. It's the kind of sweetness that previously would have made me want to touch him, kiss him, hold him, but now, I know that this perfect husband of mine is really just a murderous psychopath in disguise.

My chest shudders with a silent sob.

Levi frowns at my reaction before he turns and shoves his hand back into Callum's gaping abdomen, rooting around towards his chest cavity.

I pinch my eyes shut and mumble desperate prayers under my breath, pleading to the god my grandma used to pray to at the dinner table, the one my mama used to cry to when she thought I was asleep, the god I'm not entirely sure exists. Still, human instinct demands I cling to anything that might comfort me right now.

To my immense disappointment, my prayers aren't

enough to drown out the sound of Levi thrusting his knife into Callum's flesh again.

I hear every atrocious slash and ensuing scream, then the sudden silence when death finally descends on him. Then, I hear something else—low whirring, almost like a rain stick turned over rooms away. The air around me drops in temperature, and I shiver, my nipples pebbling beneath the thin satin of the nightgown. The tattoo on my chest prickles, and it feels as if the atmosphere is being displaced. There are no windows in this room, and it can't be the vents, because they're all covered by thick plastic. My morbid curiosity pleads with me to look, but I resist.

For a little while, at least.

Levi tears his way through three more, announcing their sins before he plunges his knife into them, over and over again, but I can't register anything more than the sensory terrors. The crackle and snap of bodies breaking. The constant low hum that fills the room. A wetness beginning to saturate the back of my nightgown. *Their blood.*

I try in vain to contort my body away from it, but it's no use—the human body bleeds too much. I start to worry that it will eventually fill the room and drown me in its viscous embrace, and fuck, I hope it does. At least then, I can die with them. I can escape him.

Levi's feet slap against the wet floor, and I suddenly can't stop my eyes from fluttering open to watch him walk into my line of sight.

A silence rings in my ears when I see him, and my brain short-circuits. The man who ambles to a languid stop in front of me is unrecognizable. He's at least a foot taller, slender, though still powerfully built. His skin is paler and spider-webbed all over with millions of those undulating purple veins.

They had been real—I *hadn't* imagined them. His shoulders are two different sizes, and his left leg has to bend to match the height of the right, almost as if he's... between two bodies.

He's fucking *molting*.

Long hair, the darkest shade of blue, peeks through the tousled blond of Walter's, and the eyes staring into mine right now are mismatched too. One is that familiar flat black iris, but the other one has changed—the sclera is now entirely black, filled in with ink, a luminous green hoop glowing in its very center.

I can't look away from him, though I desperately want to.

There's chunks of flesh and shards of bone clinging to his blood-streaked body, and somehow, I know it's the remnants of Walter. This new form is bursting from the last one, like some violent moth emerging from a cocoon.

With that realization, everything else snaps into place.

He told me the truth about who—and *what*—he was from the very beginning. Levi. Leviathan. Prince of Hell. Keeper of the Hellmouth. I've been sleeping with a *demon*.

I fight my restraints with renewed fervor, my back and the heels of my feet sliding uselessly against the floor, the blood sticky in my hair. *I've been kissing and fucking a demon.* "Oh my god," I wail. My wrists are starting to burn from how hard I yank on them. "God, oh please, help me. *Someone help.*"

I scream as loud as I can, hoping that if I beg heaven just a little louder, someone might come. If there are demons, there must be a god. Right? Haven't I been good enough for Her?

Levi chortles, that green ring in his eye flaring brighter. "God can't be bothered with you, baby. He can't even be bothered to answer me." With that, he turns to the next body.

His words shatter me. My chest is a pile of glass, ripping

into my lungs with every inhale. I watch with watery eyes as Levi hoists the next male into the air, trailing the tip of the knife down the man's abdomen and slicing into the awaiting neck with glee. As blood pours out, Levi holds his free palm toward the body, and the space between them starts to vibrate.

I finally see where the displacement of air is coming from.

Blue-ish gray mist is being siphoned out of the neck wound along with the blood, and Levi manipulates it with his extended hand, carefully guiding it towards him. As the mist makes contact with his skin, the veins burst apart, crackling quietly as more of his new form surfaces. That's all I see before my vision overflows with tears. It's too much.

Until today, I didn't believe in demons or magic. I didn't even fully believe in love.

Now, all of this is punching me square in the face, and I'm too shocked to accept it. I cry silently as he kills the others. I start counting them. The sooner he kills them, the sooner this is all over, regardless of what his plan is for me. I'll take anything over being a helpless bystander. *Five. Six. Seven.* There's only two more.

Every death enables Levi to stand a little taller. Walter's blond hair has fallen out, replaced by a straight curtain of blue hair clinging to his bloody back.

Before Levi pounces on the second to last body at the edge of the room, he turns to me. I shrink against the floor as his eyes drill into mine, both now that otherworldly black with green hoops, his body evenly proportioned. The purple veins are gone, and so are his tattoos, but I swear I can see something rolling in dark blue waves under his translucent skin.

He's gigantic, every part of him.

He crouches beside me and slides that bloody knife between my belly and the rope, tearing through the twine in one, easy jerk. He does the same with my ankles and then my wrists, and I'm frozen in fear as he pulls me to my feet. When he drags me toward his next target, I forget how to breathe. There's a burlap bag on this one's face—the last two are the only ones whose identities have been hidden.

Levi purrs in my ear, "It's your turn, little snake. The best meals come in pairs."

My head is cloudy and warm, and I can't process what he wants from me until he shoves the handle of the knife into my hand. Bile crawls up my throat as I try to shove it back at him. "I-I can't."

He wraps his hand around mine, ensuring I don't drop the knife as he leans over to hoist the body into the air. I find myself entranced for a moment by his sheer height, his strength, the gracefulness of his movements. He's so large; I don't understand how he moves so fluidly, and I certainly don't understand why I'm admiring him.

He's a murderer, Rose. A demon and a murderer.

Once he's done tying the rope, he's towering over me again with a sly smile. "Don't worry, I'll teach you how. You'll need my help to absorb his energy at first anyway."

He releases my hand and, somehow, I don't drop the knife. It's as if my fingers have fossilized around the handle.

"Please," I cry. "Don't make me do this."

His hands wrap around my waist and turn me toward the hanging figure. "You *want* to do this, little snake. Just wait until you see the field mice I've captured for you.'"

The body before us jerks and writhes at the sound of his voice. Post-traumatic stress, I'm sure. This one seems stronger than the others, which I can only assume means he's been taken recently... but Levi has already killed the business partners who went missing. Their dead bodies hang like promises around us, their blood covering the floor.

Before I dare to ask the question, Levi rips off his hood.

I can't believe my eyes for a moment, or my heart.

Charlie. Charlie is hanging from the rope, his salt-and-pepper hair disheveled, his brown eyes round and wild. I barely recognize him. He was always so carefully groomed when we were together, polished and composed. Seeing him now, a decade later and weak like this, I wonder if he was ever as beautiful as I imagined, or if I had fabricated it. Maybe I had just loved being bad with him. It's the hell Levi said was inside me—it loved any excuse it could get to be naughty.

I'm past naughty now.

Levi and I have rocketed straight past immoral into downright wicked, and I'd be lying if I said that twisted part of me didn't like being here, didn't like seeing these men bleed. I just wish I wasn't covered in it. In part, they are dead *because of me.* It's no wonder a god isn't answering my prayers; I'm headed straight to hell. With him.

"Charlie," I whisper, shaking my head. "How did you even know about him?" I try to wiggle away, but Levi's arms keep me in place.

He lowers his hot lips to my ear. "The bastard showed up in your dreams once or twice while I was watching." His words are soft, but the understanding it gives me is sharp. He's the shadow from my dreams, the one that's always been watching, hunting, claiming.

Levi shakes his head in mock pity, his mouth dropping to caress my collar. "I pieced the details together on my own, little snake. He *hurt* you. I couldn't allow that to go unpunished."

Grinding my teeth, I ask, "You want him dead because he broke my heart?"

A low growl vibrates into my back. "I want him dead because he haunts you, and the only creature who gets to do that is *me*. You see? I will never abandon you, menace. I will never hurt you. You are my mate, and if that means I must retrieve lost shards of your heart from every corner of this world to prove you can love again, then that is what I shall do. You are *mine*."

Goosebumps erupt all over my body, and my head spins.

"Drag the blade across his neck," he instructs me. "Press hard, and it'll be over quickly. Or, we can make it slow if you'd like. A thousand small cuts will do the work just as well. As the life bleeds out of him, I'll guide his energy toward you, and all you need to do is open yourself up to receive it. Do you understand?"

Oh, I understand. I understand that my husband has been dead for two weeks and the *thing* inhabiting his body is a demon intent on making me his bride, his *mate*. I understand that he expects me to participate in this dark, twisted ritual and enjoy it. I understand that he thinks I can love him.

I've been blind to the reality of who he is, willingly and foolishly, but I won't be anymore. I'm wide awake.

I nod, and Levi squeezes my waist, pressing a sweet kiss to my hair.

He tugs Charlie's head back a little more, presenting his carotid, and my hand tightens on the slick handle of Levi's knife.

Before I can chicken out, I twist in his embrace and thrust the bloody tip of the knife into one black eye. I feel the organ give under pressure, squelching as I slice through the juicy sinews. The blade lodges in the hard bone beneath, and Levi lets out a roar as he staggers back.

I don't hesitate.

I run, my feet slipping on the bloody plastic as I hurtle myself through the archway and through the rose curtain. I scramble down the hallway, sliding on the wooden floor as I sprint out of the house. If he catches me, I'm done for.

I doubt a demon takes kindly to being stabbed in the eye.

I'm not sure where to go, but I need to be anywhere else but here. He has the keys to the car, and there aren't any towns within running distance of here. If I were to take the road, he would find me, so instead, I fly down the private lane to the wrought iron gate. It's a rusty, antiquated thing, barely intact enough to be fitted with the mechanics needed to swing open and shut, but I'm slender enough to squeeze through two of the slats.

As I do, my gaze catches on the cemetery fence across the road, and I realize what I have to do if I'll have any chance of surviving. The cemetery is large—it backs up to a smaller road that eventually winds through a few towns. Best of all, there are a million places to hide.

I'll be seeking sanctuary amidst the dead and buried tonight.

CHAPTER 25
DON'T HIDE IN A GRAVEYARD

"Come out, come out, wherever you are." Levi's voice is a siren, and I am definitely lost at sea.

It takes effort not to succumb to it as I sprint through the cemetery, past the tilted gravestones and forgotten names. His voice is deeper now that he's in this new form, more commanding, and if we weren't covered in blood, I'd probably be turned on.

Hell, who am I kidding? I'm turned on anyway, because apparently I'm a freak, but I *can't* succumb. Not this time.

A demon has my ex-boyfriend hanging from the ceiling of our vacation home, and he expects *me* to be the one to slay him. Levi mentioned a transformation. For not only him, but me as well. If this is some kind of demonic at-home ritual, I don't want to be anywhere near it.

I have to find that road and get help.

I look over my shoulder, but I can't see any trace of Levi. I don't know how close he is, so I run until my side cramps and my lungs are burning, until the blood has dried on my skin. I veer into a section of the cemetery I'm sure hasn't been visited in quite some time. The headstones around me grow larger and more brittle, worn by time and rain and salty ocean air. My head is too inflated to figure out where the road is. As I turn down one of the many aisles of stone, I see a silhouette, and my heart skips.

That isn't Levi staring at me from the end of the aisle with a single lit match and a scythe in hand.

No, it's that person we saw at the haunted farm. The one Levi ran away from. They're still wearing that tattered cloak, only now, there's fishnet tights on their legs and a pair of boots that stretch to their thighs. The match in their left hand flickers in the dark, barely illuminating the outline of their hood. I don't know if it wants to hurt me, but it's not human. *Definitely not human.*

They lean down and blow out the match.

I bolt, my heart in my throat.

A line of small buildings appear on my right, the moonlight bouncing off their white stone. I choose one of the crypts at random and squeeze myself through the door, shutting it behind me. The mausoleum is cast from ivory, untouched aside from a small pile of dusty beer cans in the corner. A single coffin hewn from white stone sits in the center of the room.

In my moment of hesitation, I hear movement outside.

I lurch for the other side of the building, ducking behind the coffin, clamping a hand over my mouth and nose to stifle my breathing. I hear footsteps drawing closer; they're right outside. I try to track the direction, but then, the steps cease altogether.

Long moments pass, and my head balloons from lack of oxygen.

Maybe they've already passed by. Maybe the coast is

clear, and I can run to the road, attempt to flag down a vehicle or run to the closest neighbor. It's worth a try.

I have to look. I'll go mad if I don't.

Heart thundering, I peer around the edge of the coffin to find Levi's shadow standing just beyond the rickety old doors. As if sensing my movement, his silhouette slides closer, blocking out the world beyond. The entire universe seems to pause for a moment, waiting on bated breath. Even from here, I can see his head tilt as he says in a slithering voice, "I can smell you, love."

Then, the doors burst open, and Levi stalks across the room to the coffin, knife still lodged in his eye.

I throw myself around the other side, scrambling to my feet as I make a break for the door. Before I even hit the foot of the coffin, Levi launches himself across it, landing on his feet in front of me. I stagger back, nearly falling on my ass, but Levi catches me by my hair.

He wrenches me toward him and then turns to press me up against the alabaster stone. His hand pulls on my hair, bowing my body to his will. My back arches in an attempt to put more space between us, between my face and that sticky knife handle jutting from his eye. I don't know how he's still standing, much less how he chased me through a graveyard. I drove that knife deep enough to touch brain—but then again, I don't know if that matters for a demon. Maybe nothing can really kill him.

I ran, knowing this particular monster loves to chase me. Not the best decision on my part, I know. Squeezing my eyes shut, I gasp for air as he lowers his mouth to my skin, angling his head so the knife doesn't touch me as his blood drips onto my collar.

"You know," his breath is hot against my neck, "I like to

think that I am exceptionally patient for an Eternal, but you may test my limits yet, menace."

His nose traces my carotid like he wants to rip it out with his teeth.

"Please," I rasp. "Either let me go or kill me."

Levi's hand loosens in my hair, not quite enough to get free, but enough that I understand my words have surprised him. "How many times do I have to tell you that I have no intention of hurting you?" His voice is gentle.

"But... I thought—"

"That's the problem," he growls, his fingers tightening in my hair to tilt my face toward his. "You think too fucking much."

Then, his mouth is on mine, kissing me sideways.

That's the last thing I expected, and, in my surprise, I gasp, allowing his tongue to sweep between my parted lips. It's *different* now. Smoother. Thinner. The tip is split in two, and I'm fascinated enough to open my mouth a little wider, and it's all the invitation he needs. Those fleshy probes slip between my teeth to writhe in my mouth, overwhelming me with sensation, coaxing and arousing. It's a strange sensation, having what feels like two tongues dancing with my one.

My hands find their way to Levi's chest, my nails digging into his skin. He's rock hard and warm, his skin blazing at the same feverish temperature as when he was in Walter's body —only now, it's been fully unleashed. I skim my fingers across his chest, drinking in the new valleys and hills, the lean build of his abdomen.

His skin is coated in the blood of the men he killed tonight, and that brings me back to my senses.

Fighting the hand in my hair, I break our kiss to start shoving his chest. "*I can't do this.*" I'm not sure which one of us I'm trying to convince.

"Stop running and look at me." It's a velvety demand. "Go ahead, look. I kept the knife where you left it so you can see what you've done." There's sly amusement in his voice, a faint chastising undercurrent that reminds me of when I got in trouble as a child. I never thought I'd be in a position where a *demon* would try to teach *me* a lesson about right and wrong.

After he killed seven men in cold blood, no less.

What a self-righteous, hypocritical dick. I am *not* about to be lectured by a demon. So I turn to look at him, staring directly at that knife and the blood seeping down one side of his face as I sneer. "Do you expect me to feel guilty?"

The green ring in his intact eye pulses wildly as Levi's blue lips peel back to reveal his teeth, his long canines. They press into his lower lip as he smiles. "My vicious little menace is so proud of the pain she's caused." He chuckles quietly. "You are more like me than you care to admit."

I lean up to snarl in his face. "You deserve it for ruining my life."

His eyes darkens. "You think I came here to ruin your life? No, little snake. I have come to give you everything you've ever wished for. I am your darkest shadow, your most devoted lover. You know me. I have been with you for a very long time."

I'm feeling stronger now that I know he won't hurt me. Even the hand he has tangled in my hair seems gentler. I shove again at his chest, kicking his shins to no avail, but I'm pretty sure his bones are made of steel. "You aren't my lover— not now, not ever. If you aren't going to kill me, let me go."

Levi's hand tightens on my hair as his other hand hooks under my thigh, laying me out over the edge of the coffin. There's no way I can wiggle away from him like this and every time I do, a certain part of him prods my swollen flesh, so I stop fighting and glare up at him instead.

He leans in and growls onto my jaw, "You remember the moment we met as well as I, menace. Your breath smelled of tequila and sugar, and you fell masterfully into my lap. You kissed me, and I read the stars in your palm."

Those words rip all the air out of my lungs, siphoning the strength from my limbs—I know which night he's referring to: that Halloween so many years ago, when I first met Walter and resolved to make him mine. Is Levi saying what I think he's saying?

"What?" I squeak.

That green ring starts sparkling. "You see, beautiful thing? It has been me from the beginning. It is me you desired, *me* you have dreamed of."

"You were my shadow in all those nightmares," I say, half out of my mind.

"They were more than nightmares, Rose. You think you can't love me, but you're wrong. Tell me you haven't fallen deeper in love with me in the last two weeks than you did the entire decade you were shackled to that self-absorbed prick."

Levi's hips grind against mine slowly, possessively, and I bite my lip to keep from reacting. His expression is one of barely veiled fury as he whispers, "Tell me that the thought of being corrupted by my cock doesn't make you wetter than you've ever been before."

I'm suddenly very aware of the heartbeat thundering in my ears and rattling every single one of my ribs. My body softens under him, and I can't stop it. I can't stop my want from rising to the surface. I've found myself in another night-mare, but the true monster isn't the one pinning me down. No, it's myself for wanting to give in, for wanting to be a part of him, despite what he is. Maybe he's right. Maybe I do know him.

Maybe we are more alike than I was willing to confess.

I would bathe in the blood of bad men night after night if that was the only way I could be touched by Levi, and he knows it. My only other option is to resist, to try and get away again, and possibly face that other creature here in the graveyard with us. I haven't a clue what that one wants from me. At least with Levi, I know I'll survive another day. The more his words sink in, the more I realize I'm not fighting against him for my own defense, not even for my own comfort. He's not a danger to me. I'm fighting in the name of a morality that doesn't apply to him. And does it even apply to me, if this is a matter of survival? He isn't human. To him, those men are just souls, just energy. Their destiny was always going to be that of the ultimate death. So, at least in that sense, I understand him. I understand his actions. Those who reign in the afterlife have never followed their own rules.

At least Callum deserved it.

If the sins he told me about the others were true, they did too.

Levi doesn't feel for others the way I do. He made it crystal clear that the only human he cares about is *me*, and I don't know why that makes me want to cry.

He sees the warring emotions on my face.

With a slow smile, Levi releases my hair and grabs one of my wrists, dragging my hand into the sliver of space between our bodies. "Touch yourself," he purrs. "Show us both how right I am."

I try to pull my hand away, shaking my head, and a harsh growl radiates from his chest.

"Touch yourself before I do it for you, baby. I'm warning

you: if you make me touch you right now, I won't exercise any control. I'll make a mess out of you right here."

I don't know what him losing control looks like, but I have a feeling that's the last thing I need right now, so I obediently slide my hand between my legs... and my jaw slackens as I discover the slick gathered there.

He's right.

My body loves the idea of him violating me in this demon form, desecrating what little is left of my human innocence. I want him to ruin me, but that's probably because he's already ruined me for anything remotely normal, anything healthy. My hand trembles as I present it to him, my fingertips glistening.

The ring in his eye tightens. "Look at how wet you are," he whispers. "Look at how beautifully your pussy weeps for me."

"That's because you've broken me." My voice cracks.

Levi shakes his head, his blue lips a sharp line. "You aren't broken, Rose. You see me, the real me, and you aren't afraid. Now, be a good girl and taste yourself." He nudges my wet fingers toward my mouth, and I suck in a shaky breath as I slot my middle fingers between my lips. "*That* is what your love tastes like. I have the flavor memorized—a blend of brined melon and spice. You are exquisite beyond compare." He brushes the hair away from my forehead and my eyes flutter. I want him to keep touching me. I want to feel his fingers all over.

"Would you like to see how much I love you?" he asks.

My skin chills at the mention of those words. *I love you.* Half because I want him to take it back, and half because I want him to say it again. It wasn't a direct confession, but it was close enough. No man has ever told me they loved me before (none that I believed, anyway), but I believe Levi. Or, at least, I believe he believes it. I see the depths of his obsession, the knife in his head and the blood on his skin.

Levi's touch is blistering as he cradles my jaw, as he grasps my hip beneath the nightgown and drags me back to my feet.

He straightens to his full height, towering over me, the top of my skull only reaching his sternum. His hand under my jaw keeps me from looking away from him, but I suddenly don't want to. I understand now why he chose hell. Nothing about him is good or pure, but he's angel-like all the same—an angel caught between death and life.

A wicked smile tugs at his lips. "Get on your knees and taste my love."

His hand on my jaw drops away, drawing my attention to his cock as he gives it one slow, firm stroke. That's larger now too—menacing, really. I return my gaze to Levi's bloody face, attempting to take a step back, but he catches my arm to keep me close.

His fingers are a brand, warm and permanent.

Before I even realize what I'm doing, I drop to my knees on the alabaster stone. He strokes his cock again now that it's level with my eyes; it's pale and thick, blue veins bulging under the pressure of his hand. The head is more bulbous than a human's, and the slit along the tip is longer, stretching a few inches down his shaft on both sides.

Gossamer precum seeps from the tip on his next stroke, dripping to the floor in front of my knees. My mouth waters at the sight of it.

I grimace. I shouldn't want this so badly. I shouldn't be falling to my knees the moment he asks me to, after everything that's led us here... but I wanted to. It's like I *needed* to. What the fuck is wrong with me?

Levi leans forward, bracing a hand on the coffin behind

me. His cock is inches from my mouth, and a sticky-sweet scent fills my nostrils, beckoning me closer.

"That's it," he murmurs. "Open your brave little mouth and let me in."

That order sparks one last rebellion in me.

I clamp my mouth shut and lift my eyes to his, attempting to infuse all my contempt for him into this one glare. He sees the defiance and his upper lip curls. Bringing his face closer to mine, he growls loud enough to shake the stone floor of the mausoleum. "Let. Me. In."

His cock bumps into my mouth, his slick smearing across my lips.

I make the mistake of letting my tongue dart out, and the taste of him instantly pervades my senses. Salt and earth. Heat and power and darkness crackle across my tongue, a peppery musk, and I have no choice but to get closer, to taste more, to take all of him into me. His essence tingles over my tissues, equals parts effervescent and sweet as it dissolves in my mouth.

His hand returns to the underside of my chin as I eagerly take him between my lips, his fingers digging into the hinge of my jaw. He's at least a little afraid I might bite his cock off.

I smile in satisfaction as I take him deeper.

It's not a bad idea but, honestly, it hadn't even crossed my mind. He tastes too good. He *feels* too good. I move my mouth over him, coaxing more of his precum to the surface. I need more. What is this stuff laced with—*crack?*

Levi's voice echoes through me. "Does my love taste evil to you, baby? Or was it all in your head?"

I lift my hands to his thighs, my nails digging into his pale flesh as I inch closer. My knees ache from the hard floor of the mausoleum, but I don't care. I suckle on him like I'm starving.

Levi's laughter fills my ears. He pulls himself out as I reach for him, not knowing why but desperately needing his proximity. Reaching up, he applies pressure to his impaled eye with one hand and swiftly rips the blade out with the other. He doesn't make a sound as blood surges out of the mangled flesh. Then, he bends down and hooks a hand under my arm, hauling me upright. I sway on trembling legs, and he quickly drapes my stomach over his shoulder to sweep me off my feet.

His hand cups the back of my leg as he carries me out of the mausoleum. I writhe, barely holding in my need. There was definitely drugs or hormones or *something* in his dick, because I'm useless right now.

My whole body vibrates as Levi walks us back across the cemetery, through the gate, and all the way into the house. I'm crying by the time we walk into the plastic room, but not because of where we are. I'm crying because I need him inside me. I see the men, recognize them. Six are board members while the seventh is Jake, the bartender who threatened me. Levi must have tracked him down too.

Charlie is dead now as well. It looks like Levi tore into him with his bare hands after I ran, but I feel nothing when I look at his empty body.

All the blood underneath us, all the death—none of it matters.

Maybe that's his magical cock juice talking.

Maybe this desire burning in my veins has made me a terrible person.

Maybe he really has corrupted me beyond repair.

Levi walks to where the last body hangs upside down and lowers me down the front of his body. His damaged eye is almost fully healed—twin rings of bright green pulse as he stares down at me, but I don't get a chance to admire them as

Levi spins me, his arm wrapping around my neck and holding me against him.

When he leans around me to tear off the burlap sack, I almost choke on my own spit.

"Mr. Busch," I rasp.

His face is scratched up and bruised, streaks of snot and ichor dried on his face from crown to chin. That's why Levi changed out of the clothes he'd been wearing earlier today. He followed Mr. Busch and abducted him as he had the others, for me. Now, Levi wants me to kill him; I know because Levi is handing me the knife again, the one now coated with his blood.

"You know what he's done as well as I do. You know he deserves this," Levi croons in my ear. "He hurts children. Every child who enters his home suffers."

I don't know how he found out the details about Mr. Busch's wrongdoings, but I'm not surprised. I imagine there is little a demon can't find out. He's not wrong, either. Mr. Busch does deserve death in my eyes. He deserves that and worse for taking advantage of a teenage girl. I want him to suffer, and Levi might as well be the devil purring in my ear.

The creep is unconscious right now, and I'm pretty sure that's because of all the blood rushing to his head. At least he won't be awake for what's about to happen.

My hand tightens and loosens on the hilt of the knife. If I cross this line, there's no coming back from it. It isn't my place to punish him. That's what the justice system is for—but then again, he already established he isn't afraid of that. Besides, I know that if I don't kill him, Levi will. None of them will be walking out of here alive.

Levi's voice purrs, "Do you think this fucker faced a moral dilemma before he touched his foster daughter, menace? I promise you, he didn't. He thinks he owns her, simply because he paid for it. She's a toy to him. Don't you wish to free her from his torment?"

I want to fix it. I want to be the one to make it right. I want to take this asshole's toys away and watch the light fade from his eyes.

My throat swells, tears welling. "How is what you're doing to me any different?"

His breath catches against my back. "You aren't my possession, little snake," he says somberly. "You are my heart. You are my *soul*."

That confession burns in my chest like white embers.

I'm his soul, and he's my demon. He's the darkest parts of me given form, given freedom. What must it feel like to be exactly what he is, without the fear of human intervention, without consequences? I want to know what that's like. My anger is still here, boiling under my skin. Levi's cum is still in the back of my throat, burning through my hesitation like the wick on a fuse. Why shouldn't I do this? Their blood is already on my hands. I'm already to blame.

I'm sick of being good while men like him get to be bad.

My hand whips out and slices across Mr. Busch's neck. I'm numb, watching him wake up from seemingly miles away. His piercing blue eyes bulge, the color made more staggering surrounded by the burst veins in his sclera. Blood sprays toward us, and wet flecks hit my bare flesh, marking me like a painter flicking stars onto a black canvas.

The knife clatters loudly to the floor as I drop it.

Then, Levi's hand clutches mine and extends our threaded fingers in front of us. "Remember," he whispers, "all you have to do is open yourself up to it. Drink in his death."

A humming fills the room as the blue-gray mist emanates from Mr. Busch's body. His skin goes paler than I thought possible as the very *life* of him is pulled out, his skeleton deflating as I watch in a blank, detached state. He deserves every bit of that pain for what he's done to Sam, for what he's done to others before her, because I know it's never just once for men like him. Once you start feeding on pain, you can't stop. A bigger monster came along to devour him, and now, he's the prey.

The mist curls toward us, and my apprehension is forgotten.

Profiting off the backs of terrible men is something I've always done. Why stop now? I want to know what this power feels like, what Levi's *world* feels like. He wants me to drink it in? So be it. I stretch my arms toward the mist, letting myself want it, letting it in like he demanded.

It's that simple.

The mist begins absorbing into my skin.

Where Levi's love tranquilized me, his death magic is electrifying. My heart rate spikes, and a pressure builds in my chest. A boulder of molten lava rolls its way under my ribs, and I feel it burning *everywhere*. It fills my pores and lungs, invading every cell. I'm on fire. I want to scream. And yet, it isn't pain I feel. Tension, yes, a vibrating, unbearable pressure.

This is power, and now it's mine.

The nerves all over my body are overstimulated, numbed, except for the ones between my legs. I need release. I can't concentrate on anything else. My ass grinds against Levi's erection, my head falling back to rock against his chest as a moan crawls its way out of my throat.

Levi squeezes my hand. "You didn't take enough. More, baby."

"I-I'm trying," I whimper. My body is overwhelmed, and I can't think about the mist anymore. I can't drink it in.

He trails his hot fingertips down the center of my chest,

pressing his hand firmly against my belly. The pressure there is delicious, and I launch onto my toes, trying to coax his touch lower. He growls in my ear, "If you can't stay focused long enough to take what you need, I'll have to fuck it into you. Is that what you want?"

I don't even have to think about it. "Yes."

Levi goes shock-still—even the mist around us seems to halt for a heartbeat before he says, "As you wish, little snake."

The mist moves then, pulling toward us abruptly as he sucks it in like a vacuum. He spins me in his embrace and lifts me off my feet, hooking my legs around his waist as he walks to the center of the room, remnants of the mist following behind us. Those rings in his gaze may as well be a cage, because I'm trapped in them. The skin around his eyes are veined with purple, pulsing, the power he absorbed pummeling just under the surface.

He lays me on the floor where I woke up. The blood is still there, cold and coagulated, but the only thing I'm thinking about is Levi's hands as he hitches the nightgown to my waist.

"You're such a good fucking girl, menace," he praises me. "You did so well."

Pleasure tingles through my stomach. I love that he's calling me good after I did something so bad. I love that I'm good to *him*.

My hands wrap around the back of his neck as he grasps my hips, guiding them into position as his long body stretches over me. The head of his cock nudges my entrance, and I realize my arousal hasn't lessened since the mausoleum. If anything, I'm wetter now. Weeping indeed.

Power is one hell of an aphrodisiac, better than chocolate and roses, better than chicken nuggets even. I never thought I'd think something so ridiculous.

But I'm not exactly thinking clearly.

I let my legs fall open, welcoming the intrusion, but as he presses in, I realize I might have overestimated myself. He's large. His girth barely fit into my mouth, so I'm not sure what made me think I could take him down there. I cry out as he pushes in another inch, and my hands push against his chest, making him pause.

I flutter my eyes open, looking up into his glowing rings. His blue hair is matted with blood, falling around us in a dark curtain, but I don't think I've ever seen anyone so beautiful. Tears well in my eyes—I hate the idea of disappointing him. "I-I don't think I can take it."

Levi's head tilts slowly, the rings in his eyes narrowing to slits for a fraction of a second. Snake eyes. As they round out again, he smiles. "But you *are.*"

He withdraws and makes a short, sharp thrust. The sensation takes my breath away. He's right: I'm stretching for him. It just feels so good that my muscles are clamping down on him with every thrust, making it difficult for him to get all the way in. I groan as he thrusts again.

"Look at you," he croons, "taking my cock, clenching so tightly for me. That's my sweet little snake." He slowly works himself the rest of the way in, and we both gasp when he finally bottoms out.

Levi's forehead drops to rest against mine as he savors me, savors this moment. It's a brief sweetness, though, because in the next breath, Levi pulls back and slams into me, and I lose what little air I had. His thrusts are deep and rough, and I love every one of them as my hips rise to meet his. I'm moaning so loud, I can hear myself over the ringing in my ears, over the hum of his magic. As his movements turn frantic and wild, he reaches between us, touching me where I throb for him.

I fall over the edge, seeing galaxies and constellations as I explode.

I don't get to come down, though. As my cunt flutters, he lets out a low moan and swells impossibly large inside me. There's a faint popping sensation, and suddenly, I'm too full. I don't know how, but his cock has expanded to twice its size, and the texture of him is different—bumpy or scaled *or something*. Whatever it is, it clings to my insides, sending new waves of pleasure rolling through my body.

"*Agh,* what is that?" I gasp, my nails digging into his shoulders as I try to pull away.

He chuckles, "You asked for it, baby."

"How are you, *still*—" My question cuts off as he tilts his hips, thrusting shallowly at a delicious new angle. "*Ohmy-fuckinggod.*"

His rough laughter spills around me, and then, with a low, whining moan, his cum erupts inside me, filling and heating what little space I have left for it, seeping out around his erection.

I feel the power then.

It sinks through my core and arrests my body with undeniable pleasure, striking my spine like a lightning rod. I'm barely conscious as I come again, my body writhing beneath Levi, my nails ripping into any part of him I can reach as the orgasm tears through me.

The power settles in my stomach, twirling and burning. Even as my pleasure ebbs and the pressure of Levi's length fades, that power remains a heavy weight in my gut.

It's a sobering sensation.

When I open my eyes again, Levi is right there, his nose millimeters from mine. His eyes search mine, the rings thick and bright—a sign of his happiness, I think. I'm too blissed out to regret what we've done yet; that can wait for the morning.

I reach up and feather my fingertips across his temple. He's handsome without the knife in his eye, all sharp slender features and expressive blue brows. They raise as I continue studying his new face.

"Imagining where you'll stab me next?" he teases, but there's a note of vulnerability in his question.

"Maybe," I grumble, letting my hand fall away.

My knuckles touch the thick blood beneath us, and I wrench my hand from the floor, choking on a sob as I squeeze my eyes shut. "Please, get me out of here," I beg him.

There's a long silence, and I don't think either of us dare to breathe. He can feel me pulling away, coming back to my senses, I'm sure of it. I just slept with a demon again, willingly, in a pool of blood that he shed. I can't believe I did that. I can't believe I *liked* it.

Levi sighs, and then his arms scoop me up off the floor. "Let's go get cleaned up."

I turn my face into his chest as he carries me out of the room. I don't want to look at the death anymore. Guaranteed, there is already enough of this horror ingrained in my memories to stick with me until the day I die.

I suppose, since it seems I was wrong about life after death, it will follow me afterward as well.

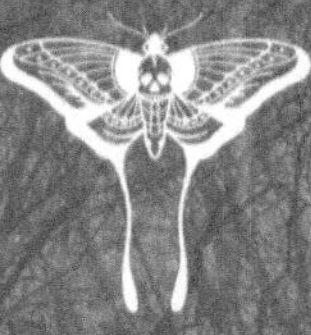

Levi walks out of the house with me in his arms. At first, I'm simply relieved to be away from that grotesque murder scene, but then he walks past the pool house and across the grounds, his black eyes trained on the ocean bordering the back of our property.

"Where are we going?" I demand, shivering as the breeze whips across my skin.

"We need to clean up, and we shouldn't do it in the house. It'll only spread the mess."

Understanding dawns on me as he strides toward the distant, dark waves. I start wiggling, trying to break free from his arms, but he's holding me too tightly, like he might never let go. "You can't seriously be considering jumping into the ocean right now," I hiss.

"It is the simplest solution," he says. "And besides, I like the ocean."

"It's not that simple, Levi. Not at all!" I protest. "It's freezing, and the water is going to be even colder. You may not realize this, but humans don't have flames in their veins like you do to keep them warm. I could freeze to death."

He gives me a dry smile. "You won't freeze to death."

"Don't tell me what I will and won't do," I shout, smacking him on his big stupid chest.

He throws his head back and laughs.

My hand closes into a fist, and I punch him a few times in the same spot, writhing now like a snared snake. "And don't laugh at me while I'm trying to hit you!"

"Oh yes," he chokes out, pursing his trembling lips. "I'm sorry, menace. Ooo. Ouch. You've bruised me with your vicious little hands. Whatever will I do?"

The air between us is lighter now that we're under the night sky. The deaths are only a memory, a phantom that twirls in my stomach and connects us permanently. He did terrible things, but he believed he did them for me, for *us*. I can't shake the sweetness of that. He understands the darkness—he wants my darkness just as much as he wants my light. Heaven and hell, he said. He wants them both, even the parts I keep hidden from the world.

I wish I could love myself that much.

Levi doesn't walk down the slope to the shallows. Instead, he stalks up an incline to the left, where the terrain forms a small cliff. I don't know if it could be classified as a real cliff, technically. It's more of a ledge. Either way, it's terrifying at night, with the black water glittering beyond it.

I dig my nails into Levi's shoulders, clinging desperately to him as I shake my head. "Levi, stop it. Put me down right now!"

"What are you so afraid of, baby?" He wiggles his eyebrows at me. "It's just a little water." We're approaching the edge now, his hands squeezing my body in preparation.

I use the sternest voice I can manage. "Don't you dare

throw me off this rock, Leviathan. I mean it. I'll never forgive you." Even as I say it, my lips twitch.

Damn him. He's so playful right now, it's difficult to be serious with him.

His grin stuns me. "Yes, you will."

And with that, he tosses me into the ocean.

I gasp for a breath before I'm plunged into the frigid fist of the abyss. My lungs immediately constrict in the icy temperature, and I can barely keep myself from inhaling the briny seawater. I rise in a flurry of foam, and just as I break the surface, I start hyperventilating. Swiping the excess water from my face, I lock my gaze on the shore a few yards away.

Before I can swim more than a foot, arms wrap around me from behind, Levi's heat bleeding into my back.

My sense of self-preservation outweighs my irritation as I turn in his arms, wrapping my legs and arms around him, soaking up every inch of his sweltering skin, shivering too hard to speak. I'm pretty sure the crescent moons my nails are leaving in his neck convey my fury, because Levi chuckles softly into my hair.

The water is as cold as I expected, but I'm handling it well now that the shock has passed.

That weight of power in my stomach is still there, burning, a flickering flame that licks at my trembling bones and chases away the chill. Now that my skin is flush with Levi's, it's as if my little flame is dancing with his inferno, fanned by his proximity—and I suddenly wonder if he carries a similar weight around with him.

I wonder if this is what true power feels like: *heavy.*

I finally muster the ability to speak. "I can't be-believe you," my teeth clack together so hard, I'm surprised they don't shatter, "di-did that. I'm gonna ki-kill you."

"Oh, my sweet little menace. You shouldn't make threats you can't follow through on."

"I mean it. I'm go-gonna wrap my hands around your neck, and—"

He leans back suddenly, grabbing my hands to wrap my fingers around his throat as the rings in his eyes tighten. "And? What are you going to do?"

I lick my lips, my gaze flicking to his mouth, his lips berry blue and large. They part as I stare at them, revealing the tips of his canines. I'm at a loss for words. I want him to kiss me— fuck, I want him to do a lot more than that. There's blood caked onto his eyelashes, and all I'm thinking about is how his tongue felt against mine. This is so wrong.

I shake my head and slip my hands around his neck, burying my face in his collar before I do something stupid... like admit that I'm falling in love with a demon.

His hands wander over my body, rubbing the blood off my skin and rinsing it from my hair. It feels wonderful, being tended to like a child. I don't know how we're staying above the surface so easily; I don't even feel his legs moving. It's like his body is buoyant, or he's manipulating the water by some other means. Maybe it's a demon thing.

When he's done scrubbing me clean, he strips me of the nightgown and lets the material disappear under the waves. Then, he moves on to his own body. I peel back enough to let him wash off, but I keep my hands hooked on his shoulders.

I don't want to let go.

He dips his head back into the waves, scrubbing at his scalp. His hair looks near black now that it's wet, but there's still a faint blue sheen to it. The angles of his face are sharper under the moonlight, and I'm momentarily fascinated by his ears, which are the same size as mine, but pointed at the top.

Levi peers down at me as he continues to rinse his hair, a

smirk curling over his mouth. "Enjoying the view, little snake?"

I shrug. "It's not every day a woman gets to bathe with the devil."

Levi lifts his head from the water with a frown, his hair clinging in a straight sheet to his neck and shoulders as the rings in his eyes seem to spin. "I think we're clean enough now," he mutters, guiding us toward the shallows.

His feet hit the sand before mine do, and we rise quickly from the water. I whimper in discomfort as the cold air hits my breasts as he leaves me there, in the waves. I watch as he emerges from the ocean. It's impossible not to admire him— the robust muscles of his back and his firm, toned ass.

Levi spins to face me once he's clear of the waves, gathering his hair off his back to wring the water from it.

When he sees I'm not following him, he grimaces, folding his arms in front of his chest. "Don't worry, menace. I figured you wouldn't want to sleep in the main house, considering the smell. We'll stay in the pool house until I can take care of the bodies."

That's not why I'm still in the water. The water is tepid compared to the vicious breeze outside of it, and I'm not ready to brave it. Stone cold reality waits for me back at that house, and if I'm being honest with myself, I miss the warmth of Levi's arms.

He made me need him, made me want him, even while I hate him. I hate him, don't I?

I'm glad we aren't returning to the main house, but the pool house isn't far from it. How am I supposed to sleep knowing what's rotting next door? My life. My beliefs. My self-control. "Or you could just let me go home," I offer.

Levi sharply shakes his head. "Your home is with me now. We need to stay together."

"Why?"

He sighs forcefully, placing his hands on his hips, his fingers splaying over the defined lines of his adonis belt. "Because I'm no fool, menace. The moment I let you out of my sight, you'll run, and I can't keep you safe if you do."

"I don't need your protection," I argue.

Levi takes one swift step forward and roars, "Yes, you *do.*"

I swear, even the ocean trembles as I shrink away from him.

He closes his eyes and retreats a step, his head lowering in something like regret. When his eyes open again, the glowing rings have contracted. "Come, Rose. We'll talk about this later, when you're dry and warm."

Then, without waiting to see if I even follow him, he turns on his heel and ascends the pebbly beach.

He's just going to *walk away?* After all the things he did to me tonight, after chasing me, fucking me, and throwing me into the ocean, he's going to turn his back on me the moment I upset him? I try not to let it bother me, but, fuck, it does.

That flame in my belly flares hotter as I stagger forward a few steps. "Hey!"

Levi slowly turns back to me, crossing his arms over his chest. He's smirking, so I know his previous frustration is fading. Those mesmerizing green rings expand in interest.

"The least you could do is hold me until we get inside," I grumble. "You're a lot warmer than I am."

Levi's amusement softens as he rakes in a deep breath and stalks back to me, his steps slicing easily through the water. I let him close the distance between us, unwilling to yield even one more inch until I'm in his arms. I sigh in relief when he embraces me—I hook my legs around his torso, and every muscle in my body unravels at once.

The walk back to the pool house is silent.

Levi opens the door with one hand, the glass panels clattering as it hits the inside wall. Then, he carries me through the living room and kitchen and down the hall into the only bedroom, pausing to close the door behind us before setting me down on the four-poster bed.

The bedding is fresh, so I can see he really had anticipated my desire to be away from the main house tonight.

With gentle hands, he tugs the blankets and sheets out from underneath my body, tucking them in around my shivering limbs before he turns to the brick fireplace on the far end of the room. With a wave of his hand, bright blue flames erupt in the hearth. The loud crackle and flare of light makes me jump, and I watch wide-eyed as the blue flames slowly fade to orange.

Levi acts like he's simply flicked a light switch.

He returns to tucking the blankets in around my torso, his expression flat. "I know you must desire a little space right now," he murmurs, avoiding my gaze. "A lot has happened tonight. I'm just going to make sure you're warm enough before I let you sleep."

I don't know how he does it—how he understands what I need so well while being what he is, understands me so well while I know almost nothing about him. I reach up and rub a few strands of his hair between my fingers. The blue is vibrant against my creamy skin, illuminated by the firelight. "Do all demons have colorful hair like this?" I whisper.

Levi lifts his gaze to mine, his brows furrowing. "A few of us do. Do you—" He hesitates, swallowing hard. "Do you like it?"

I nod. "It's beautiful."

His green rings blaze brighter as he smiles. "So are you, little snake."

He pulls away, but I catch his wrist. "Who are you, really?" I ask. "How are you here? Help me to understand."

Levi blows out a heavy breath and sits back down. "I am not so different from you," he murmurs. His voice is deep, filling my ears with rounded consonants, alongside a slight accent that I didn't notice before—one of ancient formality. "The way I came to be... I had no one, nothing but myself and the power I carried. I think you can relate to that. When your mother died, you were truly alone, and you did what you needed to, but we both know that it did not make you happy. It made you *hungry*." That last word comes out a bit throaty, a bit strained.

Levi watches me from the corner of his eye, considering my reaction.

I don't give him one.

He clears his throat after a moment, shifting his gaze to the wall in front of us. "Serving my purpose did not satisfy me either, no matter how much I wanted it to. I tried so hard to be happy with my existence, but I felt *incomplete*. And then, one day out of the blue, I was summoned to the surface by a very foolish, ignorant young man who demanded the world from me. Success, money, a pretty wife: he wanted it all. It is not often that I deal with humans, but I was annoyed and bored—so I did. I promised him everything he wanted and left a brand on his soul, one with an expiration date. I took his body for a short time to arrange his future." His eyes drop to the hands threaded in his lap. "And that's when I met you."

As his confession sinks in, I feel my heart shrink. Was that all Levi saw when he met me? A pretty wife for Walter? A debt to be repaid?

"You're telling me I was a pawn in some demonic deal?" I ask in a quiet voice.

His face whips to mine, his green rings bright. "No," he disagrees, tone impassioned. He leans in, bracing his hands on either side of my hips. "Admit it, little snake: you have never been innocent enough to be taken advantage of by *anyone.* Even from the beginning, I knew—you're as much a predator as I am. That's why I chose you. Your needs aligned perfectly with mine, and after that first night, I knew what you were. You became the only thing I could think about. For years, I have waited for the moment I could return to you."

The way he's looking at me makes my skin itch. The room closes in around us until there is only him and those alien eyes, the proximity of his soft blue lips.

"You said you have no one in hell?" I whisper. "You don't even have friends?"

When he speaks, it's with an absent lilt. "I do have friends, but how real can their love for me be when we were thrust together by the universe? My friendships are designed by fate itself, not choice."

"You believe fate is that powerful?" I breathe. "You think it can control you?"

That question takes him aback. "I don't know," he says with a huff. "Perhaps it is more my own fear talking than any real belief. It's difficult for me to trust my fellow Eternals with something as trivial as loving me. The big stuff, the world stuff, we are good at—us Hellish Eternals are, at least. Communication, though? Not so much."

It's a lot to process: his world, the realization that there are more creatures like him.

What does he want me for? A *human* mate? I must seem so small and powerless in comparison to his kind. I can't hide the tremble in my voice as I ask, "Is that why you chose me? Because I'm human? Because you knew you could make me... *feel* for you?"

His brows slant with sadness as he runs his fingertips over my cheek. "I chose you because you were the first creature my heart ever broke for, little snake. *I* was the one who felt for *you*, and I have never stopped."

There are no words in my head, but there are a million in my heart. My chest swells so full, I can barely keep them in. Somehow, I keep those words from crawling up my throat, from ripping me to shreds—I can't say them. I can never ever say them. He will own me if I do. He will hurt me, the way my mother was owned.

In my silence, Levi's smile falls. He pulls away, and I don't stop him this time.

He ambles over to the fireplace and folds himself into the large chair beside it before he turns his black gaze to the fire. "Get some rest. I'll watch over you."

I should try to stay awake. If he plans to leave me alone at any point tonight, that would be the perfect opportunity to escape, but my eyes are already wilting. My body feels so heavy, and the warmer I get, the further I sink into the mattress. Plus, in my delirious state, I think I don't really want to leave.

How very strange it feels—to have this desire to protect a demon from the pain of being alone when he has destroyed me so completely because of it.

I drift to sleep, knowing he will indeed watch over me, the way he always has.

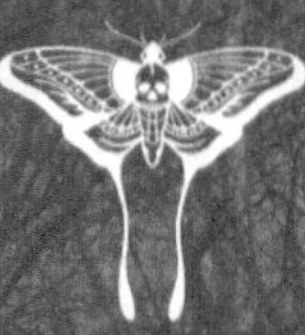

Walter Burroughs.

My eyes latch onto him the moment he walks into my sorority's Halloween party. It's impossible to miss him. He's always surrounded by the same flock of obnoxiously loud men, standing a head above them in his Italian-made clothes. He learned that habit from his father—the mega-billionaire who owns several tech companies. I'm pretty sure his family created crypto-currency or something, and from what I can gather, Walter is just as ambitious. He's already started crowd-sourcing funds for his first start-up.

I hear he's very persuasive. Resourceful. Absurdly *lucky*. He's a gold digger's wet dream.

I track him over the lip of my red solo cup as he and his friends settle in on the couches, their mere presence driving away the freshmen already seated there. I'm not drunk... or at least, I shouldn't be. I've only had one drink, but my vision is blurry around the edges.

A dark voice in the back of my head nags at me, telling

me to go to him, and for some reason, it feels like I'm not quite in control of my thoughts, like I'm an actress performing in a play. I've done this all before.

A hand appears on my bare waist, dragging me toward my boyfriend, Augustus. He kisses my temple, his heavy cologne filling my nostrils. My nose wrinkles; I've let him touch and kiss me enough tonight to pay for the lingerie on my body. He's nice, sweet even, but his family isn't loaded enough to make up for how boring he is.

I turn to Augustus, holding out my cup. "Refill?"

Augustus gives me an indulgent smile and walks off to grab more beer.

As soon as he's out of sight, I spin to face the living room as I suck on my teeth and adjust my bra. I'm barely crossing the threshold into the living room when the crowd shifts, and I see someone has beaten me to Walter. One of my sorority sisters is standing next to him, her hand braced on the chair cushion behind his head, wearing a bunny costume.

He smirks at her, nodding at whatever she's giggling at, his eyes dark and dull.

I have nothing against Angelina, but she doesn't need this. She has two doctors for parents and is on the med-prep track herself. She doesn't need to seduce the most eligible trust fund at our party. *I do.* Besides, everyone knows Walter is a prick.

I'm doing her a favor.

Hiding my annoyance, I smile and sway my hips to the music playing through the speakers. As I spin past Walter's chair, I trip over my feet and fall backwards, landing in his lap.

Walter grunts, his arms wrapping around me as he jolts upright.

My hands slither their way around his neck. "Whoops," I

giggle. "Sorry about that. I'm just *soooo* dizzy. Mind if I rest here for a minute?" I use my sweetest voice.

That's the easiest way to seduce a man: sugar. Play with his ego. Become what he needs to feel like his best self. Make him feel powerful. It's all about mirroring their deepest desires. If he indulged Angie because he actually likes girls like her, then I could pretend to be her for a little while.

I throw my head back, locking eyes with my sorority sister. "Be a dear and find Augustus for me?" I wink at her.

Angie pouts. I know she's probably disappointed, but she won't stay angry with me after I've just offered up my boyfriend. This isn't the first time I've traded in boyfriends like this. She gets attention from a pretty frat boy, and I get what I want. It's a win-win.

She rolls her eyes and sashays away, leaving Walter and I alone.

When I return my gaze to Walter, he smiles politely, his eyes glazed as they wander over my outfit. "I like your costume." He says it like a business card he's handed out a dozen times already.

I reach up and run a hand through his hair. The roots are blonde, but the rest has been colored with splotchy blue hairspray. "I like your hair. Blue is my favorite color."

He scoffs. "Sure; of course it is."

I narrow my eyes at him, forgetting my sweetness for a moment. "You don't think I'm telling the truth?"

"I think you'd say anything to keep sitting on my lap."

My jaw drops, and a soundless laugh huffs out of me. "You really are a self-absorbed prick, aren't you?"

His smile widens. "I suppose. But I also have no idea who you are—I don't even know your name—so how can you expect me to react to a total stranger dropping into my lap?

Would you rather I fall to my knees and worship you for your terrible balance?"

Okay, so maybe he's a little funny. Still a prick, though.

"I expect you to be grateful, obviously." My smile spreads into a warm, seductive thing. "My name is Rose, but you can call me whatever you'd like if you take me home tonight."

He barely gets the chance to smile before a voice calls my name. I glance over to see Augustus standing on the threshold to the living room, his brows stitched together and my beer in his hand. Angie appears beside him in the next breath, shooting me a contrite look over his shoulder. Her attempt to distract him clearly didn't work.

I have to give credit where credit is due: he's loyal, poor guy.

Without saying a word, I turn my attention back to Walter, running my hand through his hair again and leaning in to press a kiss to his collarbone. I sense more than see Augustus storming out of the house.

Walter catches my hand in his hair and brings it to his mouth. He kisses my knuckles and whispers, "You're a bit of a menace, aren't you?" His eyes are bright now, twinkling darkly.

I chuckle. "Only to those who need a little terrorizing."

"Was there something you actually *wanted* from me?" He drops my hand and rolls his skull against the back of his chair. "Or am I your next victim?"

I shrug. "I'm just looking for a little conversation, baby."

His eyes narrow at me. "Hmm," he hums thoughtfully. "I didn't realize any of the brats on this street even knew how to carry a conversation."

I search his face for any sign of that being a bad joke, but I think he's serious. My neck begins prickling with anger.

"There's rarely a man worth talking to who comes to these parties anyway, so why would we waste our breath?" I snap.

Walter's lips purse. "So you think I haven't met the right woman yet because I'm unlikeable?"

I smirk at him. "I *know* you're unlikeable."

"But you've graciously decided I'm worth your breath tonight?"

I shrug again.

He chuckles. "Then I'm flattered. Well, as flattered as I can be that you've deemed me worthy of sitting on like some fleshy throne."

"You're very comfortable," I taunt, wiggling suggestively on his lap. "If you want me to get off, you probably shouldn't be so mean to me. I have abandonment issues. Your standoff-ishness only makes me want to kiss you."

He laughs louder, his arms winding around my waist, his hands settling on the bare skin of my thigh and back. "Well, go ahead then, menace. I certainly won't stop you."

His hands squeeze my flesh in encouragement. He wants this as much as I do. He wants it, even if his eyes remain as hard as stone.

I lean in, my thumbs tracing over his jaw and lower lip, drawing him close enough to share air with him. For a moment, I hover there, waiting long enough for him to lean in too, attempting to close the distance between us. At the last second, though, I pull back. My stomach does a little jump as his mouth tries to follow mine, but my hands on his face keep him at bay.

"You beautiful tease," he growls.

"And proud of it," I breathe onto his lips. Then, I kiss him.

His mouth is soft and warm, and the push and pull of our lips is a languorous tango. He allows me to direct the kiss, echoing every movement with a slide of his own. His hands tighten on my back to draw me closer, and I go willingly, grinding my ass into his lap as he hardens beneath me.

A low moan crawls up my throat as he slides a hand into my hair, his nails scraping my scalp. His hand on my thigh rises toward my hip, and all I can think about is what it would feel like to have his fingers on the rest of me, all over me—to have him take this lingerie off my body and cover me with himself. I forget about the other people in the room, forget where we are and what we are, and I kiss him in earnest. My hands feed greedily on his skin as I grind down on his lap again, reveling in the tiny sparks lighting up my body when his hips tilt in return.

Then, the hand in my hair tightens and pulls my head back.

"It didn't get that far the first time," he rumbles threateningly. The words feel too real for this moment, too much, one second of clarity in a blurry world.

I blink up into his sleepy black eyes. "Right when it was getting good too," I pout.

The moment of seriousness passes, and he chuckles, acting like it never happened as he reaches between us to grab my right hand. He pulls it toward his face and flips it over, stretching my palm out in front of him. "I want to read your stars."

"My what?"

We're back to performing, saying words that have already been said before, in a different time, a different place.

His fingertips graze across my palm, tickling my skin, and I make a small noise of pleasure. I try to pull my hand back, but he keeps a tight grip on my fingers. "Your stars," he purrs. "I can read your future through the destiny lines in your palm."

"Huh." I watch as his eyes scan the lines of my hand, his lashes sweeping low, his mouth quirking in a lopsided smirk. "I never pegged you for a spiritual."

"I'm not," he mutters.

"Oh, my mistake. This must be something all blue-haired frat boys do."

He lifts his face and squints at me. "Do you want to know your future or not, menace?"

I consider the annoyance in his eyes. I know it's feigned, because the interest sparkling in his gaze is a huge improvement over the indifference of before. The kiss softened him quite a bit.

It softened me too.

"Alright," I murmur. "Tell me, is there a handsome and powerful man waiting for me in this future you see?" My tone is baiting.

He drops his eyes back to my hand, and with a gentle touch, he strokes a finger across my palm to the space between my thumb and my forefinger. He smiles and glances up at me from beneath his lashes. "It's a possibility."

I frown. That's not the answer I wanted. The least he could have done was flirt back.

He returns to reading my palm, his expression paling as he focuses on another line. After a beat, his brows twitch, and his eyes flutter. "Incredible," he mutters. "Your stars cross with hundreds of other constellations. Maybe even thousands."

"And that means?"

Meeting my gaze, Walter says, "You will have an influence on the world that is..." he exhales heavily, "significant. What is it that you wish to do?"

"Do?" I repeat.

"With your life."

I blink, finally understanding what he means. My life. For so long, I've been focused on this *one thing*: securing a rich husband to appease my mother's ghost. I want other things. Of course I do. I just haven't had a moment to think about it since my mom died.

"I don't know exactly," I say slowly, "but I think I'd like to make a difference for those who need it most. Kids like me— or, you know, the kid I used to be."

He reaches up and tucks a lock of my hair behind my ear. "I don't know nearly enough about you," he says softly. "What do you mean by that?"

I laugh nervously, shaking my head. "Trust me," I say forcefully, "my childhood is way too depressing to talk about at a party. What else do my stars say?" I nod at my hand, urging him to continue the reading. I don't want him to pity me tonight. I want him to *desire* me.

Luckily, he doesn't press for any more information. As he returns his attention to my palm, he traces a line near the top and mumbles, "Well, here's your lifeline—" He trails off, and then his head bobs back. When his eyes lift, they swirl with confusion.

"What is it? Is something wrong?"

After a long moment, Walter gives me a tight smile. He threads our fingers together, covering my palm with his before kissing the back of my hand. "Of course not. I see a very long life ahead of you, sweet menace."

"Oh, good," I say through a chuckle. "You had me worried for a moment."

His fingers graze affectionately along my spine. "You don't have to worry about a single thing. I'll be there to protect you now." There's an arrogance in his voice that sends a twinge of pleasure through my gut. It sounds like he plans to keep me around for a while.

"Are you sure you're not too busy for me? I can be a handful," I joke.

I think he might secretly like that.

He gathers the hair away from my neck and pulls me closer, his face softer now than it's been all night. "I look forward to it," he whispers.

I shiver as he trails a line of kisses up to my ear, and as he nibbles on my earlobe, I wiggle in his arms. He definitely wants to sleep with me, and if the twirl of his tongue against my flesh is any indication, he'll be a great lay. But if I want to see him beyond tonight, I need to hook him with something more than just my body. I need to connect with him on a deeper level. *Before* sex gets in the way.

"I didn't think someone like you would show up here tonight," I mutter as I play with his blue hair, "but I can see why Halloween must appeal to you. It must be a relief."

His eyes swell with emotion, and I know I've struck just the right spot. "What do you mean?"

"All the responsibility you take on," I whisper with a conspiratorial grin. "On Halloween, you get to be whatever you want for a while. There's no one around to tell you what you are or what you need to do—you just get to be yourself." I rest my head against his shoulder. "You can always be yourself with me."

"You have no idea what that means." His words are guarded, but I can tell I've affected him. His gaze is dark and heated, as beautiful as a starry night.

I lean in and press a soft kiss to the corner of his mouth. "Then teach me."

I jolt awake.

Peeling my eyes open, I see Levi sitting cross-legged in the bed beside me, and I startle again, my hand flying up to press against my heart. "You really have to stop watching me sleep," I mutter, dragging a hand over my face.

It's too bright in here. The curtains are open, and it has to be at least mid-morning.

"You knew I was here."

I glare at him from between my fingers, but his expression is calm, thoughtful. I suddenly recall the dream I just had and drop my hand. He's right. I knew he was here, watching me, because somehow, he'd inserted himself into my dreams the way he always does.

This one was meant to replay a memory, though. The night we met.

That's why Dream Levi had gotten upset when we kissed a little too long—he'd wanted to keep it as close to the memory as possible. Our first kiss had been sweet and sensual, but brief. My chest tightens; he had been the one I kissed that night. *Him*, not Walter.

I push myself upright so we're sitting face to face.

He's taken another shower, I think, because he smells like soap. It had to have been a few hours ago though, because he's completely dry already. With the sunlight pouring into the room behind him, his hair creates a blue halo around his face, and I itch to run my fingers through it.

I fist my hands in the sheet wrapped around my chest to keep them to myself.

Levi wears the tight leather pants from yesterday, the buttons undone, the material parted on either side of his delectable happy trail. Even the hair there is blue. I hadn't noticed last night, seeing as I was distracted by other parts of him.

I force my eyes away from his crotch. "What did you see," I ask him, "in my stars?"

A silent beat passes, and he starts shaking his head. "Terrible things. Things that would not serve anyone any good if I told you about them."

"I think I should be able to decide what good the truth will do for me."

"No," he replies emphatically, leaning forward until our noses brush, his hands pressing into the mattress on either side of my hips. "I'm taking care of it."

I clench my jaw to keep from arguing; I know there's no point. He may be a demon, but he has the conviction of a saint. "Where are my clothes?" I demand. "Or do you plan on keeping me naked in this bed forever?"

Levi grins. "As tempting as that sounds, no. I put the clothes you packed in the dresser." He nods to the armoire in the corner. "You can get dressed if you want to... or not. Whatever you want."

"What about my clothes from yesterday?"

"They're in there, too."

"Okay." I nod, my heart in my throat. "I want to take a shower first, though. I don't think the ocean water got all the blood out of my hair. Can you start the faucet for me, make sure it heats up before I leave the warm bed?"

He stares at me for a long time before he rolls off the opposite edge of the bed. "Sure, little snake."

Levi strolls into the bathroom, flicking on the light. His eyes glance at me through the mirror before he turns and disappears farther into the room, walking to the shower on the far end. I hear him messing with the faucet, the dial squeaking loudly. Thank god the pipes here are old and finicky. It'll take him a minute to get the temperature right.

I leap off the bed and cross the room on my toes.

With a cringe as the hinges on the armoire creak, I quickly gather the clothes I need off hangers and a pair of jeans from the shelf. The sound of the shower will cover me for a little while, but not long. As soon as he steps away, he'll know I'm moving. I grab the jacket I wore yesterday and run back across the room.

I'll get dressed later, once I'm far, far away from this nightmare.

Levi left the bedroom door open, so it takes me less than thirty seconds to sprint across the pool house to the front door.

My hand closes around the doorknob at the same time I'm wrenched backward by a strong arm. The clothes explode out of my hands, and I yelp as a burning palm closes over my mouth. The world whirls as Levi turns me away from the door and carries me a few swift steps to the kitchen counter. He bends me over the island, his chest flattening me against the cold marble.

"You think I wasn't prepared for that, menace?" he growls against my neck. "You're a terrible liar."

I squeeze my eyes shut, fighting the instinctual sob in my chest.

He's got his hands on me again, and I'm a lost fucking cause. If I can't get away soon, then I'll never want to leave. I barely managed to try it just now. The longer I stay in his arms, the more likely I am to fall in love with him, to give him too much of myself. And yet, I'm so glad he caught me. I love it when he chases me, when he catches me, when he shows me exactly how much he wants me.

Levi turns his face into my hair and inhales deeply. "You're right. You do have blood in your hair. Are you sure you want a shower, or would you like me to cleanse you with my tongue?" I feel that wet organ drag up the length of my neck, his teeth grazing, and it takes every ounce of my willpower to keep my legs closed.

He removes his hand from my mouth, presumably to allow me to say yes, but I refuse to give him that.

"Get the fuck off me," I hiss, bucking.

He clicks his tongue. "That's so disappointing." Levi lifts me off the counter and throws me over his shoulder, returning down the hallway to the bedroom.

I hate that he said that. I hate that he's disappointed in me.

I pound my fists into his back, bitter tears stinging my eyes. "*Put me down.*"

He tosses me off his shoulder and sends me staggering into the center of the bedroom before he shuts the door behind him and locks it. When he turns back to me, the rings in his eyes are pulsing. The shower is still running, and its steam curls into the bedroom, making the air warm and wet.

Levi takes one slow step toward me, but he pauses when I echo that step with one of my own in retreat. "When are we going to get past this?" he growls.

"Past the fact that you're a demon?" I sneer, crossing my arms. "I don't think I could get past that if we had all the time in the world."

That fucked up bitch in my head is screaming at me, telling me to take it back and tell the truth, but I've locked her up and swallowed the key. She's reckless, dangerous, and she likes Levi way too much. I need to get my feelings under control *right fucking now*.

Levi's nose flares, but vicious amusement crawls across his face as he shakes his head. "You don't really want to run from me, menace."

I pique an eyebrow at him. "Don't I?"

He slowly advances on me, herding me toward the bed. "You would miss the way I fuck you too much. You like to pretend that's the reason you feel *anything* for me, after all— the sex. Do you think that's why you get wet at the mere sight of me? Do you think that's why you scream my name when I'm inside you?"

My legs hit the side of the bed, and I nearly fall back onto it.

Tilting his head, he purrs, "It can't possibly be because you *love* me, right? You refuse to say it, but that's only because you're lying to yourself. How long will you deny the truth for the sake of your humanity?"

I have nowhere to retreat, so I lean in instead, baring my teeth as I fight back. "The only thing I want is for you to let me go."

"You know what? I think you ran so I would catch you

again, so I would *punish* you." His eyes are glittering, the rings spinning wildly within their inky tissues as my heart pounds hard and fast. I'm giving myself away. He lifts a finger to my face, drawing a line down my cheek. "Do I have to remind you what my love feels like, little snake? What it tastes like?"

The words rise to the tip of my tongue. *No, I never want to feel your love again. Your love is twisted and wrong. It frightens me.* I scream those things in my head, but my lips don't move, because they're blatant lies. I would be betraying my body if I said them.

My hands are itching to touch him as my eyes burn with unshed tears. My legs are shaking, and not because of the adrenaline pumping through my veins.

He knows what he does to me, and that's dangerous, because he'll win that way.

He's winning now.

Levi gives me a lazy smile and leans around my body to throw a few pillows into a pile against the center of the headboard. When he straightens, his chest is less than a handbreadth away from mine. I squeeze my eyes shut and lower my face as his heat envelops me.

A finger appears beneath my chin, lifting my face. I look at him, studying the graceful brutality of his features.

What's the worst that could happen at this point? I've already let him fuck me once in this new form, and I didn't burst into flame or grow horns. He's right about one thing: the sex is incredible. I want more. I want everything I can get from him before this is really, truly over.

Besides, I'll have an easier time getting out of this house if I play along.

Levi sees the softening in my eyes, the sensual curve

forming on my lips, and he smirks. "Get back on the bed, baby," he growls. "Prop your head and shoulders up on the pillows."

Without dropping his gaze, I crawl backwards to the headboard. When I reach it, Levi's eyes dip to mark the space between my legs, the arousal already clearly visible to him. I smile at him—a soft, wicked thing.

His hands fist the blanket as I settle myself against the pillows and let my knees fall open. Then, before I can anticipate his next move, he vaults himself up on the bed. Every step and shift of his limbs as he advances on me is as fluid as water, as weightless as mist.

Now that he's towering over me, I lose a bit of my nerve.

I swallow as he walks across the mattress, his head tilting one way and then the other. It feels like he's sizing me up, like he's estimating exactly how much he can consume in one swallow. He halts when his feet bracket my thighs.

He drops to his knees, jostling the bed beneath me and straddling my lower abdomen.

"Do you feel powerless right now, little snake?" He takes my face in his hands, leaning in to speak against my lips. "I'll show you exactly how much power you have over me."

He kneels up, bringing his happy trail right under my nose.

It would seem he wants me to taste his love again and, considering the way my mouth waters when I see the bulge in his pants, I want to taste it too. I glance at him from beneath my lashes, my breath coming faster.

Levi clenches his jaw. "Go on. Take control of me, menace."

It's an illusion, of course, a silly game of pretend, because there's no way I could *ever* truly overpower him in any capacity. Still, it's tempting all the same. He wants me to make him feel weak? Fine. Tucking my fingers under the waistband of his pants, I roughly tug them down, holding his gaze as his length springs free. Then, without blinking, without hesitation, I seize his hips and pull him toward me, taking him into my mouth.

Levi inhales sharply, his pitch-black eyes fluttering as he grabs onto the headboard behind me. The wood creaks as I make a shallow pass over him.

"Good girl," he groans.

He allows me to guide his thrusts, and for a while, I do feel in control. I feel powerful watching his jaw slacken and his eyes roll as my mouth sheathes inch after inch of him, as his hips twitch under my touch. He moans again, the sound spearing down my spine and singing across my core. I dig my nails into the meat of his backside, pulling him deeper, pushing my limits as he hits the back of my throat and I gag around him.

But I don't want to stop.

I suddenly see what he meant: there's no greater power than the one we wield on our knees for someone who loves us. Every roll of my tongue, every scrape of my teeth, makes him love me more. I'm lighting wildfires in his body just to watch them rage. I'm watching him turn to ash in my hands.

It isn't enough for me.

I want him to come undone and take the weight of power away from me. It took me until this exact moment to admit I prefer him in control. I like him wild and hungry. It *frees* me.

So the next time he slides into the back of my throat, I score his skin with my nails, looking up at him through teary eyes and begging for what I want. When he sees the desperate state of me, he brushes a thumb across my cheek before plunging his hand into my hair.

And with that, the illusion slips away.

He ruts into my mouth, holding my head firmly in place as his tip hits my throat, as I swallow him as much as I can. Tears pour down my cheek, and I can no longer keep my eyes open. His cock is thrumming in my mouth, undulating.

And that's when I remember what happens when he climaxes in this form, and my eyes flash open. Before I can attempt to push him away, he pulls out of me, and I blink rapidly to clear my vision. Levi grips his length and roughly strokes himself two more times.

The head of his cock expands like a balloon, and then it explodes.

His long slit splits open and dark blue tissues burst out from the center. I flinch, but my eyes round as I examine his anatomy—fatty twin orbs of spiky flesh protrude from the head of his cock. They look a little like sea urchins. Those spikes are what I felt tickling my insides last night, so I already know they're a lot softer than they look.

Levi continues stroking his shaft, every tug swelling those orbs a little more. His breathing is heavy, uneven, and a light sheen of sweat coats his pale forehead.

He licks his lips and whispers, "Touch me."

It's a command. It's a plea. I'm still in control, and he wants me to know it.

My heart feels lighter than air as I allow my senses to absorb his scent, his salt and warmth sinking through my pores. My fingers tingle as I reach for those pulsing orbs.

Levi starts growling before I even touch him, and I draw out the moment, halting my fingertips just millimeters away, fluttering my eyes as I smirk at him. His eyes darken, the rings tightening to pinpricks. "Gorgeous fucking tease," he grunts.

I finally let my fingertips brush against his cock. The orbs are definitely soft, those spikes the texture of a cat's tongue, slightly tacky and stimulating.

My core clenches as I imagine them inside me again. I squeeze one, and Levi lets out a deep groan, his eyes sliding closed as he bows over me. Cum squirts thick and fast from the center of each orb, painting my chest in translucent sap. There's so much of it—some clings to the spikes on the orbs, dribbling onto my skin. My lungs tighten; I can no longer breathe. I can only watch, breathless, as he continues spilling himself, pulling back to spread the fluid down over my stomach. He stares at the mess he's making with bared fangs as the green rings glowing brightly in his eyes.

The more he spills, the more his orbs deflate, until finally, the two sides of his slit glob back together, only a few sticky strings seeping from his tip as his eyes raise to mine.

I manage to rake in a shaky breath.

His scent is all over me; I love it, but I can't let him know how much. It'll make him feel more entitled to my heart, to my body, than he already does. So, I start sitting up, only for him to stop me immediately, pressing a hand to my chest to push me back down.

"Don't you dare," he whispers.

He drags his hand down the center of my chest, gathering his cum between his fingers as they travel across my stomach and over the mound of flesh between my legs. I try to close my legs, but he catches one of my thighs with his free hand, eyes flaring in warning.

Levi's fingers drip cum into my slit, frozen there above the bundle of throbbing, swollen nerves—so close, but not close enough to ease the ache.

"Hold yourself open for me," he demands.

Trembling, I do as he commands. I press my fingers to my swollen lips and open myself up, and only then do his fingers slide downward, grazing over my pulsing clit to my opening. I lose the capacity to focus on anything when he smiles devilishly and shoves his cum into me. I groan, opening my legs wider. He gathers more of his cum from my belly and does it again, driving his fingers deeper.

I can't hide my pleasure anymore. My head rocks against the pillows as I surrender. I'm shaking, arching into his touch, my hips twitching in an effort to take more of him.

"You nasty little thing." His taunt is melted chocolate, delectable and sweet.

Levi adds another finger, then another, until eventually, he's using his entire hand to stretch me, pressing in to the last knuckle. I feel my cunt clamp around him, slowly softening to allow him in. My ache is hidden deeper, and I yearn for him to touch it—I want him to rip me apart to get to it if he must. It's overwhelming, the pain and pleasure and pressure.

My moans drown out the vulgar sounds of his fist passing in and out of me, my neck and face filling with molten steel. Fierce pleasure swirls low in my gut, rising steadily to the surface. Just when I'm ready to come, Levi stops moving.

I let a growl of frustration and glance down, intending to grab his wrist to fuck myself if I have to, but I pause when I see his face.

Confusion is furrowing his brow. "What is that?" he asks as his fingers twitch inside me.

"What's what?" I gasp out.

"This string."

Understanding rushes over me. "Oh," I breathe. "That's just my IUD."

"IUD?" he repeats.

"Birth control. It keeps me from getting pregnant."

Levi blinks a few times. "I see. You never felt the desire to procreate?"

I grimace. His arm is wrist-deep in my pussy and (big surprise) I don't find the topic of children to be particularly arousing. I wrap my hand around his forearm as I hiss, "If you aren't going to make me come, get the fuck out of me."

His smile is that of unholy glee. "Oh. Is that all I must do to remain inside you?"

Levi twists his fist inside me, and I gasp, wincing at a sharp twinge of pain as he pulls his hand out. It takes me a moment to recognize the piece of plastic he lifts in front of my face.

My IUD. *He pulled out my IUD?*

And then, before I can even fully react to what he's done, he tosses the plastic over his shoulder, knocks my legs wide with his knees, and thrusts himself inside me.

My body accepts him with a thrill of sensation, though I don't know why. I don't understand how he can make me feel such intense pleasure when I know I shouldn't, when I should hate him, fear him. But as he slides in and out of me, I feel nothing bad about him. His forehead drops to rest against mine, and I realize we're both struggling to catch a full breath. I affect him just as much as he affects me. He tilts his face up to kiss me sweetly, and that's all the warning I get before he starts fucking me hard.

By the second thrust, I'm panting, lifting my hips to join his brutal song of lust. I feel like I'm losing my mind. My hands find his backside and urge him faster as sweat beads on my face and slides into my hair, into my eyes. I'm blind and broken, desperate to be his.

Nothing matters apart from this.

His voice fills the darkness of my mind. "Do you like the idea of me breeding you?" My body clenches, and I whimper as his cock rends my tight cunt apart, forcing his way in and out. "Do you want me to fill your womb with my dark seed?

Invade every part of you, possess you in every single way possible?"

Heat stirs in my belly, and I know it's more than pleasure. It's him—the power inside me, responding to him. My toes curl, my thighs squeezing his hips. "Please," I cry.

What he's saying is so wrong, but it feels so good. I'm addicted to this feeling.

Levi chuckles. "You know what, little snake? I think you love that idea. You love that idea because it's *me* doing it to you, because it's *my* seed. *My* offspring." He moans as his cock bursts open, and an orgasm sweeps through me. Those spiky orbs jostle inside me, clinging to my walls and heightening my release until I swear I've ascended to another planet altogether.

Levi snarls, his hands fisting in my hair. He thrusts into me one more time and stills, emptying himself. His heat fills me, leaking out between us as we wait for his length to deflate enough for him to move away, but for now, we're trapped in this moment.

A moment later, his eyes flutter open and latch onto mine. "You are so beautiful."

"I can't believe you just did that," I say breathlessly.

Levi gently pulls out but remains hovering over me as he tucks a piece of my hair out of my face. "I figured I would give you a thrill before breaking the news that I can't actually get you pregnant." He smiles sadly. "Ever."

"Oh." I feel my forehead crease.

How interesting. I wonder if that's the case with all Eternals.

"Does that disappoint you?" His gaze is trained on my face, studying every minute shift in my expression. It's almost like he's... nervous.

"No," I sigh. "I swore to myself a long time ago that I

would never have kids. I'm just... surprised by you sometimes."

His smile widens. "You were quite the surprise for me too."

I'm spared from finding a response when my stomach growls loudly. Levi glances down at my belly and chuckles before he rolls off me, sitting up against the headboard next to me. "Hungry, menace?"

That's when a wonderful idea occurs to me. I see it—a chance to save myself from his intoxicating presence.

I shift, rubbing my legs together to savor the dampness between them as I twist toward Levi and prop my head up on my hand. "I might be. Plan on feeding me anything other than your cock?"

"I bought some food for us; we just need to fetch it from the main house."

Perfect. "Absolutely not," I grit out. "I'm not eating anything that's been in that house. I'll taste death on it."

His eyes narrow. "Any death worth consuming is already in your belly, little snake."

My stomach churns at that reminder. "I mean it. I'm not eating anything that was in that house when—" My voice cuts out. I do a damn good job of making it seem like I'm close to tears, if I do say so myself.

Levi huffs a sigh of exasperation.

"There's a grocery store in town," I offer quietly. "We can grab fresh groceries from there and cook it in the pool house for the rest of the weekend." It's my newest escape plan—at least, the best I can come up with right now.

Levi doesn't respond right away, the tension radiating off him probably enough to power a small engine. Then, he runs a hand through his long blue hair. Spinning away from me, he slides off the edge of the bed and skirts around the foot of the mattress to the side I'm lying on. He leans forward, forcing me to look up into his green eyes.

"Fine, we'll go to the store. *But*," he scoops me up off the mattress so swiftly that I yelp, "you need to take a shower first, and I want to watch."

CHAPTER 29

TRY NOT TO FALL IN LOVE. IF YOU DO, FUCK IT UP

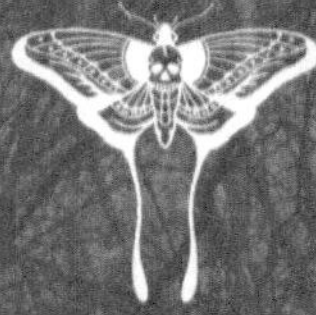

Walking into something as domestic as a grocery store with a seven-foot tall, black-eyed, blue-haired demon is weird. What's weirder, though, is that no one seems to notice him. I mean, they definitely know he's there—several people step aside and walk around us—but they just don't seem to see anything strange.

It's gotta be some kind of magic, something Levi is doing to make himself blend in.

He inches closer to me, sliding a hand over my lower back as we enter the produce section. I walk a little faster, and his hand falls away. I feel him frown at me. My gaze skips across the produce baskets. It's nearing noon, and the store is fairly busy, which I expected, seeing that it's Saturday and this is the only supermarket within fifty miles.

I grab a green bag from the dispenser and start loading it with apples. I'm not looking at the type or size or condition. No, I'm trying to formulate a plan. I need to get away from Levi. All common sense flies right out of my head when he touches me, and I forget my morals, or rather, I don't care about them anymore when I'm in his arms.

The sooner I get some space, the better.

A pale arm curls around me, startling me from my thoughts as it snatches the apple in my hand. I huff a little, conveying my annoyance.

Levi's low, taunting laughter wraps around me as he leans against the stand beside me and lifts the apple to his mouth. He takes a bite, the red flesh breaking with a snap. I flinch; it sounded a little too much like the bodies he broke last night. Flashes of that blood-soaked room fill my head, and my heart thuds a little harder, a little faster, as fear squeezes my lungs.

Levi doesn't seem to notice my stress. He turns the fruit in his hand, studying it.

"You know what I find funny about you humans?" he muses. "That you chose *apples* to symbolize corruption and sin. They don't even taste that sinful. Pomegranates, berries, grapes—now *those* are sinful fruits."

"Apples?" I peer up at him, curiosity winning over my pounding heart. "Are you... referring to Adam and Eve?"

Levi flashes his fangs. "I am indeed. Well, actually, the first human to ever survive long enough in the garden to claim a soul from the tree of life. Some religions call her Eve, but she was more like a Dawn. The dawn of humanity." He pauses, his eyes glazing over, as if remembering something as a low chuckle rumbled out of his chest. "Don't let the humans fool you about your history—there was no Adam. Every man who ever walked into our world was lured to their death. You human women, though—you are a different breed, strong and determined, perhaps more powerful than you ever should have been after what your male counterparts did to you. Dawn was the beginning of a new world. The tree wasn't what enlightened her, though. Its fruit only gave her the ability to enter the Eternal realm once she died, to continue existing alongside us in the underworld. And I know, because I was the one guarding the tree at that time. There's a snake in your version of the story, remember?"

I tie the top of the apple bag and place it in the basket hanging off Levi's forearm, looking at him with a skeptical furrow between my brows. "That was *you?*"

Levi nods, smiling.

His grin is equal parts smug and vulnerable, and I can't decide whether he's excited to tell me his past, or if it hurts him to relive it. As I continue to stare at him, his smile starts to fade, replaced by an urgency in his eyes that I'm finally starting to recognize. I don't know the source, and maybe it's better that way. I shouldn't care about what's weighing on him. He's a monster, a demon, and I have let him take up too much space in my chest as it is.

I turn away and move to the oranges, whipping a new bag open.

When Levi steps up behind me, I try to ignore his beckoning heat. "Why tell me any of that?" I ask quietly.

"You said you wanted to understand me better," he replies.

I nod. "I did." *But you're also a supernatural creature from hell, and I was drunk on sex last night. I was saying and thinking a lot of things I didn't mean.*

I can't mean them. I just can't.

Another woman approaches the opposite side of the produce cart in front of us, and I clamp my mouth shut, glancing behind us to see if there's anyone else I may have missed who might be listening.

Levi smirks at me, leaning forward to add another orange

to my bag. "Don't worry about them, menace. They won't listen."

I toss the bag into the basket and cross my arms, anchoring my gaze in his again. "The same way they don't seem to see you?" I ask tersely.

His spinning green rings and one-sided shrug are answer enough.

I sigh and walk away, heading to the deli counter. A few people are already in line, so we settle at the end.

Levi clears his throat and says, "I was a much younger Eternal back then. I hadn't descended to my place at the Hellmouth yet because no one with a soul had died. I was freer. I walked the Earth for a long time before the garden was destroyed and the split of Heaven and Hell occurred amongst our kind."

None of the people in line even bother to look at us—I don't know how he's doing it, how he's making everyone ignore us.

I spin to face him. "The split between demons and angels, you mean?"

He shrugs again. "After the garden was destroyed, there were Eternals who decided to collect good human souls like they were pets, because humans had consumed the fruit of the tree, and they carried what little was left of it. The tree was our only source of sustainable energy before it withered. Some Eternals chose to feed off human souls one nibble at a time, keeping them whole but only barely—reeling them in with the illusion of eternal life in paradise. Still, there were a great many Eternals who didn't like that system. They did their best to help the human race thrive here on Earth: watching, meddling, sorting through souls, looking for the worst ones. Those Eternals feed only on the rotten, breaking them down completely and using that energy to sustain their side of the Underworld. So, yes, to ease your understanding, I suppose you could view them as something as simple as demons and angels, but I'll let you guess which does what."

That's a lot to take in all at once. I let it sink in for a moment, staring at a child in a grocery cart behind us as they squeal at the banana in their hands. When I peer up at Levi again, I can't shake the dread of his confession.

"Are you telling me angels and demons are just glorified soul-suckers?"

Levi huffs a sharp laugh. "Don't worry, little snake. I won't bite... unless you ask me to." Then he leans forward and nuzzles my hair, inhaling deeply, and I swallow back a shiver.

So not only are demons evil, but angels are too. They're two sides of the same predatory coin, feeding off our souls? I would have preferred to never know that—I wish I could still believe that death is darkness, nothingness. That's more appealing than the horrors of the afterlife he described.

I turn to face forward, my head whirling with anger and disappointment. Someone is ordering three different types of cheese at varying thicknesses at the counter as another person gets into line behind us. This might be the best opportunity I'll get.

"I'm craving chips," I announce, stepping out of the line. "I'll run and grab some quickly. Order half a pound of honey ham, okay?"

"Rose." His tone is a warning.

I give him my brightest smile before I calmly walk away. "I'll be fast, I promise."

As soon as I pass the first end-cap, I start jogging. Then, I'm running. My eyes flick down each aisle as I search for something—*anything*—that might help me. I thought getting some space would make me feel better, but now, I'm feeling so much worse. There's an enormous pressure bearing down on my chest, and I start to panic, because I'm realizing I don't have an exit plan. *There's no fucking exit plan.*

Leviathan is my coffin, and I need to find a way out of this goddamn grave before he seals me inside.

In one of the middle aisles, I see a college-aged girl with a package of Oreos tucked under her arm, typing vigorously on her phone. I launch myself toward her, forcing myself to slow to a walk before I reach her. "Hi. Can I use your phone?" I ask breathlessly.

She looks at me, her golden brows furrowing. "What? Why?"

Feigning a smile, I reply, "Mine died, and this is an emergency. Can I use yours to make a phone call?"

She hesitates, and I don't blame her—I'm sure I look just as crazy as I feel.

"Here." I shove my purse towards her. "I'll let you hold this so you know I won't run off. This is a Gucci crocodile bag, so it's worth at least a kidney or two—and there's money inside. I'll pay you however much you want."

Her eyes round at the edges as something like pity crosses her face, and she shakes her head, pushing my bag back towards me before she extends her phone. "It's fine."

I take the device. "Thank you."

As I spin away, I dig into the pocket of my jacket, my finger closing around a piece of cardboard paper. Before I left the office yesterday, I moved the FBI agent's card out of my desk and into my jacket. I quickly dial the number and press call, turning to face an array of crackers as the phone rings.

I hear a click, and then, "Agent Diaz speaking."

Hearing her voice shocks me, and reality crashes into me like a Mack truck; it's all I can do not to crumble apart entirely. I remember that I killed somebody last night. I slid a knife across a pedophile's throat, drank his fucking soul, and I *loved it*. Levi might be a monster, but so am I. I'm guilty too, and after today, my life is going to be over.

I shove all of that down for now, all the sadness and fear and anger bubbling to the surface. I need to get the words out first. I need to escape. "Agent Diaz, this is Rose Burroughs."

"Mrs. Burroughs! This *is* a surprise."

Not wanting to alarm the young girl listening in, I walk a couple steps away until I'm staring at a wall of crackers and whisper into the phone, "I need your help."

There's a brief pause. "What's happening, Mrs. Burroughs?"

I try to find the right words, but they mix and warp in my head. Everything that's happened in the last twenty-four hours flashes through my mind in blood-drenched tapestries. He killed people in front of me as their blood painted my skin. "He did it. All of it, everything you said. You have to help me get away from him, please. I need help."

"Okay, ma'am," Diaz speaks soothingly. "Just take a deep breath and try to calm down. Can you tell us where you are?"

I'm trying very hard not to hyperventilate, but I'm not so sure it's working. "We're staying at our vacation home in Maine for the weekend, but right now, we're at a market off Highway I-295."

"All right. We can pinpoint your location if you give us a moment. Where is your husband now, Mrs. Burroughs? Is he with you?"

That deli line will only take so long, and then he'll come looking for me. He'll drag me out of this store and back to that house, and I'll go, because everything about him seduces me. The only time I'll be able to think clearly is when I'm far, far away from him, when he's out of my life and I can remind myself of what my life is supposed to look like, what I'm supposed to believe in. "He's going to catch me soon. Hurry, please. I can't go back."

"We've got you, Mrs. Burroughs. We're dispatching local police right—"

A hand grabs my wrist and spins me around.

Levi's black eyes glare down at me. He rips the phone from my hand and pitches it to the ground, the sleek screen shattering on impact as he snatches the card from my hand. He reads it and laughs. "Human law enforcement does not scare me, little snake."

I spin on my heel and run, but he catches up to me in the main aisle next to an endcap of apple juice, plunging a hand into my hair and using that leverage to turn me back around. He drags my face millimeters from his and snarls, "No one is going to save you. No one but me."

"I didn't ask for you," I snap back.

"But yet here I am. Because *I love you*. It doesn't matter what you do or what you say to me. I will always care for you. I will protect you for the rest of my existence, whether you want it or not, so I suggest you get used to it, menace."

"That's not love," I whisper, the words thick and strangled. "That's control."

Levi's jaw clenches. "You want to see *control*, little snake?"

He grips my arm and drags me down the aisle. Once we're clear of the tall shelves, I see the rest of the small store spread out around us. Everyone shopping has gone totally still, not even blinking. It's not just the people, either. The entire *world* seems to stop spinning as quickly. The clock on the wall is ticking at half-speed. The banana that child in the grocery cart held is mangled and careening to the ground, but it almost looks like it's floating.

Every single adult in my line of sight starts slowly

twisting toward us, blank expressions on their faces. Honestly, they remind me of the way the actors from the haunted farm stared at us on Halloween, the way Walter's company watched us leave the banquet hall: like puppets on strings. Levi *made* them do that.

Mind control—that's how he forced this entire store to ignore us, how he got us into the haunted farm, and likely how he kidnapped all those men without getting caught in the act.

"I will make the world bow before you, Rose," he whispers in my ear. "All you have to do is let me in."

Let me in.

He wants all of me, and maybe he already has it. If he can control minds, how do I know he hasn't been controlling mine this whole time? Maybe that's why I have so many mixed feelings. Maybe that's why I want to please him so badly when we're together.

It's forced.

I wrench my arm out of Levi's grip and stagger away, shaking my head so violently that I feel a little lightheaded. He steps forward, and I raise my hands. "No. Get the fuck away from me. *Get out.*"

The instant I say those words, Levi's head jerks to the side, twisting on his spine in obvious discomfort. The air freezes between us, and when his eyes open, they're shining with pain and anger. That's when I notice blue varicose veins undulating across his neck.

It almost looks like hives, like a... *reaction.*

I recall that night in our bedroom, close to the beginning of this whole mess, when I'd yelled at him to get out. And he had—it was like he couldn't stop himself. He couldn't disobey. He's trying to resist my demand again now, but his entire body is trembling.

I take another step toward him, indulging that spark of hope. "Get out," I repeat.

With a snarl, he falls back a few steps. His eyes are trained on mine, but there's fear swirling in them now. In fact, fear might be too soft a word for what I see. He looks *terrified*.

My stomach twirls. "That works somehow, doesn't it? You have to listen to me."

I open my mouth to say it again, to say it over and over until it pushes him out of this store and out of my life.

"Don't say it again. Please." His warning pours out in a rush, and I hesitate. Curiosity gets the better of me. I want to know *why*. With a shaky breath, he says, "Three times, and it's over, Rosie Posie. If you send me away like that, I won't be able to come back. I can't take care of you. Do you really want that? Do you want me gone?"

"Don't call me Rosie Posie." I snap, my chest burning with ire and hurt. "How do you even know that nickname? How long have you been watching me?"

Levi's hands fist helplessly at his sides. "Your mother," he whispers.

My heart drops into my stomach. "You've talked to my mom?" My voice shakes. I can't help it; I've never felt so vulnerable, so raw.

This demon has talked to my mother? How? Is she in hell or heaven? Either way, I suppose she's being fed on, used. The fact that even her death did not free her from suffering makes me want to scream, makes me want to vomit.

Levi shakes his head. "You're getting off track, little snake. I asked you a question."

My body is on fire. If I'm not broken yet, then I am breaking now. I stalk toward him. "And I asked *you* one, but I see you have no intention of giving me answers to anything that matters. Nothing you say ever makes sense. You play games. You speak nonsense and draw nonsense. You *are* nonsense. You're a fucking myth, and guess what? This isn't a fairytale. This is a nightmare, because you're a demon. I won't love you. I *can't* love you, because what you are is *unlovable*."

Levi flinches, falling back another step.

As soon as the words leave my mouth, I regret them—I feel them, but not about him. I was talking about *me*. I'm the one who feels unlovable. That's why I've always run from it, why I convinced myself I could live without it, and until this moment, I was too scared to connect the dots between my heart and my mind. I said it, though, so there's no more hiding.

"Are you really that unhappy with me?" Levi whispers.

I'm so ashamed. I should take it back, make it right somehow, but I can't even find the words. I just stand there, gaping. I can't find the heart to keep going. He's taken it, and I've shoved my heart into his chest to replace the one I just shattered. Surely, there's no way to repair his.

The look in Levi's eyes rips everything that's left out of my chest, the decaying sinews and broken vessels, and he lays it out in the space between us.

"Go on," the demon urges, tears brimming in his eyes. "Tell me you don't love me."

My own hot tears start streaming down my cheeks. I don't know what I would say. I hate you? I love you? I won't know this is real until you're gone? All those things are true, and yet I can't bring myself to say any of them. Levi's eyes harden in my silence, and he nods to himself, turning his gaze to the floor. The spectators around us turn as one and start marching out of the store as I watch them go through blurry eyes.

Once the last person exits, Levi lifts his eyes back to mine. "Kiss me one last time before I go," he whispers. "Kiss me goodbye."

There is no passion in that request. He's suddenly so cold, so distant, and I decide that I don't like this side of him. It frightens me.

"Levi," I sob.

He closes his eyes against my garbled cry, his own voice steady as he says, "Do this one thing for me, little snake, and I will never ask anything of you ever again. You will be free of me for the rest of your human life, if that is what you wish."

Once the words are out, he waits for me to send him away.

If I still had my heart, I think I'd be able to hear it breaking. He said so many things to me over the last couple weeks, made so many promises I started to believe. He told me he wouldn't let me go. He told me I was his. And yet, here he is, asking me to kiss him goodbye.

For some reason, I thought he would keep fighting, even now, but I've broken him, I suppose. He's giving me up. *And isn't that exactly what I wanted?*

Isn't that what I *should* want?

Ignoring the sick feeling in my gut, I walk forward until my chest is flush with his. I want to feel my heart beating one last time. I reach up and cradle his face, dragging my thumbs over his cheekbones and the corners of his mouth. I suddenly wish his eyes were open, but maybe it's better that they're not. His obsidian eyes would only make this more painful.

Holding my breath, I close my own and gently press my lips to his.

His arms snake around me, lifting me off the floor as he eagerly returns the kiss. Our mouths battle one another for purchase. Grief and hate, love and lust; there's a million truths wrapped in this one. All too soon, he sets me back down on my own two feet. I cling to him until he grips my shoulders and pushes me back.

Then, Levi presses his forehead to mine and rasps, "I will always love you, menace, even if you cannot find enough forgiveness in your beautiful, bleeding heart to love me back."

His hot palms disappear from my shoulders, and when I open my eyes, I'm alone.

In his absence, the world feels empty. Heavy. My grief rises swiftly, choking me, seizing my heart with ruthless fists and shaking me free. I gasp for air, but that quickly turns to sobbing. My knees buckle, and as I slide to the floor, feeling as grimy and insignificant as the dirt beneath me, I hear the distant symphony of sirens as the authorities pull into the grocery store parking lot.

CHAPTER 30

DEMONS KNOW NO MERCY

There's a chip in the wall of the interrogation room—a little speck of white in the dreary expanse of gray. I've been staring at that little speck for a long time—minutes or hours, I'm not entirely sure. It doesn't feel like I'm really here. No, I feel like I'm floating, watching myself at a distance.

I know the agents are talking to me, but I barely hear them. I've been ignoring them as much as I can since they picked me up, brought me back to Boston, and told me what they know. They've been trying to get me to talk about what happened to the bodies.

I wish I knew.

I led them to the vacation house when they arrived in Maine, thinking it would be easier to show them the evidence rather than try to explain it, but the bodies and blood and plastic were gone when we got there. The furniture had been returned to their picturesque placements in the sitting room, as if all that death had never even happened.

Instead, there were hundreds of red roses waiting for me,

large bouquets wrapped in white paper and scattered all over the sitting room. That was more haunting than the blood would have been. I wish it *had* been blood.

He had to leave me with one last reminder of his love, of my own treachery, a reminder that everything would eventually wilt and die, and I would be left with nothing.

A hand smacks into the table in front of me and startles me out of my own thoughts—Agent Peregrine. He glares down at me over the table, his face reddened and the veins in his forehead pulsing. They're both getting desperate, I think. Diaz tried to comfort me at first. She thought I was ready to spill everything, and, to her credit, I was until I saw those roses.

I was until I heard the whole story.

The vacation house was not the only place where Levi wrought his death. He set Exies on fire, burned the whole building down. They found almost every single board member and employee dead inside, but not at the fault of the fire. Their throats were sliced, every single one of them, in the banquet hall. And, worst of all, the evidence says they did it to themselves. They found Cindy's body too, dead on the side of a road somewhere. Same condition.

I can see it in my head: every person in that banquet hall lifting a knife to their own throat and wrenching it across, minds blank and eyes dull.

Peregrine told me all the gritty details in an effort to get me to talk, but it only made me withdraw further into my mind, into the bitter emptiness and detached analysis. I should have known better than to assume Levi would let any one of them live after what they'd seen of me. I should be horrified by it, but I'm not. The violence makes sense to me. It's simply what he is. Although, to be fair, I don't think I'm feeling much of anything right now. I cried myself out, and now my emotions are nowhere to be found.

Logically, I know what's happening to me, even if I can't feel it. I'm disassociating. This is my brain's way of protecting me.

I was ready to turn myself in. I was ready to confess to killing Mr. Busch and face the consequences, a compulsion spurred by shame and regret. Now that I can't feel anything, though, I find myself incapable of forming the words. I'm an animal cornered, and I'm trying to fight my way out of it. Right and wrong doesn't matter right now. Nothing matters.

"You need to tell us where he went," Peregrine growls, "before we run out of time. If he leaves the country, our chances of finding him reduce to nothing. You have to know *something*."

I don't want to be here. I don't want to be anywhere. My head shakes of its own volition. "He's gone," I rasp.

He's gone. He's gone. He's gone. And it's all my fault.

Peregrine leans over the table, spitting saliva with each word. "You're protecting him, but you're an accomplice now, little lady. If you refuse to help us, all those deaths, all the pain felt by those families, are on *you*. Believe me, Mrs. Burroughs, I will make sure you are held accountable for every single one of them."

I know it's true. I already am to blame. Those deaths have stained my hands, and no amount of scrubbing will make them clean. They don't know the truth, and they never will, because the truth is unbelievable.

I have denied him. He is gone forever. They will never find him, and neither will I.

My vision blurs. The air suddenly feels as thick as cream. I gasp for air, pulling at the collar of my shirt as I scoot back. Metal scrapes loudly as I slide my chair away from the table, trying to tune Peregrine out as I bend over my chest is flat against my knees. My hair spreads out around my face, shielding me, and I try to soothe myself.

It will be okay. I'll be okay. This will pass. It will pass.

But that's the problem. The feelings I have for Levi aren't fading.

He tore through my brambles and wrapped himself around me, subjecting his flesh to my vicious thorns in exchange for what little I could give to him. What used to be a warm cocoon where his arms were has been ripped to shreds, and now, I'm freezing.

Faintly, I hear the door open to my left, and the room falls silent.

A moment later, I feel a large hand slide across my back. I jump and look up to find Astra's brother, Aldrik, staring down at me, concern written all over his face. He's in lawyer mode. Thin gold glasses frame his eyes, and he's wearing one of his perfectly tailored suits rather than the jeans and graphic tee I'm used to seeing him in.

"Are you alright?" he asks, his voice a low tenor.

I shake my head, and his dark brown eyes harden as he quickly shrugs off his jacket to drape it over my shoulders before turning to the agents, professionalism and fury radiating from his every flawless pore. I pull the blue blazer tight around me as I lift my chest off my thighs.

"Am I to understand you've been harassing my client *after* she demanded her representation be present?" Aldrik asks. "You two are begging for a lawsuit."

Diaz pushes off the wall she's been leaning on and joins Peregrine at the table, her hands bracketing her hips. She speaks softly, but I know better than to trust her kindness now. She's a shark. The only thing she cares about is making an arrest. "We needed information, and she's the only person who might have it. We're on a clock here."

"You can't honestly believe a *psychopath* would tell his wife anything. After what she's been through, Mrs. Burroughs needs rest and psychological treatment," Aldrik snaps.

I have never been so thankful or felt so unworthy as I do now, watching Astra's brother defend me like I'm his sister too.

"If you want to keep her here, you'll need to officially place her under arrest—otherwise, we're leaving, and I sincerely doubt you have the evidence required to charge her with anything."

I've said so little since being brought in. They don't know what I've seen. They only know that I believe them, that my husband is the one who abducted all those people, and that he probably killed them. They'll search the vacation home, but they won't find anything. Exies has burned down, so they won't find any evidence of worth there either. Levi took care of it. He's taking care of me, even now.

I will always love you.

I will protect you for the rest of my existence.

What have I done?

In the tense silence, Aldrik says, "That's what I thought." He turns to me and helps lift me out of the chair to my feet.

"We'll be speaking again soon, Mrs. Burroughs," Peregrine warns me.

Aldrik shields me from them. "Not without me, you won't. Let's go, Rose."

He guides me out of the interrogation room, and I squint my eyes against the bright fluorescent lighting in the hall as we walk briskly through the rest of the police station and into the dusky evening. A whole day has passed since I woke up with Levi watching over me. Loneliness crashes over me as we walk down the front steps toward the parking lot, as I leave behind the harsh lights of the station and the agents breathing down my neck.

I see Astra waiting for us, sitting on the front of her brother's Audi.

She leaps up and starts running to me, her eyes alight with worry. Seeing her breaks my composure, and a sob rips out of me as I fall into her arms. Somewhere, I find the strength to cry again—really, truly cry. I dissolve like hot sugar in her arms.

Astra strokes a hand over my hair, rocking me, allowing me to soak her shoulder with my tears. She's a little piece of home, a glimpse of safety, so I allow myself to not be okay. Because all those feelings I was so sure weren't real, all the feelings I was so sure I *couldn't* feel... they're right here.

I may never be okay again.

CHAPTER 31

HURT FEELINGS ARE BETTER THAN A CLOSED MIND

"I got Thai for dinner. I hope you're ready to sweat, because I went with a level four this time."

I turn over in bed and watch Astra barge into the bedroom with large paper bags hanging from both forearms. She deposits them on the mattress and peels off her leather jacket, letting it fall to the ground. Astra stayed with me last night and most of the day today. I told her she didn't have to, but she wouldn't listen.

She left a few hours ago to lock up the clinic and feed her cat, and I should have guessed she would come back. She's still waiting for me to talk about what happened, but I haven't decided yet if I will, or if I can.

Her eyes study my place in the bed. I've barely moved an inch since she last saw me, and the water on my nightstand hasn't been touched. I know she can tell; I'm sure she can read my aura or whatever. I can only imagine it's taken the form of a big, red, flashing sign above my head that says *I'M A GIGANTIC PILE OF SHIT*.

I force myself to sit up as Astra crawls onto the bed and

starts pulling food out of the bags. She places my favorites in front of me: potstickers and panang curry, alongside a colorful array of sushi.

I'm not hungry.

Astra tosses me a set of chopsticks and opens a box of fragrant tofu for herself, eagerly digging in.

A pang of guilt hits my gut as I realize I haven't seen her eat a full meal today either. She's starving because of me. I'm a fucking wreck, and she's taken it upon herself to take care of me, and I can't even be grateful for the food she bought. I'm a terrible friend. My guilt finally convinces me to grab my chopsticks and pick at the sushi, nibbling at the rice morsel by morsel.

By the time Astra is halfway through her carton, she notices my lackluster appetite.

"Alright," she sets her food down, "you have to talk about it before I lose my goddamn mind. What happened in Maine?" Her eyes burn with agitation, and I know it's masking a deeper, more painful emotion. Seeing me hurt hurts her.

She's the kind of friend I've always wanted, always needed: someone I can trust.

"Where are your cigarettes?" I ask, because I need *some* kind of substance to alter my brain if I'm going to have this conversation. I know that she keeps a special pack around when her vape isn't quite scratching the itch.

Her brows pinch together, but she slides off the bed and retrieves them from her jacket, handing them to me with an unsettled look in her eyes. I take the carton and pull out one of the cigarettes and the lighter she keeps with them, and I light up, right there on top of my expensive memory foam mattress.

"Are you sure you don't want to do this outside? The house—"

"I don't give a fuck about this house," I say on my exhale, watching the smoke billow above us. I burn through half of the cigarette in a matter of minutes, flicking ash onto my nightstand like the white trash I tried so hard to prove to the world I wasn't. Astra just sits there, not judging or berating me. The only thing I feel from her is love and patience, both more than I deserve.

I think that's what finally gets me to open up.

"It's more than just what happened in Maine," I whisper.

She considers my expression, the tiredness and vulnerability there, and nods. "Let me guess. Since the accident?"

"Yeah." I drop my eyes to my lap and pick at a loose strand in the bedsheet. "You were right. Something... *changed*. I'm not sure how much to say. I can hardly believe it myself."

Astra's hand covers mine, and I lift my gaze to hers. "You can tell me anything."

The words are a promise, genuine and real and warm, so I do.

I tell her everything.

I start at the beginning, with the night I first met who I thought was Walter, and I recount every moment of significance from then to now. I watch as Astra's face falls, as her eyes fill with fear and concern. When we come to the night we arrived in Maine, Astra gets up, pacing the length of the room as I tell her the rest. I tell her about the sacrifices and the magic and the way I was chased down in the cemetery. She chews on her thumbnail, refusing to meet my anxious gaze as I finish telling her the rest. I even tell her what I did to Mr. Busch. I wasn't sure I was going to tell her that part, but once I started talking, it erupted from me like a geyser.

Astra inches closer and closer to the door, but by some miracle, she doesn't leave.

She keeps pacing, and when I'm done talking, I wait for her reaction. I'm glued to my place in bed, arms wrapped tightly around my shins. Eventually, she stops pacing, her dark brown eyes training on the wall across from her for a few heartbeats before she finally turns to me. "Okay," she says.

Her forehead is creased with worry, and her pink lips press into a thin line as she seems to search for her next words, but she doesn't look scared. That was my greatest fear —that she would be afraid of what I'd seen, what I believed. What I did.

I wouldn't blame her if she rejected me, rejected our friendship. I'm used to being left.

Astra walks to me, halting at my side of the bed. After a moment, she perches on the edge. "I'm not going to say this doesn't sound crazy, because it does." She takes a deep, trembling breath. "But I know you, Rose. You have to be the most skeptical person I've ever met, and I already knew there was more to this world than what we can see. So, I believe you."

I feel a weight lift off my heart, one tiny pebble of the avalanche burying it. "Do you think I'm a terrible person?" I whisper.

Her eyes pinch. "Why the fuck would I think that?"

I swallow around the lump in my throat. "I killed some-one." My voice is quieter than a whisper now, barely audible.

She exhales heavily. "Oh, that. Honestly, that kind of got overshadowed by the fact that your husband was possessed by a prince of hell." I almost want to laugh at that, but I don't. She gazes at the wall again, thinking about her answer. "No... I don't think you're a terrible person, Rose. I think Mr. Busch was a terrible person."

I can feel her belief in those words, and my chest loosens a little bit more.

"Can I say something, though?" she murmurs. "Something that might hurt your feelings?"

I blink at her. I feel so incredibly raw right now that even the hint of a harsh truth scares me. Astra wouldn't be cruel to me for no reason. I know that. Still, it takes a few long moments of reasoning with myself to muster the ability to nod.

Astra scoots a little closer and takes my hand. "It sounds like you fell in love with him a long time ago and you pushed him away because you were afraid, but I think you were afraid of all the wrong things."

I can hardly breathe. "What do you mean?"

"He wasn't going to hurt you, Rose. Those men he killed —they weren't good people, and I think Levi knew that. I think, deep down, maybe these demons aren't as bad as their namesake leads us to believe. Maybe they *want* to be good. Why else would he punish people who hurt others? He single-handedly disarmed an entire trafficking ring and exposed the men responsible for creating it. I know you aren't eager to look at the news right now, but that's real. Even if Levi isn't good, he's at the very least deeply principled. Like you."

My skin starts crawling—I don't want to be talking about this, not when she's on his side. Levi served an ultimate good, that's true, but he also murdered people right in front of me and fucked me in a pool of their blood. It was *wrong*. That twisted bitch in my head rises from her grave, staring at me with a *who do you think you're kidding* sneer.

She's right, of course. It was fucking incredible.

What does that say about me, though, that I can miss him like this? That I *want* him like this? I shut my eyes and fall back into the pillows. Covering my face with my hands, I turn into the mattress, willing the memory foam to swallow me whole.

The bed jostles as Astra climbs over my body and settles into place beside me. When I peel my eyes open, I see her watching me. Then, she reaches across the space between us and swipes away the tear on the bridge of my nose. "You know," she whispers, "it's not too late to run away and live a cottagecore lesbian dream together."

A rough laugh crackles out of my chest, but I shake my head. "It's too late for me."

Her brown eyes soften. "Yeah. I know."

After a long moment of silence, I whisper, "How are you so okay with all of this? You don't even seem surprised."

Astra purses her lips, as if debating with herself in her head. Then, she smiles and shrugs weakly. "If you knew the small town I grew up in, you'd understand. My adopted Auntie practices there; she's their resident witch."

My eyes bulge. "A real one?"

"They're all real," Astra replies with a laugh. "But yes, she has real Magick. I spent most of my childhood watching her take care of the community. For a while, I thought I would become just like her someday—her daughter in The Practice, her protégé of sorts—but... that wasn't in the cards for us. For *me*."

Genuine disappointment colors her words, and part of me *wants* to pry, but I'm exhausted. I don't know how much more information I can process right now. My head is like an overflowing sink, spilling truth and fear and unfamiliar emotions all around me, flooding my world with uncertainty. "You've never talked about that before," I murmur instead.

She sighs. "I haven't had a reason to. We both know you wouldn't have believed me if I told you this a month ago."

Unfortunately, she's right. I don't know what to say. I feel the intense urge to apologize for being so narrow-minded when it came to her methods, to her beliefs. I was so closed-off. How much of reality have I turned a blind eye to just because I didn't have physical proof?

Astra continues talking in my guilty silence, her eyes going distant and her tone taking on a thoughtful lilt. "I swallowed a lot of bad with the good there, but I also learned that anything is possible, especially the things that can't be seen—the things that can only be *felt*." Her hand presses against her chest, over her heart, before her eyes focus on me again. "Maybe I'll tell you more about it some other day. When you feel better."

I'm not sure I'll ever feel better, but I smile encouragingly anyway. "I'd like that."

We lay there for a long time, watching the late afternoon turn to dusk, the warm colors of sunset glittering over the walls, shifting from orange to purple. When darkness finally sweeps in, Astra sits up. She reaches for one of the bags at the end of the bed and pulls a grocery bag out, setting it next to me before retrieving her jacket from the floor.

"I picked up your prescription like you asked," she says. Then, after a pause she adds, "I didn't know you took sleeping pills."

I pull the white prescription bag out of the plastic and withdraw the bottle before shoving all our trash onto the floor. "Levi made them a necessity. He used my dreams to get to me. I guess there's some truth to the whole astral travel thing, at least for Eternals."

Astra sweeps her curls out of her jacket and smiles. "You'll never doubt me again."

"No, I won't." My returning grin is brief and brittle. "Are

you sure you're okay with all this? You don't think I've lost my mind or something?"

Her lips twist to the side. "I'm probably going to spend the next six years meditating on everything you've just told me, but no, I don't think you're crazy." She shrugs. "And besides, don't we all lose a little piece of our minds when we fall in love?"

It doesn't feel like I lost a piece. It feels like Levi has taken a jackhammer and pounded my gray matter to dust. I exhale slowly, turning my attention to the pills in my hand.

Astra walks to the door, but she pauses on the threshold and glances at me over her shoulder. "Rose?"

When I look up, she murmurs, "Maybe you shouldn't take the pills anymore. Maybe you should let yourself dream, allow your heart to take you wherever you need to go."

My brow furrows, and I try not to frown at her. "Goodnight, Astra."

With a wave of her fingers, she disappears down the hall. I wait until the front door slams shut before I open the bottle and shake a little white tablet into my palm. I stare at it for a long while. It would be so easy to just take them and not feel, to sleep and not dream. It feels like there's a thousand thoughts just waiting for me once my head hits the pillow, truths that I've ignored but that refuse be ignored any longer. My heart pounds hard in my chest.

In a split second, I make the choice to run from those thoughts again.

Tossing the pill into my mouth, I reach for the water on my nightstand, but the tablet is already dissolving on my tongue. Bitter. Chalky. *Rotten.* I fill my mouth with water, but the taste remains, thick as a film over my teeth and tongue. I don't want to swallow it.

My stomach sinks. What am I doing? Who have I become?

Fighting back a gag, I lurch out of the bed and spit the contents of my mouth into the bathroom sink. I watch as foamy white spit trails into the drain.

Astra's right.

I fell in love with Leviathan, and I love him still. I miss him. Isn't that why I've spent all day in bed, waiting for sleep to take me to wherever he was? He might be good. He might be bad. He might be a demon and a monster and a murderer, but whatever he is, he's *mine*.

My whole life, I ran from love, but Levi ran after me anyway.

I was so certain I would never find someone who could make me feel safe in my feelings. I didn't think there was anyone out there who could see me at my worst, at my darkest, and still choose me, but a demon did.

Levi gave me his all, and I couldn't bring myself to do the same. Instead, I pushed him away. I hurt him. The thought makes me want to laugh and cry at the same time. *Me*, an inconsequential little human, hurting *a demon*. It's preposterous.

And yet, that sums up our entire relationship, doesn't it?

I lift my eyes to the woman in the mirror, the woman I'm not quite sure I know anymore, a woman carved from material ambition and fear. Where is the child I used to be? The one who loved without hesitation? The one who felt deeply and freely. She's inside me still, even if I can't see her. Even if I can't find her right now. Someday, I'll find her again, and when I do, I want her to be proud of me. *Her*, not my mom.

Tonight, I'll let myself dream and hope my demon is still watching over me.

———

I'm in my bedroom, but it feels different, darker. I'm standing in front of the full-length mirror next to my vanity, but I can't see my reflection. The glass is black. Slowly, I walk up to it.

There's something inside, movement veiled by thick black smoke.

I lean in closer.

The sound is faint, but I hear a voice. It's calling to me. *Rosie Posie, full of thorns. Come in, come in.*

"*Levi?*" My voice is an inaudible, echoey thing.

Nothing answers me. The mirror only swirls, beckoning me forward.

"*Please, are you in there? I'm sorry for what I said. I didn't mean it. Come back. Leviathan?*"

The mirror seems to respond, and as the smoke swirls again, it lightens so I see the outline of my reflection. Beyond that, I see something on the other side. I recognize his body right away, the pulsing green rings. Banging on the glass, I call his name. Ripples spread out from every impact of my fist, the glass softening more and more with every collision.

Levi's voice finally reaches me. He's telling me to stop, telling me to turn around.

The air chills at my back, and I suddenly realize I'm not alone in this dark room. Something is behind me. I spin around, my eyes flicking from one corner to the next.

I don't see it right away. At first, it's only a glimmer, a dark fly in my periphery. Then, it grows—the more attention I give it, the more substantial it becomes.

A black cloak. A silver scythe glinting in a fist. Then, the figure rushes at me.

I scream and trip backwards, and the mirror swallows me,

the thick surface splitting like a creamy pudding to allow me passage. For a moment, I can't breathe. I'm falling through what feels like empty air, and there's only darkness. All I know is that there's a hard stop rising to meet me, and I won't survive it.

No one who makes this fall ever survives.

———

I JERK awake as I hit the ground.

The plastic bag I'd thrown to the floor earlier crinkles under my face. I groan and turn over, staring at the ceiling as I come back to full awareness. That little crack in the ceiling smiles down at me. It's dark in here, but not nearly as dark as the dream had been.

I think it's safe to say Levi had no interest in hearing what I had to say.

That thing in the dream with me—it hadn't been him. That presence had been cold, scary, and not in the way that Levi was scary. This had been a different kind of fear, like standing on the grave of a loved one, like being buried alive alongside them.

I might as well be. Dead, that is.

Tears roll down my temples, and I try my best to feel nothing at all.

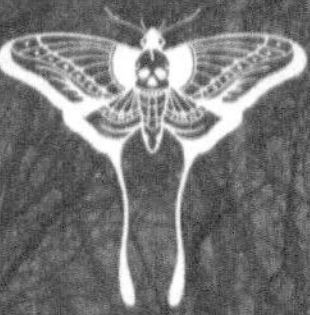

Astra opens the door to the clinic but turns around to face me before walking in, blocking the entrance. She looks far more rested than I do; I barely had enough energy to throw on a dress and brush the knots out of my hair before she arrived to pick me up. She's wearing a jumpsuit today with a pretty, colorful headband to match, a few of her curls carefully braided around it. My partner is as bright and beautiful as ever.

"Are you sure you're okay to be working so soon?" she asks quietly.

It's been three days.

Levi left me three days ago, and I feel as if I've been on my own for ages. I'm sick of home. For as long as I can remember, this is what I thought I wanted: a large, beautiful home all to myself, a bad man's money, and the freedom to do with it as I please. I could do *anything* now. Walter isn't coming back for his fortune. As far as anyone else knows, he's alive and in hiding for the rest of his life. It's all mine.

But I don't care. I don't want the money. I want the demon who gave it to me.

"It's the best thing for me right now," I tell her. "I need the normalcy."

She flattens herself against the door to let me walk in beside her, and as we walk across the large foyer, she wonders aloud, "Can anything feel normal after what you've been through?"

I exhale. "I hope so."

Astra catches my arm before I can walk into the hallway. "Hey. I have appointments all morning in the community room, and it might run into the afternoon, but I was thinking afterward, we could go out for lunch. There's that Italian place that just opened up down the street. You wanted to check it out." She's doing her best to give me something to look forward to, but I'm already on autopilot. I don't need to be comforted because there's nothing left in me to hurt.

I force a smile for her sake. "Sure."

Astra stares at me for a long moment, her fingers twitching around my arm. Then, she lets me go and enters the community room. I stride down the hallway and dig through my purse for the keys, pausing when I realize the door is already cracked. My heart leaps before I can stop it, and I surge forward, entering the room, my eyes scouring the space for a blue-haired demon.

But Levi isn't in my office.

"Sam? What are you doing here?"

She's sitting on the couch, my snack container on the table, a sea of empty wrappers spread out around her. Her hair is knotted, and her clothes are wrinkled—it looks like she's been *sleeping* here.

Sam stands up, wringing her fingers. "I didn't know where else to go."

I drop my purse on the couch and walk to her, reaching out but not quite touching her. "What's going on? You're *shaking*."

Tears well in her eyes. "I can't go home. You said I could stay here, right? I want to stay with you."

Those words crackle like a flame in my heart. *I want to stay with you.* Her eyes are saucers, and her lips are quivering. She's so scared. I take a deep breath and say in an even voice, "Sam, you need to explain what's going on. You can stay here and talk with me for as long as you want, but I need to understand."

She reaches out and wraps her hands around my wrists. Her grip is painful. "You can't call social services, okay? Promise me."

"What? Why not?"

"He adopted me." The words erupt from her in a sob. "I didn't even know he was planning on doing that, but I guess he did it a while ago. He set aside all this money for me. I knew he was going to do that—he promised me a lot of stuff—but after he went missing this weekend, men showed up at the house and told us they were taking everything. Mrs. Busch completely lost it. She went through his office, all of his papers, and she found out *everything*. She got so angry, waving a gun around the house. I had to climb out of my bedroom window to get away, and this was the only place I could think of. Please don't send me back to her."

My chest tingles.

There's other children in that house, other kids who could be in danger now, even if Sam has always been the odd one out. I look around the room, trying to determine what the right next step is. My eyes catch on the smart phone sitting on the edge of the couch.

I nod at it. "Did you get that phone from Mr. Busch?"

"Yeah, why?"

Grimacing, I pull away and scoop the phone up, swiftly turning it off. "Because it could be tracked. If Mrs. Busch doesn't know where you are, she will soon." I turn around and stalk toward my desk. "We have to call the police."

I'm strangely calm. I suppose nothing really compares to having eight men murdered in front of you, hearing their muffled screams as they slowly bleed out. Those men deserved all that Levi did to them and worse, especially Mr. Busch.

Sam staggers in front of me. "No, you can't." Her fingers are stained red as they rise in front of me, as she tries to keep me from the office phone.

I take her hands in mine. "I'm not going to let anyone send you back to her, Sam. I swear I won't. But if she pointed a gun at you, she needs to be reported. You need to be protected."

"I want to stay with *you*," she repeats.

My hearts stutters then begins pounding in earnest. For a moment, I forget everything else. Why shouldn't she stay with me? I understand her. She feels safe with me. Maybe this is my meaning, to teach this girl all the things I wish I'd known at her age, to teach her that love is the greatest currency in the world and it's okay to wish for it, to value it.

"I'd like that too," I say gently. "But we need to do it the right way, okay?"

Her breathing is erratic as I slide past her and reach for the phone. I quickly dial in the emergency number, but as I lift the phone to my ear, a series of deafening cracks erupt from the front of the clinic. I freeze as someone screams, another terrified voice joining the first. I hear Astra shouting over them, and then additional shots ring out, and I can't hear her anymore. I can't hear anything as my blood rushes violently in my ears.

Sam spins toward the cacophony, her eyes widening, and her fear snaps me out of my paralysis.

I shove the phone into her hands then push her backwards. "Hide behind the desk," I command. "Tell the operator there's an active shooter here. Give them our street and tell them to hurry."

I sprint across the room and shut the door, locking it. Then, I rush to the couch and begin pushing it in front of the door. The doorknob starts rattling and I push harder. One of my heels break off, but I keep going.

Until gunshots erupt right outside the door.

Something hits my leg, and it feels like my bones are shattering from the inside out.

Falling back, I land on my ass and scramble away from the holes being made in the door. My right leg is dragging. Shock numbs me for a moment, but then I bite down on a sob as the pain suddenly assails me, as I look down to see the bullet wound on the outside of my thigh, gushing blood. I think it only grazed me, though. Glancing back, I see a hole in the wall behind me, confirming it. I'll be okay. My thigh is just on fire.

There's another deafening crack as a bullet hits the lock on my office door. Smoke spits from the metal on this side, and the knob finally turns the rest of the way.

The person on the other side of the door throws their weight against the couch. After a brief struggle, I see Mrs. Busch's arm appear as she attempts to squeeze her way in.

We have mere seconds before she's inside.

Turning my head, I meet Sam's gaze behind the desk. I point at the window to her other side, urging her towards it. It's unlocked. She could escape, but she shakes her head, tears streaming down her cheeks. Her entire body is trembling. She can't move—she's too frightened.

So I struggle to my feet, shifting all my weight onto my uninjured leg.

"It's okay," I murmur, accepting our fate. "Just don't make a sound."

I'm partially shielding the desk when Mrs. Busch finally shoves her way through. I stand as straight as I can, my hands raised. She isn't fully present—I can tell that immediately. Her eyes are distant, her movements jerky as she raises the gun at me, but she doesn't shoot immediately, which surprises me.

"Where is she?" she demands, walking around the couch.

I attempt to keep my voice calm as I ask, "Where is who, Mrs. Busch?"

Her face twists. "That little whore who tricked my husband out of his money and left us with nothing. Where is she? I know you're hiding her somewhere." Her hands are shaking around the pistol. I don't dare glance to the side, where I can sense Sam holding back her sobs.

I'm glad I don't look away from Mrs. Busch, because I notice when someone moves across the threshold of the room behind her.

Astra.

Her hair and clothes are disheveled, and there's a wound on her shoulder, pouring blood down her torso. She was shot. Her watery brown eyes drill into mine; she's carrying something heavy in her opposite hand, but I look away before I can determine exactly what.

I have to keep Mrs. Busch talking, keep her distracted. "I had no idea she did that, Mrs. Busch. That's awful. Would you like to tell me what happened?"

Astra inches around the couch. She pauses for a moment,

her face twisting in pain as she accidentally bumps her injured arm against the armrest. Blood gushes from the wound, but Astra can't stop it, because she's holding onto a massive geode that had been in the community room. The purple and black crystal is as large as Astra's head, large enough to do the right amount of damage.

Mrs. Busch's laughter is unhinged. "Would I like to tell you what happened? Oh, sure. My husband put a pretty penny away for *his girl*, and then he disappeared on us. He abandoned us. Two days after that, we get a visit from some men he owes money to. They took everything that's worth anything. Then, I found the letter from the IRS. Guess who's been committing tax fraud for the last two years? The only thing that's going to be left once they're done with us is that little whore's trust fund. She doesn't deserve it. *I'm* the one who bends over backwards for him day after day, the one who supports and cares for him."

"Of course." I nod. "You deserve that money. You deserve to be cared for."

She blinks, and a brief vulnerability flits over her features, but that's quickly lost to her anger. Mrs. Busch shakes the gun at me. "Tell me where she is."

My stomach turns rock hard as the hair lifts on the nape of my neck—I swear I can feel someone blowing a torrent of cool air down the length of my spine. There's a certain peacefulness about it, and that frightens me more than the gun does. It feels like I'm standing on the ledge of some cliff, like I'm about to topple right over it.

I swallow hard. "I'll tell you where she is, Mrs. Busch, but you're going to need to lower your weapon first."

Her jaw tightens. "I can't do that." She thumbs the hammer of the pistol.

The world is spinning, the seconds slipping like sand

through my fingers. I say the first thing I can think of, the only thing I think might stall her. "Your husband didn't abandon you, Mrs. Busch. He's dead."

Mrs. Busch's brows pull together, and her hand drops a millimeter. "What did you say?"

"Your husband is dead," I repeat, a little louder now.

Astra nods behind her, stepping forward to close the space between them.

"How do you know that?" Mrs. Busch demands.

I reply, "Because I watched it happen."

Astra takes the last step, raising the crystal over her head, but she steps on one of the plastic snack bags scattered across the floor, and Mrs. Busch hears her. It's as if the entire world slows to crawl. Mrs. Busch spins, lifting the pistol just Astra brings the crystal down, but I can see... she won't be quick enough.

I move without thinking.

My hand wraps around Mrs. Busch's arm, the one with the gun, and I wrench her toward me. I just have to hold her off until Astra can incapacitate her. We just need one more moment.

It's such a small thing. Time. Having it. Needing it. I steal one moment, and the rest of them disappear right before my eyes.

There's a flash of light. Pressure. Searing pain. I stagger back, collapsing as I collide with my desk. My vision spins with little black dots as I hit the ground. I watch Astra hit Mrs. Busch hard enough in the temple to knock her out. My ears are ringing. I gasp for air, only to find that I can't get a full breath. There's more pain there, in my lungs. I cough, and I taste iron.

I hear crying.

Turning my head, I see Sam sitting beside me. She's trembling in the same spot, hiding against the back of the desk, the phone trembling against her ear. Her sobs are uncontrollable now, and that's when I realize that I've been shot. That's when I realize that I'm dying, and this poor girl—she will remember this, remember me.

She's going to watch me die, just as I watched my mother die.

I reach for her and promptly realize my depth perception is off. She's not as close as I thought she was. "It's okay. This isn't your fault, Sam."

Then Astra is there, falling into place on my other side.

"Oh my gods," she wails as she looks over my body. "*Rose.*"

"Not looking so hot, am I?" I wheeze. Tears streak down my temples, wet and warm.

Astra is doing her best not to break, but I see the panic in her eyes as she starts ripping her jumpsuit straps down her shoulders and pulls the shirt underneath off, hissing as she works it around her wound. She presses the bundle of fabric somewhere on my torso. I can't feel much anymore; a numbness spreads upwards, touching my ribs and everything beneath it. My body is growing colder, my eyes starting to droop.

Astra waves a hand at Sam. "Sam, I need your help. My shoulder... I can't press down hard enough to stop the bleeding." Sam scoots closer after a brief hesitation and follows Astra's instructions. "Push right here, okay? Don't stop. I'm going to run next door to the physical therapist. Maybe he can help us."

She readies to stand up, but I catch her wrist by some miracle. "No, you can't go," I murmur. "Don't leave me alone —don't leave her alone." I glance pointedly at Sam.

Astra follows my stare and frowns, tears glittering in her eyes. "You need help."

My head rocks against the ground as I fight to keep my eyes open. "Don't. I'm so tired."

A tear tracks swiftly down her cheek, but I don't back down. I've already fallen. The air is cold, the ground rising quickly to meet me, and the only thing I can do is make sure that the people I'm leaving behind don't fall off the ledge after me.

After a moment, Astra nods, understanding in her eyes. "Okay," she rasps. "*Okay.*"

She leans over my body and pulls the office phone toward her. When she sees that a call is already going, she brings the phone to her ear and begins informing the operator of our situation. Her words meld together in my ears, becoming nonsensical.

My eyes begin to close, and I'm vaguely aware of Astra shaking me back awake. "Hey, don't you dare, Rose. The operator says you need to stay awake, okay? Stay with us."

I can't stay. I know it down in my bones, but still, I try. For Astra and the child beside us, I try. It won't matter in the end. I'm losing the battle, and I'm also losing the war. I might as well let someone else win. "In my desk," I gasp as I remember it. "There's a USB drive in my desk."

Astra presses the phone to her shoulder, gazing down at me in bewilderment. "What?"

I'm having a hard time swallowing; the saliva in my mouth is mostly blood. "The USB. Give it to the authorities. My phone too. It has all the evidence they need."

"Give it to them yourself," Astra snaps, quickly returning to the operator.

I know she's scared, and so am I. I can feel myself fading. That's the best way to describe it: a fade of everything I am, little by little. All the unimportant parts leave first, followed by the bigger things, until I can only remember one thing—the most important thing.

It's an effort to lift my hand again, but I manage it. I touch my partner's face. "Astra," I whisper. She looks at me, her chest heaving with panicked breaths as the air between us vibrates with meaning. I try to smile. "I love you. I should have said that to you more."

"Shut up," she growls, more silvery tears brimming over.

"I love you. Say it back."

"No, you're going to be fine. You're going to be completely fine," she shouts.

My smile fades. "Astra, *please.*"

Her hand holding the phone drops, and her head falls back so she can stare at the ceiling for a moment as a sob shakes her chest. When she returns her gaze to me, it's grim. "I love you too, bitch." She leans over and kisses my forehead then pulls back and starts to pet my hair as my eyes slide closed.

"*Thank you.*" I don't know if I manage to say it, but I tried.

Pain returns in the darkness, a small twinge in the center of my heart.

It's just a little pain, though. Temporary. It will pass. Someone screams my name, a voice I no longer recognize.

It will pass. It will pass. It will...

CHAPTER 33
KNOW YOUR DESTINATION

waken.

A I peel my eyes open, and a black ceiling comes into focus above me. I study it as I sort through the cloudiness of my thoughts. Somewhere nearby, there's the gentle lap of water, rhythmic and soothing. Stalactites drip toward me, veins of glowing blue minerals threaded through the ebony stone, the color softly illuminating the darkness. How did I get here?

BANG.

Oh my gods, Rose.

I love you, bitch.

I lurch upright with a gasp, hands flying to my stomach. Instead of blood, though, my fingers twist in gossamer white fabric. I'm wearing a dress I don't recognize, and I don't get a chance to study it closer, because I start coughing. There's something in my throat. As I cough, it rises up my esophagus and into my mouth, and then a little gold coin falls out into my hand.

It's roughly formed, hexagonal. An intricate pattern fills the center.

Blinking, I lift my gaze back to my surroundings. I'm sitting on a porous black island in the center of an underground lake. It's surprisingly soft, almost spongy. Luminous blue water laps at the island, every wave glittering like stars as they crash against the stone.

I stand, my feet sinking into the foamy black matter as I approach the edge.

It's not the water itself that's glittering—rather, it's what's *in* the water, swimming and swirling, glowing with every movement. Ribbons of blue light. They're beautiful, but as I watch them writhe, unease spreads through my stomach.

I don't think I'm supposed to touch them.

Beneath the water, I see a blanket of coins just like the one in my hand. I stare again at the gold coin in my palm, and then, without second-guessing my instinct, I toss it into the lake. The instant the coin hits the surface, water erupts from the point of contact and whirls, hardening into something like pure, hard crystal before my eyes.

A boat.

The belly is long and narrow, the ends flared like elegant horns. The crystal gleams with a faint blue hue as water runs off either side back into the lake.

It waits for me.

I'm in the Underworld. The realization settles over me suddenly and completely —I'm dead, and this boat is taking me to my eternity. There's no doubt in my mind.

A naked woman has been carved into the crystal facing

me. Her body is slender, every inch transparent and glistening, what I imagine a phantom would look like. There's a certain energy around her, a... *being*ness. I step a little closer, admiring her delicate crystal eyelashes. My heart leaps as those eyes flutter open, and a pair of translucent eyes focus on me. For some reason, though, I don't back away. I'm not scared. Startled, yes, but that's all. She doesn't speak, and yet I understand her. I need to get into the boat now.

Without saying a word, I skirt around the crystal lady and grab onto the edge of the boat, the crystal smooth and cool to the touch. As I take a seat on the bench in the center, the boat pulls away from the island and moves smoothly into the dark expanse of the lake. I watch through the bottom of the boat as the water splits around it.

On every inch that the crystal touches the lake, those ribbons of blue cling and glow, bursting outward like shooting stars. It's mesmerizing.

The boat suddenly slows and starts spinning, the island I left behind nowhere to be seen. I'm spinning between two new islands, one with a large golden gate leading into a deeper darkness, another leading to a massive set of black doors embedded in the wall of this cave. With each rotation, I turn slower and slower until the boat finally comes to a gentle stop facing the golden gate.

I rise from the bench as the boat starts moving again. I clutch to the edge, watching attentively as a light flickers to life behind the gate. I swear, I can feel the boat's crystal lady watching me, but I don't care. That warm, buttery light in the distance grows brighter and brighter the closer we get, and then I see the figure waving at me, wearing a dress like mine.

A wild, strangled noise leaves my mouth. "Mom?" At first, it's only a whisper, and then, I'm shouting. "*Mom?*"

The boat is moving swiftly toward the island, and I see

that it *is* her. It's my mom. She's jumping now, her long auburn hair bouncing around her shoulders. The last time I saw her, that hair hadn't been there. She looks so youthful now, so happy and healthy.

Tears streak my cheeks as I lean over the end of the boat, waiting impatiently for the boat to shore on the island. I climb up onto the ledge, and when the bow finally hits land, I leap off and scramble up the hill to the golden gate now opening for me. My mom's arms are stretched to either side of her, ready to embrace me, light wrapped around her like a divine aura.

I run to her... and collide with what feels like a hard wall.

The rebound sends me flying backward, and I hit the ground a few feet away, clutching at my chest, which suddenly feels like it's been set on fire. I push myself up, lifting my eyes to the gate to find my mom staring at me with the same confusion I feel. The air in front of her seems to shimmer, and I realize it's a barrier. She reaches out, her palm flattening against it as she says something. I watch her lips move, but I can't hear her voice. As I stand, her eyes flick down to my body, and she starts banging on the invisible barrier, her head shaking in disbelief.

I look down.

The outline of Levi's tattoo on my chest burns beneath my white gown like it has been painted with blue fire. I can see all of it; the nightgown is sheer and white. And a small little dot of blue burns further down, right above my belly button. He hadn't tattooed me there. I think that little blue dot is... *me.*

My gown turns black where the tattoo touches and then spreads out into the rest of the white material, staining it.

The golden gates start closing.

I rush forward and try to stop them, but it's useless.

Whatever force is closing them is stronger than I am or ever could be, and I eventually have to step away before I'm crushed between them. I press myself against the bars, trying to get to my mom, trying to touch her, and she's doing the same on the other side. The light is fading behind her as the ground rumbles, and I know without hearing it that something is calling to her. But she isn't leaving. She won't.

How could anyone expect a mother to leave her child alone in the afterlife? Why are they keeping us apart?

If Levi hadn't warned me before, I know it now.

Heaven isn't only good.

Behind my mom, in the center of that light in the distance, another figure appears, a silhouette coming to take her away. My mom waves her hands wildly to catch my attention. She's screaming at me, pointing to something behind me, and when I look, I see that the crystal boat is pulling away from shore. I turn back to my mom and read the words on her lips: *Go. You have to go.*

I don't want to leave her here, but the terror in her eyes leaves no room for hesitation. If I stay, something bad is going to happen. Maybe the figure walking toward us isn't for her. Maybe it's for me. She would know better than I do.

With great effort, I manage to peel myself away from the gate and run for the boat.

I wade into the lake to catch the flared horn, but the instant I enter the water, those ribbons of blue light appear around my ankles. They latch onto my skin like leeches, tugging at my skin. I gasp as they try to rip my feet out from under me, and I cling to the boat with all my might, fighting against them to pull myself over the boat's edge.

In the corner of my eyes, I see the crystal lady shake her head, an apologetic frown twisting her mouth.

The boat liquifies beneath me, and I fall into the lake's grasp.

I'm so shocked at first, I let the water fill my mouth—except the lake isn't water. This liquid is thicker, and it rushes into my throat and coats everything in a slimy film as I breathe it in. That's when I realize I can still breathe. Even as those blue ribbons of light hurtle down my throat and tickle my lungs as they drag me deeper and deeper, and what little light the cave offered slowly disappears. I scream Levi's name, hoping he'll hear me somehow, hoping he'll come for me.

He's here somewhere, isn't he?

I feel a warmth encroaching on my back, closing around me like a massive hand. I'm wrenched sideways, and suddenly, white light floods my eyes, and I'm blinded in a different way. I drop, sprawling on my hands and knees over a hard floor. My stomach revolts, rejecting all the not-water I swallowed as I vomit.

Through squinted eyes, I watch as the liquid spews from my mouth, a handful of those blue ribbons hitting the white ground and writhing like eels between my hands. I heave a few more times before my stomach feels empty enough that I can lift my head, and I start to tremble.

There are people here, sitting above me in raised seats, staring down at me like I'm some kind of rare spectacle. Well, people isn't exactly the right word, I suppose. I can tell they're Eternals. Some of them have brightly colored hair, like Levi does, while some have animalistic features, like the mane of a lion or the tusks of an elephant. My vision blurs as I try to take it all in. Their seats are arranged like an amphitheater, and I feel very, very small beneath them.

"*Rose*," a pained voice rasps.

Heart skipping, I twist to look.

Levi stands a few yards behind me, his vibrant blue hair half-tied and the green rings in his eyes spinning violently. Silver chains are wrapped around each of his limbs, anchoring him to the floor. He's a prisoner.

And now, I'm willing to bet that so am I.

CHAPTER 34

KEEP YOUR WITS ABOUT YOU IN THE UNDERWORLD

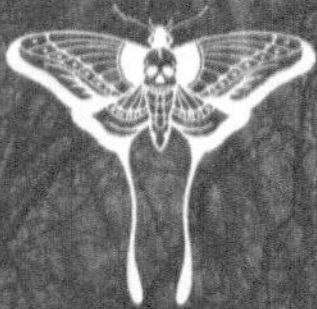

There he is. I see him, and suddenly, nothing else matters. All my hesitation from before—all the excuses and fears I used to hold myself apart from him—it's gone. He's mine and I am his. He is my monster, and I am his mate. I'm home. I'm on my feet in an instant, running to him, but before I can reach him, something stops me. Bands of heat wrap around my waist and upper arms, pulling me back.

I fight against them, snarling.

A man appears, sliding between Levi and me. He wears a dark cloak while holding a long scythe in his hand, and I recognize the figure immediately. He was the one in my room, in my dream. He's the one from the haunted farm and the graveyard, too.

Vicious, angry noises leave my mouth that have never left me before as I'm dragged away from Levi. Something dark and primal has come to life inside me, the weighted heat in my belly twirling desperately. I need to be with Levi. I need to touch him, and I'm willing to rip apart anything that comes between us.

That fury is mirrored in Levi's eyes, the green rings contracted to pinpricks as they slash to the cloaked figure beside me. Jaw clenching, he lifts his gaze to the audience. "Let her go," he growls, the mere force of his voice vibrating the air around me. "Restraints aren't necessary. She's only mortal. She's not a threat to you.

A velvety voice replies, "I have been surprised before."

It's a woman's voice, and I would turn and look for the source if I could look at *anything* but Levi right now. He looks more like himself. I don't know how I know that, maybe because he just looks more... settled in his skin, in his clothes. He wears dark leather pants and black boots, a dark shirt hanging open halfway down his chest. The ridges of muscle undulate with light blue veins, another hint of his anger. There are iron rings on all his fingers and pierced through his ears. What looks like an iron blade secures his blue hair up on the back of his head in a haphazard bun.

Levi's eyes pinch, his face twisting in desperation. "Luci, I swear on my Spark, we won't cause any trouble. Release us. *Please.*"

There's a moment of silence before the cloaked figure's hood lifts as he looks up at the audience as well, and then, the invisible bands around my body disappear. The chains around Levi's limbs do too.

We rush towards each other. He gathers me in his arms, his warmth enveloping me, and my arms and legs wrap around his torso. His face turns into my hair as he inhales deeply, and it's such a familiar affection, tears prick my eyes.

"*Leviathan,*" I whisper hoarsely.

A gentle shudder rolls through him as his lips find my ear.

"Keep your wits about you here, menace." Then, he sets me back on my feet, holding me close.

We're not safe. Not yet.

Taking my hand, he turns his full attention to the people gathered above us. I follow his gaze to find one Eternal standing from her seat in the center, a woman with strawberry blonde hair and a stoic expression. One of her delicate eyebrows is raised in silent demand, her hands clasped in front of her stomach, the picture of formality as a soft orange light emanates from her skin. Now that I look a little closer, I notice that every Eternal seems to have a unique glow, every color of the rainbow and beyond. Some colors, I don't even have a name for.

Looking over, I see that Levi glows a light blue-ish green. As I glance down at our hands, I realize that I'm glowing too, a soft, pulsing white.

How strange.

The woman's voice echoes through the room, threateningly gentle. She's the one who spoke before—Levi called her Luci. "Are you prepared for your trial, now that the witness is present?" When her eyes meet mine, I shrink. They are a bright, bloody red. There's no anger in them, nothing to suggest that she wants to hurt me, but I'm unsettled all the same. I can't breathe.

Her gaze returns to Levi, and I quietly gasp for air.

"You have been charged with dishonorable interference in human life," Luci declares. "How do you plead?"

Levi squeezes my hand, but that's the only sign of his discomfort. His face is a hard mask. "I should not be punished for what I did to protect my mate," is his reply. "Our law pardons such things." Those words tickle the flame in my gut, and I lean closer to Levi, wishing it was more, wishing I could feel his fire lick my own.

Both of Luci's brows raise, and a flicker of surprise brightens her red eyes.

Another Eternal stands, drawing the attention of the room. This one is seated at the edge of the audience, somewhat separated from most of the other Eternals present, wearing simple white robes, both feminine and masculine all at once. They have a set of wings—beautiful flaxen wings, similar to a moth's, the glow emanating from their skin the same shade.

"Protect her from what, exactly?" they demand. "You knew you could not save her. Her death was written in the stars, as sure as the sunrise." As they tilt their head in question, their long, white hair slides over their shoulder.

Levi's eyes narrow in obvious irritation and he snarls back, "Any Eternal would have intervened if they met their mate on the surface. Even *heavenly* eternals like *you*, Rainiel. Let's not forget what kind of paradise you and your siblings have created for those you deem worthy. What I did was protect Rose from the dangers of the Underworld, from all of you and from myself. I made her strong enough to live alongside us. I did what I had to."

Luci lifts a hand toward Rainiel; the white-haired Eternal frowns but slowly sits back down. Then, Luci turns her gaze toward Levi. "You have no need for a mate, Leviathan."

Levi drops my hand and strides forward. "Rose helped me see how incomplete my duty was. All those lost souls roaming the Hellmouth—I've never been able to help them. I've been waiting for *her*. She is the beacon of hope that will guide lost souls out of my labyrinth." His voice resounds through the room with crystal clarity. "I thought you out of all Eternals would understand that, Lucifer. *You* took a human mate. Why shouldn't my choice to do the same be respected?"

Lucifer? The female Eternal standing before me is *the* Lucifer, King—*Queen*—of Hell?

I should have known the devil was a woman. Human history loves to erase our sex from positions of power.

That's when I notice the man in the seat beside hers.

He lounges in his chair, his hand cradling a jaw peppered with golden stubble. Blond hair spills over his forehead and curls around his head like a halo, and his aura… it's white like mine.

The man looks between Levi and Luci, his hand shifting to cover up an amused smile.

Luci glances at me briefly, her eyes so piercing that I shiver. She considers me, her head tilting in thought as the male at her side reaches forward to caress the back of his knuckles against her thigh. His touch seems to bring her out of her head. "My circumstances were very different from yours, Levi. What you are proposing for Rose is an endless existence of hard labor. In the Hellmouth, no less. She will be exposed to the worst souls our universe has to offer. And, like you said before, she is only mortal. She did not even know about our world until a handful of days ago, and now you want to toss her into the deep end? It seems unwise."

My stomach churns. I can tell Lucifer didn't intend that to be an insult, but it definitely felt like one. The words spill out of my mouth before I can think better of it. "I'm perfectly capable of hard work." I step forward until I'm standing next to Levi.

Luci's eyes flash with something akin to delight, and a slap of flesh against marble sounds to my right. I see that Rainiel has decided to reinsert themselves into the discussion, their silver eyes set on me. "Do you even realize what he's done to you, Rose Burroughs?"

I don't care. I don't care what he's done to me. I only care about what he is to me.

In my silence, they continue, "In order to prevent your essence from being absorbed by his mere presence in the Underworld, he altered your *soul*. He placed a mark on you that prevents you from entering heaven. There was a place for you there, with your mother, and he took that away. Now, the only place you can go in the afterlife is hell. Doesn't that make you *angry?*"

When I glance at Levi, he lowers his gaze to floor.

Shame. He feels shame for what he's done. He can't bear to look at me, but I'm not angry with him at all. Maybe I should be, but he did what he thought necessary to protect me. He'd fought against fate itself knowing I was destined to die. I can't imagine the weight he felt knowing what would happen to me—knowing that if I were to die, I'd be taken somewhere he could not follow, that my soul would be fed on for the rest of time by his kind and that he would be alone, without me, forever.

I'm not angry. No, my heart aches for him. I want to tell him he never has to be alone again. I look at Rainiel with a sneer. "From what I hear, heaven isn't all it's cracked up to be."

A few of the Eternals laugh at that while Lucifer and her mate smile. Rainiel, however, isn't so entertained.

They shake their head, their pale eyes chilling me down to the bone. "So cavalier about your eternity," they muse. "So disdainful. Be careful, young lady, or heaven may be tempted to rescind its offer to take you."

"Heaven forbid," I mutter under my breath.

Luci waves her hand at Rainiel, a flippant gesture that conveys exactly how little the devil wants this angel here. "Let's not overwhelm the girl. She's been through quite a lot in a very short period of time." Then, Lucifer turns to me. "Rose, if we were capable of a miracle, if I told you that you have another option, would you be interested in hearing what it is?"

I glance to my right to see that Levi is just as confused as I am.

"What do you mean?" I ask.

"We want to offer you a second life on Earth."

Levi's jaw slackens, and he rocks back a step.

"I want to make it clear that Heaven did *not* agree to this yet," Rainiel grumbles.

The being in the black cloak behind us rumbles, "Is that supposed to matter? You hermits never agree to anything. Leave the meddling to us."

Several others in the room begin to speak, and a low rumble of conversation fills my ears as I reach for Levi's hand. But he walks forward before I can touch him, his eyes trained on Luci. "You expect Rose to give up being an Eternal for another life on that planet?" he demands. "After what her first fate decided? That's cruel."

"I expect her to be given a *choice*," Luci retorts, her tone sharpening. "As any Eternal does. She should have the opportunity to choose the life she truly wants. Mate or not, there is no love—nor is there devotion—without choice. You would do well to remember that, Leviathan."

Levi's hands fist at his sides, but he remains silent. When his eyes shift to me, they linger for a brief moment before flitting away to some spot on the floor. He takes two swift steps away, turning his back to me. He's leaving me to face Luci alone.

Despite my fear, she's smiling kindly when I look up.

After a heartbeat, she sits down, and I think it might be her attempt to put me at ease. Luci's hand drifts sideways and finds her mate's. He turns his head to stare adoringly at her as she continues to study me, and I find myself wondering what *their* circumstances were.

Lucifer finally says, "I have been watching the memories of your past since I learned about you, Rose, trying to understand you. I know what you strove for most in your mortal life: stability, security, prosperity. If you choose to return to Earth, I can ensure that you are placed with a family who gives you those things. You will never know poverty again."

My heart starts pounding. *I have a heart down here?*

"Why would you do that for me?" I whisper.

She shrugs. "We have done it before, for those who believe in it, those who *deserve* it. It is probable that at the end of your next lifetime, the mark Levi made on your soul and the Spark you carry will have faded enough for you to enter Heaven, if the heavenly realm is your desire."

I don't think that is my desire.

Seeing my mom again, of course, is something I want, but I'm not sure Heaven can actually make me happy. I've been happy the last few weeks, ever since Levi came into my life. He makes me feel heard, seen, understood. He makes me feel like the most important person in the universe, just by existing. Even now, I feel his eyes return to me.

I *always* feel him.

I'm starting to believe him—that we're meant for each other. We bring out the parts in each other that are real, that are hidden. I never thought I would be able to believe in a love like that.

"You mentioned a spark," I said quietly. "What did you mean?"

Lucifer glances at her mate, and after a moment of silence, he nods and turns to me, answering my question himself. "The Spark is what makes us Eternals," he explains, his voice a honeyed rumble. "It's like a mortal soul, but more. The original."

My brow furrows. "But if they're only for Eternals, then I wouldn't have a Spark."

"You do," Levi mutters from beside me, "because I created one for you."

I turn to him, my chest tightening, but Levi quickly looks away. I think I'm starting to understand. That ritual wasn't just for him. Those men, their deaths, all that energy he absorbed and fucked into me... they were the cost for my eternity, my *Spark*.

Luci interrupts my thoughts. "You must understand, Rose, that if you choose to return to Earth, you will not remember this life. You will not remember your mother's soul, and she will not meet you at the Gate again. You will live for your future. We simply can't allow you to remember any of this—us or Leviathan."

My heart sinks. There's too much inside of me—too much information, too much feeling, too much heat. This room is cold, and Levi is keeping his distance. All I want is to hold him, to know what's going on behind those green rings. "Leviathan?"

He leans away from me, as if he were willing himself not to wrap me in his arms and steal me away. "It's up to you," he says gruffly.

What Lucifer said must have really struck something in him. This will be my choice alone. He doesn't realize that I love him. He doesn't realize that any devotion I am capable of is his. My human heart is still beating in his chest.

I don't want to forget this life, or my mom. I don't want to forget *him*.

"I want to stay," I murmur.

Levi's head whips up as the rings in his eyes spin wildly,

dilated in surprise. I wait for him to come to me, but he doesn't. He just stands there, staring with immense tenderness, his chest rising and falling erratically. Can Eternals go into shock?

I look at Luci and say it louder. "I want to stay here, with Leviathan."

She only smiles, her red eyes flaring and her lips twisting into a knowing smirk. "Very well. For you to stay, you must formally accept your Spark and the mate bond right here, right now. We will serve as your witnesses. Is that something you are willing to do?"

"Yes." I nod as I feel every set of their eyes burning into my skin, my body vibrating under the attention. The flame in my belly—my *Spark*—burns a little hotter. "Just tell me how."

Luci gestures behind me. "Ask your mate."

I feel him before I even turn around, and as I face him, my chest loosens. He's close enough to touch me, and I so badly want him to touch me. I want to know he still wants me the way he did before, before I asked him to leave, before I hurt him.

Levi is too focused on the task at hand to answer those questions for me. "We need to join hands and interlock them, one over the other." He offers me his hands, and I don't hesitate to give him mine. As our hands join, I shudder at the heat of his palms—so warm and large and gentle. The hardness of his rings is the perfect juxtaposition to his touch.

Luci clears her throat, and Levi begrudgingly looks over at her. "If you ever force your way out of the Underworld again, Leviathan... I'll chain you to the labyrinth."

"Understood," he breathes.

Levi's fingers squeeze mine, and I inch a little closer to him, my heart wholly open for the first time in years. He can't see it yet. He has no idea how much this means to me. He's too fascinated by our interlocked hands, too blinded by his shame and hurt. "You'll have to repeat an oath in the Eternal tongue," he says softly. "I'll go first, and then I will teach you."

I squeeze his fingers in agreement.

He opens his mouth, and the most beautiful consonants I've ever heard roll off his tongue, the flow of them sticky sweet syrup traveling down my spine. I could listen to him speak like that for days. *Hmm. Are there days and nights here?* As he recites the oath, his aura grows in brightness. It wraps thickly around his arms, stretching downward, twining around our hands.

His power taps at my skin. *Let me in, let me in.*

His words stop, and those ropes of magic linger between us, illuminating us both. "What did you say?" I whisper, leaning in like it's a secret between us. "What does it mean?"

"Where you go, I go." His green rings flare. "Where you stay, I stay. I hereby bind myself to you, offering up my Spark so that we may burn together, two flames to one fire."

My stomach flutters as heat fills my limbs, tingling under my skin. I can't fight my happiness, my smile. "Show me how to say it."

Word by word, Levi guides me through the oath, and as he does, his thumb traces small circles into the back of my hand as my aura grows as well. It feels strange—like I'm pulling the life out of my body and drawing it taut in front of him like an offering. It's the most vulnerable I've ever felt, and I know it must be the same for him.

His eyes are anchored in mine, unwavering.

When the last word leaves my mouth, our energies collapse together. His power feeds into me, intensifying the heat in my belly, but he takes from me as well—not nearly as much as he gives, though. My eyes burn as our auras brighten, and I cling to his gaze, that fathomless, eternal darkness.

"Rose," Levi murmurs. "We're supposed to kiss now."

I smile up at him for a moment, quietly relishing in the tickle of power around my wrists, my body swaying forward until my chest brushes his.

"But we don't have to," he adds weakly, "if you don't want to."

"We've made it this far, haven't we? Just kiss me already, before our witnesses riot."

Without another word, he tugs me forward and claims my mouth. I lose myself in my need for him, in the burning dance of our tongues. When his hands thread into my hair and drag me closer, I forget how to breathe. Breathing is secondary, though, as my body melts into him, my arms wrapping tightly around his neck and holding him to me. I'm never letting him go. I am his mate.

It's not until he pulls away that I remember we aren't alone.

Cheeks burning, I glance over, only to find the white seats empty. Either they'd seen enough, or we were kissing for a lot longer than I realized. I return my gaze to Levi to find him staring at me with sleepy eyes, those greens rings blown large.

Levi kisses my forehead and offers me a fleeting smile. "Come, menace. Let's go home."

The Hellmouth emits a sweet, flowery scent. As we stand there, staring at it from the edge of its black island, I understand what Levi meant by honey catching flies—the pull I feel to those black doors is powerful. *Overwhelming.* I can see how wandering souls are lured in.

Levi was explaining the lake as we crossed it. That's where all the souls end up who refuse both heaven and hell. After a while, the soul grows tired of roaming between Earth and the Underworld (because yes, apparently, inter-dimensional travel is possible and ghosts are, in fact, real), and they begin breaking down. The entire lake is liquified spiritual matter.

Once I learned that, I was eager to get out of that boat and back on solid(ish) ground.

Looking up at the Hellmouth, though, I find myself hesitating. I want to go in. Now that I'm Leviathan's mate, I imagine the magnetism of this place appeals to me on an even deeper level. This is my purpose, my future, so what am I going to do if I hate what's inside? This is hell. Can I really be happy in a place that absorbs all the evil that enters it?

"Go ahead," Levi whispers, his mouth hovering over my ear. "No reason to be afraid."

His hand presses against my lower back to nudge me forward. "Even if you are afraid, I'm sure we could find a way to make it please you." There's humor in this voice, but I hear the hesitation behind it too. He's as nervous as I am.

I roll my shoulders back and approach the doors.

Winding snakes are carved into ebony wood. It's from no tree I've ever seen on Earth, but I can tell it's raw—there are ashen knots and irregular charcoal streaks every few feet of lumber, carved with hundreds, maybe even *thousands*, of the most beautiful, tangled serpents with eyes that gleam with jagged, sapphire crystals. Now that I'm closer to them, I think the honeyed scent is actually coming *from* the wood.

I have the oddest certainty that these doors came from the tree Levi once guarded, the tree that gave humans their eternal souls.

A lure no human can resist.

Lifting a hand to the wood, I trace a snake from head to tail. This is exactly like *him*, I suddenly realize—these beauti-ful, wild, vicious snakes—which gives me hope that whatever I find beyond these doors will be like him too. If that's true, I couldn't hate any part of it, even the scariest bits.

I pull the door open and enter my new home.

The scent of vanilla and cinnamon hits me instantly. It heats my blood, every muscle in my body relaxing as I look around at what appears to be a perfectly normal entryway. It's a hall with another set of black doors at the end of it. To my left, about halfway down the corridor, the wall opens to a large staircase that winds out of sight. The floors beneath us are a polished blend of black and cherry wood, the walls painted black with white wainscoting all the way down.

I can tell that this is the part of the Hellmouth designed for mortal traffic. The floor and doors at the end of the hall emanate the same undeniable scent of the entrance, guiding souls exactly where they need to go.

Levi strolls past me down the hall. His hands fold behind him as he speaks, his voice bouncing off the walls and escorting me forward. "I won't give you a full tour of the labyrinth right now, as I'm sure you need some time to process what you've seen up to this point, but you'll get acquainted with it soon. It's on the other side of these doors." He grips the bronze handles and swings the doors open.

Tall walls of concrete appear, sprawling with vines and moss; it looks like the entrance to a garden. I hear songbirds chirping from deeper in, smell the beckoning scent of rain-drenched soil and flowers. It's all deceitfully welcoming.

He glances back at me, a sly smile on his face. "It's all a bit more monstrous from here."

"I thought so." I amble up to the doors, crossing my arms to keep from touching the wood. "But it can't hurt me, right?"

"I mean, it *could*," he says with a shrug. My eyes widen, and he laughs. "But it won't," he adds. "As my mate, the labyrinth will accept you the same way it accepts me. We're an ecosystem. The entire Underworld is."

"And now I'm a part of that system," I murmur, watching as a curious darkness swirls ahead, gathering at the end of the maze's first alley. It doesn't feel malicious to me... but then again, my soul can't be eaten.

Levi shuts the doors, and I shift my gaze to him as he leans against the doorframe with crossed arms. "Do you regret it?" he murmurs, waiting for my answer with a blank expression.

It feels like he's still distancing himself from me, and I don't like it. Maybe I did push him too far when I pushed him away. Maybe he's angry with me and only took me in because I asked. I wish I knew for certain, but I'm not going to broach the subject, just in case. I don't want him to touch me because he feels obligated. Also, I'm not entirely sure I could handle his rejection after everything we've been through.

"No," I reply quietly. "I just hope I can be of help to you. I'm in your world now, and I've got about a million questions. I don't know what I'm doing."

He nods. "I only want you to be yourself. If you have questions, ask them freely. There are no more secrets between us."

The words are sweet, but his eyes are cool.

"Am I supposed to sleep here? Or some other place in the labyrinth?" I ask.

He pushes himself off the door. "Our living quarters are upstairs." Levi ambles past me, and I mutely follow him.

The wainscoting ends at the first turn of the staircase, and then there's only black and iron surrounding us as we ascend. The steps open to a second floor and an almost identical hall to the one below us. There's art on these walls, and the floor doesn't radiate the same seduction of the first floor. Hardy white columns are aligned one either side of the hall—

Oh my god.

These are the same columns that were on the house my mom and I used drive by when I was a kid, except on these pillars, a pair of snakes are carved into them, twining up to the vaulted ceiling. I walk up to the nearest column and trace my fingertips over the delicate white scales.

Levi follows me, skirting to the other side of the column to study my reaction.

I lift my eyes to his as I realize something. "That's why

you call me little snake. You were always calling me your mate."

He braces his shoulder against the column with a grimace. "Yes, I was." I stare at him, my chest tingling, and after a moment, he adds, "I spent a long time down here, waiting for you, preparing for you. Time moves differently in Underworld. Sometimes, it speeds by, but at other times, it slows to a crawl. Those years after I met you felt like many decades."

Levi's eyes burn, lined with luminous vulnerability.

In a small voice, I ask a question that has been on my mind since I sent him away. "If I was yours, how could you leave me with him?"

His eyes shutter, and those elegant blue brows pull together. "How could I stay? There was no breaking the deal I made. At least if you were a part of that deal, I knew I could keep a close eye on you. You got what you wanted out of Walter in the meantime."

"He was terrible to me."

Levi steps forward until his chest is pressed against mine. His hand loops around my waist, and I crane my neck to look into his eyes. "And he paid for it dearly, believe me," he swears. "He will pay for how he treated you for many centuries yet."

Leviathan's other hand lifts to caress my cheek, and my eyes flutter at that whisper of affection. It's such a gentle, hesitant touch.

But then he pulls away, and the absence of him draws me up short. My eyes flash open, and I see he's already striding down the hallway. "Come," he tosses over his shoulder. "Your room is this way."

There are several doors in this hallway. Levi walks to one on the right side of the corridor and opens it before he flattens his back against the door to let me walk in ahead of him. The walls are black in here, with silvery dots and lines embossed throughout the wallpaper. Large windows border either side of the wall directly across from us, and a gentle silver light filters in from outside. A bed sits in the center of the room between the windows, the headboard an intricate formation of spirals and columns, sleek panels rising nearly to the ceiling. The duvet and sheets are pitch black, and bright red rose petals are scattered across the bed and around the foot of the bed frame. I feel the supernatural pull to it—it must have been made with more of that wood from the tree of life. I'm so distracted by the bed that I don't immediately recognize the room.

When I do, tears well in my eyes.

I take a few steps inside and turn in place. The old-world charm of the dark wooden furniture. The iron pattern on the windowpanes and the black lace curtained on either side of them. I know this room.

A long time ago, the house my mom and I used to dream about was put on the market. My mom had already passed. I was barely a freshman in college, in no place to purchase any kind of property, but I went to look at it anyway. It was my goodbye to the dream we had together. This had been the master bedroom. It's an exact replica, save for the bed.

I look at Levi, who stands a few feet behind me with his hands in his pockets. "Why does it look like this?" I whisper.

Levi's eyes darken. "You don't like it?"

"I do, it's just—" I flounder for the right words. "How did you *know*?"

"About the house? You dreamed of it many times, and I saw how happy it made you." He walks toward me. "But I can make changes if you want. Whatever makes you most comfortable—this is *your* space."

I shake my head vehemently, looking around at it again. "This is perfect."

My eyes catch on a bundle of color sitting amongst the pillows on the bed, and my heart skips again as I rush across the room to it. The magnetism of the bed gets stronger as I approach, tempting me to strip down and rub my skin all over the wood, but I ignore it for now. I snatch up the beanie baby, turning it over and over in my hands. It's exactly the same: a curly little snake with a bright red tongue and green belly, the burn mark on its head from that time I had jumped onto my unsuspecting mother's lap while she was smoking. Orange stitches are sewn clumsily into its tail from when it got caught in a door, this thread the only color my mom had on hand.

I glance over my shoulder at Levi, my vision watery. "Levi, I don't know how you found this... but thank you."

He nods, and shy smile blooms over his lips. "You haven't even seen the best part yet."

Levi takes a step forward, offering me his hand. I place the beanie baby back where I found it, patting its head before I turn and take Levi's hand. He pulls me toward one of the windows on the back wall, and I realize that the pane here is actually a door.

He pushes it open, and we walk out onto a balcony together.

The balcony has no railing: it's just a flat white podium looking out over a massive green and gray maze. City lights glitter beyond that, the sky dark above us—if you can even call it a sky. It looks like a black blanket, with small holes that seem to peer out into other galaxies. Millions of swirling stars—that's where that silvery light is coming from. There's no moon.

It's beautiful and disorienting, but I'm sure I'll get used to it.

Levi points at the distant city. "That's Hell; the upper-most level, at least. The hellish Eternals live up here and commute downwards for work underneath the city. I can take you there sometime if you want. You'd love uptown. There are a few clubs there for former humans, the mates and other mortals who have a place here with us. They can help you acclimate."

"Oh, I didn't realize we were that common."

He scoffs. "You aren't, trust me. But the human citizens add up after several centuries."

"Fair point," I say around a chuckle. "I look forward to meeting them."

Levi nods, his eyes pinching a little. He slinks back into my bedroom, and I follow, my core thrumming, my heart leaping as I wait for him to grab me and throw me down on the magical bed. I'm ready for him to have his wicked way with me again, and now that I'm dead, I wonder if I'll ever get tired, or if we could just keep going indefinitely. I want to be with him until I forget what it was like to be apart.

But he doesn't touch me. He barely even looks at me.

Levi gestures to a door on the far end of the bedroom "My room is right next to yours. We have a conjoining door, so don't hesitate to knock if you'd ever like to see me."

My brow furrows. "We aren't sharing?"

He shifts his gaze to the floor between us. "I thought you might appreciate having your own space, especially at first. The adjustment to being an Eternal is... a lot of pressure, and I have no intention of forcing myself on you in any capacity. Not anymore. You've made it clear how you feel about me. We're mates, but we can just be... *friends*, if that's what you prefer."

It feels like I've been dumped into that terrifying lake

outside, like spirits are hurtling down my throat again, choking me. Does he really think I don't want him?

Or maybe this is an excuse for him, his way *out*?

Before I can speak, he starts backing away, his eyes flicking around the room in detached satisfaction. "I'm glad you like your room, Rose. I'll go ahead and give you some time to settle in. Tomorrow, we'll begin your training down in the labyrinth. There's a bathroom beyond that door," he points to another door behind me, "and your new clothing, dresses and nightgowns and the like, is in the closet behind the shower. If you need anything else, just let me know."

My head spins as he walks to the door leading to his room. My heart pounds, anxious blood rushing in my ears as he walks through it and leaves me all alone.

As the door shuts behind him, my shock bleeds into disappointment, and then my disappointment bleeds into anger. All that time he spent stalking me and pining for me, and he chooses *now* to put space between us? After my soul is irrevocably changed and I'm truly alone in this strange new world? When we finally *have* each other again?

No. It's not happening like this.

I barge into his bedroom without knocking to find him standing beside his bed, undressing. He drops his hands and turns to me with a concerned look, his black shirt hanging unbuttoned and untucked on either side of his abdomen.

Glaring, I stalk across the room. "You know, I just started getting used to the idea of you being a demon. This isn't the time to start acting like an asshole too."

His eyes widen in surprise, and then a small huff of laughter escapes him. "I assure you, little snake, I am not a sphincter." His eyes are sparkling like emeralds.

Hearing him call me that name soothes some of the tension in my chest. I'm still his mate. He still wants me—he has to. No more running, no more hiding, not unless it's a game we play for our pleasure.

I halt in front of him and say the bravest thing I can think of. "I'm in love with you."

Levi's face slackens. He looks lost for a moment, drifting at sea. Then, he blinks and a hardness returns to his eyes. I don't know what to call that emotion; it's like anger and sadness combined, and I don't understand why he would feel those things right now.

Unless he doesn't want me.

I start drifting too, into the sea of fear I thought I had already conquered. He was supposed to be my lighthouse, but now, I'm struggling to see the light. I thought he was going to be my way back home.

He takes a slow step toward me, his large pale hands clenching at his sides, knuckles lit up with that undulating power beneath his skin. "Rose, do you even realize how close you were to damnation because of me? They could have sent you into the depths of hell just as easily as heaven or Earth. Some of them wanted to hurt you just to punish me." There's violence in his confession, and I realize what's really going on here.

He's not angry with me. He's angry with himself.

I simply shake my head. "I don't care."

The rings in Leviathan's gaze still for a heartbeat, but then they start spinning again, wild and large. He steps closer to me, and I realize his body is trembling.

Halting a hands-breadth away, he lowers his face until we're sharing breath, his nose grazing mine. "I would have crawled into the pit of hell to find you if they had sent you there. And if they sent you back to Earth, I would have stopped at nothing to rip your soul from the clutches of heaven again and again to bring you back to me. I wouldn't have regretted any of it. That's who I am. That's the kind of Eternal you're saying you love."

"I know," I whisper, smiling sweetly at him.

He smiles back then, a flash of teeth that's sharp and bright and warm.

"And my room is beautiful," I continue softly, "but I don't want to spend half of my time somewhere you won't be. I don't want to sleep in that bed without you beside me." I touch his face, feathering my fingertips down over his cheekbone.

He catches my hand, flattening my palm against his cheek. "Then I suppose I'll have to move my things in."

I wrap my arms around his neck and nod, my heart lightening. "I'd like that."

Levi kisses me, and I fall into his embrace for a moment, floating in his arms as he slides his lips against mine in a slow tangle.

A rumble vibrates under our feet, and I jump back, looking down at the shifting flooring. That's when I notice the desk, bookshelves, and a set of two sitting chairs in his room. The lurid blue waterfall cascading into a small pool on the floor on the opposite side, a white stone barrier embedded in the floorboards. A painting easel and a table full of brushes sit next to his bed, and I watch as they soften and bend and shift. It would seem that the rooms are little more than an illusion—a fantasy that can be molded to Levi's will, made real with the power of his mind. His bed warps until it becomes the bed that was in my room, this time a little larger. The walls around us stretch until this room envelops the one next door, and all of our belongings meld together. A room made for not one or the other, but for both of us.

When I return my eyes to Levi, he smirks. "Is it too much?"

"No. I love it even more now." I launch up and press a kiss to the corner of his mouth.

Levi grabs a fistful of my hair and brings my lips fully over his. His kiss this time is conquering, and I let him claim every inch of my mouth with his tongue, dancing my own between those narrow, forked points. I moan softly, melting around the heat building in my belly, but too soon, he starts pulling away. I bite his lower lip, trying to urge him back to me, but to my dismay, he breaks off the kiss.

Before I can ask what the fuck his problem is, the floor starts moving again. I gasp and cling to Levi's shoulders as the ground turns like a dial. Levi chuckles, leaning in to nuzzle my neck as the room shifts, the wall opening up until we're standing outside on the balcony, looking out over the labyrinth again.

Levi's hands rise to the tiny straps of my gown.

As he pulls them down my arms and the gown drops below my breasts, he smiles a wicked, serpentine grin. "Do you want to play with me again, little snake?"

CHAPTER 36

BE A GOOD GIRL, EVEN IN HELL

Levi pushes the gown's straps until I'm exposed down to the waist. I allow my eyes to flutter shut as he leans down to bury his nose in my hair, his hot breath caressing the crown of my head.

Then, his hands shift, his palms grasping at my sensitive breasts, his fingers playing with my puckered nipples. "Every inch of you is divine," he purrs.

My Spark twirls in my stomach, growing heavier, pulverizing what's left of my self-control as I shove my gown down over my hips. Then, I wrap my arms around his neck, threading my fingers into his silky blue hair as I kiss him.

His hands travel lower, squeezing my hips, gliding around to cup my ass. He grinds my naked body against his hardness, and I'm seconds away from climbing him like a tree. I grapple with his clothing, my fingers fumbling as I start snarling in desperation.

Levi chuckles, his head tilting. "Frustrated, menace?"

As I look up into his amused green eyes, my Spark spins faster, whipping the insides of my abdomen with vicious heat. I shove the shirt off his shoulders, then his pants before I begin lowering myself to my knees, but he catches me with a hand around my neck.

Levi forces me upright, his gaze scorching as he drags my face to his.

He kisses me gently, slowly.

After Leviathan kicks his pants the rest of the way off, he gathers me in his arms. My thighs wrap around his waist as he picks me up and kneels, deepening the kiss to something that makes me think we've touched souls. My body settles over his lap, his length rubbing against my slit, and I break off the kiss to grind myself against him with a gasp.

His hands grasp my hips, but he doesn't take control like I expect. No, he draws encouraging lines up and down my thighs, his tongue reclaiming my mouth as he lets me writhe. My legs are trembling. I need him. I need to be one with him again, consumed by him.

I whimper into his mouth, and he laughs.

Wrapping my arms tighter around his neck, I rise up his length again, but this time, I lift high enough for the head of his cock to prod my entrance. I hesitate, a wicked smile crawling across my mouth. "Maybe I shouldn't let you inside me. You're the monster from my nightmares. This is *wrong*."

He gives me a vicious smile, catching onto my little game right away. "But you're the perfect temptation, little snake. So tight and ready. To deny me would be cruel."

I nod, fluttering my eyes with feigned innocence. "Just the tip, then. That's all. Any more than that, and you'll corrupt me entirely." I moan as I lower myself a little more into his lap, rising back up sooner than I wanted. "You're *my* monster, Leviathan. *Mine.*"

I keep moving just like that—up and down, slowly fucking the head of his cock.

His breath grows ragged as he watches me. He tightens his grip on my hips, his hands hot and trembling with restraint as the tiniest glimmer of savagery flashes through his eyes. "I could never corrupt you, menace. I might be your monster, but you're my good girl, and you always will be."

With that, all illusion of holding back evaporates, and my Spark explodes as I lower myself onto his cock, taking it all. Strangled moans escape both of us as I take him to the hilt. We aren't even kissing anymore—we're only exchanging air between our parted lips.

Levi recovers before I do, nuzzling my nose and kissing every inch of my face he can. He whispers against the corner of my mouth, "Show me how much you love me, mate." All the names he calls me... I love them. I love him. His hands lift my hips an inch, urging me to move.

I don't need to be told again. Squeezing his hips with my thighs, I slide up and down his length, shuddering as he tilts his pelvis in tandem. It's a delicious, slow seduction, our mouths barely grazing. Still, it feels like we're kissing, like we're merged *everywhere*. The head of his cock kicks against my front wall each time I drop back down, the heat of him heightening every sensation, driving me mad with pleasure.

The rest of my patience slips away.

Bracing my hands on his shoulders, I push with all my might, flattening his back against the floor. My hands find his chest as I ride him, chasing my pleasure as I look into his glowing green eyes. He smirks up at me, his amusement and obvious admiration only making me fuck him harder. I feel so warm—like my belly is on fire. Tingles raze across my skin, and I rise sharply to that luminous release.

"That's it. Come all over my evil cock, menace," Levi croons in a dark voice.

My mind shatters into a billion tiny pieces. As the

rhythm of my body stutters, Levi swiftly sits up, taking my hair in one hand and sliding his other between our bodies to circle my clit. Another wave of pleasure crashes over me, and my lips part in a silent scream.

Achy bliss radiates through my limbs as I collapse against Leviathan's chest.

He captures my jaw and kisses me deeply. I'm trembling as he wraps an arm around my back and flips us over, thrusting into me deep, hard enough to make my back slide against the ground, his growls loud and wild.

Inch by torturous inch, he fucks me until my head hangs off the edge of the balcony.

He smiles monstrously. "Look at your new realm, baby."

Then, he lifts my hips, rutting into me with smooth, measured thrusts. He's holding off on his pleasure, but I don't want him to hold off—I want to feel him burst open inside me, to fill me until there's nothing else to think about.

"Levi," I whimper.

"*Look at it,*" he growls, his eyes flicking to the labyrinth behind me.

I let my skull fall back against the balcony's edge, blood swelling in my head. My core is tightening, but I manage to ignore it long enough to see what's waiting below.

The labyrinth comes into focus. Giant, gnashing jaws snap up at us. Hounds pace with red eyes and black coats. Stringy black worms twist from one side of the maze to the other in mere seconds. Shadows. Nightmares. They know we're here.

Somehow, I know they don't want to hurt me. They're... *welcoming* me.

Levi latches his mouth onto my nipple and sucks, bringing me back to him. "Does the labyrinth scare you, little snake?" he muses around my flesh. "Does it turn you on?"

My head swims. "*You* turn me on," I whisper. "*Please*, Leviathan. I'm so close."

He shifts his mouth to my other breast, sucking hard and drawing a deep groan from my throat. "Anything you want, I'll give to you," he promises. He licks the space between my breasts. "I heard you praying to me after you sent me away. You asked me to come back to you when I couldn't, but pray to me again now, little snake. Ask me to come for you now, and I will."

My hands tangle in his hair. "Please, Leviathan, come with me. I want to be full of you."

With a low groan, I feel him erupt, and I gasp as his cock expands, the spheres clinging to my inner walls. The pressure threatens to push me over the edge, but before it does, Levi drags me upright in his lap, and I whimper as the new position sinks him even deeper.

His jaw clenches as he keeps himself from coming. I try to move, but he holds me in place, pushing hair out of my face so he can look into my eyes. "You're never getting away from me now. Anywhere you go, I will be with you. I will be a part of you, and you will be a part of me."

"That's all I want," I breathe.

Leviathan releases a harsh breath and lets go of my hips. I ride him again, showing him exactly how much I love him, how much I need him as his hands roam my body, squeezing and scratching and manipulating my limbs. He pulls me as close to him as possible before he comes, his groans slipping into what I now recognize as the Eternal tongue. The ancient words slither straight to my core, and I fall into pleasure with him, clenching around him as he empties himself into me.

We remain there for long minutes, wrapped in each other. At some point, the floor starts moving us back into the bedroom. I look around at it again, and my eyes burn with tears. The little beanie baby sticks his tongue out at us from its cozy perch on the bed. This place is *mine*.

I swallow my tears and whisper, "I've never had a home like this before—somewhere safe, something that... can't be taken away. Thank you." Then, my tears fall anyway.

My demon smiles at me before he turns his face into my hair, inhaling my scent and cradling my face in his hands. As he pulls back, his thumbs caress the curve of my cheeks. "That's not true, little snake. From the moment we met, I have been yours entirely. I love you with all that I am, all that I was, and all I ever will be."

EPILOGUE

I glow in the labyrinth—bright white.

The magic of the labyrinth brings Sparks to the surface, which makes finding human souls all the more difficult, considering they don't have one. Instead, I rely on the hounds' keen sense of spirit to track them down. Them, and the map Leviathan etched into my chest.

The hounds are my companions in this place; at least four or five of them stick close to me at all times. I'm pretty sure Levi put the pack up to it. He wants them close, to protect me from any violent, wayward soul that might lash out, especially when I'm participating in the hunt.

The darkness of the labyrinth stirs around my feet as I run. I glance backwards, watching the soul follow me around corner after corner of the maze.

My role in this place was so much easier to fall into than I thought it would be. I'm not just a seeker, but a lure too, when the circumstances demand it—when a mouse is hiding a little too well within the maze.

That's why I'm running from the soul behind me. I draw it deeper into the labyrinth, towards the monster waiting at its center. As I face forward again, a vicious smile graces my lips as I make the final turn. I glance down and watch the dot of brighter blue under my skin near the epicenter. My stomach warms in delighted recognition as I step into the core of the labyrinth. A wide, concrete circle with several offshoots stretch out around me, but I turn towards the one I just emerged from and wait.

The soul staggers in, puttering to a slow stop as his eyes fix on me.

Another man, another meal.

As he steps forward, wicked intent in his eye, the hounds start to growl, and the darkness at my feet billows upward, caressing my legs with possessive curls. The man halts, seeming to finally see more than my glow. As the darkness turns toward him with a dissonant chuckle, his face falls, and he starts backing away—but it's too late. The paths behind him have already sealed, and a large figure stands waiting.

There he is. *My mate.*

His form pulses with a soft teal glow, highlighting his pale skin and black clothes. He wears a hungry grin, and power undulates wildly under his skin. With all the smoothness of a slithering snake, he walks forward, his hand reaching up to pull the blade from his hair. A thrill courses through my body as I watch his dark blue hair tumble down around his shoulders.

He is so beautiful in the labyrinth; savage, but beautiful.

The human soul barely gets the chance to turn around and see him before Levi has his hand around the man's neck. He lifts him off the ground and thrusts his blade into the soft skin beneath the soul's jaw. Death ripples out over the labyrinth, and the hounds howl at the commotion. Even the ground shakes in anticipation as Levi opens his mouth. His jaw stretches down, opening until he can fit the soul between his lips at last. He shoves the entire body into his mouth in one, long swallow. The soul collapses in the funnel of his throat, and a heartbeat later, there's no trace of him left except for the enhanced glow emanating from Levi's skin and the green rings in his black eyes.

Those eyes train on me, and Levi lifts his hand, beckoning me closer with one finger.

That flame in my belly jumps to attention, and I immediately rush forward, eager for the taste I know Levi will give me. I need to feed my Spark now, too. That's been the hardest adjustment: these new meals. As soon as I'm within arm's reach, Levi pulls me into him, tilting my head up to receive his offering. Our lips meet, and I surrender as his mouth pries mine open, slipping his tongue in, guiding the death down my throat. I focus on the twirling of his tongue and the softness of his lips, forcing myself not to taste it. I don't let it linger in my mouth. Thankfully, Levi always feeds me like this. He chases the bitter taste with his sweetness.

By the time he pulls away, I'm warm and satisfied, completely death-drunk.

He smiles down at me, affectionately pinching my chin. "Beautiful job, little snake."

"How will I be rewarded?" I whisper, leaning heavily on him.

His eyes glitter as he laughs. "Oh, I have an idea or two."

I'm leaning in for another kiss when I hear it: a high-pitched cry echoing from one of the labyrinth's many paths. The sound sobers me, and I step out of Levi's arms to turn toward it. When I glance back at my mate, I can tell he heard the same helplessness in it that I had.

He smiles sadly and gives me an encouraging nod.

Levi won't be able to help me with this one.

The hounds accompany me as I take off after the new spirit. A pup noses my fingers every few turns to remind me that it's there, trying to calm me as my heart starts to race all over again. The other hounds race ahead; they've caught the scent now, and we give chase, delving farther and farther into the maze.

The little spirit is running from us.

I don't blame it. There's a lot to run from here, even if the labyrinth would never intentionally hurt an innocent. Sometimes, it's inevitable, though, if they get too close to the other end, where the maze leads into the city. The labyrinth is designed to prevent that at all costs. We're nearing that final archway now.

The labyrinth walls shift around us, guiding the soul towards a dead end instead.

When the hounds direct me around the last turn and I finally see who we've chasing, my stomach drops. It's a child, like I thought. He trembles at the end of the aisle, curled into a ball and hiding his face in his knees. A surprising number of souls who get lost in this maze are children. They fall out of the boat before it can take them to the gates of heaven, or they try to swim in the lake, caught up in the sweet scent of the Hellmouth. The first time I found a child here, I cried for hours afterward. Levi did his best to console me, but it was just a hard realization, that even in the afterlife, bad things happen to those who don't deserve it.

I suppose that's exactly why I'm here.

Eternals don't feed off of children. Eternals can't have offspring, but even *they* recognize the purity of a young soul. Levi said most children are even given the same choice I was —an opportunity to go back to Earth, to live again, if they want to. That knowledge makes sending them off to heaven a lot easier. That, and knowing enough time has likely passed here that their family would be waiting for them at the golden gate.

"Hey," I call, walking across the vine-latticed concrete toward him. "It's okay."

The child hugs his legs even tighter, shaking as I draw closer, so I get on my hands and knees and crawl to him.

"It's all going to be okay," I try again. "I'm here to help you, I promise. I'm going to guide you to a happier place. There's no reason to be afraid anymore."

I wait a few minutes as his body slowly calms. Then, hesitantly, he lifts his head. His eyes are bright blue under a mop of black hair and a million freckles, and when he sees me, his eyes round at the edges. He lifts his head even higher, and I smile encouragingly, stretching a hand toward him.

"Are you an angel?" he asks, the words tinged in awe.

I chuckle. "No, but would you like to see one?"

I lead him out of the labyrinth, the hounds jumping and yelping around us in excitement, the boxy creatures leaping forward to lick his little face. The child smiles at them, and I wonder how long it's been since he was able to do that—smile.

The hounds halt at the entrance to the house, sitting back on their haunches, preparing to wait for my return. The child looks curiously around the hall as we walk down in. "I think I've been here before."

Nodding, I reply, "You have."

"It smells so good," he whispers. "But I couldn't find the candy."

My chest squeezes painfully. "Nothing here is exactly what it seems." I open the door to the lake and lead him onto the black rock. "But everything will be okay, as long as you follow my instructions."

His eyes catch on the lake, and he starts backing away, shaking his head. "No. Not the lake. I was lost in there for so, so long."

I kneel in front of the boy and hold his shoulders. "You do not need to be afraid, little one. There's a boat for you. When it comes, sit on the center of the bench and don't look over the edge. Don't move until your boat arrives at the next island. Someone will be waiting for you—an angel, just like you want." I smile at him, swallowing the urge to tell him the angels aren't quite what they seem either.

His wide eyes flick back and forth between mine. "Do you promise?" he whispers.

"Yes," I tell him. "I promise. Everything will be okay."

Then, I withdraw a golden coin from my dress and offer it to him.

Leviathan was telling the truth about the labyrinth, about the Underworld as a whole. It really is an ecosystem, and it accepted me immediately. Whenever I need a coin, I always seem to find one in my pocket.

The child's eyes light up when they see it. He recognizes the coin—truly, it would be an impossible thing to forget. He swipes it out of my hand and runs to the water's edge, throwing it with all his might into the lake.

A boat bursts out of the water with as much force as the coin was thrown in, crashing down and gliding swiftly toward us before it beaches right in front of the child.

He glances at me over his shoulder, smiling brightly, tears in his eyes. "I remember."

I nod and back away as he clambers into the boat. The crystal lady on the bow opens her eyes once he's seated and smiles at me. She's another Eternal, one of the most ancient among them. Her name is Styx, but she doesn't talk to me much (not a single word, really). At first, I thought it was because she didn't like me, but Levi assured me she's just the quiet type, an Eternal set apart from both heaven and hell, much like my mate.

She's someone I would like to get to know, I think. Maybe sometime in the next century or two.

When she's not ferrying souls, she doesn't lounge in the bowels of hell like Levi and me. She has a space of her own beneath the lake, and she keeps company with the angels of heaven, though I often wonder why. The rare, amused gleam I catch in her eyes sometimes makes me think she wouldn't fit in there.

One thing I've learned about angels: they are serious creatures. *Too* serious.

The boat pulls out onto the lake and eventually becomes a speck in the distance. The sudden flash of light as the gates open is unmistakable, and I release the heavy sigh captive in my lungs. He's finally safe.

Turning around, I see Leviathan waiting for me on the threshold of the house, and a grin bursts across my face as I run to him. He catches me as I leap into his arms, and together, we stagger into the hall as Levi toes the door closed, capturing my mouth in a breathtaking kiss. For a moment, I sink into the sensation of being his.

"I have a surprise for you," he says when we finally break apart some minutes later.

"You always do," I tease with a roll of my eyes.

"This one is *big*."

I laugh. "Oh, really? I thought you already were."

His green rings flare a little brighter, but he bites his lip to bring his Spark under control. "Focus, menace. You have plenty of time to be naughty later."

My eyebrows raise. "Wow, this is serious, isn't it?"

In one fluid motion, he crouches and folds me over his shoulder, spinning on his heel to carry me up the stairs. I giggle into his back; some things never change.

He brings us to the third floor of the house. I haven't had much time for exploring, but I know every room in this place is magical. It's filled with a thousand wonders, portals that lead into different pockets of the world. The one he carries me into now looks like a jungle, with hanging vines and colorful foliage and lime green trees all over. It's humid as hell, pun intended. It must have rained recently, because there's a fine misting of water everywhere.

"You better not be fucking me in here," I grumble. "It's too hot."

He sets me back on my feet. "No, but now you've got me thinking about all the fun we could have with the vines."

"*Rose,*" a shockingly familiar voice calls from a distance.

I spin, already on the verge of tears as my eyes land on my mom standing between two gnarled tree trunks a few yards away. She waves at me, her eyes eager but threaded with fear as they flick between me and Levi and our surroundings. I'm tempted to run to her, but I hesitate. These rooms are capable of many things, and fabricating the visage of my mother is not beyond their scope of power.

My hand tightens on Levi's forearm as I look back at him. "Is this real?"

"I had some help." He nods at the figure emerging from the trees beside my mother.

Rainiel. The angel who was in Lucifer's audience when I first arrived.

Levi clears his throat and inches toward the door, grimacing. "I'll wait for you out in the hall. I can't get too close to her without the gate separating us."

I catch his hand, my eyes brimming over with tears as I whisper, "Thank you, Levi."

"Anything you desire," he reminds me just before he turns and silently slips into the hall.

As I rush over to my mother, Rainiel passes by, acknowledging me with a tight nod. They look annoyed, and I can't help but wonder what Leviathan exchanged to get them to agree to this little task. Probably some kind of energy transference. The heavenly Eternals are always eager for additional meals, considering the ration laws they have to abide by.

I turn my full attention to my mom. She doesn't move toward me right away; I think she might be afraid to, but once I'm close enough to look into her eyes, she breaks free of her reticence and launches herself at me, her plush arms drawing me into a hug. Oh, I've missed the way she hugs—so tight, it's almost painful, as if she were trying to convey how hard she loves me with the force of her affection.

I can't help it. I start weeping into her shoulder.

"Shh," she croons, rubbing my back. "It's okay. I'm here."

I laugh through my tears. "I know." I pull away to look at her face, re-memorizing it. "I'm so happy to see you."

She sighs, and I can almost feel her relief. "Me too. I was so worried after you couldn't get through the gate. They told me you couldn't get in, but I knew that had to be a mistake. Are they getting it sorted out? Why are they keeping you here?"

Her barrage of questions overwhelm me, so I take it one at a time. "This is my home."

She looks around once more, apprehension in her eyes. "This jungle?"

"No, no," I laugh. "This is just a room in what's called the Hellmouth—it's Leviathan's home, and now it's mine, because... well, because I'm his mate."

I swallow hard, waiting for her reaction. I watch the cogs turning behind her dark blue eyes before she glances to some place behind me, and when I follow her gaze, I see she's staring at Leviathan, visible through the open door.

"I remember him," she mutters. "He requested to see me a few times at the gate, asking questions about you—he's a demon."

Tension wraps around my spine, hard enough that it feels like my heart is bruising the inside of my ribs. What do I say? How do I explain? I take a deep breath. "Yes, he's a demon, but that's not what you think it is. He's not really that different from the angels in heaven, and the Eternals here might even be more compassionate when it comes to humans, because at least they choose—"

"Rosie Posie," she cuts off my rambling and cradles my face. "Is he good to you?"

"More than," I breathe. "He loves me, Mama, and I love him."

She smiles slowly. "Then I'm so happy for you."

New tears well in my eyes, and I surge forward to hug her again. "Thank you," I gasp. I wish I could hug my mom forever, but I know that's not possible. She'll have to leave eventually. She'll have to return with Rainiel whenever they decide our time is up.

When I pull away, I ask, "What about you? Are you happy in heaven?"

My mom nods, that gentle smile lingering. "Yes. It's comfortable there, and I've met so many wonderful people. There's one man in particular I've grown very attached to. We, uh, we live together." Her entire face reddens.

I raise a brow at her. "You're dating again?"

She laughs. "What else am I supposed to do with my eternity? Besides, there's not nearly as many selfish assholes there, so the whole experience is a lot calmer than it used to be."

"Well, good. You can use some of that eternity to visit me now." I squeeze her hands.

"Yes, I can." Her smile falters as she glances at the hallway again, where Levi and Rainiel are conversing. "Although, I'm not as eager to spend more time with that angel. They're one of the guardians—not nearly as friendly as the angels who roam within the gates."

I nod, and after a moment, I muster the courage to ask, "Do the angels treat you well?"

She sighs through her nose. "Of course, honey. Their visits are exhausting sometimes, but they are gentle." A thought brightens her eyes, and she chuckles to herself. "Honestly, the whole arrangement reminds me of when I used to breastfeed you. We sustain them. It could be worse."

Then, my mom shrugs, and my heart hurts a little bit. It makes too much sense that she would brush off the reality of heaven. She's too strong to complain, and she's certainly felt and seen much worse.

I grimace. "I guess there's no convincing you to stay here with me, is there?"

She shakes her head, continuing to smile so I know it's her choice. "No, honey."

I'll admit, she seems sure, so at peace. She deserves a little bit of peace after all she's been through, so I don't push it. I won't ruin anything for her. Instead, I gather her into another hug, closing my eyes as she squeezes me tightly. "I love you, Mom."

"I love you too," she rasps, and her next inhale catches in her throat. "And I am so proud of you for following your heart. I know I-I didn't make that easy for you."

Somehow, those words are everything, mending a deep, bleeding wound in my heart.

"You did your best," I tell her. "I forgive you."

Because after all, in the end, isn't that the most any of us can do?

THE END

THE SPICE LIST
BURNS YOU'LL WANT A SECOND
DEGREE OF

ACKNOWLEDGMENTS

Thank you to everyone who made this book possible.

First, to my wonderful husband, who has always and will always be my biggest and most valued supporter. You are a dream of love come true.

Then, to my readers. My passion is to tell stories like this one, and I wouldn't be able to do it without you.

To my author friends who have taken Rose's journey alongside me—I love you guys. Shannon (my dearest writer friend and incredible critique partner), Erin (my work wife and dark romance sister), Hannah & Clare & all of my other beta readers who have helped me fine tune the details of this story, I don't know how I would survive the lows of authorship without you.

A huge, heartfelt thank you to my sensitivity reader, Lo, and my line editor, Alexa. You guys are the real ones.

ABOUT THE AUTHOR

Beka Westrup is a genre-hopping author of fantasy and romance. Demons and Roses is her fourth full-length novel. She lives in the PNW with her husband and two children, collecting more books than she'll ever be able to read and drinking copious amounts of iced coffee.

Stay in the know with Beka's Newsletter:
https://www.bekawestrup.com/coming-soon-03

facebook.com/bekawestrup

instagram.com/bekaboowrites

tiktok.com/@bekabooauthor

amazon.com/author/bekawestrup